Also by Catherine King

Women of Iron
Silk and Steel

Catherine King was born in Rotherham, South Yorkshire. A search for her roots – her father, grandfather and great-grandfather all worked with coal, steel or iron – and an interest in local history provide inspiration for her stories.

Without a Mother's Love is Catherine King's third Yorkshire novel. Her previous novel *Silk and Steel* was shortlisted for the Romantic Novel of the Year Award.

Praise for *Silk and Steel*

'[A] wonderfully told story of pain and passion'

Helen Lederer, RNA judge

'A powerful tale . . . King superbly evokes time and place in this good old-fashioned, page-turning story' *Wigan Evening Post*

For *Women of Iron*

'She writes with authority, skill and confidence . . . a real old-style Victorian drama . . . [with] a mix and balance of wickedness and purity' Elizabeth Gill

'A gritty and realistic tale . . . The characters are so richly drawn and authentic that they pull the reader along in the story effortlessly. A very satisfying read' Anne Bennett

'A powerful and page-turning saga' Dee Williams

'Hard hitting and powerful, this gritty tale features an appealing heroine, a dashing hero and a whole host of intriguing characters ranging from the charming to the downright evil. The out-of-the-ordinary North Country setting adds flavour to the plot and the dialogue pulls no punches. Catherine King has written a first-rate novel' Maureen Lee

WITHOUT A MOTHER'S LOVE

Catherine King

sphere

SPHERE

First published in Great Britain in 2008 by Sphere
This paperback edition published in 2009 by Sphere
Reprinted 2009 (twice)

A CIP catalogue record for this book
is available from the British Library.

Typeset in Bembo by Palimpsest Book Production Limited,
Grangemouth, Stirlingshire
Printed and bound in Great Britain by Clays Ltd, St Ives plc

www.littlebrown.co.uk

To the memories of Alice Ramsbottom Piper
and Edmund Humphrey King

Acknowledgements

I should like to thank the staff and volunteers of Rotherham Archives, especially Betty Davies of FoRA, for helping me with the research for this story. A visit to the National Coal Mining Museum, once a working pit in the West Riding of Yorkshire, gave me an unforgettable underground experience. Thanks, also, to Sheila Garrity (now Whitehead), my old school friend from Rotherham High, for telling me about Epworth Rectory, the home of the Wesley family, and to the helpful staff at the museum there. Finally, special thanks to my agent Judith Murdoch, my editor Louise Davies, and all the team at Sphere, notably Emma Stonex and Alex Richardson, for their constant friendly and good-natured support during the writing and production of the finished book.

The Mexton family tree

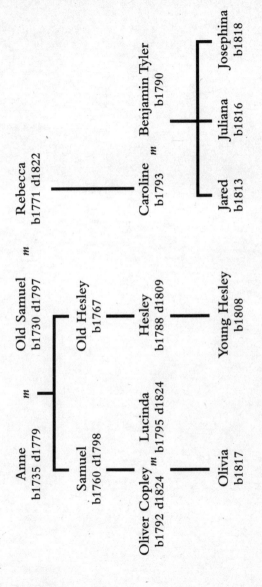

Anne
b1735 d1779

m

Old Samuel
b1730 d1797

m

Rebecca
b1771 d1822

Samuel
b1760 d1798

Old Hesley
b1767

Caroline
b1793

Benjamin Tyler
b1790

Oliver Copley
b1792 d1824

m

Lucinda
b1795 d1824

Hesley
b1788 d1809

Olivia
b1817

Young Hesley
b1808

Jared
b1813

Juliana
b1816

Josephina
b1818

PART ONE: 1830

Chapter 1

'Miss Olivia! Where are you, child? Come here this minute.'

Olivia snatched at her drawers, dragged them out of a tangle of brambles and scampered away before Mrs Cookson came to look for her. She darted through the gap in the old wall, down the track and past rows of flowering bean plants on their stick supports, until she emerged, dishevelled and grubby, at the back of Hill Top House.

'Lord above! Look at you! Filthy dirty and, oh, my heaven, are those your drawers in your hand *again*?' Mrs Cookson grabbed her arm and dragged her across the yard into the scullery where she plonked her on a wooden board by a stone sink and wiped her down with a cold wet cloth. 'There's no time to go upstairs and change. Get into them drawers and put this cap on.'

She jammed a close-fitting white bonnet over Olivia's straggly fair hair. 'Hurry up. Your uncle Hesley is waiting.'

They clattered down the stone-flagged passage and into the front hall. Olivia did not like it there. It was gloomy and dusty, and the beady eyes of dead animals' heads watched her from the dark wood-panelled walls. Mrs Cookson straightened her own apron and cap, then knocked on the door of Uncle Hesley's library.

The room had that 'Uncle Hesley smell' of stale spirits and tobacco. His clothes were the same, and Olivia did not like them either. He stood with his back to the fire, his straight limbs and upright stance at odds with the greying hair and lined face of his advancing years. He was half a century older than Olivia and, in reality, her mother's uncle.

Olivia Copley could still remember her mother. Her beautiful, kind mother. She stood silently before her uncle with her eyes on the threadbare carpet and thought of her as Mrs Cookson complained.

'I tell you, sir, I can't be responsible for her any more. She's wild. She was out there again today with her drawers off. Lord knows what she's been up to at only twelve years of age—'

'I'm nearly thirteen!' Olivia protested, and was immediately silenced by her uncle's stony glare.

'It's not right, anyway,' Mrs Cookson continued, 'making friends with gypsies and the like. She needs a good hiding, she does. I mean, look at her – that pinny was clean on this morning.'

'All right, I heard you! Get back to your work.'

'Yes, sir.' Mrs Cookson bobbed a curtsy and left.

4

The room was quiet, save for the hissing of coal burning in the grate and— Olivia thought she heard a sigh or the soft rustle of a skirt. She looked up at her uncle. He was staring past her into the dimness of the book-lined walls behind her.

'Come forward, Miss Trent.'

Olivia heard a movement and resisted the temptation to look round. She had learned to be still and silent when Uncle Hesley was cross.

'Did you hear that, Miss Trent? She's feral. Do you still wish to take her on?'

'Yes, sir.'

Olivia thought the voice sounded determined. Not at all anxious like the scullery-maid used to be. She wanted to see the face of the girl who wasn't frightened of Uncle Hesley.

'Well, show me what you can do.' He picked up his walking cane and hooked a foot underneath his fireside chair to drag it forward. 'Bend over this, Olivia.'

Olivia's mouth dried. 'But I haven't done anything wrong, Uncle!'

'Do as you're told, or I'll beat you myself.'

Olivia remembered the pain from when he had done so: first, she had stolen a whole game pie from the larder and given it to a passing gypsy, and again when she had tried to run away across the moor behind the house. And worst of all when, alone and frightened, she had woken him with her nightmares. That was when his cane had hurt most and the smell of whisky and cigars was strongest. She turned to obey, stealing a sideways glance at the stranger.

The hood of Miss Trent's cloak had fallen back, revealing a pale, pinched face and fair hair that was similar to her own. Miss Trent had brushed hers, though, and wound it round her head so that she looked plain and severe. But she wasn't very old, Olivia thought. Well, not an old woman like Mrs Cookson.

Olivia pressed her lips together, flared her nostrils and closed her eyes as she waited for Miss Trent to remove her cloak and take up the cane. When the first blow landed she hardly felt it. Surprised, she opened her eyes and examined the worn tapestry of her uncle's favourite chair.

'I can see you're just a skinny little thing, but can't you do better than that?' her uncle snapped. 'Hold the cane in your right hand, girl! You're no good to me if you cannot discipline the child.'

'I beg your pardon, sir.' Miss Trent walked to the other side of the chair, placing herself between Olivia and her uncle. Her voice took on a sterner tone. 'She may have a slate down her drawers, sir.'

'The devil she has!'

'Permit me, sir. I have dealt with her sort before.'

Miss Trent leaned over her, bunching up Olivia's drawers and petticoats to search for protection. As she did so, she left the rolled-up undergarments to form a padding under her skirt. Olivia twisted her head and Miss Trent's face was very close. She breathed, 'Yell,' and Olivia blinked to acknowledge her.

'No slate, sir.'

'Get on with it, then. Six of your best.'

The cane came down hard, and it hurt, even through

the padding. But not as much as it might have, and certainly not enough to make Olivia cry. That did not stop her, though. Each time the cane landed, she let out a long, whining yowl, and was so pleased to deceive her uncle that, by the end, she felt hardly any pain at all. She stood up, snivelling and whimpering.

'You'll do.' Her uncle nodded to Miss Trent. 'Keep her out of trouble and out of my way. Cookson will show you to your chamber, and you'll answer to me about the child.'

Miss Trent picked up her cloak and took Olivia's hand, urging her out of the door first.

'One more thing.'

'Yes, sir.'

'Find out who she's been with.'

'Been with?'

'Outside. In the fields. *With her drawers off, woman!*'

Olivia tensed and her eyes widened in alarm. She didn't want anyone finding out where she went. It was her secret. At the back of the hall Miss Trent stopped to unbundle Olivia's petticoats, putting her finger to her lips. Mrs Cookson did that sometimes and Olivia knew what it meant. She smiled at Miss Trent, satisfied that she already knew one of *her* secrets.

Miss Trent's face relaxed a little so that it wasn't quite so pinched, and she seemed almost pretty with grey eyes, a small straight nose and a neat mouth. But her plain gown was of a coarse brown material that felt scratchy when Olivia's hand brushed against it, like the jute aprons Mrs Cookson wore for scrubbing. Miss Trent opened the kitchen door and they walked in together.

7

Mrs Cookson was Olivia's friend, even when she shouted at her for getting dirty, because she baked buns and let Olivia eat them straight away, still warm from the oven. She was very big, with wispy, grey hair and round cheeks that went red when she was cooking. But she was also Uncle Hesley's servant and did as he said most of the time.

When they came in, Mrs Cookson stopped kneading dough and stared at the newcomer with a guarded expression in her eyes. 'You 'aven't come to take 'er away, 'ave you?'

'No, ma'am. I am here to look after her.'

'I do that. As best I can, anyway. The master trusts me wi' 'er.'

'But she is becoming more difficult for you?'

'Well, she's growing up. I can't watch her all the time.'

'You won't have to now. I am to be Miss Olivia's governess.'

Olivia had been wondering whether Mrs Cookson was going to make buns today and was looking for the currants, but when she heard this, she turned her attention to the grown-ups' conversation.

'Governess? We've never had no governess before! Where a' you from, then?'

'Blackstone School on the other side of the moor. I was a pupil there, then a teacher.'

Mrs Cookson snorted. 'Blackstone? Ee, there's no wonder you look half starved. When did you last eat?'

'I had bread and cold mutton with me for the walk over here.' The mutton had been mostly fat and difficult to chew so she had thrown it away. But Mrs Cookson had fetched her a tankard of water when she had arrived and she was feeling better now.

'You walked all that way, carrying your bag?'

'It's not very big.' Miss Trent had placed it inside the front door when Mrs Cookson had let her in.

'What about the rest of your belongings?'

'I have nothing else, Mrs Cookson. Where is the schoolroom?'

'Schoolroom? This isn't a mansion, you know, and the attics are too damp to use. But young Hesley had a tutor when he was a lad, so I suppose you mean those chambers.'

Olivia interrupted: 'That's where I sleep.' She raised her eyes to the ceiling. 'Up there.'

'She's right. They're directly over the kitchens, but you'll have to see to 'em yourself, Miss Trent. I've got enough to do down here.'

'Can Miss Olivia show me the way?'

'I don't see why not.' Mrs Cookson reached under her apron for her keys. 'I'll get you the linen, and we've bedpans for airing.' She heaved a sigh. 'There was a time when everything was done proper in this house. Foller me.'

Olivia trailed after them. Normally she would rather have been outside, chasing rabbits and catching butterflies. But she was too curious about Miss Trent and thought that she must be brave to disobey Uncle Hesley. If he found out that she hadn't beaten Olivia very hard he would be angry.

Mrs Cookson placed the heavy sheets in Olivia's

arms and said, 'Are you going to be'ave for Miss Trent, then?'

Olivia nodded, keeping her lips tight shut. Mrs Cookson didn't shout at her if she did as she was told, and she wanted Mrs Cookson to stay her friend. She wondered if Miss Trent would be the same.

'I hope you're up to this 'un,' Olivia heard her say to Miss Trent. 'You don't look old enough to be a teacher, like.'

'I shall be one-and-twenty next year,' Miss Trent replied firmly.

Mrs Cookson raised her eyebrows and turned down the corners of her mouth. 'You can sleep in the ante-room between Miss Olivia's bedchamber and the old tutor's room.' She shrugged. 'Miss Olivia's tea is at five o'clock in the kitchen.'

Olivia was hungry already and looked forward to teatime. She struggled up the wide wooden staircase and dropped her burden on a landing chair. Then she opened the schoolroom door so that it banged against the wall, glancing furtively at Miss Trent, who had followed with her small travelling bag.

Miss Trent was taking no notice of her. She was staring at the room, at its whitewashed walls and battered old furniture. It was the first of three linked chambers that jutted out from the back of the house and had windows overlooking the cobbled yard. This was where Mrs Cookson sent Olivia when she had been a nuisance downstairs, usually when it was raining and she couldn't go outside to the walled garden and her secret wilderness. The stables and barn were across the cobbles and she could watch Matt and his farmhands scurry back and forth in the wet.

The schoolroom housed a heavy oak table, ancient and scarred, an assortment of chairs and a globe of the world that Olivia spun as she passed. An open cupboard in a corner revealed a jumble of teaching items, books and broken wooden toys.

Miss Trent surveyed them. 'Are these yours?' she asked.

'They belong to Cousin Hesley.'

Miss Trent walked through to the next room to put down her bag. 'Where is your cousin now?' she asked, over her shoulder.

'At the university,' Olivia replied, feeling important to be asked.

'In July?'

'Oh!' She wondered how much to say. 'Well, he's finished now and gone to stay in the North Riding. Uncle Hesley's going as well when the shooting starts.'

Miss Trent did not respond. She was looking at the books scattered on the floorboards and picked up one that lay open at an illustration of the Tower of London.

'That's mine.' Olivia snatched it from her and hugged it to herself. 'That's my castle.'

'Will you show it to me?' Miss Trent sank to the floor and began to examine the other books.

Olivia shook her head emphatically.

'Can you read the words?'

Olivia continued to shake her head.

'Perhaps you can draw it for me?'

'Draw it?'

'Copy the picture on this slate. Here.' Miss Trent rummaged in the bottom of the cupboard and found some chalk. 'Go and sit at the table while I tidy these shelves.'

Olivia concentrated on her drawing, resolving to take the slate with her next time she went to the old garden. She knew how she could smuggle it outside. She would never have thought of hiding it in her drawers if Miss Trent hadn't mentioned it. Olivia wondered again why she hadn't given her a proper beating in front of Uncle Hesley.

Miss Trent came to look over her shoulder as she drew. 'That's good, Olivia,' she said.

Olivia put down her chalk. 'Why didn't you beat me harder?' she asked.

'You said you hadn't done anything wrong.'

'But we all have to do what Uncle Hesley says. That's what Mrs Cookson told me.'

'I use beating for really wicked things.'

'What things?'

'Telling lies. Stealing.'

'Not for talking to a gypsy? Or crying in the middle of the night?' Olivia saw Miss Trent frown.

'Is that why your uncle beats you?'

'Yes, and he'll beat you, too, if you don't do as he says!' Olivia gave a satisfied smirk as Miss Trent's eyes widened in alarm.

'It's time to wash for tea,' her governess said briskly. 'I'll fetch some hot water.'

'Oh, I just rinse my hands in the scullery.'

Miss Trent smiled at her. 'Not now that I am your

governess. Go and find your hairbrush and a clean pinafore.'

Olivia picked up her slate and walked through the anteroom, where Miss Trent's bag sat unopened on the narrow bed, and on into her own bedchamber. She treasured this room because it was her private place, like her wilderness in the walled garden where no one could find her. She leaned the slate against the small wooden cupboard that contained the chamber pot, went to the washstand and took off her cap. She was still trying to drag the brush through her tangled hair when Miss Trent came back with a ewer of water.

'Here, let me.' Miss Trent tackled the ends, holding Olivia's hair firmly at the roots so that it did not tug and hurt. She tied it back with a piece of bonnet tape and replaced Olivia's cap. 'Have you a looking-glass?' she asked.

'No.'

'Or a small brush for your nails?'

Olivia didn't reply, and Miss Trent said, 'At least you have soap. Give your hands and face a good wash while I unpack.' She poured some water into the china basin and took the rest with her, closing the door behind her.

Olivia swirled the water with a finger. It was still hot! She splashed it on her face and wiped it off with the cloth. Grey streaks appeared on the white linen and she grimaced. Mrs Cookson scolded her when this happened in the scullery.

Hesitantly, she took up the soap and turned it over

and over in her hands, watching the water become cloudy. She played with the creamy foam for a minute, then rubbed her palms over her face, enjoying the soft lather on her skin. She decided she didn't mind washing when the water was warm.

Harriet Trent took Olivia's hand and went down for tea as soon as she heard the clock in the hall chime the hour. She had been hungry all day but the smell of baking bread when she had drawn water from the boiler in the kitchen range had increased her appetite. In the warm kitchen, one end of the table had been set for the three of them.

'Is all this for us?' she exclaimed, when she saw it. Tea at Blackstone School was usually bread and dripping.

There was the crust end of a game pie cut into two pieces, a dish of beetroot and some garden radishes, a bowl of boiled eggs and a leg of mutton, which Mrs Cookson was slicing with a long, sharp knife.

'Not much left on this now. Will you have a taste, Miss Trent?'

'Thank you.' Her eyes were drawn to the bread-board with the crusty loaf and the slab of butter, which still bore the marks of the wooden bats from the dairy. Butter! Her mouth watered at the thought of butter on her bread.

Olivia stretched for an egg, tapped it on her plate and began to peel away its shell.

'May I say grace, Mrs Cookson?'

'If you must. I suppose that is the Blackstone way.'

'Thank you. Put your egg down, Olivia.' She waited patiently until her charge obeyed.

'Lord, bless this food for our use and us to thy service. Amen.'

Mrs Cookson reached for the beetroot, muttering, 'I hope the master knows what he's doing taking you on.' She picked up a stoneware jug. 'There's milk to drink. Or would you rather have some o' this ale?'

'I'll take the same as Olivia. You keep a good table, Mrs Cookson.'

'Aye, well, that's my job here. The mutton leg and pie are leftovers from the master's dining room. Miss Olivia will have some bread and butter with her eggs, if you'll oblige.'

Harriet sawed at the bread and understood why her pupil was so well grown for her age, and Mrs Cookson so rounded. But because she was used to having so little eat, it was difficult for her to do justice to the meal. She did her best, though, until her stomach felt uncomfortably full.

'I see there is a fireplace in the schoolroom,' she commented.

'Aye, and the chimney's swept. They were all done after Easter.'

'Then may I light a fire during the winter months?'

'You can have one now, if you want. You'll need it if we get a north-easterly. But you'll have to carry the coals yourself. I've no housemaids. Mind, with you taking the little 'un off me hands, I'll be better off, make no mistake.'

'How many buckets of coal may I have?'

15

'As many as you want. The master owns Mexton Pit. Didn't they tell you that at Blackstone? He sells 'em his slack, doesn't he?'

Harriet nodded. Slack was the cheapest coal found at the edges of the seams. It was poor quality and mixed with stones that left clinker in the grates when it had burned. The master would not be able to sell it to the furnaces and forges in the valley because it didn't give out enough heat.

'We allus have plenty of coal here,' Mrs Cookson continued. 'The pit sends it by the drayload wi' a couple o' men to shovel it in the coalhole across the yard.'

Good food. Warm fires. And her own small bedchamber. Suddenly Harriet felt anxious that something dreadful might happen to take it all away. It was a strange feeling and it reminded her of how she had felt when she had first arrived at Blackstone School. Austere as it was, it was better than where she had come from. And now, more than ten years later, she was grateful to be gone from there.

'What happened to your kinfolk, Miss Trent? All the girls at Blackstone are orphans, aren't they?'

'No, but I was. My mother and father died when I was seven.' She remembered them as being old, with grey hair and bent backs. All three of them had been laid low by a fever and only she had survived. It was a long time ago now but she had not forgotten the fear when she had been taken away from the only home she had known in the back of a farm cart.

'And you've been at Blackstone ever since?'

'I was taken to a poorhouse first and stayed there for two years.'

'We had a scullery-maid from a poorhouse once,' Olivia exclaimed.

'Aye, good little worker she were till she upped and left wi' a passing tinker. Still, we got you now, Miss Trent.'

'She isn't a scullery-maid,' Olivia stated loudly.

I was in the poorhouse, Harriet recalled. And a laundry-maid. She said, 'I have been luckier than most. My mother had a distant cousin in the clergy who heard of my misfortune. He applied to the trustees at Blackstone for a charity place there.' When she'd arrived at the school, she had thought it wasn't much better than the poorhouse, but at least she had had lessons for some of the time, instead of washing and scrubbing all day.

'What did you do at Blackstone?' Olivia asked.

'I learned.'

'Learned what?'

'All the things I'm going to teach you.' As she said this, she remembered how terrified she had been that she might be sent back to the poorhouse, and how hard she had studied to avoid that fate. She saw that now she felt the same about returning to Blackstone School, with its frugal ways and strict regime. She never wanted to go back to the humiliation of being a charity girl, walking with her head bowed and for ever beholden to her betters. She shivered at the memory of her attic dormitory, shared with more than a dozen others, where the water in the washstand ewers turned to ice overnight.

'Are you all right, Miss Trent?' Mrs Cookson asked.

'A little tired from the walk here. That's all.'

Even as a pupil teacher her only privilege had been the worn gown and boots given to the school by clergymen's wives who passed on their servants' clothing for the older girls.

Many of the pupils went to be nursery-maids as soon as they were old enough. Harriet had been fortunate, she was told, for she read and wrote well: she could stay on as a pupil teacher. She had thought sometimes that the others were the lucky ones. They were paid for their work. As a charity girl she was taught to feel honoured that she could serve the school as a teacher and thereby repay her benefactors. The only money she had known was the few coppers they gave her each week to put in the church collection. She longed for escape, and when this opportunity to leave had come she had grasped it with both hands. And to the Mextons at Hill Top House!

Fate had dealt her a good card. Here, there was hope, hope of finding answers to her questions about Olivia Copley and why she lived with the Mextons. Here, there were books and papers, and the freedom to read them. Now that she had left Blackstone she would make sure she never had to go back.

'I'm surprised they let you go, you being a teacher there, like,' Mrs Cookson commented. 'Especially to here, where the master is well known for his . . .' she glanced at the child '. . . his ways.'

'What do you mean?'

'This is not a churchgoing household.'

'Oh. I did not know that. But I wanted to come here and none of the other teachers did. The principal encouraged me. He told me the school would have free coal for the winter if I accepted.'

'Did he? I hope the master will pay you as well.'

'Oh, yes.' Harriet was excited about her salary. 'It goes to Blackstone until I come of age. But after I am one-and-twenty it will be mine. And the principal said that the master would provide me with boots and cloth for a gown at Michaelmas.'

'Is that all you've got, then? What you stand up in?'

'I have undergarments, a nightgown and an apron.' Harriet thought of the work she would be doing. 'I should like another apron. Do you have a spare one, Mrs Cookson?'

'I'll see if I can find some old linen you can make up. And while you're about it, the little 'un could do wi' some more. You can show her how to sew 'em for herself.'

'What about her gowns?'

'There's a draper's shop in town.'

'Is it far into town from here?' she asked.

'Aye, it is. Too far to walk there and back on a half-day.'

'Oh.' Harriet was disappointed. Still, she had no money to spend yet so perhaps it was just as well.

'We don't use fancy plates and silver forks 'ere, but we're well provided for. What the farm can't gi' us we 'ave sent up on a cart.'

'There must be a church that is nearer than town?'

'I told you. We're not church folk.'

'What about the little one on the moor?' Olivia squeaked.

'Aye, there's that. Not many goes, though. Most of the men have left to work in the pits and ironworks, and the cottages are falling down.'

'Does it have a clergyman?'

'Oh, aye. A curate comes from t'other side of the moor on a Sunday.'

'Would you like to come to church with me, Olivia?'

'Ooh, yes!' Then her face fell. 'Will Uncle Hesley let me?'

Harriet raised her eyebrows questioningly at Mrs Cookson.

'He's not that bothered what she does, as long as she stays out o' trouble.'

The younger woman smiled at her charge. 'I'm sure your uncle will not object if he sees how well you can behave.'

'It might do her some good,' Mrs Cookson shrugged. 'But it's not what she's used to. Me and you should have a little talk, Miss Trent. Not now. Wait until the child is in bed, then come down for a nightcap.'

After tea, Harriet helped to clear away and wash up while Olivia whooped around the yard outside the kitchen window. Harriet watched her scatter a handful of crumbs, then retreat to the barn while the doves came down to peck at them. Then she ran out and tried to catch one, chasing after the birds and jumping in the air as they flapped away. She stood with her head tilted back to watch them settle on the tiled roofs of the buildings surrounding the yard.

Mrs Cookson was preparing a cooked meal of pig's fry and onions for Matt and his lad who lived above the stables. They looked after the horses and livestock for the master, as well as working what was left of his land. They took bread and cheese out with them for their dinner.

'Keep your eye on her,' she warned Harriet. 'If she runs off there's no finding her. Look at her, like a wild animal, she is.'

'I don't think so,' Harriet observed. 'She's probably just lonely. And bored. I can see why she's so grubby.'

'I do me best with 'er.'

'Of course you do, but you have enough with looking after this large house by yourself. Is the water hot again yet?'

Half an hour later, she was carrying another ewer of hot water upstairs with some clean towels, nudging a reluctant child in front of her. 'But it's not dark yet and I washed before tea,' Olivia whined.

'I can see the bits you missed. And your hair needs a proper brushing. Besides, I want to read to you before the light goes. Has anyone read to you before?'

'Mama used to when I was little. And we said prayers.' She stopped abruptly on the landing. 'I don't want *you* to read to me. You're not my mama.'

Harriet did not argue and wondered how her pupil had occupied herself all day on her own. She blew out her cheeks as she thought of her outside with her drawers in her hand. The master was right to be

21

worried. 'Tell me what you do with your mornings,' she said.

The child shrugged.

'Do you play on the moor?' she persisted gently, untying the pinafore bow.

'Sometimes.'

'Take off your boots now. Do you have friends out there?'

'No.'

'No one at all? What about the gypsy?'

'He's gone.'

'But he was your friend?'

'No, he wasn't,' she replied indignantly. 'He said he was hungry so I took him a pie from the larder. And Uncle Hesley beat me. He said it was stealing, but it wasn't! It was as much my pie as it was his. Mrs Cookson said so.'

'Did you talk to the gypsy?'

Olivia nodded as she struggled out of her boots and stockings.

'When did you last wash your feet?'

'I can't remember.'

'I see. Now, take off your gown. Did you play games with the gypsy?'

'No. He was old and dirty. *Really* dirty.'

Harriet hid a smile and resolved to find a looking-glass. 'Did he touch you?'

'Ugh, no. I wouldn't let him near me! I left the pie on a boulder.'

She helped Olivia take off the grubby gown. Her chemise was clean but the drawers were decidedly muddy and torn.

22

'Why did you take off your drawers out there, Olivia?'

'I didn't!'

'I know when you're lying. Did someone take them off for you?'

'No.'

'Is that the truth?'

'Yes.'

'But you did take them off, didn't you? Why?'

'I'm not telling you. It's a secret.'

Harriet did not respond to this and continued getting Olivia ready for bed, insisting that she washed her ears, the back of her neck and her arms.

'Now down there.'

Olivia screwed up her nose. 'It smells.'

'I know. That's why you must wash. You'll feel more comfortable afterwards.'

When the child made no further move, she squeezed out a cloth in the warm water and handed it over, adding firmly, 'With soap.'

The child obeyed reluctantly.

'Has anyone touched you there?' she asked.

Olivia concentrated on her task silently.

'You must tell me,' she added. 'Even if it is a secret.'

'You're horrible.' She threw the cloth into the water.

Harriet persisted: 'When you took off your drawers, was anyone with you?'

'No! Nobody knows about my—' She stopped. 'Go away. I hate you.'

'Very well. No more questions.' She wondered how she could persuade Olivia to talk to her. Beating the child would not get at the truth and would ensure that Olivia lost confidence in Harriet for ever. She said, 'Tip that dirty water into the slop bucket next door and I'll pour some more for your feet.'

A few minutes later Harriet watched as the child wriggled her toes in the warm water and rubbed between them with a soapy cloth. 'Would you like me to read the words in the book about your castle?' she asked.

The child looked at her sullenly.

Harriet handed her a towel. 'Put on your nightdress and cap. Tomorrow I shall start to teach you to read them for yourself.'

Chapter 2

As soon as Olivia was asleep, Harriet went down to the kitchen. She sat at the table. 'What did you want to say to me?'

Mrs Cookson yawned, reached for a stone bottle and poured some dark liquid into a metal tankard. 'That life in this house is a bit different from Blackstone. Will you have a drop o' this?'

'What is it?'

'Rum. From the West Indies. You should try it.'

'No, thank you.'

'Well, don't expect no clean-living church ways from the master. Black sheep, he is. The Mextons used to be a respected family round 'ere. Samuel, Miss Olivia's grandfather, was a real gentleman and his daughter, God rest her soul, was a proper lady.'

'That would be Olivia's mother?'

'Aye. The master is Samuel's younger brother and, if you ask me, he's a bad lot.'

'He is caring for his great-niece, and he has engaged me to look after her,' Harriet reminded her.

'Aye, well, now she's growing up and, what with her wild ways, he has to protect her from herself.'

'She not really feral.'

'You saw her, didn't you? She goes out on the moor to heaven knows where, taking up with passing vagrants and the like. It's not right.'

'She is still a child, Mrs Cookson. There is no world-liness about her. As far as I can tell.'

'And what would you know of the world?'

'We had all sorts of girls come to us at Blackstone, including some who were far more knowing than they should have been for their years. I do not see the same signs in Miss Olivia.'

Mrs Cookson snorted. 'You'd better tell that to the master. He thinks all men are like him where women are concerned.'

Harriet tried not to show her anxiety at the way Mrs Cookson was speaking about her employer. 'Olivia is not a woman yet.'

'No, but she's growing fast.'

Harriet pursed her lips. 'Perhaps. Is there a Mrs Mexton?'

'There used to be. Two of 'em. But the master's wife passed on more'n thirty year ago.'

'And he married again?'

'No. T'other one was his son's wife. Long gone, she is. He lost his son early on, you see. Thrown from his

26

horse. I think that affected the master more than anything. Made him worse with his drinking and his women.'

'The master has women?' Harriet's shock was evident in her voice.

'Notorious around here. Hadn't you 'eard?' Mrs Cookson gulped from her tankard.

'But what sort of example is that for Miss Olivia?'

'Oh, he doesn't bring 'em here. I suppose he thinks I don't know why he goes off into town of a night and doesn't come home until morning.'

'Well, how do you know, Mrs Cookson?'

'Because Matt from the farm goes into town now and then. And he tells me anything I want ter know for a drop o' rum.' Mrs Cookson jangled her keys. 'The master trusts me wi' these, you see.'

Was this why none of the other teachers had wanted to come here? Harriet asked herself. No wonder they had been surprised when she was so eager. But she was determined to stay, whatever it took. She would guide and protect Olivia for as long as she could. Whether or not Mrs Cookson was right and this was an ungodly house, Harriet most certainly was not. And, if the master did not interfere, she would make sure that Olivia was not either. As a charity girl, Harriet knew the importance of her virtue. The school had made it clear to her that her good name was all she had.

She said, 'I shall make a point of teaching Miss Olivia to value her virtue. Blackstone may have had its faults but it taught its girls the worth of moral conduct and duty.'

27

'Aye. Pious lot, they are. All folk aren't like that, though. You'll find that out now you've left.'

'I am aware of sin, Mrs Cookson, and of its consequences.'

'Aye.' Mrs Cookson half laughed as she said it and her speech was becoming slurred. 'We'll all be damned in hell.'

'I hope you do not speak like that in front of the child!'

'Miss Olivia? Bless 'er, she's the only decent thing living here. You keep her decent. That's all I ask.'

Well, of course I will, Harriet thought irritably. That was her task. 'Do you think you should be taking quite so much rum at this hour? It will interfere with your sleep, surely.'

'When you've been living up here for a year or so, you'll understand the need of a drink or two of a night-time.' Mrs Cookson was becoming maudlin. 'Both the same, the Mextons. Their bellies and their cocks, that's all they're interested in. They get their bellies filled here and their cocks serviced in town . . .'

Harriet was shocked but knew it was the rum talking. 'Shall I help you to bed, Mrs Cookson? Where do you sleep?'

The older woman did not reply. She picked up the stone bottle and went out of the kitchen door, locking it behind her. 'Don't bolt it,' she called, as she crossed the yard.

In the fading light, Harriet watched her go into the stables, no doubt in search of a drinking companion. She went upstairs to her tiny bedchamber, planning

Olivia's salvation from the self-indulgent ways that seemed to be the custom at Hill Top House.

That night the breeze rose to a full-blown wind. It crept in around the windows and door frames. Unfastened gates and trees creaked outside and heavy rain beat on the roof. Harriet lay awake listening, imagining the wildness of the exposed moor and wondering if Mrs Cookson's disposition was the result of living in this inhospitable place.

In the darkness, when the house was quiet, she feared for the life she would have to live here. She had not warmed to Mrs Cookson and shivered, suddenly feeling very much alone. But the Lord had led her here, and she said a prayer for the pupils and teachers she had left behind at Blackstone, asking Him to find them suitable positions as He had done for her. She fell asleep eventually, secure in the knowledge that she was safe indoors, warm and well fed, and able to repay her betters for the shelter they had given her over the years.

In the bedchamber next door, Olivia fretted about the wind and rain and wished it would go away. She put a pillow over her head and imagined she was shut up in her imaginary castle, safe and sound from the storm. But, even then, she could still hear the wind, howling around her ears . . .

It whistled through the crevices, rattling wooden doors and shutters, tearing relentlessly at her bonnet, which was sodden with rain, the lashing, thrashing rain. She was crying. 'Mama, Mama, I want Mama.' But nobody came. Timbers creaked and groaned, canvas ripped and flapped.

The ship listed violently and she was thrown to the deck among all the crashing and grinding. She clutched at a piece of rope. Men were shouting and women crying, and there was water, so much water, everywhere, salty on her lips and all over her so she couldn't breathe. And the creaking and groaning, crashing and crying . . .

'Wake up, Olivia.' Miss Trent was bending over her with a candle, shaking her shoulder.

'Mama, Mama.' She had been crying in her sleep again. She wiped her eyes with the back of her hand.

'It's just a dream, Olivia.'

Olivia wept. Her mother was never there in her dream. Nor her papa. Just the men who had rescued her. They had black faces and spoke to her in a strange language. That was when she screamed. But Miss Trent had woken her before that bit. She looked at her calm, pale features and was glad she was there. The black men had been kind to her, but she had not known that at the time.

'Would you like some milk?' Miss Trent asked.

She nodded.

'And I *shall* read to you.'

'In the middle of the night?'

'I don't see why not.' Miss Trent lit the candle by her bed. 'Will you be comfortable for a few minutes?'

Olivia sniffed and nodded again. When Miss Trent brought the milk, it was warm and sweet. Then she told Olivia about the kings and queens of England.

And it was interesting, but she was tired and her eyes kept closing. She must have fallen asleep for the next thing she knew it was daylight and someone was out in the yard, pumping water into the horse trough.

The next afternoon. Miss Trent took her on what she called a 'nature walk'. They followed a track past the farm buildings that led to the moor. It went by the old garden, and when Olivia saw the overgrown wall she quickened her step. She did not want questions about her secret wilderness. The gap where the door had been was filled with brambles except where she had pushed through, and as Olivia hurried by, Miss Trent asked what was behind the wall.

'Nothing,' she answered, then added, 'but there might be dragons.'

'Dragons? Do they breathe fire?'

'I expect so.' She took Miss Trent's hand and tugged. 'Come.'

But Miss Trent could not be budged. 'Shall we explore?'

'No!' Olivia let go of her hand and ran up the track towards the moor. She scrambled over a dry-stone wall, ducked behind it and crawled back in the direction of Hill Top House until she rolled into a hollow in the ground and was out of sight. She heard Miss Trent calling, sounding frantic. Olivia peered carefully over the wall. With satisfaction, she saw her governess moving up the track away from her and settled back, leaning against the wall to recover her breath.

She wondered briefly if she'd be beaten for this. But Miss Trent hadn't beaten her last night when she had disturbed her sleep. Instead, she had been kind. Mrs Cookson was like that sometimes, although it never lasted long. Her governess would be the same as all the other grown-ups, she thought.

When the voice calling her became faint she climbed back over the wall, ran across the track and behind the old walled garden. It was a long way round through the scrub and she flopped on to her belly as she neared the spot where Miss Trent was standing, shading her eyes and scanning the moorland.

She crawled on all fours, pulling herself along the ground with her arms and legs, trying to imitate the farm cat as he stalked rats in the barn. She narrowed her eyes, prepared to pounce, and was disappointed when she raised her head to see her governess retracing her steps down the track. She had stopped calling her name and Olivia panicked: Miss Trent was heading for the door to the old garden.

She jumped to her feet, and cried, 'Over here! Come quickly, there's a snake!'

Miss Trent turned and ran towards her. 'Where? Did it bite you?'

'No, it's gone.' She watched the older woman's face change from relief to – well, Olivia wasn't sure. Not anger, she thought. Miss Trent's gentle smile disappeared and the grey eyes stared without blinking.

'I expect it was frightened of you. Vipers usually are,' Miss Trent said. 'Why did you run away? Are you frightened of me?'

'No. I gave *you* a fright, though, didn't I?' Olivia thought this would make her cross, but Miss Trent merely continued to gaze at her.

'You most certainly do now,' she responded. 'You're a dreadful sight, with twigs in your hair and your gown dirty and torn. You will have to mend that tonight instead of listening to a story. Shall we finish our nature walk?' Miss Trent took a firm grip on Olivia's hand and set off up the track at a brisk pace.

Reluctantly, Olivia followed her, growing warm with the exercise. She was relieved when Miss Trent suggested they rest on a boulder. Olivia sat beside her, watching the sheep graze and the rabbits romping in the scrubby pasture.

'Do you know what they're doing?' Miss Trent asked.

'The rabbits? They're fighting. The doves fight like that sometimes. They chase around and jump on each other's backs.'

Miss Trent didn't say much more but she asked Olivia to pick some flowers: they would take them back to the schoolroom. 'We shall find out their names from a book,' she said.

Olivia didn't reply. She knew some of them already from Mrs Cookson, but she wasn't going to tell that to Miss Trent. It was easier walking down the track, and Olivia was pleased to hurry as she was hungry. As they passed the old garden Miss Trent asked her if she wanted to go dragon-hunting.

'No!' she exclaimed.

'Another day, then.'

Olivia became thoughtful. Miss Trent wasn't like

33

Mrs Cookson, who told her to be seen and not heard and not to answer back. Mrs Cookson soon lost patience with her, when she had to get back to her work, leaving Olivia to do as she liked as long as Uncle Hesley didn't find out.

Miss Trent was different. She didn't give up like Mrs Cookson and she was quicker in every way. Olivia wouldn't be able to escape from her governess so easily. She hoped Miss Trent wouldn't be with her every minute of the day or she would never again be able to go to her wilderness. If her governess was here to stay, would she ever have any proper freedom?

A few days later Olivia was copying letters on her slate in the schoolroom when Harriet heard horses on the cobbles in the yard. Out of the window, she saw the master return with a gentleman in his middle years. Both looked angry and dishevelled and they left their horses loose when they went indoors. Matt came hurrying out to gather up the trailing reins and tend the steaming beasts.

An hour later, Harriet hurried past the sound of raised voices coming from the library as she went to fetch water for Olivia to wash before dinner. The kitchen was filled with a delicious smell of roasting pork and tangy stewed apple.

Mrs Cookson was busy laying a tray. 'You'd better have your dinner up there today. The master's in a rage. I should stay out of his way,' she said.

Harriet remembered how irrational the principal at Blackstone could be when he was angered. She considered this good advice but was curious none the less. 'What's happened?' she asked.

'There's been a ruck at the pit.'

'An accident? Is anyone hurt?'

'Nay, nowt like that, thank heaven. Keep the child upstairs. Yourself too. He's got his pit manager with him and the pair of them are already on the rum.'

Harriet ate the savoury duck in gravy with peas, and planned how she could occupy Olivia in the schoolroom for the rest of the day. The child hated to be cooped up in good weather and looked forward to her afternoon nature walk.

'I want to go to the privy,' Olivia whined.

'Use your chamber pot,' Harriet suggested.

'I might wet my drawers.'

'Take them off and roll down your stockings.' She rummaged in the cupboard for a book. 'Then I shall read to you and you must close your eyes, imagine a picture in your head and draw it for me on a slate.'

As Olivia occupied herself with chalk, Harriet realized there might be an innocent explanation for why she had taken off her drawers outside. Had she simply been too far away to come back to the privy? But she was not a lazy child and preferred the outside privy to the chamber pot. In summer, at least. Later, when Harriet had to go downstairs, the library was quiet and Mrs Cookson was dozing by the kitchen fire.

'Has the pit manager left?' she asked.

'They're sleeping it off in the drawing room. But it's a bad do.'

'What's happened?'

'Matt said the coal seam is worked out and it's mostly slack what's left, so the master's cut his colliers' wages and they've been complaining.'

'Well, I'm not surprised. I suppose they have to work just as hard to mine it.'

Mrs Cookson gave one of her snorting laughs. 'Aye, and the master can only sell it for half the price.'

'When shall I bring Olivia down for tea?'

'Best not to when the master's been drinking. He'll be wanting his own tea when he wakes. Come for a tray and I'll cut you some cold meat.'

It must have been late when the pit manager left because Harriet did not hear his horse on the cobbles before she fell asleep.

In the morning Mrs Cookson was out of sorts, and Harriet guessed that the master would be the same when he woke, so she took her pupil straight outside after breakfast.

'We're going dragon-hunting,' she explained.

'I don't want to,' Olivia protested.

Harriet had to take her by the hand and pull her along until they had left the house and its outbuildings behind them. She stopped by the old walled garden. 'This is your garden, isn't it?' she asked.

'What if it is?'

'It must be special to you.'

'It's a secret.'

'Will you show me if I promise not to tell anyone?'

Olivia looked at her resentfully and Harriet wondered if she would run away again, but she was already learning how to punish her without beatings

– or restricting her diet to bread and water as they did at Blackstone. Rather, she had noticed how much the child enjoyed being read to and used that to reward her improving behaviour.

Harriet smiled. 'Shall I go in first?'

'No! You can't! It's *my* secret!'

'Oh. Will you invite me in?'

'You'll tell Uncle Hesley.'

'I have promised that I shall not.'

'Not even if he beats you?'

Harriet Trent was alarmed by that, but answered, 'Not even if he beats me. It will be our secret, ours alone.'

Harriet found some fallen branches to hold back the brambles, observing that a few shreds of fabric were caught on the thorns. She followed Olivia through the gap into what must once have been a productive garden. Brambles, ivy and bindweed grew everywhere, except in the far corner where a gnarled spreading apple tree seemed to be winning the battle for sunlight. The ground underneath was dry and scattered with kitchen implements, including a wooden bucket, a large long-handled spoon and a metal tankard big enough for ale. Beside it, the brambles had been cleared to reveal the low stone walls of a seed bed, its glass covers long gone. An old spade was stuck in a patch of soil. 'I don't see any dragons,' she remarked.

'I only said there might be.'

Harriet surveyed heaps of dried mud at regular intervals along the seed-frame walls and detected a passing resemblance to the battlements in the book illustration. 'Did you build this castle yourself?' she asked.

'Yes. It's mine.'

'Of course.' Harriet picked up the heavy wooden bucket and sniffed, withdrawing her nose sharply. 'Are you building your castle with this mud?'

Olivia picked up the tankard. 'I use this to make the turrets and I collect water in the bucket when it rains. But sometimes it doesn't rain enough and the mud doesn't stick together.'

'So you provide a little more yourself.' A childish pastime, she thought, born of boredom. 'Is that when you take off your drawers?'

Miss Olivia stared at her. 'How did you know?'

Harriet plucked a fragment of white cotton from a bramble on the path. She was relieved that she had judged the child correctly. 'I shall keep your castle a secret, Olivia,' she said, 'but now that you're nearly thirteen, I think I can find more interesting things for you to do outdoors. Shall we go back?'

When they arrived at the house, Mrs Cookson was agitated. 'Why weren't you in the schoolroom? The master's leaving after dinner and he wants to see you first. Go in there now.'

'In where?'

'The library. He's waiting for you.'

'Wash your hands in the scullery, Olivia, then go up to the schoolroom.' Harriet rinsed her own hands, tidied her hair and presented herself at the library door.

'Where have you been?' the master demanded.

He was standing in front of the fire, lighting his cigar with a burning taper. He did not seem to want an answer for he went on, 'I've enough to do, dealing

38

with my mine, without having to wait about for you or worry about the child. That is your job.'

'Yes, sir. She is safe with me, sir.' Harriet felt more confident of this now.

He made a grunting sound that she believed was of approval and waited for him to continue. He was a handsome gentleman, she thought, in spite of his lined face. In fact, his maturity seemed to enhance his strong features, which were dominated by a pair of brown eyes, set well apart. His eyebrows were grey and the hair on his head had not thinned. His tall frame was not bent by toil and she knew he continued to ride when others of his years might have resorted to a carriage.

'Is she?' he demanded. 'Is she not still running wild on the moor at every opportunity?'

'Not so much now, sir. I have found her other occupations and I am with her all the time.'

'Make sure you are. She is my ward, my property, and she is to stay that way.'

'Yes, sir.' Harriet wondered why he was so possessive of a child he found such a tiresome burden. Perhaps it was something to do with the mine. He seemed very agitated.

'I don't want any young buck near her.'

'Good heavens, no!' Harriet was appalled that he would voice such an opinion to her. 'She is still a child, sir.'

He blew out cigar smoke. 'She's wayward. Who knows what she's been up to on the moor?' Then he leaned towards her to emphasize his words. 'If she tries to run off with anyone, I shall hold you responsible.'

Harriet's eyes rounded in horror at the idea that

Olivia would do any such thing. 'I am sure there is no risk of that, sir.'

'Are you? Have you discovered yet who took off her drawers?'

'She did, sir.'

'Is that so? Who was with her?'

'No one, sir. She – er – was using an old bucket as a privy.'

She watched incredulity spread across his face. 'Is that what she says?'

'Yes, sir. She is telling the truth, sir.'

'Is she still a maid?'

His directness stunned her and she took a moment to recover. 'I believe so, sir.'

'Mrs Cookson does not.'

Harriet was annoyed with the woman. The master might indulge his vigorous appetites at every opportunity, but all gentlemen were not the same. 'Perhaps Mrs Cookson knows only gentlemen like yourself.' She snapped her mouth shut immediately. Lord, what had she said?

His face darkened. He was not a man to be crossed and she was anxious to be gone from his study before she said anything else that might anger him. She took a deep breath and hastened to repair the damage. 'Olivia is unworldly in these matters. I have taught girls who were not innocent in the ways of men. At Blackstone, there were – girls were sent to us because they were in danger of moral decay.'

His mouth twisted. She supposed he might know that. 'Is that why you went there?' he asked.

'No, sir! I was an orphan. But as a teacher I learned to recognize the signs of sin in young girls.'

He stared at her as though he were seeing her for the first time. 'Did you, by Jove?'

'Some girls are more knowing than others in these matters. Olivia is not, I am certain of it.'

'Huh! What would a maid like you know about such things?' he barked. 'Or perhaps you are not a maid, Miss Trent.'

She felt the colour rise in her cheeks. 'You are disrespectful, sir.'

'You need not hide it from me, Miss Trent.'

'Not all the girls at Blackstone are tainted!' she protested. 'It is true that the school will take girls in moral danger when other schools will not, as long as they show repentance for their ways. But those girls are few, I assure you.'

He sniffed audibly and removed a shred of tobacco from his lips. 'I suppose Blackstone is preferable to a popish convent in the eyes of their worthy parents.'

'Yes, sir.'

'What about the vagrant?'

'She felt sorry for him.'

'He did not defile her?'

'I do not believe so.'

'But you do not *know*?'

'I am not a physician, sir, but I would swear that she is innocent.'

He puffed again at his cigar and moved closer to her. She wanted to step back. But he was like the principal at Blackstone and she knew he would interpret that as weakness. She stood her ground, even though his height overshadowed her, and his eyes were hard and glittered.

'If she is not, Miss Trent, you will be sorry. And so will she. It won't be Blackstone for her but the asylum.'

'Not that, sir!' She knew this was where girls who transgressed were sent, but only if they were beyond help. It was the very worst place for any girl. He must not think of it as an option for Olivia. 'She will behave, I promise. Just give me time with her. She is energetic and bright. She would not survive in an asylum. You cannot do that to her.'

'I can and I shall, if her behaviour dictates it. I will not be disobeyed.'

'I shall see you are not, sir.'

He appeared to accept this and his features relaxed into a crooked smile. But he did not step away from her and she became flustered at his proximity. She could smell the tobacco on his breath. His manner towards her was threatening and she believed him capable of beating her as well as his niece, if she did not obey him. He was trying to frighten her and he was succeeding. But he did not need to do that for her to be diligent in guarding his great-niece. She wanted to look after the child, to teach her and watch her grow. Harriet cared about Olivia – more than he did, she thought.

She looked down at her feet until he turned away and said, 'Very well, Miss Trent. I am going north for the shooting. Mrs Cookson is in charge of the house until I return.'

The shooting? That means he will be away for weeks! She felt so relieved. His behaviour towards her was too menacing for her comfort. Without him about the house, she could concentrate on her pupil, and need not worry about his domineering presence.

'You may go,' he added.

Harriet hurried out of the library, anxious to be away from him and thankful that the interview was over. She would not have to speak with him again for several weeks.

Chapter 3

The master was away for the remainder of the summer. Mrs Cookson told her that he had joined his grandson in the North Riding for the grouse shooting and would stay on to hunt. Harriet was left to her own devices with the child, a luxury for one used to a roomful of little girls who could not concentrate because they were cold and hungry. Her cheeks took on a healthy bloom and she began to fill her gown so that she had to let out the bodice where she had taken it in when it had been given to her.

At Michaelmas, a cart arrived from town with supplies for the kitchen, books, paper and ink for the schoolroom, and cloth for gowns. The bolt of fabric was so heavy that the carter had to help them to carry it indoors and up to the schoolroom.

'It's beautiful, Mrs Cookson!' Harriet exclaimed, as she fingered the grey woollen weave.

'Enough for the three of us an' all. There's cotton, too, for chemises and drawers.'

'I shall give Olivia sewing lessons on wet afternoons.'

'Aye, she's best kept inside in this blustery weather.'

'We shall continue to take our walks. It helps her sleep.'

'Does she still have the nightmares?'

They had become more frequent as the autumn wind and rain stirred the child's memories. On stormy nights Harriet lay awake, waiting for Olivia's cries, ready to rouse her before she screamed. She asked, 'Has she always had them?'

'Since she came to live here. She lost her parents in a storm, you see. She used to scream in the middle of the night and wake the master. He tried to beat it out of her but it made no difference and she just tried to run away.'

'Where did she go?'

'Up on the moor. She was easy enough to find then. I don't know where she went after that but she'd be out all day and come in looking like a gypsy with her drawers off. I had to tell the master then.'

'At least she returned.'

'Only when she was hungry.'

Harriet smiled to herself. She had been at Hill Top House for more than two months now and already Olivia was a different child. She had a rebellious nature, to be sure, but much of her wildness had been because she was bored. Underneath the grime, Harriet had found intelligence and Olivia had learned quickly to read and write. So quickly that Harriet thought her mother must have taught her before she died. Now she was greedy for books, and her uncle's library had become a haven. For Harriet, too, as long as the master was away.

When their new gowns were finished they wore them to church. Olivia's was almost concealed by her pinafore and the short woollen cape that matched her bonnet. But Harriet had trimmed her own with a white cotton collar and cuffs. She had made three sets so that they were always fresh and clean and, as her cloak was old, she let it fall away when she stood to sing the hymns, feeling proud of her appearance and position of governess at Hill Top House.

It was the last Sabbath in October. The congregation was small so the curate came from over the moor, accompanied by his wife, in a borrowed trap. Harriet lingered in the churchyard afterwards, eager for a little adult conversation.

'Is this the wayward child?' the curate asked. 'She looks quite different.'

'She's growing into a bonny girl.' His wife held out her hand. 'Come and walk with me, child.'

Harriet released her grip on Olivia and enjoyed a pleasant exchange with the curate. They talked of her life since she had left Blackstone, which he and his wife had visited, and her teaching. He asked after the master and she reported that he had been away since before the harvest and was not likely to return until Christmas. This seemed to please the curate, who gave a satisfied nod. Harriet was quite disappointed when they had to say goodbye and walk back down the track to Hill Top House.

Olivia fell into step beside her and Harriet resisted the temptation to take her hand. Her charge was proud of her new gown and she hoped she would not risk tearing and soiling it by running wild through the scrub today.

'What did you talk about to the curate's wife?' Harriet asked.

'The books I read. Especially the novels.'

'I see. The pupils at Blackstone don't have novels.' The principal had some in his room, though, and, as a teacher, she had been allowed to read them.

'Oh, I like them best of all.'

'I know.' Harriet's heart sank. The curate and his wife would not approve of Olivia reading novels. They thought that worthy ones were too difficult for a girl to understand and those that were not would put wrongful ideas into her head. She added, 'The Bible is Blackstone's story book of choice.'

'Why do you let me read novels, then?'

'Because you enjoy them.'

'I said I read the Bible every morning, too.'

This cheered Harriet. She wanted the approval of the curate and his wife. She valued their weekly conversations after church. 'What else did you say?'

'I told her about my lessons and our nature walks. And how you are teaching me to care for my gowns. She said it showed.'

'Well, yes, that is very true.'

'And I told her how you stopped me pretending to be a cat catching rats.'

They were approaching the walled garden and Harriet sensed disappointment in Olivia's voice, as though she missed her childhood pursuits and yearned to return to them. Through the summer the brambles had grown thick and strong around the door and they had picked blackberries from them for Mrs Cookson.

'Is your castle still there?' Harriet asked.

'I expect the rain has washed it away by now.'

'Shall we see if Matt can clear the ground in there this winter?'

'What for?' Olivia sounded sullen.

'So that you can grow fruit and vegetables to eat.'

'Can I?'

'Why not? There are books and journals in the library to tell us how. When you are mistress of your own house you will need to know about these things.'

'Mistress of my own house?'

'Of course. It's what ladies of your position do. I shall talk to Matt after dinner.'

'I'm hungry. I wonder what Mrs Cookson has made today. I like Sunday dinner in the kitchen with you and her.'

'I think there's blackberry and apple pie for pudding. When we get closer to the house we'll be able to smell the joint. Let's see if we can guess.'

But when they went into the kitchen, glowing from their walk, there was no delicious scent of roasting meat on the spit in front of the fire and Mrs Cookson was busy kneading bread dough. With the back of her hand, she pushed a strand of hair under her cap. 'Oh, thank goodness you're here. The master's back. I wasn't expecting him for weeks. You'll have to help me with the dinner. I've a brace of fowls to pluck while this dough's rising.'

'We'll do the vegetables. Olivia, take my cloak and your cape and bonnet upstairs, then come down to help.'

'Wh-where is Uncle Hesley?' she asked warily.

'He's resting in his chamber.' Mrs Cookson turned to Harriet. 'He says you and the little 'un are to have your dinner with him later.'

'I don't want to,' Olivia said stubbornly, and sat on a kitchen chair.

Neither did Harriet. She was happy and relaxed at Hill Top House when the master wasn't at home. Now tension was creeping over her and she wondered why he wanted to see them so urgently. She took off her own bonnet and gathered up their outer garments. 'No need to risk disturbing the master. I'll leave these in the hall for now. I suppose we must do as he orders.'

Mrs Cookson gave her an impatient, querying look, as though it should not have occurred to her to do otherwise.

'I'm hungry now,' Olivia whined.

'So am I.' Harriet took her pupil into the scullery to clean her boots and wash her hands. 'We'll have some bread and cheese in a minute,' she reassured her. 'You must remember your manners in the dining room later, and show your uncle how well behaved and grown-up you are.' Harriet hoped he would be satisfied with the child's progress.

'I don't like Uncle Hesley,' she said.

'Hush, you must not say that. He is your guardian and you must do as he bids you.'

'He smells nasty.'

'That is how gentlemen smell. It comes from the cigars they smoke. It is a gentlemanly pursuit and quite pleasant when it is fresh.'

'I don't like it.'

And I don't like the master, Harriet thought. She remembered their last meeting in the library and how he had threatened her. He demanded obedience, and would be ruthless with anyone who crossed him. She felt fearful of the forthcoming meeting.

'You will curtsy to your uncle when we go into the dining room, just as I have shown you. If he speaks to you, you will reply politely with a smile. And truthfully.'

'Even about the novels?'

'You need not mention them unless he asks.'

'What if he is cross with me?'

'He won't be. If he becomes angry it will be with me, not you, I promise.'

'Why does he have to come back? It's been so nice here with you.'

Harriet was pleased to hear her say that. 'I'm still here,' she reassured her. But she agreed. Without the master's grim presence, teacher and pupil had formed a bond. A fragile one on Olivia's part: her reluctance to trust anyone was Harriet's biggest hurdle. But Harriet had persevered. There was a determination in her charge that echoed her own and gave her strength.

She guessed she would need to be strong. Even

though she had not yet seen the master, his presence at Hill Top House was inescapable. Mrs Cookson fussed and flapped about the dinner and Olivia became more fractious as the light faded. Harriet quelled her misgivings and put the finishing touches to her own and Olivia's appearance.

'Remember what I've taught you,' she said, and opened the dining-room door.

The master was sitting at one end of the oak dining-table with a tankard of ale in his hand, and his feet, clad in fancy Oriental shoes, resting on a nearby chair. He wore no jacket and his waistcoat was unbuttoned, so clearly the meal was to be an informal affair. His lined face was more weatherbeaten than Harriet remembered, and his wiry grey hair was shaggy and in need of a barber, as was his stubbled chin. But his eyes were sharp and bright as they swept over her.

'Turn towards the light,' he said, as they stood before him. 'I do believe you have grown, Olivia. Has she, Miss Trent?'

'Yes, sir. She measures herself by the yardstick on the wall when we do numbers.'

'You, too, have grown, I see, in girth.'

'A little, sir.'

'More than a little. Mrs Cookson's doing, no doubt. Sit, both of you.' He gestured towards two places, one on either side of him, at the table and poured ale into another tankard when Harriet took her seat.

'Tell me about your lessons.'

'Well, sir—'

'Olivia will speak.'

The child looked at her, and Harriet gave her an encouraging nod.

'In the morning I do my letters and numbers first, and then I learn some Bible—'

'Bible, eh? Well, I suppose that's the only book you had at Blackstone.'

'We have been going to the church on the moor, sir. The congregation is small, coming only from the few houses still left there, but the discipline of the service has been a good influence on Olivia's behaviour.'

'I told you to be quiet.'

Harriet sank back in her chair and sipped her ale.

'Go on, Olivia.'

'After dinner I learn about history and geography and nature.' She paused. 'And, I am reading Cousin Hesley's books.'

'That'll please your aunt Caroline.'

'Is she coming to see me?'

'Not if I can help it,' he growled.

Mrs Cookson brought in soup, made from leeks thickened with potatoes, and a plate of bread. 'The birds are about ready, sir.'

'Good.' He reached across for bread and took up his spoon. 'Continue, Olivia.'

Olivia sat very still and silent.

'Well?'

Harriet took a deep breath. 'Olivia has been saying grace for several weeks now, sir.'

He grunted and chewed some bread.

Harriet smiled and nodded. Her pupil was word

perfect and she wished she could have kept her eyes open to watch the master's reaction.

When Mrs Cookson came in with the meat, he exclaimed. 'At last! I'm starving.'

He doesn't know what starving means, Harriet thought. She did. Starving was being unable to satisfy your hunger at any meal. Starving was being frightened to start eating because if there was not enough it only made you more hungry when what you had been given was gone. She watched him eat and drink noisily, with appetite.

She had eaten a lot when she had first come here, but not so much now: she no longer had that constant hunger and was confident that the next meal would be substantial. She would not have to let out her old gown again.

However, she enjoyed the roast fowl, bread sauce, the carrots, potatoes and greens that went with it. Olivia behaved as Harriet had taught her, and Harriet was pleased that the child's table manners put her uncle's to shame. Mrs Cookson came in with a bowl of pears and some walnuts.

'Shall we leave you now, sir?' Harriet suggested.

He grunted and waved her away with his tankard.

She stood up and nodded to the child. 'Olivia, you may bring a pear with you.'

When they reached the door the master called Harriet back. 'Come to the candles, where I can see you better,' he said.

She hesitated, wanting to be out of the room and away from him. The meal had gone well and he seemed pleased with Olivia's progress. But she did not wish further discussion with him. He had been drinking ale before and throughout dinner, and Mrs Cookson had advised keeping out of his way when he was drunk.

'I have schoolroom work to do, sir.'

'That can wait. Or would you rather come back . . . later?'

His tone alarmed her. His speech was slightly slurred and his question had made her uncomfortable. Olivia had left quickly, no doubt as anxious as Harriet to be away from him.

Reluctantly, she moved back to the table where the candles gave more light. His unshaven chin moved up and down as his eyes travelled over her. There was no mistaking his meaning. It was as though he were sizing her up at a hiring fair and she felt embarrassed by his invading stare.

'Turn around,' he ordered.

'Sir, I must protest!'

He stood up so quickly, knocking over his chair, that she jumped. He kicked aside another chair and reached across the table for the candelabrum, which he held near as he walked around her. He stopped in front of her. The candles cast weird shadows on his lined features, making him look fearsome and quite menacing.

'Good living becomes you, Miss Trent,' he said.

She did not reply. She was clenching her fists and holding her breath, wondering what he would do next. Then he dismissed her with a jerk of his head towards the door. 'Go and prepare your lessons, then.'

She was out of the room in a second, but lingered

in the darkening hall to allow her heart to slow. How could he treat her like that? As though she were one of his – his *women*! She was a *governess* in this house, responsible for the moral well-being of a *child*! She went into the kitchen where Mrs Cookson was stacking crockery on the dresser.

'Does the master take pleasure in humiliating all his servants?' she asked.

Mrs Cookson gave a half-smile. 'Only the young females as a rule. It's just his way.'

And perfectly acceptable to his housekeeper, Harriet thought. She took a few deep breaths to calm herself, then asked where Olivia was.

'I sent her upstairs. Something's up with the master, mark my words. Things haven't been right since that ruck at the pit.'

'Is that why he has come back?'

'Matt told me he got rid of the troublemakers and that quietened things down.'

'But did he not need all his men to mine the coal?' It was not the miners' fault that the coal seam was poor and it must take just as many men to dig it out. 'With fewer colliers, won't there be less coal to sell?'

Mrs Cookson looked at her sideways with an expression of puzzlement. 'That's nowt to do with you. This is summat different, though. The carter told me last week that the town bank was in trouble and the master would never have left his shooting and rode all the way on horseback if it hadn't been serious.'

'Oh.' Harriet had nothing to do with the bank so she could not comment.

Mrs Cookson went on, 'Will you help me carry hot water up to the landing? The master will take a bath before he goes out.'

'Of course. Shall you need help when he's finished?'

'One o' the farmhands'll see to it. But you could clean his riding clothes for me.'

'Bring them into the schoolroom. I'll show Miss Olivia how to do it.'

Mrs Cookson nodded. 'Wear your new gowns every day while the master's here,' she added.

Harriet was teaching her pupil how to use a flat-iron on woollen cloth when she heard a horse on the cobbles outside. She crossed to the window and saw Matt taking a letter from the rider. A few moments later, she heard his boots on the stairs, then a shout of rage from the master. He was on the landing and she heard him quite clearly: 'Tell him I'm going to the mine now,' he yelled.

Harriet watched as Matt returned to the messenger in the yard, then led out one of the hunters from the stable. Minutes later, the master emerged, dressed smartly in a fine dark coat and high hat. For a man of his advancing years he was still quite agile and sat well in the saddle.

She watched him ride away into the fading light and was aware of relief washing over her. She had not liked the way he had scrutinized her in the dining room. His return to Hill Top House had unsettled her more than she cared to admit.

Chapter 4

Jared Tyler watched quietly from the back of the crowd. Dusk was falling and the Mexton miners had not gone home after their shift. Instead they were hanging about in groups at the back of the Navigator Inn by the canal. Some were already shouting but few had been drinking for most were feeling the cut in wages earlier that year.

'It's not right and we're not standin' fer it!' someone called out. He jumped up on to the back of a cart, waving his hands in the air. 'We've done t'work an' we wants us pay!'

'Aye!' the gathering crowd yelled in agreement.

A lone voice responded: 'Well, 'e can't do that wi'out money from t'bank, lads.'

'Thee shurrup. Owd Mexton can allus find money for 'is drink and 'is women. We know that.'

'Tha can bet 'e's ovver at his whore's house now!'

'Aye, while our wives and little 'uns'll go wi'out their dinners!'

'Aye, an' winter just round t'corner.'

'Manager said he wa' working summat out,' the lone voice responded.

Jared stretched his neck to see who it was. It was a brave man who went against a crowd like this. Or a stupid one.

At sixteen Jared was tall for his age and had learned how to fist-fight at school. He enjoyed the cross-country runs and games that filled his Wednesday and Saturday afternoons and missed them when he was home for the holidays. His father's forge further up the canal in town was doing well. One day he'd be running it for him. He couldn't wait. His father had promised him his own horse for his next birthday.

But Jared knew something was wrong when Father had sent word that he would not be home for his tea as he had to see his bankers. He should have stayed with his mother and sisters but he didn't. He had gone down to the canal and followed a group of ironworks men to Mexton, where the miners were gathering.

'Work summat out?' another voice repeated. 'Like 'e did when we got to that slack? He worked summat out then!'

'Aye! Cut us wages, 'e did, and got rid o' them that complained!'

'Aye, an' 'e'll do t'same again!'

'Shurrup, thee.'

'Shurrup, thissen. Who says we all go to t' pit'ead now, an' 'ave it out wi' 'im?'

'I do!'

'Me an' all!'

'Come on, then, lads. Let's see what 'e 'as ter say this time.' The man jumped down from the cart, took up a heavy stick and led the way.

Jared felt alarmed. Although he didn't like Hesley Mexton any more than the next man, this crowd was baying for blood. He stayed back, skirting around to get to the pithead first. But there was no way he could reach the mine office before the other men. Lamps glowed from a couple of windows in the stone and slate building, and a couple of horses were tethered at the side. He kept his distance, watching the crowd grow in size. Someone lit flares, which made the scene even more sinister.

Jared recognized one or two of the ironworkers joining the march. They knew that pit problems also meant trouble for the furnaces and forges that paid their wages. Besides, they were supporting their kin. Fathers, sons, brothers and cousins, whole families depended on coal and iron in this part of the Riding. The crunch of their heavy boots blended with their mutterings and shouts.

Jared stayed out of sight. His mother might not have much to do with old Hesley Mexton, but she was his half-sister even though she was thirty years younger. Jared's grandfather, old Samuel, had died soon after his mother was born and his grandmother, Samuel's second wife, had been ill-provided for in Samuel's will. She had been shunned by Jared's uncles and had taken her infant daughter back to her own family in town.

No one liked Hesley Mexton around here, and some in this crowd might know Jared was a relative, even though it was distant. As he surveyed the men, he was glad he was a Tyler.

His father was more tolerant of Uncle Hesley than his mother was. Mexton's coal was cheaper than Swinborough's at Kimber Deep and had been just as good until recently. Tyler's Forge had had to refuse a bargeload from Mexton Pit because it was mostly slack and his father had had to buy his furnace fuel elsewhere. But this trouble was about something else, Jared thought. Something that had caused his father enough worry to make him visit the bank, and seemed to be affecting the whole town.

One of the men holding a flare tried to reason with the crowd. He was soon shouted down by an angry mob who, without their wages, would not be able to pay their rent or buy food for their children. As the men pushed nearer to the blackened stone pithead buildings, a few picked up stones and threw them at the manager's office where a light glowed from a window. The sound of breaking glass raised a cheer, and the tension heightened. Jared saw a door open and Hesley Mexton stepped outside. His manager was close behind him, carrying a lantern. The crowd quietened in anticipation.

'I can't pay you without money,' Hesley shouted. 'The bank's closed down. It's failed.'

'Don't give us that! Banks don't fail!'

'It's true,' the manager added loudly. 'The furnaces can't pay us for the coal we've delivered 'em.'

'What are we supposed to do for us rent, then?'

'Every man will get half of what he's due,' the manager replied.

'Aye, an' what we're due is on'y half o' what we're worth!'

This comment started up the muttering and grumbling again and more stones hit the building. Hesley turned aside, shielding his head with an arm, but a rock hit him squarely on his side. He cursed and stepped behind the manager as more missiles landed at their feet.

'It's all we've got in the safe,' the manager added desperately. 'It'll pay your rent.'

'Aye, an' what about bread for us bairns?'

Neither Hesley nor his manager had an answer for that. Jared's attention was drawn to the horses tethered in the shadow of the office building. The noise of the crowd had frightened them and they were restive.

Suddenly the men lost control. They surged forward, shouting and throwing stones, breaking more windows and splintering wood. Jared realized that the pit office would offer no protection for Hesley or his manager. This was a serious business and not only for the pit. His father had reason to worry. His forge relied on regular coal supplies. Also, he used the same bank and his workers wanted their pay too.

The horses whinnied and reared. Hesley and his manager, struck by flying rocks, turned and ran, grabbing the reins of their horses and mounting quickly, spurring the animals to a gallop. A brick caught Hesley full in the back. He yelled and flopped forward, but rallied and urged his horse on. The two men rode away in different directions, faster than any man on foot could catch them.

The mob, angry at their escape, vented their frustration on the buildings and wagons lying around the pithead. Flares were discarded as men rejected them in favour of stone and anything that would serve as a heavy cudgel.

One of the flares landed on a fodder cart for the horses. A bundle of straw smouldered and caught light, spreading to sacks of oats and hay. As it burned, the cart was jostled and began to move, rolling steadily towards the gin-house, containing the steam engine and pit-shaft winding gear.

Cold fear ran through Jared. There'd be coal in there. And grease for the engine, probably oil for the office lamps as well. If that lot went up, the mine would be out of action for weeks! Jared darted around the mob towards the moving cart as the flames took hold. He'd never stop it on his own.

'Take the shaft and heave! Swing it round!' Another man had seen the danger and was running with him. Jared registered an unusual accent but no more as both men leaned for all they were worth to change the wagon's course. It turned slightly and headed slowly towards the army of angry men.

'Fire! Fire!'

The warning spread as quickly as the blaze and the men scattered. The flaming cart rolled gently towards the mine office and toppled, spilling its burning straw and sacks onto the ground. A couple of miners took off their jackets to beat out the flames, but most could only stand and watch as bedding and food for the carthorses were destroyed.

'It's too late! Get back!' The man who had come to Jared's aid stood in front of the fire, facing the crowd. The leaping flames behind him cast his face in darkness and gave his gesticulating form a demonic appearance as he shouted, 'Enough! None of this will help your wives and children. Listen to me!'

'Why should we?'

'Who are you?'

'My name is Tobias Holmes and I'm from County Durham.'

'Nay, I've bin there and tha dun't sound like it ter me.'

'I was in America until recently.'

This seemed to impress and still a few of the rebels. There were stories in the taverns of riches to be made in America. Jared raised an eyebrow. So that was where the accent came from.

'You made a fortune to gi' us, then?'

'No, but I can help to feed your families until this business is righted.'

'Oh, aye? How?'

'I've taken a lease on the old farmhouse. I'll have soup and bread for your wives and children in the barn at dinner time tomorrow.'

There was quiet as the crowd took in the stranger and his offer.

'You from the poorhouse, then?'

'Aye, well, we don't want your charity, we want us pay.'

'I'm a Wesleyan,' Tobias Holmes shouted. 'I'm setting up a mission in Mexton.'

'One o' them preacher types, are you?'

'Like them that live at the Dissenters' House?'

'We're church folk 'ere. We don't want no radical preachers stirring up our womenfolk.'

'I'm not a preacher,' he declared, 'and it's not charity. It'll cost a farthing for each family. Go back to your wives and tell them there'll be dinner in the old barn tomorrow for a farthing.'

The men muttered but the offer was not to be spurned, and they retreated to their homes. Jared licked his lower lip and tasted blood from a cut. His boots and trousers were scuffed and his good jacket dusty. He looked around for his cap and found it trampled in the mud.

Tobias Holmes came over to him and held out his hand. 'Thank you, sir.'

Jared nodded. His grasp was firm. 'It could have been nasty. I'm Jared Tyler. Are you serious about a mission here?'

'Yes. Do you know of us?'

'I learned about Wesleyans at school.'

'You have been to school?' Tobias Holmes stepped back to look at him in the dying firelight. 'Yes, I see now that you're not a miner. You speak well and your coat is cut from good cloth.'

'My father is an ironmaster.'

'Then he will know of the bank's failure. A bad business. The rich will suffer as well as the poor.' Tobias Holmes grimaced. 'But I care only for the poor.'

'The Methodist chapel in town has a growing following.'

'Give us time and we shall set up missions with poor funds in every pit village in the Riding.'

'I wish you well.'

'Thank you. Will you not join us on Sunday? I hold a meeting in the barn at the old farmhouse.'

'I might.'

Jared's mother and father were church people and he was expected to worship with them. He noticed the last of the miners hurry away as a rider approached. It was the constable from town. He slowed and picked his way carefully through the debris of stones, broken glass and charred wood.

'We had better leave,' Tobias Holmes suggested.

They parted, and as Jared hurried home he thought that Tobias Holmes was a different kind of chapel man from the ones he had known in the town and at school. For one thing he was physically strong, more like the miners he wanted to help than the church leaders Jared had known. But, then, he had travelled to America and probably knew how to look after himself. Jared did not have much time for God in his adolescent life but he reckoned he might have time for Tobias Holmes. If he wasn't a preacher, he wondered what kind of meeting he would have. He would go and see for himself.

'Is that you, Jared?' his father called, as Jared closed the door from the kitchen behind him. He stood quite still, hoping his father would go back to his reading.

The door from his study next to the kitchen stood open, casting a glow from the candles into the hall.

'Come in here now. We must to talk. And close the door quietly.'

Jared dusted down his clothes with his hands, but could do little to improve his appearance. Why hadn't he thought to clean himself up in the scullery? He joined his father in the small study. It had once been a morning room, but now that Jared and his younger sisters were growing up, and they had a maid who slept in the attic, they breakfasted in the dining room.

'Where have you been? Your mother's been worried.'

'I'm sorry, Father. Where is she?'

'Gone to bed, so leave her be.' His father approached him with the candle. 'Which is just as well, with the state of you. Have you been fighting? You shouldn't have stayed out so long. Don't you know there's a deal of unrest?'

'Yes, Father.'

'You may think you're a man at nigh on seventeen but, believe me, my lad, you still have much to learn. Did you see any trouble?'

'A gang of ironworkers gathered down by the canal. They went down the towpath to Mexton.'

'And on to your uncle's pit, no doubt,' his father continued sourly.

'Uncle Hesley hasn't paid his men. I heard about the bank. Has Mexton Pit failed too?'

His father gave a short, dry laugh. 'Not yet, son. Hesley always manages to scrape by somehow. He's lost his capital, though, and he was going to use it to sink another shaft and install a new steam engine. I – I was going to invest in it, too.'

'Did Mother know that?'

'No. And don't you tell her now it's not to be. It would have been sound business, though. I can't run my forge without good coal and I'll have to pay more to have it brought from Kimber Deep.'

'The men were angry, Father. They threw stones at him. The constable was there.'

'Aye, I expected that. And Hesley?'

'He was hit, but he rode off. Lost a feed wagon, though. It caught light.'

His father gave a disapproving grunt. 'Sit down, son. This bank business has affected me as well.'

Jared obeyed, fearful of what his father had to say.

'Some of my investments have gone, and the money I owe to Sir William for my pig iron. But he is a fair man and I have a contract with the railway company for my castings. My reputation is good, so my forge will survive. But—' He stopped and Jared sensed bad news. 'I'm sorry, son, I'll not be able to keep you at that school now. There'll be no university either.'

For the first time that day Jared felt elated. He was tired of learning and anxious to be in the forge with his father. What could university teach him anyway? He needed to know how to make cast iron that was strong enough to carry a railway wagon. He tried to look dejected.

'These things happen in business. You'd best learn it now as later,' his father added.

'Yes, Father. I can work for you instead. Let me start

on the smelting. You need not pay me a wage. That'll help, won't it?'

'Can't be done. I'd have to lay somebody else off to give you a job, and it's bad enough having to cut the wages of good men. Besides, after all this trouble some wouldn't take kindly to my son labouring alongside them when their lads languish without work.'

'I can look after myself, Father. I'm the fastest runner at school and I've learned to fight.' He put up his fists.

'Quite so, my lad. I'll not have fighting in my iron-works. It never helps matters and the sooner you know that the better.'

'But I must do something.'

'What about learning to be a shipping clerk at the canal company?'

Not an office! Jared's heart sank. 'I want to be an ironmaster like you, Father.'

'Aye, and I'm proud of you for that. But my plans were for you to help me run the forge when you'd finished at university, not to graft in the thick of the heat with the men.'

'But I want to work at the furnace face, to cast the iron.'

'You need an apprenticeship for that.'

'Well, why not take me on, then?'

'I've told you why. I've already got a lad, and a good one at that. Besides, you've got a sound head on your shoulders and there are other things for you to learn.'

'What things?'

'Well, the Swinborough ironworks are the biggest round here and Sir William has his coal mines too.

He can always use a bright fellow like you. He's called a meeting of his debtors tomorrow. I owe him, so I thought you could be of service to him.'

Jared's eyes brightened. That was more like it. Proper men's work. 'Yes, Father. Where shall I be working?'

'I'll talk to Sir William after the meeting. His iron-works are in town but he has pits on his land, along the cut that goes up past Fordham before you get to Mexton.'

Jared nodded. 'I know. You'd let me go down the pit, then?'

'You won't be doing that. You have to be born into mining. Sir William has men to run his transporting and his engineering. He's up to date on these new steam engines. That's what you need to learn about, my lad.'

Jared's excitement mounted. 'When can I start, Father?'

'Steady on. I haven't asked him yet. If he does take you, you'll have to walk there and back every day because I can't afford the horse I promised you for your birthday. I'm sorry, son.'

'Oh.' Jared was disappointed. 'I could lodge over there, I suppose.'

'Your mother wouldn't like that.'

'I'll come home on Sundays.'

'Let's see what Sir William can do for you first. And, for heaven's sake, brush your jacket and clean your boots before your mother sees them.'

'Yes, Father.'

Chapter 5

Harriet Trent was in the schoolroom when she heard a horse on the cobbles, followed by shouting and the sound of boots running. When she looked out of the window, Matt was helping the master down from his horse. He looked dishevelled and – injured? He was holding one arm close to his body and stooping awkwardly as he shuffled, with Matt's help, towards the kitchen door.

'What's happening?' Olivia asked.

'Stay where you are.'

'Oooh, is it a visitor? Who is it, Miss Trent?' She put down her book and darted to the window before Harriet could stop her. 'It's Uncle Hesley. He's hurt himself!' She ran out of the room, leaving Harriet to hurry after her.

They reached the kitchen at the same time as the master.

'Cookson! *Cookson!* Where is that woman?' he demanded.

Harriet knew she was drinking with the farmhands in the stables and would be the worse for it by now. 'I believe she is in the wash-house, sir,' she answered.

'Fetch her. No, you'll do. Get some water and towels for this bleeding.'

He had a cut on his head and another on his hand.

'What happened, sir?'

He ignored her and sat heavily in one of the kitchen chairs, giving a strangled groan.

'Shall I send for your physician, sir?'

'I'm not dying, merely bruised. By God, one of those rocks got me square in the back.'

A stone? Had he been down his mine? Surely not. He was wearing the smart clothes he had gone out in. They were rumpled and dusty, but not blackened with coal dust.

'Get on with it before I bleed to death!'

Harriet thought there was no risk of that. He was holding himself stiffly in the chair and winced when he tried to change position, but there was no sign of blood soaking through his clothes. She said briskly, 'Olivia, put some cold water into a bowl and bring me clean linen.' Matt hovered by the back door until she added, 'Please go and tell Mrs Cookson. Or fetch her keys, and then take a message to the master's physician. At once.'

Hesley Mexton's face was pale and tense with pain. His eyes were watering and rolling, but he muttered, 'I don't need him.'

'You are hurt, sir, and you should not have ridden.'

He grunted and his head fell forward. Wordlessly she and Olivia attended to the raw grazes on his hands and the cut on the side of his head. It was near to his eye and must have been quite a blow.

The cold water revived him and he even smiled the wry sneer she was becoming used to. 'Ah, the virtuous Miss Trent. What do you think of your master now, eh?'

'That he is injured and should be in bed. Mrs Cookson – at last, thank goodness. Fetch some brandy, would you? Then help Matt get the master to his chamber.'

Olivia obeyed her governess as she tended her uncle's wounds. Slumped in the kitchen chair, he was not the overpowering giant she was used to seeing in the library. He was angry about his injuries, to be sure, and grumbled constantly, but he did not shout, except when Matt and a wobbly Mrs Cookson helped him to his feet, and then it was more like a scream. His gasps and groans continued as they inched him through the gloomy hall and up the stairs.

She followed them, as instructed, with brandy and more linen, and watched with Miss Trent through the open door as they eased him, still clothed, onto his large, four-poster bed. Her hand crept up towards Miss Trent's and grasped it. Olivia felt safe with Miss Trent. She was strict in the schoolroom, but sometimes, like now, she was kind.

Her uncle gave a prolonged sigh, saw her with the brandy, beckoned her over and snatched the bottle from her hand. She stared at him as he swigged and wondered if he would die. She thought she wouldn't be too sad if he did, now that she had Miss Trent.

'Come away, Olivia,' Miss Trent ordered. 'Your uncle needs peace and quiet. Go to the schoolroom and get ready for bed.'

She opened her mouth to protest and Miss Trent glared at her. Olivia closed her mouth and obeyed.

When the apothecary arrived Harriet let him in and introduced herself.

'My name's Harvey, Adam Harvey. How d'y'do? I'd heard in the town what happened. A bad business, very bad.' He shook his head and followed her up the wide wooden staircase.

'What did happen, sir?'

'He hasn't said? Proud man is old Mexton. But it's not his fault the bank failed – and he's not the only one being mobbed by his workers.'

'By his own miners? But surely it is the people he laid off who hate him.'

'You know about that, do you? And that he cut the wages of those he kept on? Now there's no money to pay even them. The constable has a riot on his hands. Mexton's lucky to live so far out of town, and well away from his colliers.'

Harriet was shocked into silence.

Mr Harvey looked about him as he climbed the stairs. 'Is Mrs Cookson about?'

'She – she's not too well, sir.'

'Drunk, I suppose. What about the grandson?'

'He's in the North Riding for the shooting.'

'When will he be back?'

'I don't know, sir. He hasn't been here all summer.'

'Just you, then?'

'There's Matt in the stables.'

'Best place for him,' he replied shortly. 'Wait on the landing.'

He was with the master for a long time and Harriet was dozing in a chair when he came out of the bedchamber. 'He'll rest now and I've left a sleeping draught for when he wakes. Five drops in a glass of wine. He has deep bruising on his back and his ribs are cracked. He must rest.'

She nodded.

'Mrs Cookson will know how to keep him quiet. When she's sober, of course.' He paused. 'Hesley Mexton is no longer a young man, yet he behaves as if he is. It'll be a while before he's right again. I'll be back to see him tomorrow.'

Adam Harvey had left after his third visit since the pit disturbance and the governess stood in the doorway of the master's bedchamber. Shall I send for your grandson, sir?' A large fire raged in the grate. Hesley could feel the heat from his bed. He wondered how long the coal would last.

'What can he do?' He was propped up with pillows in the middle of his four-poster. He tried to shift his position but the pain was too great. The laudanum was wearing off again.

'He would wish to know that you are ill,' she answered.

'I am not ill.'

'Mr Harvey said your ribs are hurt, sir, and your back.'

'It's nothing I have not suffered before.' But he had been younger then, and stronger. 'Leave young Hesley to his pleasures. They'll be over soon enough.' For me too, he thought. The mine is already losing money. And now no hope of investment from the bank. But the sight of the governess in her chaste grey gown with its puritan white collar brought a wry smile to his lips. *She* would not notice a little hardship at Hill Top House.

'I'll go back to the schoolroom, then,' she said.

'Wait. I shall write to young Hesley. Help me to the desk.' It was by the window and had the best view in the house, with an outlook onto the track down the valley where distant chimneys belched smoke. Today, as often, it swirled away to the east and did not reach the clear air at Hill Top House.

'You really should not, sir. Mr Harvey said—'

'I know what he said!' Hell and damnation! The pain was bad. Every movement hurt. He flopped back against the pillows and closed his eyes. If he took the draught he would sleep. But he had affairs to put in order if he was to avoid the bailiffs at his door. 'You will write to Hesley for me. Tell him only of the pit troubles. He must stay away from here until this business is settled.'

She wrote as he directed, sitting stiffly on his leather chair. He guessed she was ill at ease in his bedchamber and it diverted him to imagine her dressed in one of Mrs Wortley's ornate silk gowns. Mrs Wortley . . . He

75

had not paid the rent on her house that was due last Michaelmas. Or her draper's and milliner's bills, languishing in his desk. It was time to draw a line under that particular liaison. She would soon find herself another rich old patron and he would have to make do with the whores.

The governess put down his pen. 'Is that all, sir?'

'No. There is another letter. To Mrs Wortley.' As he dictated, he saw a blush rise to her cheeks, which amused him. She did not know who the woman was, but she had realized what she was to him. He was sorry to be ending his arrangement, terminating the lease on her house and telling her to leave, but there would be others. The governess's cheeks were still pink and her brow was furrowed when she brought the letters to the bed for him to sign.

He managed a twisted grin. 'There'll be another like her soon. Tell Matt to deliver the letter to her.'

He supposed she was wondering if she would be the next to go. She was not one-and-twenty until April and the principal at Blackstone would expect his payment for her until then. He would have to persuade him to make do with the free slack for this winter.

'Do not frown, Miss Trent,' he said. 'You have not my worries. I am deep in debt, with no credit at any bank. I cannot sell my meagre coal to the ironworks and my colliers are up in arms because I cannot pay them.'

His face contorted with pain as he handed back the pen. He had already sold everything that was not entailed by old Samuel's will, and he could not raise another mortgage on what was left. There was Olivia's income, of course, and that was significant. It had paid for young Hesley's education and his own pleasures with Mrs Wortley, but he needed it now to keep Hill Top House going. The clever lawyers for her grandmother's family had tied up her capital so tightly that he couldn't get his hands on any of it. And it was capital he wanted. He decided to review the trust document.

He must have more money now. There was his half-sister, Caroline, married to that dull ironmaster. Her mother's folk had been shopkeepers and he came from the labouring classes. Neither of them had much influence in the Riding, but Benjamin Tyler's cast iron was the best and his credit was good. And he had a contract with the railway company.

Before the bank had collapsed Benjamin had agreed to invest in his mine project. He wondered how much his brother-in-law was good for. As soon as he was up and about again he'd write to him. He'd pen that letter himself. The governess knew too much already.

Adam Harvey had said he would recover and he supposed he would. But how long would it take? He'd die of boredom, cooped up in this house. He wanted his drive and vitality back. The irony! Mrs Wortley would soon have taken his mind off his worries and seen him to rights.

He dare not go into town and risk another attack. The constable himself had ridden out to Hill Top House to warn him to keep away, saying he had no militia to deploy at Mexton. There was a decent whore-house on the Mansfield Road. It was discreet enough, but too many of his creditors took their pleasure there. He was trapped in his home and he did not like it. Until his strength returned, he supposed he would have to sit it out.

'I have recommended that he stop taking the sleeping draught. He should not become dependent on it and his pain has lessened. His usual nightcap will suffice.' Adam Harvey was sitting in the warm kitchen, sipping a hot rum toddy before he made the journey to town on horseback. He had attended the master diligently for a month. 'I shall visit only once a week now, unless he sends for me. He should keep to his bedchamber for another fortnight.'

'You have told him so?' Harriet queried.

'He does not wish it, I know. Perhaps the child can help.'

'How? He – he does not seek her company.'

'She could read his news-sheets for him. His eyes are ageing and I think he might welcome that.'

Harriet pondered the idea. If he agreed, the master might appreciate what a bright and gracious girl his great-niece was, rather than think of her as a tiresome child to be tolerated at best. Her only misgiving was that she would have to supervise Olivia, and Harriet preferred to avoid the master. But, then, so did her charge.

'This injury has taken its toll on your master's health. He needs to change his ways.' The apothecary had finished his toddy and stood up.

Harriet walked into the yard with him. He was not much younger than the master and used the mounting stone to climb onto his horse, then walked the animal carefully towards the hardened, rutted track. They were into December now and it would soon be dusk. A light covering of snow had dusted the hills and frozen puddles crackled underfoot. She pulled her woollen shawl close about her shoulders and went to the coalhouse to collect another bucketful for the master's bedchamber. They were well overdue the next cartload.

He was sitting at his desk in the window, wrapped in a heavy gentleman's dressing robe with his Oriental slippers on his feet. The documents spread in front of him looked formal and legal to Harriet.

'Sir?' she ventured.

'What is it?' He sounded tetchy and she hesitated.

'Mr Harvey has suggested that Olivia read you the news-sheets.'

He growled, and began to shuffle and bundle the thick paper. Then he pushed it into a drawer, which he locked, and slid the key into his pocket. He placed a hand over his eyes and said, 'Bring me the brandy.'

'The news-sheets, sir?'

'I said bring me the brandy.'

'Very well, sir.'

Harriet returned promptly with Olivia, who was clutching a recent news-sheet, and a small bottle of rum with a glass on a tray that she placed on the desk.

'What's that?'

'Rum, sir.'

'I told you to fetch brandy,' he shouted.

She jumped. 'Mrs Cookson says there is none left.'

'I don't want that West Indies poison.' He swept his arm across the desk and knocked the tray to the floor. The heavy glass bounced on the wooden boards but the cork was drawn on the rum and the dark liquid flowed out. 'And get that child out of my sight.'

Harriet glanced at Olivia, who moved closer to her side. 'The carter has not delivered, sir. Not since the – since you were injured. We are low on flour and sugar, too.'

'I don't care about your damned flour! Where is my brandy?'

She swallowed. 'The carter told Mrs Cookson that none of the merchants in town will deliver until your accounts are settled.'

'Damn them! Damn them all to hell! And damn that child, too.'

He staggered to his feet, wincing. Olivia stepped backwards and stumbled against the bed. Harriet did not know why the child was the target for so much of his venom, but she guessed it was to do with the documents he had been studying. Perhaps his responsibility to her had not been bequeathed with the means to pay for it.

She moved forward and placed herself between him and her charge. 'It is not the child's fault, sir. If you will not take the rum, will you have one of Mr Harvey's draughts? I believe there is a dose or two left.' She held her breath, heard the news-sheet crumple and felt Olivia grasp the back of her skirt.

'The laudanum? If there is no brandy it will have to do. Then get the child out of my chamber and tell Matthew to send for my lawyer. I will have money from somewhere. I will.' He sat down heavily on a chair.

Harriet gestured with her head to Olivia, who hurried for the door. Then she mixed his sleeping draught quickly and handed it to him. So much for Mr Harvey's recommendations, she thought. The master became angry at the least provocation, these days. She had tried his suggestion but was thankful he did not wish Olivia to read to him. Any item of news might set off one of his rages. Life at Hill Top House had taken a downward turn for all of them. She could endure his anger and the household economies for she had known much worse in her life and they were no hardship to her. Her only concern was for Olivia, who relied on her protection from a selfish and unpredictable guardian.

The child was everything to Harriet. She had worked hard to gain Olivia's confidence, and intended to be worthy of it at all costs. But she worried when the master focused his anger on his ward and recalled his earlier threat about the asylum. She knew a little about wills and trusts and could only guess at the reason he continued to house Olivia under his roof. He certainly had no love for the child and she feared for both her own and Olivia's future there.

Chapter 6

Jared found his mother in the drawing room, teaching his sisters some new music on the pianoforte. Josephina and Juliana were practising a duet while she stood behind them, nodding in time with the metronome. He listened until they had finished their piece, acknowledging that they played well. They sang well too, but parlour pursuits were not to his taste and he was glad he wasn't a girl.

His mother turned and smiled. 'Jared! you were up early this morning. I heard you moving about.'

'I breakfasted with Father before he went to the forge.'

'What were you doing in the attic?'

'Just looking. There's a pile of clothes and boots up there.'

'You children have grown out of them so quickly. I am going to give them to the vicar's wife for the church school.'

'I could take them to Mexton.'

'Mexton?'

'For the miners' families.'

His mother gazed at him steadily. 'Your father has told me that you went to the pit when the fighting broke out a few weeks ago. We are not responsible for your uncle Hesley's difficulties. It's not our fault.'

'It's not the miners' fault either. Did you know the old farmhouse there had been leased?'

'I had heard. The vicar's wife told me a brother and sister had moved in. Dissenters, she said.'

'Oh, I didn't know he had a sister.'

'You've met him?'

'Mr Holmes? Yes. He helped the constable calm things down. He's running a mission there for the miners' families.'

'I see. You're suggesting I give your outgrown things to Mr Holmes?'

'I can borrow a handcart from the forge and take them there on Sunday.'

'Instead of coming to church with us?'

Church bored Jared and his mother knew it. His father didn't mind when he found something else to do, but his mother did.

'Very well,' she said. 'As long as your father has no objection. It will be a long, cold winter for all of us this year.'

Jared approached a group of lads on the rough ground outside the old barn. They were throwing stones into the air and hitting them with a stick across the scrubby pasture. Any that were missed or landed short were greeted with derisory laughter. He had no doubt that they were miners' children from Mexton, most of them old enough to be working down the pit with their fathers.

He dropped the handles of his cart and wiped his brow with the back of his hand.

'Who are you?' one asked.

'My name's Jared. I'm looking for Mr Holmes.'

'Oh, aye? 'E's in t' barn ovver theer. What you got in t' cart?' The lad lifted the edge of the sacking and peered.

'They're for the mission.'

'We'll push it fer yer, if yer like.'

'Thank you. It was heavy-going uphill.'

'Where yer from, then?'

'The town. Are you Mexton folk?'

'How did yer guess?' They laughed.

The wide wooden doors of the barn were open, throwing a shaft of light into the dim interior. Jared recognized Tobias Holmes, sitting on a stack of straw, talking intently to a young woman next to him.

Her relaxed bearing and easy manner intrigued Jared, and her youthful freshness was in stark contrast to Tobias's sober presence. She wore a plain dark gown, which showed a frill of white petticoat where the skirt was caught up on her makeshift seat. She hugged a brown shawl round her shoulders. Her fair hair was not coiled up as his sisters' was, but tied back loosely, only half covered by an old bonnet fastened with a frayed ribbon.

Even though it was Sunday, Tobias was dressed in tough country clothes, moleskin trousers and waist-coat, a thick jacket and a scarf, for the weather was cold. He seemed unaware of the young woman's pretty charm, but she, Jared thought, was wholly engaged by his conversation. He took off his cap, shoved it into his pocket and straightened his back. 'Tobias?'

'Jared! What a pleasant surprise.' The older man stood up to greet him.

'My mother has sent some things for your mission,' he explained. 'They're outside.'

'They will be most welcome. We'll take them to Mrs Wilton in the village. Come with us as far as the farmhouse.'

Jared's eyes lingered on the woman. She was very pretty.

Tobias smiled. 'This is Sarah Wilton, one of my Sunday-school teachers. Sarah, Jared is the young man I told you about. He helped me when the feed wagon caught light at the protest.'

Jared bowed politely as she slid off the straw, showing more petticoat and a shapely stockinged leg above a brown boot. She acknowledged him with a bob and seemed to have none of the coy shyness shown by other girls he had met.

They walked together, behind the boys pushing the cart, towards the decaying building. Beyond it, scrub-land gave way to spoil heaps, and between them a cluster of brick and slate terraces that housed the Mexton miners and their families. He tried to think of something to say that would impress his new friend.

Tobias opened the conversation. 'You've missed our meeting, but you are welcome to join us for some dinner.'

'Dinner?' He was thinking he should get home straight away.

'It's soup,' Sarah explained, 'in the farmhouse kitchen. You might as well because you'll have to wait for the lads to bring your barrow back from me mam's.'

He glanced ahead and noticed a straggle of young folk in the overgrown farmyard. A couple of the older lads were tucking in their shirts and combing their hair with their fingers.

'There's a pump round the other side,' she added. 'I'm off to help in the kitchen.'

She disappeared, and he was glad of the chance to sluice the dust from his hands and face. A cloth for drying was slung over the pump handle. It was grubby and damp, but he flicked it over his coat and boots and raked at his hair as he had seen the others do.

Tobias was waiting for him with two thick pottery mugs of soup. A hunk of bread was balanced on each. He handed one to him. 'It was generous of your mother to send us the clothes. Are you from a coal-mining family?'

'Not exactly. I'm starting work at Swinborough's soon.'

'Where?'

'I'm not sure yet. My father's arranging it.'

'Well, if you are on this side of the town you are most welcome to join our meetings. I am trying to bring in a travelling preacher once a month and we have a Sunday school in the afternoon for the little ones.'

'At which Sarah teaches?'

He nodded. 'In the barn.'

'Is Sarah from Mexton, then?'

'Of course. Her father's a collier.'

'Oh!' Jared faltered. 'It's just that, well, where did she do her learning?'

'The pit manager's wife taught one or two of the girls until she died. She lent them books to read, too. Now Sarah helps at the pithead.'

'I see.'

'I don't think you do. She's not a pithead lass. She's a clerk.'

Jared was surprised. He didn't know any offices in the town that had girls as clerks.

'Her father paid for her lessons so she didn't have to go down the pit like her mother. Now come and meet my sister, Anna. She set up the Sunday school and has her own mission on the other side of the Riding.'

The younger children were crowding through the back door of the old farmhouse. The older lads and lasses hung back in the yard, talking. Two of the girls had their arms firmly linked and a couple of the older boys stood to either side of them, effectively detaching them from the group. Jared smiled to himself. He knew what was on their minds.

Tobias said, 'There's bread and dripping inside. Would you like some?'

'I must go home now.'

'Well, the Wilton brothers aren't back with your barrow yet and my sister is making tea to drink.'

'Tea?' Tea was dear to buy and his face must have shown surprise.

'Don't you like tea?'

'Oh, yes. Does everybody have tea?'

'The younger ones have barley water. We don't drink ale.'

'I'll have some tea, then. Does the Wilton family live in the village?'

'At the far side, down a lane. There's a row of older cottages that used to be for farm workers.'

'Are they all Dissenters over there?'

'No, but Mr Wilton is. We live by the teachings of John Wesley.'

'You're not a minister, though?'

'I went to America to consider it.' Tobias gazed into the distance for a moment and muttered, half to himself, 'But I found myself wanting.'

Jared was intrigued by this. 'In what way?'

'I should have married, but I did not. I went to America instead.'

'And left behind a broken heart?'

'It was my weakness, not hers.'

'Weakness? If I may say so, sir, you are not making much sense.'

'I took advantage of a fine young girl rather like Sarah but I did not marry her. I wished to become a minister first.'

'So you left her?' Jared was shocked to hear this.

'She found another sweetheart and I thought that

in America I would be away from the distractions of the flesh. I was wrong. The temptation over there was even greater.'

'Another girl?'

'God tested me and found me wanting.'

'So you didn't become a minister, after all.'

'I came back to England a wiser man to serve my faith in other ways. I truly believe it was God's will. When I returned Anna was – well, she needed me. Our parents had both passed on and I had not known her situation was so desperate. She was in very poor health.'

'She is well now?'

'The illness weakened her, but she is stronger now and runs her own mission. She is going there when this Sunday school is established.' Tobias smiled suddenly, and said briskly, 'Sarah will be leaving us soon as well. Anna has found her a place where she can learn to be a proper teacher.'

'I see,' Jared responded.

'So, will you come in for tea?'

When Jared stepped into the kitchen he immediately felt at home. It was a big room with recently whitewashed walls and a cooking range in good condition. There were two bubbling kettles on swing hobs over the fire, and the youngsters had assembled themselves into a line around the table.

A grey-haired woman was pouring steaming barley water into metal mugs that Tobias handed out, and the children were helping themselves from a stack of bread and dripping. They all seemed hungry, even the girls. Jared stood back and watched the food disappear.

Tobias beckoned him. 'Sister, I should like you to meet Jared Tyler. He has brought some winter clothes for the children. Jared, this is Anna.'

The woman looked up at him and he saw that her face was lined with age. But between the lines her skin was flawless, milk white and smooth, and her features were lovely. She had a calm, peaceful expression, which gave her a delicate beauty that even her dowdy brown gown could not dim. He gave her a formal bow, and she curtsied.

'You are most kind, sir. Will you take tea with us?' She handed him a hot tin mug full of dark brown liquid.

'How are the miners' families coping?' he asked.

'Most are finding it difficult on half-pay. But they fear that if the pit closes completely they'll be destitute.'

'Will it come to that?'

'No one knows,' she replied.

Tobias added, 'I am told that the good coal has been worked out. The manager said there were plans for a new shaft, but no money to pay for it.'

'It must be hard for everyone.'

'Families like the Wiltons are all right. Sarah has two brothers down the pit as well as her mother and father, so they are not starving. It's those with babies and very young children who can't manage. Those mothers cannot go down the pit with their husbands. That's why we need the mission.'

Jared felt humbled by his own comfortable exist-ence. He had developed genuine admiration for Tobias and Anna Holmes. They appeared to be using their own funds to support these families. He wanted to help them properly.

'You will thank your mother for us, won't you?' Anna said. 'Why don't you come to our meeting next Sunday?'

That was the second time he had been asked. But Mother and Father went to church and Father didn't hold with some of the chapel ministers stirring up his labourers. 'My family are church folk,' he said.

'You are still most welcome to join us whenever you wish. We always need help in our Sunday school.'

His eyes widened. Jared didn't think he'd be much use as a Sunday-afternoon nursemaid. But these people had mined the coal that had kept his father's forge going, which had enabled him to be educated. They were not the cause of the bank's troubles and he wanted to give something back if he could.

'What kind of help?' he asked.

'Are you any good with numbers?' Tobias responded.

He nodded. 'Mathematics was my best subject.'

'Sarah has no facility with figures.'

And I'm no teacher, he thought, but he said, 'I can show them what I did at school.'

'Would you, Jared?' Anna exclaimed. 'That would be so useful, especially for the boys.'

'Very well, then,' he agreed. 'But I really must get home now. Is my cart back yet?'

Sarah's brothers were waiting with it by the track and she walked with him.

'Is Miss Holmes a teacher?' he asked.

'I don't think so. She organizes things.'

'She's much older than her brother.'

'Not really. She's nine-and-thirty. My mam says she had a hard life while he was in America and that's why she looks older. I think he's about five years younger. He carries his age well, don't you think?'

Jared nodded.

'How old are you?' she asked bluntly.

When he hesitated she added, 'I'm nineteen.'

He considered lying as he could pass for older if he wanted to, but after a pause he replied, 'Seventeen.' Almost, he thought.

'That's old to be starting work.'

'I've been at school.'

Sarah seemed impressed. 'Is your dad well off then?'

'Nobody's well off in this town now.'

'Where do you live, though?' Sarah persisted.

'On the valley road. I expect I'll lodge somewhere when I start work.'

Sarah sighed. 'You're lucky. You'll have a future at Swinborough's. Not like us. I don't know what we'll do if the pit closes.'

He took hold of the cart from her brothers. They were big, brawny lads and went to stand at either side of her. Their unspoken message was clear: she was a pretty girl, bright and friendly, and he was a stranger, not to be trusted. He supposed he'd get to know them better if he helped in the Sunday school. Had he really volunteered to teach arithmetic to miners' children? He had surprised himself, he thought, as he pushed the cart along the towpath towards home.

He spent the next day rummaging though his

school books and copying number exercises onto some paper.

His father was late home for tea, but when they had finished, he had news for them.

'I've arranged for Jared to work in the winding house at Kimber Deep. It's Sir William's biggest pit and he'll learn all about steam engines.'

Jared grinned with delight.

His mother was not so happy. 'It's so far out of town, Benjamin, and that towpath can be dangerous after dark.'

'Don't fret, my dear. He will lodge with the supervisor and his wife.'

Caroline frowned, then smiled. 'He'll have Sunday off, won't he, to come home?'

'Indeed he will. Every week. Isn't that generous?'

'Thank you, Father.' Jared felt mounting excitement. 'When do I start?'

'Me and your mother'll take you over in the trap before tea next Sunday. You'll be up at six for work the day after, checking loads and keeping accounts.'

'I thought you said I'd be on the steam engines.'

'All in good time, my lad.'

'Will I be paid?'

'A bit. Most of it will go for your lodgings, but you'll have some left over. There's not much to spend it on at Kimber Deep so I don't want to hear tales of you making merry in the alehouse. Do y' hear?'

'Yes, Father.'

Jared was happy on two counts. First, he would be working at last, doing real men's work. And on Sir William's steam engines! He couldn't wait. Second,

Kimber Deep was up the Fordham cut, which was on the way to Mexton. It was much nearer to the old farmhouse than his home was so he'd be able to see his new friends.

His father said, 'You'll get home in time for church on Sunday.'

'Unless the weather's bad,' his mother cautioned. 'We don't want him catching his death.'

'No, of course not, my dear. It's too far to walk in the rain.'

'There must be a church over there somewhere,' Jared suggested.

'Aye,' his father agreed. 'I'll ask the supervisor where he worships.'

'Oh, but you will come home when you can,' his mother begged. 'I shall miss you.'

Jared stood up, towering over her. He bent to kiss the top of her head. 'You'll see more of me than you did when I was at school, Mother. I shall be here every Sunday if the weather is fair. You can depend on it. Would I miss one of your Sunday dinners?' He exchanged a glance with his father, who smiled and nodded, then jerked his head in a gesture for him to leave.

His sisters were sewing in the drawing room. He went through the kitchen into the backyard and down the garden to the stable where they kept the pony and trap. He had already bedded the horse down for the night, but stroked the pony's nose and spoke to it. 'Well,' he murmured, 'if Sundays are rainy this autumn, Mother won't be happy but I shall. I shall be able to go to Mexton.' He felt a pang of guilt as he hoped for bad weather.

His mother had baked a cake full of dried fruits for him to take to his lodgings the following Sunday, which pleased the supervisor's wife. Her children had grown up and left so she was glad to have someone to look after. The house was a decent size, with a front room they called a parlour and three upstairs chambers. It was fairly new, built of local stone for an overseer, and near to the pithead. They had tea in the parlour, with fresh baked scones, before his mother and father left.

'I'll ride with you as far as the turnpike,' Jared said. 'I could do with the walk back.'

It was getting dark, and as soon as they were out of sight he ran down the cut to the canal, over Fordham Bridge and across country to Mexton Pit. The barn was locked and in darkness, but there was a light in the farmhouse.

Tobias was sitting at the kitchen table adding up figures in a ledger, and his sister was opposite, writing a journal. After they had greeted each other, Jared said, 'I'm sorry I missed your meeting. I couldn't get away any earlier.'

'You're always welcome,' Anna replied.

He showed them the exercises he had written out. 'I've begun on the lessons, but I start work at Kimber Deep tomorrow.'

'You're going down the pit?'

'I'm in the engine house. I shall be able to come over here, but not every Sunday.'

'We shall look forward to seeing you.' Tobias echoed his sister's sentiments. 'Will you sit down with us now?'

'They're expecting me at my lodgings. I have my school books there so I can copy out some more exercises.' He hesitated, then added, 'Do you have your meetings when it rains?'

'Of course.'

'Good,' he replied. 'And now I must get back. I don't want them fretting about me on my first night.'

He took his leave and ran all the way back to Kimber Deep, taking off his jacket, shirt and vest when he got there to wash his arms and chest at the pump before he went into the house. This seemed to impress the supervisor, who gave him a small tankard of porter as a nightcap. Jared slept well in his new bed, thinking of his new job, his new friends and his new life.

Sunday became the focus of Jared's week and he looked forward to his visit to the Mexton mission. The weather was fine and his parents would expect him at home, so he rose early to join the morning meeting in the barn. He stood and listened to Tobias giving Bible readings he recognized. Anna led the hymns. She had a good singing voice, Jared thought.

He guessed that three or four Mexton families were present. Mr and Mrs Wilton made room for him among their children and he lingered afterwards, outside in the wintry sun, talking to Mr Wilton about his new position. He forgot the hour and had to run down the towpath to reach home before dinner. The Yorkshire puddings were already on the table when he slid breath-lessly into his chair.

'I'm sorry, Mother. It's further than I thought from Kimber Deep.'

'You must set off earlier next week,' his father replied seriously.

'You're here now,' his mother said. 'Pass the gravy to Josephina and tell us about your work.'

It had been less strenuous than he had expected, and his supervisor didn't let him anywhere near the steam engines so he was stuck in an office with little chance to talk to the other men at Kimber Deep. 'I've been checking loads and recording numbers in a ledger,' he reported, with a groan.

'That's responsible work. You make sure you do it right.'

'Yes, Father,' he replied automatically. He found his new job easy enough, but there wasn't much else to say except that he wondered how long he would put up with the boredom. He changed the subject. 'What have my little sisters been doing while I've been away?'

His lateness was forgotten as they told him about their drawing lesson and their music. They finished the Yorkshire pudding and concentrated on the joint of roast pork that their father was carving before them.

Josephina said, 'Will you sit for us after dinner? We want to draw your likeness for Mother.'

'I can't stay. I've some reading and calculations to do before tomorrow.' It was the truth, he thought, even if it was for the Sunday school. He saw that his sisters looked disappointed and felt a pang of guilt. He went on lightly, 'Why not wait until you've had a few more lessons?' He was relieved when they laughed.

'Give him time to settle in at Kimber Deep, my dears,' his mother chided gently.

Juliana, the younger, protested, 'But the weather will get worse and then you won't come home at all.'

'You'll be here when you can, won't you, son? Just make sure you get to a church over there when you can't be with us,' his father added firmly. His tone told them all it was his final word on the matter. He picked up his carving knife and asked, 'Now, who would like more crackling?'

Jared stayed to listen to his sisters play their new duet, then sprinted down the towpath towards Mexton. The barn was empty when he reached it and he headed for the farmhouse.

Anna must have seen him through the kitchen window for she came outside to greet him. 'Jared! Come.'

'Phew! It's warm in here.' He blinked. The kitchen was crowded. All the bread and dripping had gone and the youngsters were lining up in the scullery to wash their hands and faces in warm water.

'The children were hungry. They don't get much dinner nowadays.'

Jared felt the second pang of guilt that day as he thought of the good dinner he had devoured.

Tobias was collecting the empty tin mugs. When he saw Jared, he said, 'Hello, again. Will you help me with these?'

The two men carried a pailful of mugs outside to

rinse them at the pump. They took off their jackets, rolled up their shirtsleeves and filled the pail with water.

'It's good of you to call,' Tobias said.

'I'm sorry I didn't get over earlier. I'd like to do more to help.'

Tobias stopped rinsing the mugs. 'We are grateful for your support. What do your parents think about you coming here?'

'We haven't discussed it.'

'You should.'

Jared nodded and put a handful of mugs to drain on a clean plank. He wondered what his father would say. Well, it would be best to tell him, rather than let him hear it from somebody else. He just needed to find the right moment.

Chapter 7

Jared liked his Sundays at the old farmhouse. He even enjoyed the rush to get there before the end of Sunday school. He took number exercises he had learned at school and gave them to the village lads after Sarah had taught them their letters. He'd never met anyone like Tobias and his sister before and he was glad to be of help to them. He thought their mission was not only necessary for the survival of Mexton villagers but seemed well organized and orderly. He continued his visits as the autumn days shortened and winter mists slowed down traffic on the canal.

He went home too, fearful he might be neglecting his family, but by the middle of the month he realized that, although they were pleased to see him, his father was not in a good humour when he greeted him. Jared ate his dinner and talked about his work.

His father pushed away a clean plate and said, 'That was a very good dinner, Caroline, my dear. Don't you agree, son?'

'I do. Thank you, Mother.'

She smiled. 'It's such a pleasure to see you on Sunday, Jared. Juliana and Josephina would like you to sit with them for their drawing this week.'

'I must get back before dark. The mist soon comes down along the towpath.'

'He can take a lantern, can't he, Benjamin?'

'Of course, if he wishes.' His father turned to him. 'You never stay long enough on a Sunday.' The dinner had not lifted his father's mood.

'It's difficult, staying with the supervisor and his wife. I have to fit in with their ways.'

'And they know that you are expected to spend Sunday with your family.' His father's voice was sharp. 'I want to talk to you, son, in my study at half past the hour.'

'Yes, Father.' He sighed. A telling-off, no doubt. He supposed he deserved it. He sat in the drawing room while his sisters drew his likeness and examined their efforts afterwards. They were talented, he thought. His mother was too, but their other drawings of garden flowers and ladies' outfits held no appeal for him. Now, steam engines and the machinery they drove would be another matter. He was reading everything he could find about them and wanted to learn more. Perhaps his father wanted to talk about that. He was more cheerful when he went into the study.

'Now, son, I know it's hard for you, settling into

your new lodgings, and it's a long walk for you to come home, but your mother and me expect you here well before midday. You could at least make the effort to get home in time to go to church with us.'

'I'm sorry, Father.'

'And then you're off again as soon as you've eaten your dinner.'

'I'm not going back early today,' he replied smartly. His father gave him a keen look, so he added, 'It's just that I – I've made some new friends.'

'Family comes first on a Sunday. Who are these friends?'

'I have told you about them. Tobias Holmes and his sister.'

'Not them dissenters at the old farmhouse?'

'They're nice folk, and they're doing a lot to help the families of miners who have no work. They have meetings in the old barn and a Sunday school and—'

'Is that where you're spending all your time?'

'Miss Holmes gives the miners' children tea in their farmhouse. They've cleaned it up and put in a cooking range like ours. You should see it, Father.'

'They're radicals, preaching all sorts of ideas to my labourers. I'll not have you going there, do you hear?' His father had raised his voice.

'They're not all radicals. Some just want to help.'

'How, though? By stirring up trouble?'

Jared was annoyed at his father's assumptions and responded angrily: 'By feeding starving children!'

His father narrowed his eyes. 'I know some do charitable work, but so does the church and we're church folk. What would your mother say? I don't want you involved with them.'

He wished he hadn't started this conversation now. 'You don't know them,' he replied.

'I know that being rebellious is part of growing up for you,' his father snapped.

'Well, I'm old enough to make up my own mind.'

'No, you're not! You stop this right now, my lad. You do as you're told and behave yourself or I'll give you the whipping of your life.'

Jared didn't care about a whipping. He'd been hardened to those at school. But he was angry that his father had judged him and his new friends so harshly. He'd only made his situation worse by trying to discuss it. He heaved a sigh and muttered, 'Yes, Father.'

His father nodded and pursed his lips. 'Good. Now we'll go into the drawing room together and listen to your sisters play their new piece. Your mother has something to say to you as well.'

Josephina and Juliana sang and played. They were attractive to look at and, although a little younger than he was, they were growing up fast. As he was. Jared realized that he would be as watchful as Sarah's brothers about anyone who came courting them.

'Excellent,' his father said, when they had finished. 'We'll have some jolly evenings this winter, to be sure. Now, Caroline, my dear, tell the children about our invitation.'

His mother beamed at them. 'We are going to your uncle Hesley's for our Christmas feast. He has written to invite us and I have said yes.'

'Uncle Hesley's? Why? You don't like him.'

'Jared!' His father scowled.

'Well, it's true that I do not approve of the life he leads,' his mother said, 'but he is my half-brother and we are the only family he has outside Hill Top House. He wishes us all to be together for the festivities. I believe that, since his troubles at the pit and his injuries, he may have reformed a little. His grandson has finished at the university, and Hesley tells me he has engaged a governess for Cousin Olivia. He knows that I worry about her. I should think he wants to show us how well he can look after her.'

'More likely he wants to borrow money from Father,' Jared muttered.

When his father gave him a dark look but did not chastise him again, Jared knew he had been right.

His father said, 'I haven't any to lend him. He had a fright over the bank failure, so perhaps he has come to realize how important his family is to him. To all of us. I am sure that is why he is being so generous this festive season. So,' his father stood up, 'we shall make a special effort to be united, for your mother's sake and for little Olivia.'

'How old is she now?'

'Thirteen. A year younger than Juliana. I shall offer to bring her here to stay with us for a while. She must be lonely there and my daughters will be good company for her.'

Chapter 8

The following afternoon, governess and pupil were walking in the pasture above Hill Top House. A fresh breeze was blowing and they could see the smoking chimneys of the ironworks in the distant valley. The town was spreading, with rows of cottages to house labourers for its prospering manufactories. The master's pit was out of sight, on the other side of town where the navigation disappeared between the hill slopes. As they rested on a dry-stone wall, they saw riders approaching. There were two, and their horses slowed on the steep, rutted track to the house.

Harriet recognized one horse and its rider. 'It's Matt back already. Do you know who is with him?'

'That's Cousin Hesley,' Olivia said quietly.

Harriet glanced at her. 'Aren't you pleased to see him?'

'No. He pulls my hair and pinches me.'

'Surely not. He is a young gentleman.'

'He whips me, too, with his riding crop.'

'He gives you punishment?'

'Only when I get in his way. Then he laughs at me.'

Harriet frowned at the idea of such thoughtless behaviour. She reached across for Olivia's hand and said, 'We shall show him how grown-up you are now, and then he will treat you as a lady.'

They continued to watch as a cart laden with travelling boxes and sacks trundled a few hundred yards behind the riders. Cousin Hesley had brought provisions with him as well as luggage, but Harriet wondered why he had returned from his shooting and hunting.

'We had better hurry back,' she suggested. 'Mrs Cookson will need our help.'

But Mrs Cookson sent them to the schoolroom with game pie and pickles for their tea, saying, 'The gentlemen are receiving visitors later. If I were you I'd stay out of sight until tomorrow.'

During the evening Harriet saw from her window several riders arrive. They were smartly clothed with fine coats, boots, and tall hats. Before long they were making a lot of noise in the drawing room.

After tea, she taught Olivia the words to more hymns and they sang them together as best they could without any music. This helped to drown the shouting downstairs and soon her pupil was sleepy from their earlier long walk. When Harriet went to fetch hot water from the kitchen, she hurried past the dining room.

Mrs Cookson was nowhere to be found and had

left untidy debris from the gentlemen's cold supper on the table. She put the food in the pantry, took the dirty pots to the scullery and wiped down the tabletop. The fire was low, but the water in the range boiler was still hot. She filled a ewer and hastened upstairs.

After Olivia had gone to bed, Harriet read, as she did on most evenings. She looked forward to this time and had found several books in the master's library to occupy her. She sat by the window and lit a candle when the light faded. The noise downstairs lessened and she heard horses' hoofs on the cobbles in the yard as, finally, the gentlemen left. She put down her book to watch them.

Young Hesley was out there, in his shirt sleeves and waistcoat, holding a lantern. When he turned he looked up at her window and Harriet drew back, wishing she had extinguished her candle. A few minutes later he walked into the schoolroom, closing the door behind him.

He was a handsome fellow, she thought, with the tall, straight stance and good features of his grandfather. But he carried a horsewhip in one hand and a silver hip flask in the other. His swagger made her nervous. His dress was dishevelled and she guessed he had been drinking all afternoon and evening.

'So you're the governess?' he said. 'Miss Trent.' He spoke her name with a mild scorn that she found disrespectful.

'Please be quiet, sir. Olivia is sleeping.'

'Is she now? Just you and me, then?'

'You will be good enough to leave my school-room, sir.'

'It's *my* schoolroom.'

'Sir, you are intoxicated!'

'And you are not.' He offered her the flask. 'Join me, governess.'

'No, sir.'

He flicked his whip across the table leg. 'I said join me, damn you!'

Harriet jumped, shocked by his language and behaviour. She moved to the door, intending to hold it open for him to leave. But as she neared him he snaked an arm about her waist and pulled her close.

At first she was angry that he gave no thought to his sleeping cousin, but then her fury heightened. He had assumed she would obey him without question. She tried to remove his arm but it was anchored firmly around her body. 'Not thinking of running, are you?' He grinned.

She strained her head away from him. Her anger was turning quickly to fear. He was tall and strong, he smelled strongly of spirits, and his grip was tight. She was frightened of what he might do next.

She had never experienced such an attack from a gentleman – or, indeed, from any man – and could only say, 'Stop this at once, sir.'

It was inadequate, she knew, for he was not listening to her. But in her increasing panic she could not think what else to do. Mrs Cookson could not help her. She was in the stables, probably drunk by now. And she dared not call for the master for he was sure to blame her for the incident. It was always the servant's fault.

'Comely armful, aren't you? What was your name? Ah, yes. Miss Trent. The comely Miss Trent. The governess.' His speech was slurred and he spoke with an exaggerated slowness as if he wanted to be sure that he articulated the words correctly.

Her heart was pounding with dread and she tried to steady it by breathing slowly. She knew she was no match for his strength. He tossed aside the whip and took the flask from his other hand, draining it into his open mouth. Then he threw it across the room. Dread turned to horror as his hand fell on the swell of her breasts and he dug his fingers roughly into her flesh. She squealed and tears sprang to her eyes. 'No, sir. No,' she begged. 'Please let me go.'

'Over here,' he growled, and dragged her towards the schoolroom table, pushing her backwards and pressing his body to hers. 'C'm'on, governess,' he slurred. He grasped her chin. His florid face and open lips had made contact with hers before she knew what was happening.

She screamed in her throat and struggled to break free of him. As she did so the schoolroom door banged against the wall and, over his shoulder, she saw the master standing in the doorway with a lighted candle in a brass holder. 'Oh, no!' she cried.

Hesley's grip slackened and he slumped over the table. She scrambled away from him to stand alone in the centre of the room. The master would dismiss her for this. And without a testimonial. Oh, Lord, no! Where would she go and what would become of Olivia?

'Stand up straight, Hesley, and get yourself off to bed,' the master barked.

Hesley turned his head slowly and gave his grandfather a look of contempt. The master took him by the scruff of his shirt, hauled him across the room and flung him out of the door. Harriet heard the younger man stagger along the landing as the older one turned to face her with a questioning look.

'Sir, please believe me, he came here uninvited . . .' Harriet began anxiously.

'I know my grandson, Miss Trent.' He sniffed audibly and looked her over in the candlelight. 'And your gown becomes you.'

She was relieved that he had sent away his grandson but she had the same uncomfortable feeling she'd experienced with him before: humiliation, as though she were a beast being sized up for market. She remembered Mrs Cookson's warnings about the Mextons, and although she was grateful for the master's intervention, she wished he would not stare at her so.

Harriet swallowed. 'What will you do, sir?' she asked.

'Do?'

'Am I dismissed, sir?'

He guffawed. 'Why should I want to dismiss you? You are an excellent servant, and mine until you are one-and-twenty at the very least. As I said, I know who is at fault here.'

She breathed an audible sigh of relief. 'You will be kind enough to ask your grandson not to visit the schoolroom.'

'He will keep away from you. I shall see that he does.'

'Thank you, sir. Goodnight, sir.'

110

He stood looking at her for what seemed a long time, then turned away. She closed the door quietly after him and went through to her bedchamber. She hoped Olivia had not woken and heard any of the unfortunate incident.

'You must do something with your time, Hesley.'

'What do you mean? Am I not a gentleman?'

'You must use your education.'

'Why, for heaven's sake?'

'Because it cost me a great deal of money.'

Grandfather and grandson had had a good day out in the fields with their guns. There were not many birds in these parts but hare was plentiful and Matt's cousin had been over with his dogs. They had deposited their bag on a stone slab in the outside larder.

The master of Hill Top House had glanced into the kitchen window and noticed the womenfolk eating their tea. 'We'll talk in my study. I've taken delivery of a case of sherry wine. Adam Harvey says it's better for my health than spirits. Try a glass with me.'

As they stretched out their feet to the fire the mud on their boots began to dry and crack in the heat.

'What do you want to do, Hesley?'

He sipped his wine appreciatively. 'This is rather pleasant. A case, did you say?'

'Well?' Old Hesley was not to be distracted.

'Travel. Do the Grand Tour. Italy is the country to visit, these days.'

'Can't be done, I'm afraid. The pit is still losing money. You need a profession. What about Parliament?'

111

'Good God, no! I'd rather run the mine for you.'

'Would you, by heaven? Do you think you'd make a better job of it than I can?'

'It can't be that hard. You don't spend much time there.'

'No, but I can do the manager's job if I have to!' he snapped. 'Besides, I have other interests to deal with. The plantation, for example.'

'Olivia's trust, you mean? When does she inherit?'

'Not until she is five-and-twenty.'

'But the revenue comes to you until then. It's safe, isn't it?'

'It's dwindling, Hesley. I cannot have you wasting your time.'

'I can occupy myself well enough.' Young Hesley grinned and refilled his glass.

'Not on my doorstep with my servant. I will not have it.'

'Very well. I'll find my women in the town.'

'As long as you stay clear of Mexton. You will not be welcome there.' Old Hesley became impatient. 'Don't you understand? The plantation is our future and now that the slave trade has stopped, emancipation will follow, mark my words. Then I shall have to pay the slaves as free men. What do you think that will do to our income?'

'I heard that freeing the slaves will benefit the plantation owners. The government is to give compensation.'

'So they say. But with such upheavals and uncertainties I need a man out there I can trust.'

'*Out there?* I hope you're not thinking of me!'

'Of course I am. You are one-and-twenty and you need occupation.'

'Good God, Grandfather! Not the West Indies. I will not go there.'

'You will do as I say.'

There was a silence as both men reflected on this difference. Then the elder spoke again. 'Where's your sense of adventure, Hesley? Your father would have welcomed the chance to leave Hill Top.'

'My father died because he did as you demanded of him.' The younger man choked into his sherry.

Again there was a short silence.

'You forget that he was also my son. His death was an accident and his loss to me is as great as it is to you. You were just a babe in arms at the time and I have kept what is left of this family going since then. You have not wanted for anything, Hesley. It is time to repay.'

'There must be someone else more suited than I.'

'Who? Where? You and Olivia are the only family left.'

'There's your half-sister,' his grandson added, and was silenced by his glare.

'You are our future, Hesley, and I have made my decision. You'll sail in the spring and we shall speak of it no further until after the Christmas feast.'

Young Hesley grimaced, but was cheered by the thought of festivities. 'Are we invited to Swinborough Hall this year?'

'No. We shall stay here for a family party.'

'What family?' he demanded petulantly.

'Aunt Caroline's.'

'God, no! We haven't seen them for years.'

'Tyler's lawyer talks to mine. His forge is one of the few that have survived this banking catastrophe. I need some of his capital.'

'But do we have to put up with all of them?'

'Apparently your aunt Caroline heard rumours about Olivia's wild ways and consulted the lawyers.'

'What for?'

'She wanted to help. Tyler's a family man and shares her concern. One day and one night, Hesley, is all it will take to bring them both to my side and stop them meddling. I am Olivia's guardian and I have plans for her.'

'So that was why you employed a governess. A good choice, Grandfather.'

'I have warned you to keep away from her, Hesley. Surely there are enough women in the town to satisfy you?'

Young Hesley contemplated the idea. The hunting had excited him and the sherry wine was warming his blood. An innkeeper's daughter had caught his eye . . . His loins stirred. He stood up quickly and the caked mud on his boots fell to the floor. 'I shall go out, Grandfather. Take one of the hunters for a gallop. Don't expect me back for supper.'

His grandfather smiled indulgently. They were cast in the same mould. His son, Hesley's father, had not been. By tradition Mexton men should be strong and vigorous, with the means to indulge their capacity for drinking, gambling and women. Where his son had

114

failed his grandson would succeed. He was a Mexton, through and through.

While the master ordered his grandson's future, Olivia's mind had been on more domestic affairs. From the kitchen window she had seen the hunting party tramp across the yard. 'They're back,' she exclaimed.

'Looks like a good bag. They'll be ready for Sunday dinner,' Mrs Cookson commented.

'I don't like hare,' Olivia moaned. 'Do you, Miss Trent?'

'Yes, with redcurrant.'

'I've a few jars of jelly in the pantry. And I expect they've a rabbit or two for you, Miss Olivia.'

'Perhaps you would care to taste roast hare this Sunday,' Miss Trent suggested. 'You are a young woman now and you should try all the dishes.'

'I don't see why,' Olivia replied rebelliously.

'One day you will be mistress of a large house like this one and you must learn when hare and other game are at their best. A good mistress should know more than her servants about domestic affairs.'

Olivia wrinkled her nose. 'Do you mean that, one day, I would give orders?'

'Yes, indeed.'

Olivia considered the notion of being grown-up and running the household at Hill Top. She liked the idea and wondered how she would learn to be a good mistress.

'Can you teach me?' she asked.

'Of course. There are books in the library and I shall

ask the master to take out a journal subscription for you.'

Mrs Cookson looked up from her faggots and gravy. 'She can help me in the kitchen. The master's so much more work now he doesn't go into town. And young Hesley will keep having card parties, needing supper for his friends.'

'We shall both help you, Mrs Cookson.' Miss Trent reached out for Olivia's hand. 'I learned much about prudent domestic management at Blackstone.'

'Aye, well, the master won't be wanting too many of those economical ways. We have two barrels of ale in the scullery and the carter delivered sherry and brandy with the provisions.'

'Cousin Hesley has a new saddle for his horse, too,' Olivia said, 'and a new gun. I saw him cleaning it in the gun room.'

'The master must have paid his suppliers, then,' Miss Trent observed. 'Finish your tea, Olivia, then go to the schoolroom for paper and ink. With your permission, Mrs Cookson, we shall make an inventory of all the household linen and china this very day.'

Olivia mopped up the last of her gravy with a crust of bread. This was different, she thought. Miss Trent was always thinking of new tasks for her to tackle. At first she had resisted such intrusion into her days. But not the nights: when she woke from her nightmare, cold and alone, her governess always stayed with her until she went back to sleep. And many of her school-room exercises interested her. Although she missed the freedom to roam on the moor or hide in the old garden, she liked her hair and clothes to be clean and pretty and she loved reading. On the whole, she was pleased that Miss Trent had come to Hill Top House.

Mrs Cookson stood up. 'Well, the gentlemen will be wanting their supper after all that hunting.'

Olivia sniffed the air. 'It's duck.'

'Aye, I'm doing it slow in the bake oven. That's your first lesson, Miss. Don't put duck on the spit because the fat splatters in the fire.'

'I'll clear the tea things,' Miss Trent volunteered.

Olivia went upstairs for writing paper, and Miss Trent drew hot water to wash the pots. When she returned, Olivia helped her governess by drying the plates. They were stacking clean china on the kitchen dresser when she saw Cousin Hesley cross the yard to the stables and later gallop away towards the track down to the town.

Minutes later Uncle Hesley came into the kitchen. 'Cookson, a word.'

Mrs Cookson was checking the duck. She turned smartly. 'Yes, sir?'

'We are having house guests for Christmas this year. See to it.'

Olivia inhaled quickly. House guests! She wondered who they might be.

'And help Matt to clean the carriage,' Uncle Hesley went on. 'We shall be using it for our visitors.'

Olivia put down a plate, unable to contain her excitement at this news. 'The carriage! Oh, Uncle Hesley, please may I ride in it?'

He frowned, first at her and then at her governess,

who had stopped what she was doing as soon as he had entered the kitchen. Now she urged Olivia to be quiet.

Uncle Hesley did not smile much, but his face took on an odd twist, which, Olivia had noticed, he seemed to reserve for Miss Trent. She thought it was more like a sneer than a smile.

'The child needs a gown, a fancy affair for the festivities. Mrs Cookson will advise you.'

Olivia's eyes widened. A proper grown-up gown. Like those she had seen in the journals. Uncle Hesley was going to let her join the party. Her first Christmas with the adults! Oh, she was impatient to know more and had to clench her fists to stop herself asking questions.

She felt Miss Trent's hand take hers and glanced up into her face. Her eyes were bright and she was smiling at Uncle Hesley. Olivia could not remember seeing such pleasure in her face before.

'Of course, sir,' Miss Trent replied.

Chapter 9

For Olivia, the past six weeks had been a whirlwind of pleasure. A dressmaker had called at the house with journal illustrations, materials and ribbons for her to choose from. She was measured for her gown. And a corset! She could scarcely wait for Christmas to arrive. Miss Trent curled her hair and dressed it elegantly in coils around her head, determined she would be a perfect lady for Aunt Caroline's visit. And now the day she had looked forward to so much had arrived.

Miss Trent straightened her blue silk skirts, twisted a curl over her ear, then opened the schoolroom door. Olivia was feeling very grown-up in her beautiful gown, but her stomach was filled with butterflies as she stepped out onto the landing – and jumped.

Then she collected herself. 'You're Jared, aren't you?'

Miss Trent was watching from the doorway: Olivia's

half-cousin from the town had come to take her downstairs for Christmas dinner.

'That's right. And you are Olivia?'

Olivia nodded. 'Do you like my gown?' She twirled, lifting the full silken skirts and petticoats to show matching slippers. Underneath, she wore the new corset, which drew in her waistline and made her small breasts swell above the low neckline.

Jared tried not to show his reaction. He hadn't seen her for years and was surprised by how much she had grown. He had thought she would look much the same as his sisters, but she was taller – and prettier. She was almost a young woman in that gown, with her fair hair done up in coils. She wore jewellery, too, at her throat and in her hair, and long lace gloves.

He had expected her to be shy as he knew they rarely had company and the poor child never went out anywhere. But she didn't seem to be a 'poor child' any more. She was confident with her appearance. It must be the governess, who had already retreated into the schoolroom and closed the door. Olivia was his responsibility for the evening.

'Last night Hesley said I looked charming. He's my cousin.'

'Second cousin,' he explained. 'His father and your mother were cousins.'

'Are you my cousin, too?' Olivia hoped he would sit next to her through Christmas dinner. She thought he was handsome, especially when he smiled. She so much looked forward to meeting her half-cousins that she had watched them arrive in Uncle Hesley's carriage from the schoolroom window. They were beautifully dressed, neat and tidy, perhaps a little plain but undoubtedly elegant, and they behaved in a mannered, orderly way that was unusual at Hill Top House.

Jared had climbed out first to lower the step for his father, and the two gentlemen had helped their womenfolk down, then straightened their cloaks and bonnets for them before they came into the house. Olivia thought that was a nice thing to do. Both gentlemen wore trousers and long jackets instead of the breeches and stockings her grandfather preferred. His mother and sisters looked very nice too, in their fashionably full skirts that easily escaped the confinement of their cloaks.

'A sort of half-cousin,' he answered. 'My mother is your great-aunt.'

Olivia decided to ask Miss Trent about that later. 'How old are you?' she said.

'Seventeen.'

'I'll soon be fourteen,' Olivia announced, feeling important.

He thought her birthday wasn't until August but didn't argue. 'Come,' he said, and offered her his arm.

She laid her hand on his and fell into step beside him. 'Are you at the university?' she asked.

'I work at Kimber Deep.'

'That's a pit, isn't it? Cousin Hesley went to the university, and so did his father. He's dead now, though.'

'He was killed when Hesley was a baby.'

'He was thrown from his horse,' Olivia replied confidently.

'My mother wanted to take care of baby Hesley, but his grandfather wouldn't let her.'

From his tone, Olivia thought Jared did not like his uncle Hesley and retaliated, 'Well, why should she?'

'Because she's a woman. It's what women do. Besides, Uncle Hesley was getting old even then. He was two-and-forty when Hesley's father died. Mother told me she wanted to look after you, too, but Uncle Hesley would have none of it. Her mother had only been a shopkeeper's wife, you see. Not good enough for you,' he finished.

His resentment was not lost on Olivia but she asked, because she wanted to know, 'What kind of shop?'

'Groceries and provisions.'

'Oh.' Unimpressed, she went on, 'Couldn't Hesley's own mother look after him?'

Jared shook his head. 'Aunt Sukie? She was always ill, I think. I don't know what happened to her and no one speaks of her. I think she might have gone away somewhere. She was religious, my grandmother said.'

'Do you think she went to a convent?'

'She might have. They look after ill people. I expect she died.'

They reached the stairs and Olivia gripped his hand as she negotiated the steps in her full skirts and slippery silk slippers. He put his other hand on hers and smiled reassuringly, which she appreciated. The wide wooden staircase turned a corner halfway down and they paused. The hallway appeared to be full of people milling about outside the dining room.

'What is the fuss about?' whispered Olivia.

Jared surveyed the scene and saw his mother's frown as she took her half-brother's arm. 'Mother disapproves of Juliana going in to dinner with Cousin Hesley.'

'Why?'

'He has a bad reputation and she doesn't like him.'

Neither did Olivia, but she did not say so. Miss Trent had instructed her not to be rude about Cousin Hesley or his grandfather. This was Olivia's chance to show how accomplished she was in company, how grown-up she had become. She inhaled and stretched upwards, lengthening her neck and straightening her back to show off her height.

She saw that Jared's attention was distracted by her movements. Her new corset emphasised the small swell of her breasts.

Miss Trent had told her that she should not be ashamed of them, especially when they grew bigger. Like Miss Trent's, Olivia supposed. Miss Trent had proper breasts. Plump round ones that were soft and squashy under her nightgown.

They went down the last flight of stairs carefully and followed the party into the dining room. It was Olivia's first formal dinner with guests and Mrs Cookson had put out silver, glass and a set of decorated Swinton porcelain she had never seen before. There were eight places, spaced around the oblong table. Uncle Hesley sat at one end with his half-sister on his right and Olivia on his left. Uncle Benjamin was at the other end with his daughters at either side of him. Jared and Cousin Hesley occupied the seats

123

between the ladies, Jared beside Olivia with Josephina on his left, and Hesley between his aunt Caroline and Juliana.

Olivia smiled at Jared's sisters. They were younger than Jared but older than she was. They wore pretty dresses, but not as pretty as hers. Not silk, she was sure. Olivia wondered if they were poor, but she guessed not. Their father was an ironmaster and they were dressed very smartly, if not richly.

Mrs Cookson came in with the dinner and watched her new servant girls like a hawk as they helped her serve at table in their coarse brown work-gowns and clean calico pinafores. Olivia noticed that they didn't spill anything and wondered if they would stay after Christmas. It was nice having other people to talk to sometimes, even if they were servants. She thought briefly that she would have liked Miss Trent to be with her in the dining room.

Aunt Caroline was speaking: 'It's no kind of life for her, out here on the moor, Hesley. If Olivia were with me in town, she would have my daughters for company. They go for lessons with a tutor in the church vestry, and we have a pianoforte at home. You do not have one here, do you?'

'She does not need your tutor. She has her own governess here, and has done for this past half-year,' Uncle Hesley replied, as he carved the stuffed goose and roast ham in front of him.

'So you say. You might have consulted me, Hesley.'

'Why? Do you think I do not know what constitutes a good governess? Benjamin, please pour more wine.'

Aunt Caroline turned to her. 'Olivia, how do you like your governess?'

Olivia looked at her great-uncle, who said, 'You may answer your aunt.'

'Miss Trent has taught me to read and write and do my numbers. She knows so much about everything, and in the afternoons we go for nature walks in the fields and on the moor.'

'And do you behave well for Miss Trent?'

Again, Olivia looked at her uncle.

'Of course she does!' Uncle Hesley exclaimed. 'Look at her! Is she not a young lady now, rather than the wild child of before? Her manners are polished and she reads her Bible every Sunday.'

Olivia stared at her plate.

'I should like to meet Miss Trent,' Aunt Caroline said.

'It is sufficient for you to see that she has done an excellent job with the child.'

'Of course, Hesley. But Olivia has no one of her own age here. Now she is so – so well grown, a year or two with us would—'

'Sister,' Uncle Hesley interrupted, 'I know what is best for Olivia. Shall we talk of other things? Benjamin, will you and Jared come to hunt hare with me one day? They have bred well this year and we are overrun.'

After pudding, which was spiced fruit soaked in brandy and set alight at the table, Aunt Caroline nodded to her daughters and they stood up to leave the gentlemen to their port and cigars.

Uncle Hesley clicked his fingers at Mrs Cookson, hovering in the shadows, and said, 'Fetch Miss Trent to take Olivia to the schoolroom.'

'But, Hesley,' Aunt Caroline protested, 'may she not join us in the drawing room?'

'And have her mind filled with ideas about going to live in town?'

'She needs company of her own age. My daughters have been practising carols to sing.'

Uncle Hesley ignored his half-sister and addressed Olivia: 'You will wait by the door for Miss Trent.'

The other ladies filed out of the dining room while Olivia obeyed her uncle. As she waited, she heard Uncle Benjamin say, 'Hesley, you cannot keep the child wrapped up here for ever. She is fast becoming a young woman.'

But Uncle Hesley ignored him.

Jared remained standing when the others sat down. 'Father, may I have leave to take a lantern and look at Uncle Hesley's carriage?'

'Hesley?' Benjamin raised his eyebrows.

The older man picked up the bottle with his right hand. 'If you must. Do you wish to go with him, Hesley?'

Cousin Hesley shook his head and moved up the table to be next to his grandfather. Benjamin did the same and they helped themselves to port and cigars.

Jared left the room quickly. As he walked past, Olivia said loudly, 'Here is Miss Trent. Goodnight, Uncle Hesley,' dropped a curtsy, and followed him into the hall.

Jared looked about. 'Where is she?' he asked.

'In the kitchen, I expect. Can I come with you to the stables?'

'What for?'

'You can show me the carriage.'

'You're to go to the schoolroom with your governess.'

'Please. I've never been in a carriage.'

'But it's yours! It belonged to your mother and father. Don't you use it when you have to go into town?'

'I've never been into town.'

Jared was surprised, but only said, 'You'd better ask your governess.'

In the kitchen the servants were sitting at the big table, finishing off the fruit pudding and drinking tankards of ale. There were seven of them, including Matt and two of his farmhands, now with reddened faces and glassy eyes.

Miss Trent rose to her feet as soon as she saw Olivia with Jared. 'You should be in the drawing room with your aunt,' she said, 'certainly not here in your new silk.'

'Oh!' Mrs Cookson exclaimed. 'The master sent for you to take her upstairs.'

'Really? On Christmas Day?'

'Please, Miss Trent, can I go and look at the carriage with Jared? Please?'

'I don't see why not, if Jared does not mind.'

Jared was busying himself lighting a lantern to take across the yard. 'Of course I don't,' he said, 'but you'll need a cloak over that gown.'

'Take mine. It's on the hook,' Miss Trent suggested. Olivia guessed that she felt sorry for her, not being allowed to join her other cousins for the evening. Perhaps they would talk together over breakfast. 'Don't be long,' Miss Trent called, as they went out to the yard together.

In the dining room, old Hesley leaned back in his chair and unbuttoned his waistcoat. He had been drinking steadily through the meal and it showed in his florid features and clumsy movements. 'He doesn't have much to say for himself,' he said, when Jared had gone. 'What's wrong with him?'

'Growing pains,' Benjamin replied. He brushed a few crumbs from his best black jacket.

He frowned as young Hesley followed his grandfather's example, and muttered, 'Boy needs a woman, don't y'know?'

Benjamin ignored him. He didn't expect any better from either of them. Both Mextons wore fine gentlemen's clothes, well cut in good cloth, but they had spilled port on their breeches and dragged the cuffs of their cutaway coats through smears of Stilton cheese. They didn't wear powdered wigs any more, thank goodness, although, looking at the state of old Hesley's straggling grey hair, it would have been an improvement.

'I promised him a horse for his birthday,' he continued, 'but with this bank failure I can't afford it. He had to leave school as well. Sir William has employed him at Kimber Deep. He lives with his engine supervisor at the pit so Caroline doesn't see as much of him as she'd like.'

'A gentleman's pursuits, that's what he needs,' old Hesley responded. 'Can't you hire a horse for him from Sir William? He'd ride over to see you in no time.'

'There's an idea. It would cheer him up, too.'

'I'll be seeing Sir William at the railway-company meeting next week so I could put in a word.'

'No need. Jared's his own man now.' Benjamin spoke lightly but his comment was loaded and not missed by either of the Mextons.

Young Hesley looked sullen, knowing the barb was aimed at him, while his grandfather retaliated, 'Take care he does not turn into a loose cannon, brother-in-law.'

Benjamin acknowledged this with a tilt of his head. He was already aware that his influence on Jared was diminishing. The lad was strong-minded and of an independent nature. Like me, he thought. He would have to learn future lessons the hard way, as he had. But Jared was right-thinking and moral, as his mother was, and at least he listened to his father's counsel even if he didn't always act on it. Benjamin was proud of his son and did not feel the need to defend him to Hesley Mexton. 'Do you think the railways will take over from the canals for transporting coal and iron?' he asked.

'Yes, I do. It'll take time, though. Landowners in this part of the Riding are not happy about the lines running through their farms and scaring the deer and sheep. That's what they say. But too many of them have stock in the canal companies to let in the railways. It'll be a while before they get to the Mexton side of town.'

'Have you survived the bank collapse?'

Hesley's mouth turned down. 'Can't say,' he answered shortly.

'Well, it'll be a couple of years before my forge is back on its feet. Your pit troubles seem to have subsided, though. Can you keep the mine open?'

'Not without more capital. We've hit a rock face. I know there's more good coal on the other side of it but I'd have to sink another shaft.'

'What about blasting through the rock?'

'Too risky, I'm told, and costly. It's cheaper to reach it in another way. Won't you change your mind about coming in with me?'

'I haven't the capital now.'

'Damn it, I must get money from somewhere or the pit will close down for good.'

'I hadn't known things were so bad.' Benjamin had seen the figures for the new mine shaft and winding engine and knew there was no more collateral from the pit. 'You've got this house and the farmland. Can't you borrow against them?'

'I already have and it's gone.'

Gone where? he wondered. But Benjamin Tyler did not need an answer to that question. Strong drink, the horses, card tables and, God forgive him, women. The whole town knew he had kept a mistress in a house on the road out to Grassebrough. His grandson was just as bad, notorious in the taverns and inns. He said, 'Well, it'll take a few years for the mine to get back into profit, even with a new shaft.'

'I'll be bankrupt!'

'Calm yourself, man. I'll ask about, but borrowing rates have soared. The only money to be had is too dear for your mine project. You cannot sell the coal for more than the forges will pay, and we cannot ask more of the railway companies for our castings.'

Hesley took the port from his silent grandson and refilled his glass. 'I'll have to find it somewhere or I'll be selling up, mine and all.'

'I didn't know you were so close to disaster. But you have income from Olivia's trust, do you not?'

'I'd be grateful if you'd put the word about in town that my mine is a sound investment. Give the other bankers confidence in me.'

'Of course. What will you do?'

'Hesley's finished at the university and is of age now, so we'll survive.'

He finished his port in one gulp. The sound of carol singing came through the wall from the drawing room next door.

'Wait for me, Jared.' Olivia picked her way carefully across the cobbled yard.

'I was looking for a way through.' He stopped and swung round with the lantern. The animal litter wouldn't hurt his leather boots but she wore silk slippers He waited with the light held low. 'Follow close behind me.'

They went into the stables, where Jared paused to look at the horses, then passed through the gap in the wall to where the carriage was housed. It must have cost a pretty penny when it was new. The more recent models were bigger and heavier, but they didn't travel as fast. He bent to examine the suspension under the coachwork. Olivia was opening the door and letting down the steps to climb inside.

'Take care,' he called. He checked that the wheels were braked and kicked wooden chocks into place as an extra precaution. 'Here, let me help you.'

'I can do it myself,' she replied. 'Please bring the lantern round.'

The flickering light picked up the Mexton coat-of-arms on the open door. Jared's grandfather, Samuel Mexton, had liked such things. Or so his mother had said. And his son Samuel, who had been Olivia's grand-father, had carried on in the same manner. But when he had died and Uncle Hesley had taken over . . . At least he hadn't sold the carriage.

He climbed inside and sat opposite Olivia, placing the lantern carefully on the floor between them. The soft glow cast weird shadows on their faces.

Olivia threw back Miss Trent's voluminous cloak and spread her silken skirts over the plush seating. 'It's lovely, isn't it?'

'Yes.' Jared nodded.

'I'm going to ask Uncle Hesley if I can go out in it with Miss Trent, now that I'm grown-up.'

Jared imagined Olivia visiting the draper's in town and causing a stir in the marketplace. Most shopkeepers didn't see carriages like this. Or, he realized, young ladies as attractive as the one sitting in front of him. She was no longer a little girl.

'You'll be able to buy your own carriage when you

inherit.' She would suit money, he thought. She was already showing signs that she would become a beautiful, intelligent young woman. It was a pity she was out here all the time, with only the governess for company.

'Inherit what?' Olivia asked.

'Your mother's plantation in the West Indies.'

In the dim light he saw her surprise.

'Hasn't your uncle told you? I expect he's waiting until you're older. We've always known about it. It was your grandmother's dowry, but your grandfather allowed her to keep it. She left it to your mother, in trust for you. You'll be rich when you're five-and-twenty.'

'I didn't know,' she breathed. 'You mean it will be mine?'

He lifted the lantern and watched a puzzled frown cross her pretty features. 'I believe so,' he replied. 'Not even old Hesley can break a trust, though I expect he's tried.'

'Is that why he doesn't like me?'

'He doesn't like anybody. He uses people for his own ends.'

'But – but that must be why he won't let me go anywhere or do anything.'

'He's supposed to take care of it for you, because you can't touch it.'

'He should have told me about it,' Olivia said.

'Yes, he should. Look, you'd better not say I said anything, if you're not supposed to know about it. But it's no secret in my family. What do you think keeps this house going? Not the coal mine, that's for sure.'

'So he doesn't want me, just my money,' Olivia retaliated. 'He wants it for himself. Well, it's mine, not his.'

'Don't get too cross. He can only spend the income from it and it will be yours eventually.'

'He should have told me,' she repeated decisively. Uncle Hesley never talked to her about anything, so she liked Jared for telling her that. She wondered if he liked her. He was certainly friendly and he didn't seem frightened of Uncle Hesley. She shivered and drew the cloak up around her shoulders.

He noticed. 'It's cold out here. Shall we go back to the house?'

'Not just yet. Will you visit us again soon?'

'I doubt it. This is the first time I've been here and I reckon Uncle Hesley only invited us because he wants to borrow money from my father for the mine.'

'Does it need money?'

'The whole town needs money. Haven't you heard about the bank failure?'

'Miss Trent told me about it when Uncle Hesley was injured.' She had talked about her becoming mistress of a large house, too, and Olivia wondered if Miss Trent knew about her inheritance. She thought not. Miss Trent would have said if she knew. Mrs Cookson was different. She always did what Uncle Hesley ordered, and if he had told her to keep quiet about it, she would.

Olivia was beginning to see that growing up was not just about leaving her childhood behind and becoming a lady. It meant learning that some people were on her side and others were not, that some could be trusted while others had to be watched.

'Will you be my friend?' she asked suddenly.

'Your friend?'

'I haven't any friends. Aunt Caroline said so at dinner, and Miss Trent commented on it once.'

'My sisters would be better as your friends,' he replied warily.

'Would they come and visit me in the spring and go for walks on the moor with me and Miss Trent? I should like that very much.'

Jared thought about his parents' opinion of Uncle Hesley and his grandson, and decided that this was not a good idea. He didn't want his sisters anywhere near Cousin Hesley and his hard-drinking ways. 'It would be nicer for you to come into town and visit us.'

He watched her face fall. 'Uncle Hesley won't let me. Miss Trent has asked him before.'

Then it would have to be him, and he would have to come out here. As he reflected on this he found he liked the prospect. The walk would be invigorating and he would get to know Olivia properly. He found her intriguing, innocent of the world outside Hill Top House but intelligent and questioning. And she was very pretty. More than pretty. She was beautiful.

'I'll come and visit you, Olivia,' he said.

'Would you? Would you really? Oh, thank you, Jared.' She leaned forward and kissed his cheek.

Now it was his turn to look surprised. He touched his face with the tips of his fingers and laughed nervously. 'It'll be weeks before the weather improves and there'll be enough daylight.' But his cheek tingled where her lips had brushed it and he had to conceal a sudden desire to return the kiss.

His eyes took in the small swell of her breasts, her skin velvety in the lamplight. It was pleasant to know he could never indulge himself with her. But he could not stop himself thinking of her in that way and his fingers itched to take hold of her. His tongue ran lightly over his lips as he suppressed the urge to kiss her.

'Olivia!' Someone was calling her. The governess. He was annoyed and relieved at the same time, and found himself breathing deeply as footsteps approached.

Harriet had heard the carol singing from the kitchen and thought she should fetch Olivia. She hurried into the hall, tapped lightly on the dining-room door and entered. Three sets of male eyes stared at her. The master and his morose grandson were now quite drunk and old Hesley demanded, 'What do you want?'

'I should like Olivia to join in the carol singing.'

'Go on, Hesley. It's Christmas,' Mr Tyler said.

'Very well. One hour only, then take her upstairs.'

'Thank you, sir.'

She hurried across the yard, chilled without her cloak. The stable door was open and there was a lantern glow from inside the carriage. When she looked in she found the two young people sitting quietly, opposite each other. They were smiling at each other, as though enjoying a private confidence. As she watched them, she half expected them to reach forward and hold hands.

Wordlessly, Harriet stared at them. In the lamplight,

she saw an expression on Olivia's face she had not noticed before. It was in her eyes, an intensity and a seriousness that startled her. She opened the carriage door and took Olivia's hand. 'Come with me now,' she said.

Olivia climbed out of the carriage. 'Goodnight, Jared.'

'Goodnight.' He added, 'Take the light.'

Miss Trent took it from him and nodded her thanks.

The carriage was empty and cold without Olivia. Slowly Jared brushed the plush pile on the seats, then climbed down and closed the door carefully. Outside, in the yard, he listened to the carols. They sounded as good as any church choir, he thought.

He wandered across the cobbles. The horses were stabled for the night and the stock locked up until morning. He saw the housekeeper stagger to the stable with a stone flagon. The lamplight moved from downstairs to upstairs. He inhaled deeply, gazing up at the stars. It was a clear night with the promise of a frost. Soon it would be New Year. He wondered what fresh misfortunes it would bring to the Riding.

After the carol singing, Miss Trent helped Olivia to take off her gown and wrap it in calico, then left her alone to do the same for Jared's sisters. There was a good fire in the grate and Olivia lingered by the window, unpinning her silky hair and brushing it slowly.

Jared was still in the yard, walking about in the moonlight. It was a cold night and she wondered why he didn't go inside. He was so different from Cousin

Hesley. He talked to her and listened to what she said. She hoped he would come over every Sunday in the spring. He was interesting and she looked forward to proper conversations with him. She brought her long fair hair over one shoulder to tackle the ends with a comb.

He was looking at the stars. Then he must have noticed her, standing in the candlelight, watching him, for he stared at her, then smiled. She saw his teeth flash white in the moonlight. He raised his arm and she waved her comb at him. She thought of him until she was in her nightgown, drifting off to sleep.

Chapter 10

The next day Jared left with his family after breakfast. Uncle Hesley and his grandson had drunk so much the night before that they were not up to see them go. Olivia stood at the front door with Miss Trent and Mrs Cookson to watch them on their way. Everyone smiled and said how much they had enjoyed the festivities.

Jared helped his sisters and parents into the carriage, then climbed up beside Matt. He looked back and waved as the horses pulled away. Olivia remembered his wave of the night before, which had been just for her. 'It would have been nice to go with them.' She sighed.

Miss Trent nodded wordlessly. Her eyes were shiny. Mrs Cookson went indoors straight away but Olivia stayed outside until the carriage had disappeared.

'Perhaps they will visit again,' Miss Trent said.

Olivia's heart leaped. 'When?' she asked.

'I cannot say.'

'They were nice. They talked to me. And they were interested in what I said. Like you.'

'It was over too quickly.'

Olivia reached for her hand. 'You wanted them to stay longer, didn't you?'

'Yes. Hill Top House was built for such a family. It came alive while they were here. And now it's empty again. Even the serving girls are leaving tomorrow.'

Olivia heard shouting from indoors and gripped Miss Trent's hand. 'Uncle Hesley's about.'

'We'll go to the schoolroom.'

They hurried past the open library door. The sound of raised voices was not unusual in this household, but this time they could be heard clearly from the hall. Uncle Hesley and his grandson were arguing again.

'Grandfather, are you out of your mind?' Cousin Hesley shouted. 'You cannot ask me to do that!'

'Oh, but I can!' her uncle boomed.

'Well, I am no longer under your control! May I remind you that I am one-and-twenty?'

'And you are dependent on me for your income so you will do as I say. My only source of revenue is the sugar, and since the slave trade was stopped that has fallen too. I must have more capital to keep the pit going and it is time you repaid me for your education.'

'But I shall repay you! Just let me spend some time in Europe first. In Italy or Spain.'

'I have settled your bills and given you all the money you've asked for without questioning how you used it. But do not make the mistake of thinking I do not know where it goes. I know about your drinking, and your gambling. And the kind of women you like.'

'I am sure you do, because in that respect we are cut from the same cloth!'

There was a short silence before Uncle Hesley went on, 'Indeed we are. We understand each other. That is why I know I am right about this. Do this now and our future – your future – will be secured. You will have the means to live as you please. That is what you want, is it not?'

'Does it matter? You will do as you like anyway.'

Miss Trent urged her towards the stairs. 'Quickly, Olivia. Out of the way.'

But they were too slow. Cousin Hesley stormed out of the library, closely followed by his grandfather. They stopped abruptly when they saw Olivia and her governess.

'Miss Trent, and Olivia. Come into the library. You, too, Hesley.'

They obeyed silently. The master took his favourite stance in front of the fire. Olivia stood before him nervously, gripping Miss Trent's hand. Cousin Hesley slumped into his grandfather's chair and stared at the flames.

'My grandson is going to the West Indies.'

Olivia was pleased about this. The drinking and noisy arguing would stop. But her uncle added, 'He will manage my sugar plantation out there.'

His sugar plantation? That was not what Jared had told her, and she burst out, 'It's not yours! It's mine!'

The fury on her uncle's face struck fear into her heart. He turned on Miss Trent and glared at her. 'Who told her that?'

'I do not know, sir.'

'It was my mother's and you are only looking after it for me until I am older!' Olivia yelled.

'*Who has been talking to her?*'

Olivia saw that she was making him even angrier, but she did not care. He was her guardian. He should have told her. He hadn't even told Miss Trent. Instead he had been taking her money and spending it on himself and his grandson without a thought for her.

Miss Trent replied, 'I repeat, sir, I do not know. Perhaps your relatives yesterday.'

Olivia was holding her breath. Would they guess it had been Jared?

'But I was with her all the time,' Miss Trent added. 'They sang carols together, that is all.'

She felt a gentle squeeze of her hand and relaxed. Miss Trent would not betray her, even if she knew.

'I knew it was a mistake to ask them here!' her uncle roared. 'Meddling in my affairs! I will not have that family over my threshold again.'

He's a wicked man, Olivia thought. He takes everything from me. First my money and now my only hope of friendship and a little happiness with Jared. She wanted to hit him, to push him backwards into the fire. She pursed her lips and flared her nostrils to stem her mounting rage. The gentle squeeze of her hand tightened. Miss Trent felt the same about her uncle. They could push him together! Then she felt a gentle tug.

'Come along, Olivia. We have reading to do in the schoolroom.'

Harriet dared not look at her charge for she knew that they thought as one about the injustice of her situation and it would not do for her to show this. She focused her eyes on the gentlemen and wondered why young Hesley seemed so shocked by the suggestion that he should go abroad. Resentment, she could have understood. But he appeared astounded and his pallor indicated more than anger. It was none of her business, except that it involved Olivia. And her inheritance. She had not known her charge was an heiress. It was not unheard-of for gentlewomen to have means of their own but not, she had thought, in the Mexton family.

'Sit down, Miss Trent!' the master barked. 'Olivia, go to your chamber. You, too, Hesley.'

'Thank God,' young Hesley exclaimed. 'I'm off to Swinborough Hall for New Year.'

Harriet frowned. The master did not often ask to speak with her. It made no difference to her that Olivia was an heiress. But if the girl was to grow up as a wealthy lady, perhaps she needed more education than Harriet could provide. Someone more used to the ways of society. She hoped he would not dismiss her in favour of another governess.

'Sherry wine? Take it. I insist.'

Harriet took the glass he offered. He was tired, she thought. He has never fully recovered the energy he had before he was attacked, and now he looks more like the ageing gentleman he is.

'You have a way with her.'

'Sir?'

'Olivia. She has turned away from her wild ways in your care.'

'Thank you, sir.'

'She will become a lady, after all.'

'I hope so, sir.'

'Like you.'

Disarmed, she replied, 'I did not have her advantages, sir.'

'But her behaviour, her demeanour . . . Commendable, Miss Trent. Are you settled here?'

'Yes, sir.'

'I am not. I am used to more company. Since my accident – well, you know of the pleasures I have given up.' He paused. 'You wrote the letter for me.'

Harriet was silent. Mrs Cookson had told her that his mistress had left the Riding. The master had terminated the lease and closed the house.

'I am advised not to join my grandson and my friends at the races and the pugilistic meetings. Adam Harvey orders for me this sherry wine instead of whisky. What sort of life is that for a gentleman? Eh?'

Harriet looked at her hands.

'Nothing to say, Miss? Well, what would you know of a gentleman's life, anyway?'

What indeed? She wondered where this was leading.

'And I shall not even have Hesley to talk to after I have packed him off across the ocean.'

'You have Olivia, sir.'

'The child? Is that your answer?'

Harriet finished her sherry, placed the glass on a side table and half rose to her feet. 'If that is all, sir?'

'It is not. Sit down.'

She did so.

He slammed his own glass down, grasped the whisky decanter and poured himself half a tumbler that he swallowed in one gulp. 'I need company.'

'You sent your visitors away, sir,' she pointed out.

'Not them, for God's sake! They make my hours even more dull, not less. You, Miss Trent, you are a different matter altogether.'

For a moment she was astounded. Her? The penniless orphan he employed to discipline his wayward niece? How could she enliven his days? His tastes, she thought, were not for her skills as a teacher. What could she offer him? Conversation? Reading? A game of chess? Surely he would have no interest in such occupations. 'I'm afraid I should not be good company for you, sir. I do not share your tastes.'

'Do you not? I like my books.'

She was mildly surprised, but believed him. He had a good library.

'I should read if my eyes allowed it,' he went on.

Ah, now she understood. He *had* changed since his accident. With his grandson abroad, life would be quieter. There would be time for reading.

'Mr Harvey once suggested that Olivia read the news-sheets to you.'

'I have in mind someone more adult.'

'It would benefit her education, sir.'

'You will read to me, Miss Trent,' he said firmly.

He gave her a small smile, the sneer that told her the matter was closed. Her heart sank. She would have to spend part of her day reading to him.

'When shall I attend you, sir?' she asked.

'Oh, I like to read before I sleep.'

It was reasonable, for she, too, preferred that time. But she felt uneasy. Then saw the mockery in his eyes, the suggestive way in which he slouched on his chair and raised his glass to her. A frisson of fear ran through her. No, she was being fanciful. He did not mean – he could not mean . . .

Her heart began to thump. He was goading her to entertain himself. As her anger mounted, she tried to sound calm. 'You will be tired, sir. May I recommend the afternoon instead?'

'After supper, Miss Trent. You will come to my chamber and read to me. Tonight.'

She gave a nervous half-laugh. 'You toy with me, sir. You cannot expect me to visit your chamber at such a late hour.'

'You will do as I say.'

She stood up, panic clutching at reason. Whether she had misunderstood him or not, he would not mistake her answer. 'No, sir. I shall not. I am governess to your ward.' She dared not look at him for his anger would have alarmed her more.

Her heart was still pounding as she closed the library door behind her. She leaned against the wood panelling. Even the eyes of the animal heads mounted on the walls seemed to mock her. What kind of woman did he think she was? She was a charity girl but that did not mean he was entitled to her virtue as well as to her labour. She must calm herself before she went to the schoolroom. She turned towards the kitchen.

'Mrs Cookson, may I have a little of your rum?'

'You look as if you've had a fright.'

'It's nothing. Really.' But she was shaking.

'You'd better sit down. I'll make you a hot toddy.'

'Thank you.'

'The master been telling you off?'

'Yes – yes, that's it,' she hedged. Surely she had imagined his proposition.

'It doesn't do to cross him.' Mrs Cookson mixed the toddy and handed it to her. 'Although with young women like yourself, it fires his blood, if you take my meaning.'

'No, I do not.' But she did. And she did not regret disobeying him or walking out of his library without leave. She would do the same again. He should not have humiliated her for his sport, even though he was her employer.

'About Olivia, was it?' Mrs Cookson asked.

Harriet wished it had been. 'She still has those bad dreams, you know. Do you know when they started?'

'She came back from the West Indies with them. All them black men scared her half to death, I expect.'

Harriet sighed. 'It is much more likely to have been the loss of her parents that traumatized her.'

'The master's apothecary said she would grow out of them.'

'I hope so. Have we sweet milk for her tonight? It helps her to sleep more soundly.'

'Aye, I've put some by.'

'I will have rum with mine.' Harriet wished only for oblivion to forget about the master's sinful insinuation.

She was awakened, suddenly, by a chill across her body as the bedclothes were thrown aside. Startled, she blinked in the glow of a candle on the box near her head.

'Olivia, is that you? What is it?'

'It's I, Miss Trent.' His voice was slurred and gravelly.

The master? The aroma of cigars pervaded her nostrils. He was in her chamber? Her mind assembled itself. Her disobedience. Would he drag her out of bed and beat her? She had not been beaten since she was a young pupil at Blackstone. But she would bear it with fortitude. She lowered her voice to a whisper: 'If you wish to punish me, sir, can it not wait until morning? You would not wish to wake Olivia.'

'Then come quietly to my chamber as I ask.'

No! Her body tensed. He meant her to obey him! She raised herself on one elbow and whispered, 'Not at this hour of the night, sir. Please go back to your chamber before Olivia hears you.'

'You're a stubborn soul, aren't you? Well, so am I and I am master in this house, as you well know.'

Her eyes were becoming used to the candle and she saw beyond its pool of light his jacket discarded on the floorboards. He wore no boots and was already unbuttoning the flap at the front of his breeches.

Alarmed, she sat up properly. 'Are you mad, sir?'

He pushed her back onto her mattress, half falling on top of her as she spoke. 'Do you think I do not mean what I say? You have much to learn. And if you are so concerned about the child you will make no sound yourself.'

'No, sir, stop! You must not!'

'Quiet.' He pinned her to the bed and covered her mouth with his hand. The other hand was already searching under her nightgown, shoving the soft cotton upwards and around her waist, grasping the flesh of her thighs and groping between her legs. His knees were between hers, pushing them apart. She struggled and squirmed and squealed, her own hands flailing at first, then trying desperately to prise his away from her mouth and from her most private areas.

He paid no heed to her pleas to stop and she could smell the whisky on his breath. It did not seem to matter how much she struggled because his greater weight was pressing her into the mattress, crushing her. She could hardly breathe. His fingers probed and poked until they found what he was searching for and she yelped in pain. She thrashed her legs, her feet tangling in the bed linen. But to no avail. Quite suddenly a charge ran through her, a stab of pain she had never known before, which stunned her into momentary stillness.

He had entered her, *entered her.* He had done it so swiftly that, at first, she could not believe it was happening. But it was. He was thrusting inside her, grunting harshly. It was over quickly. He exhaled noisily, then flopped all over her, smothering her, squeezing the breath out of her, until she thought she might faint.

She could not move. She lay there, shocked, silent and in sheer disbelief that this had happened. She inhaled with a shudder. He had taken her virtue. In a few short seconds it was gone. What kind of man was he to demand that of her because she had disobeyed him? He was an evil man. Certainly no gentleman. *How could he?* She was not one of his tavern girls. She was his niece's governess.

The man had no shame, no scruples. But she had known that already from his behaviour. Yet she had never supposed he would do this. Not even after their conversation in the library. She lay there not knowing what to think or what to do. Tears welled in her eyes as her distress mounted.

His mouth was close to her ear and she felt his lips move against her neck as he said softly, 'There, Miss Trent. That was not so difficult, was it?' Then he climbed off her, picked up his jacket and left. The candle flickered in the draught from the door.

She was wide awake, the tears rolling down her face now. But still she was unable to move her limbs until the sound of the bed creaking next door forced her into action. She pulled down her nightdress and covered herself with bedding. Had she wakened the child? Dear heaven, she hoped not!

How could he take her good name so coldly and callously? *How could he?* She had no family or position, and no money of her own until she was one-and-twenty. Her virtue was all she had had and *he had taken it*. She saw it so clearly now. He had taken it because she had refused to go to his chamber and give herself to him.

It was a lesson, she realized. He had done this to punish her for disobeying him. Olivia had said she must do as Uncle Hesley bade. Olivia! The reason she was here. She was growing into a sensible young woman under Harriet's care, but how could she continue to teach her after this?

She must go away. Tomorrow. She would demand an interview and give notice to quit with immediate effect. She turned her head from side to side on the pillow. She could not leave Olivia now. They were so much more to each other than pupil and governess. Their bond had grown strong, as she had hoped it would, and it would break Harriet's heart to desert her now. She could not do it. Not now she had become so close to her.

But she would have to. The master surely would not expect her to stay. He would turn her out. He would not wish a defiled woman to teach his niece about moral conduct and duty.

Harriet lay wide awake, wondering where she would go and how she would get there without money. The wind and rain battered her window, the noise reminding her of whippings in the laundry at the poorhouse. She had been younger than Olivia was now, but the memory of cold and hunger lingered. After a while she got up and washed herself where he had invaded her. The water was cold and she shivered. Her most delicate skin was stinging and she could still feel him there. She could not get out of her mind what he had done. She wrapped herself with linen as if, somehow, it would protect her and climbed back into her narrow bed. She had thought that life at Blackstone had prepared her for anything, but not this. She did not know what to do except cry into her pillow. And weeping did not help.

In the morning Harriet's desolation and anger had festered. Her mind was made up. She would demand an interview with the master. Despite her anguish at leaving Olivia, she had to go. Perhaps they could write to each other. She would find a way. When she went down to the kitchen to fetch their breakfast porridge, Mrs Cookson was frying black pudding and liver on an iron plate over the fire.

'I should like to speak with the master this morning.'

'You talk to him when he says, not the other way round.'

'This is important.'

'Something's gone on, then?' Mrs Cookson looked at her keenly, and nodded. 'Aye. I thought as much yesterday.'

Harriet became impatient. Surely Mrs Cookson could not know. 'I'll take the master's breakfast in for you,' she said.

'It's not fer him. It's fer Matt and his lads in the stables. The master's been gone a while now.'

'Gone? Gone where?'

152

'It's none of your business.'

'When will he return?'

Mrs Cookson turned from her task and gave her a withering look. After a pause, she said, 'You're a bit peaky this morning, aren't you, lass? Do you want a piece o' this liver?'

She shook her head irritably. 'I'll have porridge with Miss Olivia in the schoolroom. Will the master be back for dinner?' All she wanted was a testimonial and money to make her escape.

'Miss Trent, Blackstone may have taught you a lot about book learning, but not, it seems, that gentlemen will have their way.'

'I don't know what you mean.'

The older woman shrugged. 'Go and get on with your teaching, then.'

She wished she could. She had such affection for Olivia. She was here because of her and it was going to be so hard to leave. As the day wore on she wondered if, and how, she could take Olivia with her.

The master came home while they were having tea in the kitchen. Harriet offered to help Mrs Cookson with his supper instead of going up to the schoolroom to read.

'Still want to see him, do you?'

'It is important, Mrs Cookson.'

'You've been like an unbroken filly champing at the bit all day so you'd better go and say your piece to 'im.'

Harriet carried into the dining room the last of the apples from the store. 'I must speak with you, sir.'

153

'What is it?'

'I wish to give you notice that I shall be leaving.'

'Leaving? You shall do no such thing!'

'I cannot stay after last night.'

He stared at her. 'That? Don't be so damnably self-righteous! Why don't you admit you enjoyed it as much as I did?'

'Because I did not, sir.'

'Be honest with yourself, woman!'

She tried to remain calm. 'I should like to leave as soon as possible.'

He frowned. 'You are not free to go. You are in my employ and you are not yet one-and-twenty.'

'You cannot mean to force me to stay?'

'I do not have to. I am your master. I give you good food and lodging, provide you with gowns and new boots. You owe me your labour as I see fit.'

'Not as your mistress, sir. I do not owe you that.'

He laughed at her. *He laughed.* 'You are staying and that is an end to the matter.'

'But I cannot! I shall not!'

'And where do you think you will go?'

'I shall find another position.'

'Without a testimonial? I think not.'

'You will be good enough to furnish me with one, surely.'

'Recommend you to others? And why should I do that when I want you here?' He sounded genuinely surprised.

'I do not wish to stay. I should rather return to Blackstone.' But at that her heart shrivelled.

He snorted. 'So shall I write and say what good service you have given? The principal will be very interested in what occurred last night, I'm sure.'

Agitated, she took him at his word. 'But you cannot – you must not. I shall be ruined.' No, that was not quite accurate, she thought. She was already ruined.

'You will not get another position in the Riding, Miss Trent. I shall see to that.'

'Sir, please do not be so cruel! You can find another mistress, one who is willing and more suited to your tastes.'

'Oh, but you suit my taste very well, Miss Trent. Your pious resistance makes the challenge, and the victory, so much sweeter.'

'You are despicable. You have no consideration for your great-niece either. I cannot set such a low moral example to her. What if she should discover it?'

His patience snapped. 'You will see that she does not. Why not be sensible, Miss Trent, and come to my chamber as I ask?'

'*No!* I shall not do it.' But inside she was failing. She could not stay here. Neither could she leave Olivia. She imagined herself running away in the middle of the night and taking Olivia with her, away from the evil influences in this house. But how would they survive without money? She had none. Olivia had none. They would starve out on the road in the cold. She could not let that happen.

'Then I shall come to you,' he said slowly and deliberately. 'And you will be silent.'

'You are a wicked man.'

'If you think that, why have you stayed?'

'You know that I cannot leave until after I am one-and-twenty. I have no money.'

'Ah, now, there we have something in common. I have no money either.'

'Then who pays for all of this?' she indicated their comfortable surroundings.

'I am talking about coins and banknotes.'

She was becoming scornful of his excuses. 'How do you pay your servants?'

'I don't. Not this year, anyway. There will be no payment for anyone in this household.'

'You cannot mean that. We shall have earned our wages.'

'So will my miners, and there is no money for them either.'

Harriet reflected on this for a minute. With the ruck at the pit and Adam Harvey's comments before Christmas, it was probably true. 'Are you saying I shall have nothing at midsummer?'

'None then, maybe none after that. The bank has failed, Miss Trent, and I have lost a fortune. The men's wages have been halved. Do you think I shall pay my governess when I have men with families to feed, baying at my door? The farm will keep us with meat on the table, and my colliers will continue to mine my coal for half a loaf to give to their children. You are a sensible woman, Miss Trent. You would be well advised to stay here rather than end up starving as a street woman in the town.'

She saw the sense in his words and hated him for

156

being right. Yet, she thought, she might as well be on the streets after what he had done to her. She walked out of the dining room without another word.

Olivia was engrossed in a book, and while she was occupied, Harriet searched for a key to the schoolroom. She didn't know why she hadn't thought of it before. If she locked the door at night, she would be safe. After an hour of surreptitious searching, she asked her charge where it might be. 'Uncle Hesley has it. He used to lock me in when I cried at night.'

Harriet swallowed. 'Do you know where he keeps it?'

Olivia shook her head and went back to her book.

That night, Harriet hardly seemed to close her eyes at all. She kept on her drawers and corset and suffered a night of discomfort. Yet she would not have slept a wink without them for every creak and rattle had her sitting bolt upright and half out of bed.

The master did not appear. Perhaps he had listened to her protests and thought better of his actions. But the night after that she was in despair when she discovered she was wrong.

The winds across the moor were wild that year and Olivia woke with a start. The salt and the wet on her face were not from the sea of her nightmares but her own tears. She wanted her mama, but dared not call out for Uncle Hesley was at home. If her crying woke the household and Uncle Hesley was disturbed he would beat her and tell her that it was seven years now and she must stop these night-time disturbances. Then she remembered that Miss Trent was next door and she lay still in the dark and listened. She could hear the ship's timbers creaking, the groaning and crying . . .

But this was not the ship, it was her bedchamber, next to Miss Trent's and the schoolroom. Miss Trent would never beat her. Not even when Uncle Hesley insisted. The wind spattered rain on her window. She licked at her tears and wiped her face on the sleeve of her nightgown. She knew it had been the bad dream again and that she had woken from it, but she still heard the creaks and the groans. The noises were coming from Miss Trent's chamber. She lay awake in the dark, frightened and alone, and eventually the sounds stopped. Then there was silence. Until the crying began, a muffled, choked sobbing that made Olivia forget her own sadness.

She slid out of bed, walked barefoot to the door and opened it a fraction. A candle burned low on Miss Trent's washstand. It was not one from the schoolroom. It was in a tall brass candlestick from downstairs.

'Go back to bed, Olivia.' Miss Trent seemed to be choking.

'Don't make me. Please don't make me. I've had a nasty dream.'

'Your nightmare again?' Miss Trent struggled to sit up, pulling down her nightgown under the tumbled bedding. It looked to Olivia as if she'd been crying too, but she held out her hand, smiling in the flickering light.

'Don't cry, Miss Trent.'

Miss Trent wiped her face with the sheet.

'It won't be so bad in the morning.' She took her governess's hand. 'That's what you say to me.'

'Dear sweet child, you mean more to me than anything.'

'Can I climb in beside you?'

Miss Trent nodded and held up the sheet. The sheets were very wrinkled and – she sniffed – they had that 'Uncle Hesley smell'. Had Uncle Hesley been here? Uncle Hesley only came to the schoolroom to punish her when she was wicked.

Olivia wrinkled her nose. 'Uncle Hesley's been here, hasn't he? Is that why you're crying? Did he beat you and make you cry?'

'No, of course not,' she whispered. 'What an imagination you have.'

'He did. He was here, I can smell him.'

'Hush, child. It was all in your dream.'

'It wasn't! He's made you cry and you'll go away! Oh, please don't go away and leave me.'

'Quiet now, Olivia,' she soothed. 'You've had one of your nightmares, that's all. It isn't real.'

'Oh, it is! It happened when I was seven. I was on a ship with Mama and she drowned. Papa too.'

'I know, my dear. We have something in common, then, for I am an orphan.'

'Uncle Hesley says I'm lucky to have a guardian and I must behave or he will send me away and I would have to live in a place worse than Blackstone. Blackstone isn't very nice, is it? It's always cold and they eat only porridge and broth, and bread and dripping.'

'I won't let him send you away. I promise.'

Olivia snuggled into Miss Trent's warm soft body and tried to ignore Uncle Hesley's smell. 'I'm lucky to have you, Miss Trent,' she whispered finally.

She was almost asleep when she heard her governess's soft voice above her head. 'No. I am the lucky one. I have found you. You are worth any amount of humiliation and hardship and I shall not leave you. The Lord will give me the strength to stay.'

As Olivia drifted off to sleep, Miss Trent was praying. She could hear soft murmurings about forgiving her sins. She must have behaved badly and her uncle must have beaten her, for she winced and gasped when she changed her position in bed.

Olivia thought that Uncle Hesley's smell never really went away from Miss Trent's chamber. Now it was not her nightmare that woke her. It was Uncle Hesley knocking over a chair in the schoolroom, or Miss Trent's anguished pleading for him to leave. But he did not heed her. Neither did he beat Miss Trent in the same way he did Olivia. Miss Trent's punishment was different. When she was woken by the noise, Olivia crept out of her bed and opened the door a fraction to watch.

Uncle Hesley did not use his cane on Miss Trent. He beat her with his body. The bedding was thrown back and he was stretched out on top of her in just his shirt. His legs were bare, long, white and hairy, and he made noises like a pig as he punished her, making the bed creak as the ship's timbers did in her nightmare.

In the light of the candle by her head, Miss Trent's

frightened face peered out over Uncle Hesley's shoulder and tears spilled down her cheeks. When he had finished, he climbed off her, picked up his boots and breeches and lumbered away through the schoolroom. Olivia knew it was punishment because Miss Trent always cried afterwards.

When Miss Trent saw her she became angry. 'Close the door, Olivia. Don't you know it's wicked to spy on others?'

'I wasn't spying!'

'Well, you must not talk of this to anyone. No one. Not even Mrs Cookson. Promise me.'

'I promise.' Olivia meant it. She did not want others to know that Miss Trent had had to be punished. Miss Trent was her friend, and Olivia could keep a secret when she had to.

Chapter 11

'Before my grandson leaves for the West Indies he will marry. Is that not a good idea, Miss Trent? For a young gentleman like Hesley to have a wife?'

'Yes, sir.' They had been summoned to the library. The master and his grandson were there, scowling at each other.

'Olivia?' he prompted.

'Yes, Uncle Hesley.'

'Good. Then we are agreed.' He raised his voice slightly. 'Are we agreed, Hesley?'

'Yes, Grandfather.'

'You must sail soon after the wedding, while the weather is fair. I would not wish you to suffer the same fate that befell Olivia's mother and father. It follows, therefore, that the marriage will take place quickly. Within the month.'

'Yes, sir,' young Hesley muttered.

'You will see to all that is required, Miss Trent.'

'See to what, sir?' Uncle Hesley looked irritated with her and Olivia clutched her hand tighter. 'Is Olivia to be a bridal attendant?' Miss Trent added.

'No, Miss Trent. Olivia is to be the bride.'

Olivia's eyes flew wide. 'What do you mean, Uncle Hesley?'

'You're to marry your cousin Hesley. You will be his wife.'

'But I don't want to!' Alarmed, she turned to her governess. 'I don't have to, do I?'

'Sir!' Miss Trent had paled.

'Yes, Miss Trent?' Uncle Hesley was glaring at her.

'She – Olivia – is still a child, sir.'

'Nonsense. She is of marriageable age.'

'But she is still young. I mean, she is not a full-grown woman yet.'

'She is old enough, and I see the signs of woman-hood already.'

'You cannot do this to her. May I speak alone with you, sir?'

'No, you may not. If it is about Olivia, it is now my grandson's affair.'

Miss Trent turned to her. 'Go upstairs, Olivia, and finish copying your Bible passages.'

'Olivia, stay where you are! You are to be married within the month. Do you understand what that means?'

Olivia held her breath, then spoke in a rush. 'Yes, and I don't want to marry Hesley. I don't like him.'

'You will do as I say or I'll see you in the asylum.'

Olivia and Miss Trent responded together: 'No!' they cried. Olivia was truly frightened and she had never heard Miss Trent so angry. Her governess's eyes were filled with fury as she faced both men. 'You will not do this, sir. I shall send word to Olivia's aunt. She will not allow it.'

'You dare to threaten me?'

Miss Trent was fidgeting and her breathing sounded laboured.

'But why must I marry him?' Olivia pleaded.

'It is your duty,' he snapped.

She saw Miss Trent swallow. 'Duty. I see. It is an arrangement for your convenience.'

'For all of us, if we are to prosper.'

'Then there is no need to consummate the union.'

That was a new word for Olivia and she listened intently.

'Of course there is,' Uncle Hesley answered sharply. 'And make sure you do, Hesley. I don't want any of your aunt Caroline's lawyers and physicians claiming annulment before you return.'

'Sir, she is too young. She is not ready,' Miss Trent pleaded.

'Then you will prepare her.' Uncle Hesley gave her a long, level look that ended in a sneer, as he added, 'I know you have the necessary knowledge.'

'Sir!'

Olivia had never seen Miss Trent so flustered. She was looking from Uncle Hesley to her cousin and back again. A distinct blush was rising in her cheeks.

Cousin Hesley's head shot up quickly at Miss Trent's indignation, and he turned it back and forth between her uncle and her governess, smiling broadly. 'You are an old rogue, Grandfather.' He laughed. 'So that's why I had to stay away from her. You want her for yourself. I suppose you'll be keeping her on after the wedding, then?'

'What do you say to that, Olivia? Would you like Miss Trent to stay on after your marriage?'

If Olivia was repelled by the idea of becoming Hesley's wife, she was terrified at the thought of losing Miss Trent and nodded silently.

'There you are, Miss Trent. We all want you to stay. But you may go back to Blackstone, if you wish. I shall be happy to talk to the principal about your services here. Perhaps you will find special favour with him on you return.'

Miss Trent's face became even redder in the firelight.

'He can't really send me to the asylum, can he?'

In the privacy of the schoolroom, Harriet allowed herself to hug Olivia. The child was being brave, but tears were threatening and it broke Harriet's heart to think of her future with Hesley.

She had seen it happen at Blackstone and she knew how ruthless the master could be. 'I believe he would,' she replied quietly, and heard a suppressed sob. 'Perhaps it won't be so bad once Hesley is overseas. I shall be with you.' She tried to sound confident.

'You will stay, won't you?'

'Of course. He will be away for at least two years, I am sure.'

Olivia tried to smile. The relief in her eyes made Harriet want to cry with her.

The banns were read the very next Sunday in the small church up the hill to a straggle of a congregation that included Olivia and Harriet. The curate who visited from the other side of the moor exchanged a few words with Harriet as they left. 'You have done well with her. I was so worried she would grow up wild and uncontrollable and have to be confined to an institution. And to make such a good match for her, too! I shall perform the ceremony myself.'

'You will not ask your vicar?'

'Of course not. He has no interest in Hill Top, and he will not travel across the moor in any weather. No one ventures here without reason. It will be a small affair, will it not?'

'I believe so, sir.'

'Excellent. She will be a wife and out of harm's way before we know it. Good day to you.'

It was only then that Harriet believed the master meant the marriage to take place. They went back to Hill Top House for Sunday dinner in the dining room, which she and her charge ate with the gentlemen when they returned from their ride. Wine flowed freely and Harriet realized that Hesley and his grandfather were going to drink themselves into a stupor for the afternoon. She excused herself and Olivia as soon as she could, sent Olivia to read her Bible in the schoolroom, and went to the kitchen to talk to Mrs Cookson.

'Olivia is to be married to her cousin Hesley at the end of the month.'

'I'd heard as much, though not from you.' Her tone was scolding, as though Harriet should have told her. 'So I sent one of the stable lads to church this morning.'

'We did not see him.'

'No, you wouldn't, you being in the front pew and he having to leave sharpish to help Matt with the horses.'

'Are you not surprised at the news?'

'I'd guessed. Stands to reason. Mind, I thought they'd wait till she were a bit older.' She shrugged. 'Nothing this family does surprises me any more. The pit is on its last legs through lack of attention and this is the only way the master can get his hands on real money.'

'You mean Olivia's inheritance. What do you know about it?'

'I suppose I may as well tell you. When Miss Olivia's grandfather inherited the pit from old Samuel he married well, a lady from Bristol whose family had sugar. It was in a trust so her husband couldn't get his hands on it. Not that he would've frittered it away like this one does. Young Mr Samuel was a fair-minded man. It's only this lot are the bad 'uns.'

'Young Samuel was the master's late brother?'

'Aye. His daughter was Miss Olivia's mother. Lucinda, she were. Nice little lass. She married a lawyer man from Bristol. Not exactly gentry, his family were jacks of all trades, but he were a charmer. And what with the government stopping the slave trade, they were going out to the West Indies to see what could be done when – well, you know the rest.'

'I don't see why Olivia has to marry, though. The master is her trustee.'

'He only gets the income. He can't sell the plantation. And without the capital to invest in the pit, it'll close. Matt told me. When she marries, her husband gets the lot straight away. So if she weds young Master Hesley, old Hesley will keep control.'

'If he does as his grandfather tells him.'

'Oh, he will. He wants to make sure nob'dy else gets their hands on it. Once she's married, it's safe. And don't you forget that means you and me are safe an' all. Where would we go if he had to sell up?'

Where indeed? Harriet thought. A life on the road as a tinker's wife, like the scullery-maid they talked of? She felt uneasy. As wife and mistress of the house, Olivia would have no need of her as a governess. The master had only agreed she might stay for reasons of his own. For how long? She was just a convenience for him. She had no illusions that he cared for her. With Olivia's money he could invest in the pit and feel safe again. He would return to keeping a mistress and discard her without further thought.

'Is there much work for women in the town, Mrs Cookson?' she asked.

'Not for the likes of you and me. If they're lucky some lasses are taken on at the pithead, sorting coals and lodging with a miner's family. If they're not so lucky they end up in a tavern or on the streets.'

Mrs Cookson twisted her head to look directly at her. 'You could do a lot worse than the master, Miss Trent, and the child relies on you.'

Oh, how could Harriet stay here? She was desperate to get away from this house. But what would happen to Olivia if she left? Harriet was in anguish at her dilemma. 'No, I would not leave her,' she said. 'She still has much to learn. Perhaps you might help me with her.'

'You're the governess.'

'But you have more experience of – of married life than I. It's just that Miss Olivia is so young for marriage and I only have a few weeks to prepare her. I wondered, Mrs Cookson, if you would talk to her about some of her – her more personal, wifely duties. You were married once. You are better placed than I to explain—'

'Don't play the innocent maid with me, Miss Trent. I know what's been going on between you and the master.'

Harriet looked at her feet and blushed. 'Does everybody?'

'Course we do! But there's no need to be ashamed of it in this house. You're not the first and you won't be the last.'

'I do not serve him willingly,' she said.

'Well, I'm sorry about that, lass, but he is the master and since he's taken up with you he doesn't disgrace himself in town any more. That's a blessing if ever there was one. But he'll never marry you and chances are you'll not fall for a babby wi' 'im. The Mextons may be a name in the Riding, but none of 'em's been up to much at making babies.'

'His sister has three children.'

'Ah, but she's only a half-sister. Anyway, they say it's the men. Weak seed. Which is as well, considering how they put it about.'

Harriet did not enquire where Mrs Cookson had gained her knowledge. But she guessed it must be true, for his demands on her body had been regular and there was no sign that she was with child. She had believed her prayers had protected her. When she begged the Lord to forgive her sins, she prayed also that she was barren. His visits to the schoolroom would have to stop now, for soon Olivia would understand. Surely he would listen to reason, for the child's sake.

Her priority was Olivia and she began her instruction the day after on their nature walk. They rested on a dry-stone wall and saw the rabbits mating on the moor.

'It's what married people do. And when Hesley is your husband, you will share his bed and he will lie with you. He will – you will be as one person with him. You must not be frightened of him, Olivia.'

'Why? Will it hurt?'

'All married people do it and you will become used to it.'

'But will it hurt?'

'Perhaps a little. At first.'

'It will hurt, won't it?'

'No, not really.'

'It will – I know it will. It's punishment, isn't it?'

'No, Olivia.'

'Yes, it is! It's what Uncle Hesley does to you and it makes you cry!'

Harriet closed her eyes. The child was right. It was her punishment. She had deceived everyone and this was her punishment. The Lord had seen fit to take her virtue from her as the price to pay for her wickedness. She thought about things she had done in the past that were wicked and confessed only to deception. As a pupil teacher and teacher, she had constantly deceived others about the punishment she had meted out to her charges, and had done the same to the master here.

The Lord was all-knowing. Was this her punishment for those lies? How could she explain herself to this innocent child? If it were not for Olivia she would have packed her bag and left after that first night he had come to her bed. Her courage had failed her when she most needed it. She could have taken her chances on the road or in the town. And, she realized, probably perished from cold, or become a street woman in the taverns, for how many families hereabouts employed a governess? Even a shopkeeper would not take her without a testimonial. She had been trapped, and without money of her own, she would remain so.

'Does Uncle Hesley hurt you very much, Miss Trent?'

'You must not ask others about these things, Olivia. But you have to do it. It is your duty as a wife.'

'You're not Uncle Hesley's wife and you do it! Why can't you do it for me with Cousin Hesley?'

Now Harriet covered her face with her hands. It would have to stop. It was never too late to retreat from sin. She must speak to the master soon.

Chapter 12

She knocked on his library door and waited.

'Yes?'

'May I speak with you, sir?'

'If you must.'

He was lounging in his favourite chair, long legs splayed in front of a good fire. A decanter of whisky and a half-filled glass stood on a small table by his right hand. An oil lamp glowed beside the decanter, softening his lined, ageing features. He had been handsome when he was younger. His son had been too, judging by the portrait on the stairs.

'Well? Is this about Olivia?'

'No, sir. That is, yes, sir.'

He sighed. 'Don't talk to me in riddles, woman.'

'I have begun instruction for Olivia's wifely duties. Now that she understands more about gentlemen and ladies together, I do not think it would be in her interests for you to continue to—' She swallowed. 'For you to visit the schoolroom at night.'

He picked up his whisky glass and stared at it. 'Does she know?'

'She believes you are punishing me.'

'Is that what you think, too, Miss Trent?'

'Of course it is punishment!' she responded irritably. 'You take something I do not wish to give.'

'The devil you don't!'

Her eyes flashed. Surely he did not think she welcomed him. 'You have never sought my permission, sir.'

He guffawed and drank his whisky. 'Women always protest. They never mean it for they know it makes the contest more appealing. Is that not what you were taught?'

'I was taught about the value of virtue and the sanctity of marriage.'

'And now I suppose a pious creature like yourself thinks herself ruined.'

'Think it? I know it.'

'If you don't like it here, you can leave,' he retaliated. 'Go on! Take your chances out in the Riding. You won't get far once the word is out about your services here. The Mextons are notorious. Did no one warn you about us? Your reputation, such as it was, was probably lost the moment you agreed to come here.'

'Well, if it wasn't then, it most certainly is now!'

His sagging eyes glittered in the lamplight. She did

not know whether it was the flickering firelight or actual movement in his breeches and stepped back in alarm. In the silence that followed, she recovered her composure. 'I do not think Olivia should consider her wifely duty as punishment, sir.'

He poured more whisky from the decanter. 'Very well. I shall not visit you in the schoolroom.'

Harriet felt as though a heavy burden had slid from her shoulders. She had not expected him to be so accommodating and felt elated. 'Thank you, sir.'

But her joy was short-lived, replaced by the misery and wretchedness that were so familiar to her.

'Perhaps I shall have you now. Here on the hearth-rug.'

He took pleasure in humiliating her, in overcoming her protests. She thought that if he did carry out this threat it would be the last time, for had he not agreed to cease his night-time calls? Well, if he welcomed her resistance, she would be compliant and see how that pleased him. She scowled. She was already thinking like a whore. She must get away from this house. When Olivia was settled in her marriage she would plan her escape from Hill Top House and Hesley Mexton.

He laughed. 'Don't look so worried. You are safe from me for now. Yes, I see how much that pleases you.' He drank again from his whisky glass. 'Would it surprise you to know that I look forward to pleasing you?'

She relaxed a fraction. She should know by now that he liked to toy with her feelings. She thought, though, that he appreciated the work she did for his great-niece. Her years at Blackstone had taught her there was good in everyone if only you could find it. The corners of her mouth turned down. She did not believe there was a decent side to the master.

But he kept his word and did not visit the school-room at night. In those uncertain hours when she lay awake, alert to every sound, she planned how she would escape from this prison. Only money gave her the answer to her situation. She did not need much, just enough to distance herself from the reputation of Hill Top House.

It would take twelve months, she reasoned. By then Olivia would be in her fifteenth year, no longer a child. She would forge a testimonial and travel outside the Riding for work. She could read, write and keep account books. There must be something out there for her.

So convinced was she that she had found a way out of her situation that there were times over the next few weeks when Harriet forgot the sinfulness of her position, and the injustice of Olivia's fate. She enjoyed the wedding preparations. The young bride was to wear her new silk gown and slippers, and Harriet practised dressing her hair in coils entwined with flowers.

The dressmaker delivered two more gowns for daytime, several new undergarments and items of nightwear, all of which Harriet and Mrs Cookson wrapped carefully in calico and stowed in young Hesley's bedchamber. It was one of the finest rooms in the house with a large bay window overlooking the front drive.

Harriet fingered the red brocade hangings around the four-poster bed. 'Don't you think girls are allowed to marry too young, Mrs Cookson? Boys are usually older.'

'Aye, well, they 'as to be earning to look after a wife. Anyroad, I reckon it's for the best wi' this little 'un. You don't want to be risking babbies out o' wedlock. She were a wild little thing afore you came, talking to any vagrants that came begging at the door and going out to meet 'em on the moor.'

'They were innocent acquaintances. That's not the reason for Miss Olivia's marriage, is it? It's for her inheritance.'

'Same thing, if you ask me. Stop any Tom, Dick or Harry getting her with child and his hands on her money.'

'But I don't think she's ready for a husband.'

'Are any of us when we wed? At least this 'un knows a bit about what to expect from you. My old ma never told me nowt and I thought my husband were trying to kill me on my wedding night. While we're up 'ere, I'll show you your new chamber. It's down at the other end of the landing.'

'I didn't know I was moving into the main wing.'

'The master's orders. And there's cloth for you to make new gowns. I expect you'll be dining every day with the family after the wedding. You'll be expected to dress as befitting Miss Olivia's companion.'

Mrs Cookson opened the door to a small, light chamber with a sash window that overlooked the front approach to the house. There was a rug on the floor-boards and curtains at the window made from the same fabric as the bed coverings. It was a larger bed than the one in her old chamber, and it had a soft feather mattress and white linen sheets.

'It's beautiful,' Harriet said. 'Oh, a cupboard for hanging my Sunday gown and a chest of drawers. This is indeed luxury for me. What's in here?' Harriet rattled the handle of a door in the wall next to the washstand.

'That's locked from the other side.'

'But what is at the other side?'

'The master's bedchamber. This was a dressing room once.'

'Is there a key for this side, Mrs Cookson?'

The older woman did not answer and Harriet sagged onto the side of the bed as realization dawned on her. The master had kept his word about not visiting the schoolroom but after the wedding ceremony . . . She began to feel ill.

'It's the master's wishes, Miss Trent. I said it'd be too much work for me, but he insisted. I'm sorry.'

Mrs Cookson sounded sympathetic. It wasn't her fault.

'I'll stay in the schoolroom,' Harriet decided.

'You can't. I'm having those two lasses from the poorhouse back all the time. But the attics are too damp to use. They'll sleep on pallets in the kitchen until the wedding and then they'll have Miss Olivia's old bedchamber.'

'Well, you've done wonders with her since you've been here. All dressed up like a proper grown lady with her hair curled and prettied. Miss Olivia's a lucky lass, if you ask me. She'll be mistress of this house after today, and if you play your cards right, Miss Trent, and stay in the master's favour you'll be with her for her own babbies.' Mrs Cookson beamed at them as they climbed into the carriage, then returned to her kitchen.

'Will I have a baby, Miss Trent?'

Harriet took her hand. 'You might.'

'Hesley'll hurt me, won't he?'

'You must tell him if he does.'

'He'll only hurt me more. I'm frightened, Miss Trent.'

'You'll be his wife. He'll be different now.' Harriet tried to reassure her as the carriage bumped along the track to church. But she knew he was like his grandfather and would have no thought for the sensibilities of his bride. She felt a loathing for both men that surpassed her reason.

'No, he won't,' Olivia responded. 'He disgusts me and I hate him. I hope he's drowned at sea.'

Harriet was horrified to realize she felt the same.

They arrived at the tiny church after the handful of morning worshippers had left. Harriet wore her new gown, a soft hue that brought out the blue in her eyes and enhanced her fair colouring, but did nothing for the dark shadows that indicated her sleepless nights.

The master and Hesley had followed on horseback. They had all taken spirits to keep out the cold wind that shrieked across the moor, but only young Hesley was drunk enough to slur his speech as he took his vows in front of the curate.

The ceremony was over quickly and the party returned to more wine and a roast baron of beef in the dining room. Harriet had not seen a joint as huge as this before, even at Hill Top. The master must be very pleased with what had happened.

Olivia was allowed to take wine for the first time and Harriet, who preferred it to ale with her dinner, took more than she should have. When she saw that the gentlemen were going to continue drinking until the pair of them fell into a stupor, she stood up.

'Will you excuse us, sir? I shall take Mrs Mexton up to her – her chamber to rest.'

She helped Olivia out of her wedding dress and into one of her new silk nightgowns, unpinned her pretty hair and brushed it out over her shoulders. 'You should try to rest if you can, madam.'

'Is that what you have to call me?'

'Now that you are married, yes.'

The girl yawned and Harriet pulled back the covers. 'I'll bring you some tea later.'

In the kitchen, Harriet laid a tray while Mrs Cookson snoozed in her chair by the fire. One of her new housemaids was on her hands and knees scrubbing out the scullery. The other was fettling Olivia's old chamber over the kitchen.

Harriet wandered into the front hall where silence had fallen. Wherever the gentlemen had gone, they were asleep as she had anticipated. She went outside to sit in the afternoon sun as it sank below the horizon. The days were lengthening already.

Harriet guessed that no word had reached the town about Olivia's marriage or her aunt and uncle would have been there, she was sure. They would be as shocked by it as she was.

Chapter 13

'Are you awake, Mrs Mexton?' A few hours later Harriet tapped lightly on the bedchamber door.

'Yes.'

She carried in a tray of tea, placed it carefully on a small table and began to pour. Olivia was sitting up in bed with the pillows piled behind her. She looked relaxed and refreshed and, Miss Trent noticed, slightly wanton with her hair tumbled and her silk nightgown clinging to her.

'I heard the gentlemen talking in the drawing room. Perhaps you would care to dress and join them.'

'Is that what I should do?'

'Yes, madam. Your days will be different now.'

'And nights. It will feel strange to sleep in Hesley's bed. But it's so big and comfortable. You'll be cold all alone in the schoolroom, Miss Trent.'

'I'm to move into the front wing now that I am your companion, and we shall continue some of your lessons in the morning room.' She handed Olivia a cup of tea. 'Are you hungry? There is bread and butter. And then you must get dressed.'

'Do I have to put on that corset again?'

'Every day now, madam. You are a married lady and must behave as one.'

'Shall I wear my silk gown?'

'No, one of your new day gowns. I'll get it for you.'

As Harriet reached inside the cupboard, the chamber door opened and Hesley walked in with his grand-father. 'I was just helping madam to dress, sir,' she said, laying the gown over a couch.

'Not now, Miss Trent. Come with me.' The master stood in the doorway and waited for her. She glanced at Olivia, who looked alarmed. She gave her a reas-suring smile but Olivia did not return it. She was watching Hesley shrug off his coat.

'Miss Trent?' There was pleading in Olivia's voice and Harriet moved towards the bed, but the master took her arm roughly and pushed her out of the door.

She followed him downstairs to his library and remembered vividly their last encounter in that room. He picked up the poker and disturbed the glowing embers in the fireplace, then added more coal with the tongs.

'You will question Olivia tomorrow about her wedding night.'

'But surely, sir, you can ask your grandson—'

'And he will tell me what I want to hear. While you, Miss Trent, speak the truth because you do not know what else to say.'

She thought that he was not quite right. She lied about beatings. But that was all.

He put down the tongs and looked at her. 'You are not afraid to be truthful with me. Blackstone tempered you well. You are resilient. I would have likened you to a piece of coal but you do not burn. You do not even smoulder. I should like to see you smoulder, Miss Trent.'

'I do not understand you, sir.'

'No, you are devoid of passion.'

Only in the way you wish, she reflected. I have passion, she reasoned silently, for I hate you with a vengeance. And I love your niece more than you could ever know.

'You are more like a piece of jet,' he went on. 'Hardened and cold. Do you know what jet is?'

'Of course, sir. It is jewellery made from fossilized coal.'

'Fossilized. Yes. That is what Blackstone has done for you. It has fossilized you.'

No. It made me strong, she thought. It is you who have made me cold.

'Have you seen any jet?'

'No, sir.'

'Well, you shall. Olivia now has a collection of jet jewellery, her mother's and her aunt's, handed down from Mexton women before them. Now she has married it is hers.'

'I shall see that it is properly cared for, sir.'

'Of course you will.' He smiled. 'You know where your duty lies. When you have spoken with Olivia about her wedding night, you will come and talk to me. Are you clear about that?'

'Yes, sir. I—' She hesitated. 'I was wondering if, after tonight, you might consider a separate bedchamber for madam. Until she is a little older, sir.'

'Out of the question. She will be alone soon enough as Hesley is leaving for the West Indies when passage can be arranged. Besides, I want her with child as quickly as possible. Hesley needs an heir. She is ready to bear them, is she not, Miss Trent?'

'Possibly. But I am not sure that she should until she has matured a little more.'

He gave her a sneering smile. 'I'm sure she is growing up as we speak.'

'Sir.' She remained standing before him.

'That is all, Miss Trent. Go and listen at the bedchamber door if you care for such entertainment.'

'I wish to speak with you, sir.'

'Well, make haste. A bottle of brandy awaits me.'

'You promised your servants that you would recommence paying their salaries on the first quarter-day after the wedding. Did you mean it, sir?'

'I did. Your mistress inherited her capital on her marriage and my grandson is a wealthy man. I have power of attorney over his affairs while he is abroad.'

'You have thought of everything, sir. Now that I am companion, as well as governess, to Mrs Mexton, I should like an increase in my salary.'

'The devil you would! I suppose Cookson has put you up to this.'

'No, sir. I have extra responsibilities as Mrs Mexton's companion, and I believe that I am worth it.'

His lined face took on its usual mocking leer. 'Do you, indeed?'

'You would not wish her to revert to her wild ways when her husband is away, sir. And, of course, she may be with child by then.'

His eyes narrowed. 'What do you want?'

'Another twenty pounds a year, sir.'

'I mine coal, not gold, Miss Trent. You can have ten.'

'Thank you, sir.'

She turned to leave before he changed his mind. As she reached the door, he called after her, 'I shall enjoy making you earn it, Miss Trent.'

Humiliated, she hurried to the sanctuary of the kitchen, where Mrs Cookson was preparing supper. She had learned to ignore his taunts and harden her core, like the piece of jet he thought she was. An extra ten pounds a year would enable her to start a new life eventually, away from the South Riding where no one knew of her time here. But she vowed not to leave until she was sure that Olivia would be happy as mistress of Hill Top. And wherever she went she would find a way of coming back. She could not leave her for ever.

Upstairs, Olivia heard the squeaking and grating of the pump as the girls filled their buckets with water. It was still light but Hesley closed the heavy brocade curtains, casting a dull red glow over the bedchamber.

'Well, cousin, we're stuck with each other so we'd best make a good fist of this.'

'A fist? Don't hurt me, Hesley. Please don't hurt me.'

He sighed. Perhaps it was as well he was going overseas. At least she'd be grown-up when he got back. Meanwhile, if he wanted to be sure of her plantation, he had to get on with this. Still, she wasn't much younger than some of the tavern lasses he'd been with in town.

He removed all his clothes and stood naked in front of her.

She sat up in bed, fascinated. She had never seen a man undress before and now she saw how different he was from her. She felt un unusual nervousness come over her as she watched his limbs and muscles move, and those brownish dangling things he had where she had none. Was that what he did it with? It didn't look very frightening. She was puzzled and her mouth turned down at the corners.

'Smile at me, Olivia. You're pretty when you smile.'

She did.

He threw back the bedcovers and added, 'Take off your nightgown and lie on your back.'

She obeyed, and as she shuffled down the bed she noticed the thing stirring and swelling and sticking out from his body. He grinned at her when she protested as he tweaked her nipples with his fingers, then climbed over her, straddling her body with his hairy legs. She tensed, unsure of what he would do next.

'Put your arms above your head,' he said, and ran his hands all over her naked body, following the contours of her small breasts, waist, young rounding hips and finishing at her thighs.

He sat back on his heels so that his arched swelling was pointing at her face and she saw a bead of moisture at its tip. He hadn't hurt her yet and she looked up at his face. It was set in a grimace and his eyes were glassy as though he were looking through instead of at her. He grabbed at a pillow, shoved it under her back, and then his fingers were between her legs exploring her very private areas. Her breathing became laboured as she tried to recoil. But he persisted, and when he found what he was searching for he played around with her, making her tingly and she felt a restlessness in her limbs. And then he stopped doing that and she held her breath as he pushed her legs apart and stretched out on top of her, his heavy body forcing her deep into the feather mattress.

She felt the pain, a short, tearing twinge, as he pushed himself inside her. It seemed as though he was tearing her in two and she cried out for him to stop. But he did not hear her. Or, if he did, he did not heed her cries. His face was somewhere above hers, angry-looking, as he kept driving into her, again and again, making the wooden bedstead creak. She remembered the creaking and crying from previous nights. Miss Trent had lied to her. It did hurt and it was punishment.

Sweat from Hesley's face dripped on to hers and she licked its saltiness from her lips. He was so heavy that she could hardly breathe. He was beating her with his body as Uncle Hesley had done to Miss Trent and all she wanted was for him to stop. Eventually he did. Quite suddenly, with a forced groan from his throat as he flopped on top of her, smothering her with his sweaty, hairy chest and stomach.

Then he rolled off her and she lay perfectly still, naked and uncovered, not sure what she should do. The sharp hurt had ceased, but there was a dull ache in the pit of her stomach and stickiness about her private areas. Miss Trent had told her to wash afterwards and she half rose to search for her nightdress.

'Stay where you are. I haven't finished with you yet.' He laid a heavy leg across her.

'But you've done it once! You don't have to do it again!'

'Don't argue with me,' he growled. 'Ever.'

She lay there anxiously, wondering what he would do next. After a while he turned towards her and told her to watch as he stroked himself until he began to stir and swell again. 'Now you do it. Like this.' He guided her hand towards him, and she did as he had bade her, feeling his hot flesh harden and lengthen under her touch. And then he fingered her, making her tingle again, and pushed inside her. 'Wet. That's better,' he said, and rolled onto her to do it again, pushing into her time after time, heaving and sweating and crushing the breath out of her body.

She kept begging him to stop but he didn't until, eventually, he let out an animal yowl and held himself up on his hands with his head flung back. His face was red and angry and she thought he was going to hit her.

'Good girl,' he said, and flung himself across the bed on his back 'You'll do.'

'Well, I don't want to do it again!' she protested. 'I won't!' She hardly dared move. Her insides were hurting and her back ached. She felt cold and exposed, splayed over the pillow without any clothing, her legs apart and her arms above her head.

'You will do as I say,' he replied harshly, and got out of bed to use the chamber pot.

She pulled away the pillow and slid out of bed, feeling sick and dizzy. She was sore and wished suddenly that she was out in her hidden garden, building mud castles. But she wasn't. She was a wife now and this was her duty. And she had pleased Cousin Hesley. He had said so. Good girl, he had said. She hoped Miss Trent could stop the stinging. But it didn't hurt as much as she had thought it would, certainly not enough to make her cry, and she wondered why Miss Trent had always cried so much afterwards.

Later, Harriet undressed in her new bedchamber. As she brushed her gown and hung it in the cupboard, she glanced at the closed door that linked with the adjoining chamber. The master's chamber. She washed her hands and face, smoothed on a little salve and combed out her hair, fixing it under her nightcap. In the looking-glass on her chest of drawers, she watched the closed door behind her. It stayed firmly shut.

She crossed to the window. There was no moon or stars. All she saw was blackness, and all she heard was silence. She had risen at six and, although she was tired from this unusual day, she knew she would not sleep. She crept across to the door, very carefully turning the knob. It was locked. She heaved a sigh, went back to pull the curtains at the window and eventually slid into bed. Yet she dared not blow out the candle for in the dark she would not be able to watch the door.

The key grated in the lock and the door swung open silently. There was a lamp glow from the room beyond that was blotted out as the master's frame filled the doorway. He was clothed in a dressing robe and held a brandy glass in his hand. 'Good evening, Miss Trent,' he said.

She feigned sleep. He had been without her for a month. He could do without her for longer. Surely even whores could choose when they worked.

He came into the room and lifted the bedclothes. 'Don't pretend with me. Your candle still burns. Open your eyes.'

She did. 'It has been a long day, sir. I am tired.' Too exhausted to sleep, in fact.

'Have some of this.' He offered her his drink.

She suppressed a sigh, rolled to the edge of the bed and sat up.

'That's better.'

She gulped it down. She needed courage tonight. 'I shall not do it, sir.'

'You will. Blackstone ceded guardianship to me when you came here.'

'But I am not your slave, sir, to do with as you wish, when you wish.'

He turned on her angrily, surprising her with his response. 'What do you know about slaves?'

'I was a teacher at Blackstone, sir. I read pamphlets and news-sheets that came my way.'

'And I suppose as a penniless orphan you have sympathy with these abolitionists?'

'I have sympathy for the slaves, sir.'

'The devil you have! You are paid for your services, Miss Trent. If you were my slave, I should not have to pay you anything.'

'But you have not paid me yet,' she pointed out, as angry as he was.

'You know the reason for that. I have given you bed and board and clothes for your back. Indeed, have I not just agreed to pay you an extra ten pounds per year?'

'I believe I am worth that amount, sir.'

'I shall be the judge of that. Come here to me.'

'No, sir. My extra salary is for my services towards Mrs Mexton.'

'You waste my time with words. I care not for your views, Miss Trent. You will do as I ask.'

He took the empty glass from her hand and pulled her to her feet. She moved away from him but he did not release her hand. He grasped her chin and held her face steady as he tried to kiss her. She turned her head away and tried to push him off. But he was taller and stronger than she and he pinned her to the bedpost, blocking any way out. She grappled to remove his hands and they struggled. She heard the stitching rip on her nightgown.

'For God's sake, do not fight me, woman, or I shall have to hit you.'

'I should rather you hit me than invade my body without my leave.'

He cursed her and pushed her back onto the bed. 'Why must you be so tiresome? I do not want this constant battle between us.'

'Neither do I! You are a cruel and wicked man!'

'Aye. So you've said before. But I have no wish to hurt you, Miss Trent. You will find that, if you do not fight me, I shall not hurt you. You may even begin to enjoy yourself.'

'Never. I do not want this, sir.'

He sighed and smiled. 'I think you do, if only you will allow yourself the pleasure.'

'You are wrong, sir.'

He became impatient. 'What if I am? I am an old man with needs. Needs that you can so easily satisfy and I do not care for coyness.'

'Then do not take that which is not freely given to you.'

He looked at her in silence for a long minute. 'I'm afraid you have no choice in this matter. Your maidenly protests are tedious. It is time to be adult about our arrangement. You are, after all, now paid more for your services.'

'I did not ask for money for this, sir.'

'Perhaps not. Because if you did you would know that you are worth more, much more, than you requested. However, I know the acquisition of money is important to you, so let us strike a bargain. You may have the other ten pounds a year you asked for if you do not fight me so. What do you say, Miss Trent? A truce?'

She closed her eyes, feeling defeated. He was not going to give up. She contained her instinct to strike him across the face in the certain knowledge that it would only inflame him further. 'You are a vile and despicable man,' she said.

'But you agree?'

She looked away. He took off his dressing robe, sat on the bed and stroked her breasts. She did not move.

'You do agree,' he said. 'You have the salary you want and we shall speak no more of it.'

He left her feeling weak and exhausted, worn down. It was not the physical invasion of her body that tired her, but the attack on her sensibilities that kindled an inner anger, which grew and festered. She hated him. But she hated herself more for complying with his wants. She had not thought it was possible to despise herself any more than she already did, until she reflected on their bargain.

She tried desperately to reason with herself. She would be one-and-twenty soon, and a portion of her stipend would be hers in the spring. The increase would enable her to leave at midsummer. There would be enough to prevent starvation until she found another position.

She still had her testimonial from Blackstone. It would be difficult to explain away the last year, but she would not lie. Perhaps not tell everything. A sin of omission. She prayed for guidance and wondered whether the Lord had already forsaken her. For, although she tried desperately not to think of it, she knew what she had become.

Whore. Whore. Whore.

She breathed the word over and over to herself as penance.

Chapter 14

'I don't believe it! You are younger than my sister Josephina.'

'Well, it's true. I was married to Hesley a month ago in this very church.'

Jared had ridden over from his lodgings that morning. He looked forward to Sundays now he could borrow a horse. She was a fine beast, chestnut with a white blaze on her nose, and he had arranged to ride her every Sunday. She belonged to the pit manager at Kimber Deep and would never win a race, but she had a good nature and plenty of stamina.

He called at the mission when he could, but his parents expected him to attend church with his supervisor when he did not go home and he hated to deceive them. He had explained this to Tobias and both he and his sister had been very understanding. Anna, he knew, had returned to her own mission on the other side of the Riding. They were good people. He liked them and missed their meetings.

When he reached the canal, he had turned his horse away from the towpath towards the open country and spurred her to a gallop until he was well away from the waterway and Mexton Pit. Olivia had been on his mind since Christmas. He knew that, despite her grown-up appearance, she was too young to regard in that way. But no matter how hard he tried not to think of her, he could not stop himself. He did not forget his promise to her and watched the weather for the first signs of spring.

His spirits lifted as he rode towards Hill Top House, admitting to himself how much he looked forward to seeing her. Olivia's conversation was bright and fresh, and there was no duplicity about her. The governess watched over her like a mother hen, but he saw the woman needed adult company and lingered with other worshippers at the church door. He was pleased to find Olivia alone, walking among the trees behind the churchyard. He was not so pleased with her news.

'Why were we not told? Not even invited to the ceremony?'

She was so delighted to see Jared that her miserable life with Hesley faded. 'Please don't be angry. I am truly grateful you have ridden over. I have looked forward to your visits and to having you as my friend.'

'But don't you realize your marriage changes everything?'

'Why?'

'You are Hesley's wife now. I cannot meet you like this.'

Olivia turned on him. 'But you promised!'

'Please don't be upset, Olivia. Hesley will be your friend now.'

'No, he won't! I hate him. He's horrible to me!'

The shock that Jared felt about the marriage now turned to fear. 'What do you mean?'

'He does not care for me as a husband should,' Olivia said quietly.

'How could he not?' Jared answered. What had old Hesley done now? His grandson was a dissolute drunkard and this – this bright accomplished *child* was his *wife*. 'He is your husband,' he added. But as he spoke the words, he became fully aware of what that meant for her. She was no longer a child. She was a married woman. He tried to imagine his sister Juliana as a wife and could not. 'He doesn't beat you, does he?'

Olivia looked at the ground. 'Miss Trent says it's what married people do.'

Jared had not meant the intimate aspect of her marriage, but clearly Olivia did. He could not bear the thought of Hesley using her in that way. He wanted to sweep her up onto his horse and take her away from such barbarity.

She continued to look at the ground and scuff her feet among the loose stones. 'She says it is my duty and I must pretend to enjoy it for now. And that in time I shall.'

'And how would she know?' he breathed sourly. And then he realized the answer to that particular question.

He knew of old Hesley's reputation from the men who worked at Kimber Deep. He knew, also, that he had given up his mistress in town after the bank failure. He felt sick as he imagined the goings-on at HillTop House.

'Where is your governess?' he demanded sharply.

'With the curate's wife. Won't you stay and talk to her?'

'I do not think I can trust myself to be civil to her.'

'Oh, but, Jared, you must. She is my companion now! She is teaching me how to be mistress of the house.'

'I am sure she is very good at that.'

His tone was disrespectful and not lost on Olivia. 'Why do you think so ill of her?'

The governess should have told his parents, he thought angrily, but he reined in his annoyance. 'Never mind,' he said. 'She will not approve of our meetings now that you belong to Hesley.'

'Belong to him? He does not own me!'

'Yes, he does,' Jared answered bluntly. 'You are his wife. Do you not understand what that means? He may order your life as he thinks fit.'

'Well, that is no different from what his grandfather has always done. And still does. Uncle Hesley tells us all what to do. He is the evil one. But he does not say I must stop going to the church, so we can still see each other here.'

She was pleading with him and he so much wanted to agree. But he feared the consequences for her. 'Not while Miss Trent comes with you. If she sees me she is sure to tell old Hesley and cause trouble.'

'Then you must stay out of sight. She always talks to the curate's wife after the service, and she forgets the time with her. Oh, please, say that you will ride over when you can.'

Jared gazed at her, pretty as a picture in a soft blue gown and matching bonnet that brought out the pale tint of her eyes, and his heart grieved for her loneliness. His sisters went out to lessons and bought ribbons and lace at the draper's. They were invited to play their duets at gatherings. Olivia did nothing like that. But she should be visiting his family in town, not beseeching him to call on her in this clandestine manner.

When he did not reply, she went on, 'Hesley will never find out. Even if Miss Trent sees you, she will not tell if I ask her not to. She cares for me.'

'Cares for you? I think not. If she does, why did she let this happen to you?'

'You do not know what she endures for my sake! I believe she would have left months ago if she were not so concerned for me. She knows I need her.'

'Does she? She could have got word to my mother for help. Father would have spoken out against your marriage, I am sure.'

'Do you really believe that would have stopped Uncle Hesley having his own way? He was ready to declare me insane to get his hands on my fortune. To me, marriage was preferable.'

Jared heard a firmness in her voice that made him frown. He had underestimated old Hesley's ruthlessness. He wanted to talk further but the conversations drifting over from the church door had ceased. Miss Trent would be looking for Olivia and he was angry with her. She was in old Hesley's pay. Her duty was to him, in spite of Olivia's faith in her. He did not want Olivia to be chastised for their meeting by either of the Mexton so-called gentlemen. And neither did he wish to destroy her belief in Miss Trent, whatever he might think of the woman.

He said, 'Do not tell Miss Trent that we have met, for the present. I shall ride over again, I promise.' He bent to take her hand and kiss it, but she moved nearer to him quickly, and he found her delicate cheek raised towards his lips. Her skin was as soft as rose petals and his mouth lingered. He was not aware of moving his hand to the back of her bonnet, but he did. She withdrew quickly, flustered. He, too, became anxious by the sudden intimacy. She was a married woman.

'You're not angry with me, are you?' Olivia murmured.

He shook his head and gathered the reins of his horse. 'I shall never be angry with you, Olivia. I shall always be your friend. You may depend on that, if nothing else.'

When he arrived home his mother and father were back from church. Their faces were dark and he realized they had received the news. His sisters scurried away immediately after dinner.

'The vicar's wife told me.' His mother frowned. 'I did not believe it but she had heard it from the wife of the curate who performed the ceremony.'

'Father! Is there nothing you can do?' Jared's anger simmered at the secrecy and deception.

'It's too late. The deed is done. By heaven, the rogue must have been planning it when we visited at Christmas!'

Jared could hear his sisters practising the piano in the next room. 'Do Josie and Julie know?'

His mother shook her head. 'I thought Hesley had turned over a new leaf,' she fretted, 'and all the time he was deceiving us into thinking how well he was caring for Olivia. But marriage to his grandson! I never dreamed he would do that.'

His father shook his head sadly. 'I knew he coveted the guardianship for her income, but this . . .'

'I suppose he wanted to make sure no one else had it when she came of age,' Jared said.

'More than that, son. The plantation belongs to young Hesley now. Olivia did not have to wait until five-and-twenty to inherit if she married. I understand he's leaving for Liverpool as soon as the weather improves and will sail to the West Indies to manage it.'

'Do you mean she will be moving away from us?' His heart turned over. He might never see her again. He could not bear that. 'You must stop this, Father.'

His father was shaking his head. 'We are too late. But she is not to travel with him. At least they have learned something from the tragedy of her parents.'

Jared felt weak with relief when he heard this. He had not known how strong his affection for Olivia had become until he had met her again near the church.

'She is to stay and continue her education, I am told,' his mother added, with an artificial brightness in her voice. 'When Hesley returns she will be quite grown-up and well able to carry out her duties as mistress at Hill Top House.'

His father added, 'Hesley, too, will have matured. Responsibility for the plantation will be good for him. It is for the best, I am sure.'

Jared snorted in derision and saw his father and mother glance at each other.

'Olivia won't be alone at Hill Top. The governess is to stay on as her companion,' his mother said, and exchanged another meaningful look with his father.

'I know as well as everybody else what goes on up there,' Jared spat. 'Olivia would be better off without any tutoring from *her*.'

'She will stay as long as she is needed, I suppose.' His mother's fingers twisted a handkerchief in her lap.

'I thought you approved of her,' Jared observed.

'Hesley has a bad effect on everyone. Even virtuous governesses can be corrupted.'

So he was right and his parents, too, had their suspicions of what went on at Hill Top House. 'Does everybody know she is a whore?' he muttered.

'Jared! Your mother is present.'

She stood up. 'Yes, Jared. Guard your tongue. You will not use that word in this house. Your sisters may hear you. I shall go and speak to them now. They must be told about Olivia. Then we shall forget the matter and they will play for us. We shall enjoy the rest of our evening together.'

Jared grimaced as his mother left the room.

'Have some compassion for your mother,' his father implored. 'She is more upset than you are, my lad.

Juliana is the same age as Olivia. Leave it to the women-folk. They pull together at times like these and, as a wife, Olivia will be invited to their "at homes". It may be the child's salvation.'

'I don't think you should call her a child any more,' Jared snapped. 'She is a married woman.'

It made him so angry to be reminded that her innocence had been taken from her in this way. And by Hesley of all people, a drunkard who cared only for himself. Olivia's only glimmer of hope was that Hesley would sail for the West Indies soon. But to leave her in the care of the executor of this abomination and his whore?

He stood up abruptly. 'I cannot bear to think of her living there alone with such corruption.'

Benjamin Tyler frowned. He was used to his son's energy and drive, but not to this simmering rage. 'Do nothing rash, son, I beg you. Old Hesley is not a man to be crossed. He is no gentleman. You will only make the damage worse.'

'How can it be any worse for Olivia? I shall bring her here, as we should have done at Christmas.'

'No, Jared. It is too late. She is married to young Hesley and that is an end to the matter. Nothing can be done now.'

'We'll see about that.'

His father stood up to bar his way. 'You must leave it, son.'

But Jared was already turning towards the door. Before his father could stop him, he pushed past him, saying, 'I shall not,' and headed to the stable where he had tethered his horse.

The day was overcast and gusty and he felt as black as the clouds. He urged his mare up the hill out of the town, ignoring the wintry wind that caught at his riding cloak and flapped it over his shoulders. Rain stung his face and spattered on his jacket and he would have enjoyed the challenge of the climb if only he were not so consumed with fury.

The Mextons were in this together, for the younger always did as the elder directed and the pair were notorious in the Riding. The governess, too, was guilty. She had been used to deceive his mother into believing her half-brother had changed his ways.

Hill Top House kept different hours from the Tyler household and they were still at their dinner table when he rode past the windows into the yard at the back. In the glow of the candles he saw four faces turn to stare at him from the dining room. Matt came out in his shirtsleeves to take the horse and Jared went in through the kitchen door.

Mrs Cookson was already on her feet. 'Are you expected, sir?'

He knew they had seen him arrive. 'I believe so,' he answered, and walked past her, through the hall and into the dining room.

Young Hesley was already at the door. 'What brings you here at this hour?' he demanded.

Jared pushed past him and surveyed the scene. Olivia was there. Her pretty face was flushed and there was a wine glass by her right hand, almost empty. The governess, too, was eating dinner with the master. She had bright spots of colour in her cheeks and looked much smarter than she had when he had seen her at Christmas. Her hair was dressed in coils and she had lace at throat and wrists. But she was not smiling and seemed tense.

Jared ignored Hesley. 'Olivia, you need not stay here,' he said to her. 'You may come with me to our house.'

Her eyes widened and she nodded.

'Look here,' young Hesley began, 'who do you think you are to walk in here and carry off my wife?'

Jared ignored him and addressed the master. 'This is your doing, isn't it? How could you? Did you ask Olivia what she wanted?'

Old Hesley's lined face, flushed with drink, now darkened with anger. 'What business is it of yours? She is my responsibility, not yours, and your meddling family is not welcome here. Leave now.'

'Come with me, Olivia.' Jared watched her glance at the governess, who was concentrating on her plate.

The older man rose to his feet and raised his voice. 'I ordered you to leave. *Now!*'

'Or what? You'll summon your farmhands to beat me? You excel at that, I'm told.'

'Guard your words, Tyler,' old Hesley snapped. 'You may be as tall and broad as my men but that does not mean you have become one yet. Get out of my house.'

Young Hesley was holding the door and blocking his way, but his eyes were glazed and Jared smelled the drink on his breath. He answered, 'Not while you behave like this towards Olivia.' He turned to face her. 'Come with me, Olivia. I'll take you to my home.' He held out his hand towards her.

Olivia half rose from her seat and smiled, but was stilled by the governess's hand on her arm. Confused, she bit her lip and sat down again.

Young Hesley followed his grandfather's example: 'How dare you make such a suggestion? She is my wife!'

'You do not deserve a wife. You are a drunkard, a gambler and a user of women.'

Hesley grinned. 'And you are the grandson of a shopkeeper who must brush his own jacket and attend church each week with his parents.'

Jared ignored the taunt and turned back to Olivia. 'Does he beat you?'

'It is no concern of yours if I do!' young Hesley yelled. 'She is *my* wife!'

'Does he hurt you, Olivia?'

'Of course I do not!'

'You do,' Olivia said loudly.

'Hush, ma'am,' Miss Trent interceded sharply.

But Olivia was not to be silenced. 'At night, you—'

'*Madam!*' Miss Trent interrupted, in her strongest governess tone. 'Quiet.'

Olivia's mouth closed and she appeared to shrink before Jared's eyes. Clearly the governess continued to have influence with her. And clearly he was right about the woman's position here. She was not just Olivia's companion in this household. She was more than that. Much more. What on earth was going on in this God-forsaken place?

Jared could restrain himself no longer. His fist was already clenched by his side and within a second he had raised it to connect with young Hesley's jaw. Hesley staggered back and retaliated with blows from both fists, the first missing and the second catching Jared on the side of his head. He reeled, but he had suffered worse in his pugilistic sessions at school. However, Hesley knew what he was doing and Jared guessed he had been in many a fist-fight himself.

As they grappled with each other, he was dimly aware of chairs scraping along the floorboards. They fell against the sideboard and he heard the cutlery and china rattle inside. Then the pair were rolling on the floor, each unwilling to let go of the other until Jared was able to raise his fist again and bring it down hard on Hesley's nose. He let out a yell. *That's* for Olivia, Jared thought.

He would have repeated the action if the barrels had not appeared in front of his eyes. Two. The twin barrels of a shotgun. He looked up, tasting the blood on his lips.

Old Hesley continued to point the gun at his head. 'I said get out of my house.'

Olivia had moved with the governess to the window at the far end of the room. She gave a high-pitched squeal, more like a squeak than a scream, and Miss Trent turned her head into her bosom. The master's face was as black as thunder and Jared saw that he was capable of anything. He staggered to his feet, and as he did so young Hesley stopped nursing his bleeding nose to kick him hard in the leg, causing him to yelp.

Old Hesley gestured to the door with his gun. 'Go,' he ordered.

Jared looked at Olivia, who had now pushed herself away from Miss Trent. She was staring at him in a strange way. Her brow was furrowed and there was uncertainty in her eyes, yet a half-smile trembled on her lips. It was similar to the way she had looked last Christmas when she had twirled for him in her new gown. He gave her a painful, bloody grin and would have spoken to reassure her if he had not felt the cold steel of the gun against his temple.

He weighed up his options. He did not think old Hesley would use the weapon. He would be sure of that if the man were sober, but he was not. He mouthed, 'Friend,' to Olivia and was consoled by a barely perceptible downward movement of her head.

'This isn't finished, Mexton,' he growled, staggering to his feet.

'Yes, it is.'

Jared felt the metal barrel push into his ribs, and then at his back as he turned to the door. He moved reluctantly, eyes on the floor. He dared not even glance at Olivia now.

Old Hesley followed him outside and kept the gun trained on him until he had mounted his horse. 'Keep away from here, you and your family. I don't want any of you Tylers on my land again. And that includes your mother.' He fired the gun into the air, startling Jared's docile mare into a gallop. Jared had to use all his strength to slow her.

His face hurt and his leg ached where Hesley had kicked him, but he did not regret his actions. He could not change what they had done to Olivia, but he hoped he had shown her that he had meant what he said. He would not abandon her. The governess was a paid servant and her loyalties were with the master. Olivia needed a friend more than ever now. As his mare slowed to a canter, he reflected that he would be back. Neither Hesley Mexton nor his gun would stop him.

Harriet and Olivia jumped at the sound of the shot, then ran to the kitchen and into the yard. They were in time to see horse and rider disappear down the track.

'I wanted to go with him. Why did you stop me?' Olivia demanded shakily.

'You are married to Hesley now. Your great-uncle would have brought you back and locked you away while Hesley was abroad. I could not let that happen to you.'

'But Jared is my friend, my special friend.'

'It is not wise for you to make a friend of Jared. It is too dangerous. You saw how your uncle reacted to him.'

'Oh, Miss Trent, I hate this place – and I should hate it even more without you.'

The master turned to them with a satisfied smirk. 'That should teach him not to play his youthful games with me.'

He was angry yet, Harriet saw, he seemed excited by the dining-room spectacle. He laughed harshly and waved his shotgun with a display of the burgeoning energy he showed when he returned from hunting hare. His blood was up and her heart sank.

'Hesley, take Olivia for a walk,' he ordered.

'What about my nose?'

'The bleeding has slowed.'

'But it will soon be dark, Grandfather.'

'Then entertain your wife in the drawing room.'

'Me? That's *her* job, isn't it?' young Hesley replied, with a nod at Harriet.

'She has an urgent matter to attend to with me.'

'Very well.' He grinned.

Olivia watched and listened. Her uncle thought she didn't know what he meant. She may not have been a wife for long but she was aware of what went on between him and Miss Trent. Now he called to her companion.

'There's brandy in the library, Miss Trent. Bring it to my chamber.'

Chapter 15

'Miss Trent! What is the matter?' Olivia had heard the weeping in the butler's pantry where the silver plate was kept. The key was in the lock and she had opened the door quietly.

'Oh!' Miss Trent was sitting on an old chair. She wiped her tears hastily. 'It's nothing.'

Olivia took her own clean handkerchief and went to kneel beside her. 'Tell me what is wrong.'

'Oh, madam, I don't know how I can go on here any longer. I've tried so hard, but—' Her face crumpled and she was crying again.

The only times Olivia had seen Miss Trent weeping in this way had been in the middle of the night, in her narrow bed next to the schoolroom, when Uncle Hesley had used her. She hadn't fully understood her distress then. But now she did. Miss Trent no more welcomed the attentions of her uncle than Olivia did those of his grandson.

She put her arms round her governess's waist and hugged her. 'My uncle is a wicked man. He uses you without any regard for your wishes.'

Miss Trent sniffed. 'You sound quite adult when you say that.'

'I have a husband and I have had to grow up quickly. I am an adult now.'

'And a very capable mistress of Hill Top House.' She rested her cheek on top of Olivia's head, then turned it to kiss her hair. It was an unusually intimate gesture from Miss Trent, who always took her responsibilities as companion so seriously.

'Indeed I am.' Olivia snuggled closer. 'I have your wise counsel to thank for that.' She laughed lightly. 'Without you I should still be building mud castles in the garden and pretending to be a cat.'

'But you were happy then. I have failed you in that respect.'

'No, Miss Trent, you have not.' Olivia could not imagine Hill Top House without her now, and added, 'You make an unbearable situation tolerable for me.'

'You do the same for me. I should have left months ago if it were not for you.'

'And I should have turned into a drunkard like my husband if you had. How else would I get through my days?'

They sat in a silence broken only by an occasional shudder from the older woman as her sobs continued. Suddenly Olivia knew why Miss Trent was enduring such unhappiness. It was for her sake. She was glad that her companion could not see her frown. She said, 'Miss Trent, you do not have to stay with me. My life here will improve when Hesley leaves for the West Indies, and—' She had been going to say that his grandfather was becoming an old man but realized that mere mention of him might increase the other's distress.

'Will it?' Miss Trent replied. 'Will it be easier for you?'

'Oh, yes, I shall be much happier when Hesley leaves.'

'Then so shall I.' Miss Trent smiled at her shakily.

Olivia released her hug and breathed a sigh of relief. 'Why don't we do an inventory of the plate while we are here? Perhaps it will distract us both from our woes.'

As they worked together, Olivia demonstrated to Miss Trent how much she had learned about plate and china from her books and journals. She was determined to make her see that she did not have to endure her uncle's disgraceful behaviour for her sake. She had no money to give Miss Trent, but she could show her how independent and strong she was as Hesley's wife, and in doing so allow Miss Trent her freedom to leave.

'Wake up, Miss Trent. Stir yourself, woman!'

Several nights later, the household was disturbed in the grey light before dawn. Young Hesley was shaking her roughly by the shoulder. *Young* Hesley? What did he want at this hour?

'She needs you. For God's sake, come and quieten her.'

Harriet pulled on her dressing robe and hurried after him.

'Madam? What is it?'

Olivia was in the large four-poster bed. Her skin had a ghostly pallor and her long fair hair was tangled and awry. 'Help me, Miss Trent,' she whimpered. 'It's never been like this before.'

Harriet looked at Hesley. 'What has happened?'

He shrugged. 'How should I know? I'll be downstairs.'

'It hurts,' Olivia moaned. 'I have the cramps each month, but this is much worse.'

'When did it start?'

'Last night. It felt like my courses and I tried to tell Hesley I was unwell but he wouldn't listen.'

Harriet pulled back the bedcovers. 'How long have you been bleeding like this?'

'Since last night after – well, when Hesley fell asleep. Tonight it was so bad I got up to wash and fetch some calico. I even drank some brandy but the pain came back and I yelled and woke him up. It has never been like this before.'

Harriet laid a reassuring hand on hers. 'I'll fetch help.' She hurried out of the bedchamber and leaned over the banister rail. 'Mr Mexton! Sir! Fetch Mr Harvey at once!'

Hesley appeared from the library with a glass in his hand. 'I'll send Matt,' he answered.

'Hurry, sir.' She woke the maids to fetch more linen and heat water, then did what she could to clean up the blood and make Olivia comfortable until the apothecary arrived. There was too much for a monthly show, although Olivia's body had not settled into regularity yet. She sat with her in her pain until after daybreak when Mr Harvey came galloping up the track.

He stayed until dinner time the next day. Olivia's pain had eased and the bleeding had slowed. Harriet did not leave his side as he administered his potions.

Eventually Olivia slept and he turned to Harriet. 'These things happen. She is young to be a wife but she is healthy, and a week of rest with her usual nourishment will see her well again.'

'Was it a child, sir?'

He nodded. 'Where is her husband?'

'In the dining room.' Harriet looked directly at him. 'He – he demands too much of her. Would you speak to him, sir?'

For a moment Adam Harvey stared at her seriously. 'I see. I'll do what I can, but she is his wife.'

Harriet stayed with Olivia until she woke that evening. Since their conversation in the butler's pantry, she had been elated that Olivia could survive as mistress of Hill Top House without her and had dreamed of her escape from the master. But now she knew how alone Olivia would be without anyone who would consider her welfare. How could she leave her now?

Jared had taken up his position in the coppice on the hillside to watch Olivia as she wandered around the churchyard. She had been reading the inscription on a recent headstone. He had whistled softly to draw her attention. 'This way.'

Olivia hurried through the wooden gate to the trees. 'I hoped you would be here.'

'I promised, didn't I? Now, tell me, are you well?'

She nodded. 'I have been out of sorts. Miss Trent said it is part of growing up, but she called for the apothecary all the same.'

A pained expression crossed Jared's brow.

'I am better now,' she added swiftly.

He wanted to take her in his arms and hold her close to protect her from the ills of Hill Top House. He would have done so with the young girl he met last Christmas, but she was no longer that girl. Now he saw in her a maturing loveliness that stirred him more than he cared to acknowledge. As he gazed at her he became uneasy with his desire to embrace her. 'Perhaps I should not be here,' he murmured.

Impulsively, Olivia reached forward with both hands. 'Of course you should!' she exclaimed. 'You said you would be my friend!'

He stepped back but could not resist taking her hands. He grasped them firmly. 'I know. But you have Hesley now.'

'Hesley is not my friend.'

No. He is more than that, Jared thought. He is your husband. The furrow in his brow deepened as he reflected on that and all that it meant. He found that the image thrusting forward in his head was an unpalatable one. But he could not push it away and anger mounted. What could he do? At least if he met her every week he would know that she was well.

He squeezed her hands. 'I shall always be your friend,

Olivia. You can rely on me.' He heard Miss Trent calling her, and added, 'Will she search for you?'

'I think so. She guards me well. As though I were precious to her.'

'Then you must return before she sees us. I shall ride here every week and watch for you.' He saw her eyes light up as he bent to kiss her hands. He had surprised himself: he had not planned to do such a thing and it had been an impulsive action. But he did not regret it. She raised them to meet his lips as though she delighted in the gesture. The sight of her wedding band brought him to his senses.

Already he harboured doubts about meeting her like this. There was danger to her in his actions. If old Hesley found out he would judge Jared by his own standards and think the worst, but Olivia, not he, would suffer. What Jared was doing was unwise, but how else could he be sure that she was well? She needed his friendship and he had promised it. He straightened and hid his misgivings.

'Where will you be?' she asked anxiously.

'I shall not say in case Miss Trent is with you all the time. I fear she is reluctant to let you out of her sight. But I shall be close by. Always, Olivia.'

The radiance of her returning smile was enough for him. It faltered only when they heard her name called again, nearer and louder. Hurriedly, Olivia searched for herbs to gather, and he watched her flit back into the churchyard clutching a handful of leaves.

He lingered, gazing at the space where she had stood, and inhaled the faint scent she had left. Before he returned to his horse in the trees he heard her enthusing about the herbs she had found. He smiled to himself and looked forward to next week.

'Has she seen us?'

'I think not.'

It had rained and Jared dreaded that on Sundays, for Olivia did not walk in the wet. He still rode out there, though, donning a huntsman's coat with shoulder cape and standing dripping in the trees to glimpse her. He could not go longer than a week without sight of her.

She had carried her trowel and made an excuse to search for a particular root, which would be easier to dig in the wet soil, and had pulled up the hood of her cloak over her bonnet. Miss Trent had protested, but Olivia was not to be put off. The finest Yorkshire worsted would keep her dry, she had said.

Jared tugged at her hand. 'Quick. This way. There's an old cottage.'

They hurried through the trees until they were out of breath.

They heard Miss Trent call her twice, then silence.

'Will she follow?'

'I think not. She enjoys her conversations with the curate's wife. What is this place?'

'Perhaps once it was a shepherd's cottage.'

Olivia wandered around, examining the disused fireplace and brambles pushing in through a broken window. The clay floor was damp, the walls mossy. 'I expect he left for better wages in the ironworks or coal mines,' she mused. It was poor shelter and they shared it with the mare, standing docile in the driest corner.

'You're wet,' he said ineffectually. He was so glad to see her that his wits had deserted him. He could think of nothing else to say.

'So are you.' She eased back the hood of her cloak to reveal her Sunday bonnet with the silk ribbons she had sewn on specially. The bow was damp under her chin.

'You'll catch a chill,' he said.

'It's warm rain and I couldn't bear not to see you for another week.'

And I, he thought, but did not say. Whenever he saw her he was drawn to her in a way that pleased and troubled him at the same time. Sometimes he hardly dared touch her. He tried to think of her as a friend – but a friend he cared about desperately: her well-being was always uppermost in his mind. 'Has Hesley left for his ship yet?'

'He's delayed,' she answered. 'Lawyers and their papers take an age.'

'He is going, though?'

'Oh, yes. Quite soon,' she replied cheerfully. 'While he is away, I shall manage the household and learn to play my new pianoforte. I shall become a society lady. Well, a South Riding society lady anyway.'

'You won't need me, then.'

'What do you mean?'

'You will be safe when Hesley is out of the way.'

'But I shall still need you!'

'Will you?'

'Of course. Why should Hesley's leaving make any difference to us?'

'Us?'

They stood a yard apart from each other as the question hung in the air. After a few moments, Olivia said, 'I don't understand you sometimes. You said you would always be my friend. It is all I have to look forward to in my life.' When he did not reply she shivered. 'It's cool in here. I shall indeed take a chill if I linger.'

He took off his heavy coat to wrap around her but it weighed so heavily on her shoulders that she laughed, then begged him to remove it before she collapsed.

He said, 'Shall we meet here in future? It is well away from the church and the other cottages.' He paused before adding, 'And Miss Trent.'

Olivia did not miss the derision in his voice. 'Why do you not like her?'

'She is so pious, and—' He stopped. She was the closest thing Olivia had to a mother. 'She would not approve of our meeting like this.'

'She believes in the sanctity of marriage and maintaining one's virtue.'

Jared swallowed an expletive. He thought that Miss Trent was the last person fit to comment on the behaviour of others. 'And you are a married woman.'

Olivia chewed her lip.

He realized then that this was his main concern. She was another man's wife and it troubled him.

Olivia went to the broken window and peered through a gap in the brambles. 'The rain will not stop for a while. Miss Trent may send someone to look for me'

'I'll walk back with you.'

'No. You may be seen. Stay here. I insist.'

'All right. Until next week, then.' He bent to kiss her damp cheek and his lips lingered on her skin. He inhaled her freshness and closed his eyes to savour the pleasure.

She turned her head so that her lips slid around to his, and for a brief second his mouth brushed hers. He opened his eyes. Hers were gazing into them with the same surprise. She drew away from him quickly and was out of the door, head bent against the driving rain, hurrying towards the churchyard, leaving him puzzled. He put on the heavy coat and took up the reins to lead his mare outside.

Had she known that if she lingered he would have kissed her properly? Deeply. With the passion that was becoming difficult to control. And if he felt like this about her, they should not be meeting. It was wrong. She was another man's wife. But he had to see her. She depended on him and he wanted that. He wanted her.

'You will stay and speak with the curate's wife after the service, madam?'

'Oh, but it is such a fine day after all the rain, Miss Trent. I must take advantage of it.'

'If I may say so, I believe it is myself you take advantage of, madam.'

Olivia glanced at her companion. It was naïve of her to think that the woman by her side, who knew her so well, would not question her walks after church in search of roots and herbs. 'The weather has been mild this year and I feel so well,' she responded.

But Miss Trent had sharp eyes, and Olivia guessed she might have glimpsed a lone horseman through the trees or on the ridge. Had she made a connection? Olivia hoped not. Jared was not the only horseman to cross the ridge to the moor on a Sunday.

'You are so much more cheerful when you return from your walks.'

'To be away from Hesley at any time cheers me,' she replied pointedly.

'You will not say that when he has been in the West Indies for years. You will long for his company.'

'No, I shan't!'

'He is your husband, madam.'

They were approaching the cluster of cottages, the remains of the village served by the tiny church. The church in which she had obeyed her uncle and taken her marriage vows, not knowing fully what they meant. It had been only months since, but she hated Hesley now as much as she did his grandfather. She knew Miss Trent feared what they would do with her if she strayed from her marriage and she did not want to quarrel with her.

'He will be different when he comes back,' Miss Trent reassured her. 'He will be the gentleman you deserve.'

Olivia thought that sounded pleasant enough but she didn't believe it. Miss Trent wanted that for her, of course. She had always wanted the best for her. But is it what I want? she wondered. She had thought constantly about this since Jared had challenged Hesley that Sunday . . . She scanned the hillside for sight of him and Miss Trent noticed.

'You should not walk alone, madam. Now the days are lengthening, more strangers pass this way. I shall stay with you today.'

'And miss your chat with the curate's wife? I should not want you to do that.'

After a short silence, Miss Trent asked, 'You meet someone, don't you?'

'And if I do?'

'Not a stranger, surely.'

'I am not stupid.'

'Who is it? What does he want with you?'

'Do not quiz me so, Miss Trent. You are no longer my governess. I am your mistress now.'

Olivia was satisfied to see Miss Trent blink at her authoritative tone.

'You have always learned quickly, madam,' was all she said.

Olivia read more than her companion now and often surprised her with her questions and opinions. 'Yes, I have had a good teacher.' Her tone was critical.

'I am glad you think so,' Miss Trent replied.

It was the first time that Olivia had felt unsure about their relationship. It had changed in the few months since her marriage. She had thought Miss Trent was a friend as well as a servant, but now she began to doubt that.

There was an uneasy silence between them as their boots crunched on the rocky path. Then Olivia sighed. 'You will tell my uncle, won't you?'

'He still thinks of me as your governess even if you do not.'

'You are so predictable!' Olivia exploded. 'He said you would.'

'Who said? It's Jared, isn't it? You have been meeting him every week.'

'Why shouldn't I? He is my friend.'

'You should not be alone with him.'

Olivia made an impatient growling noise in her throat, but did not reply for she knew that Miss Trent was right. Jared, too, had implied as much.

After a while, Miss Trent added, 'It is wrong.'

'Nothing that goes on at Hill Top House is right.' Olivia's tone was belligerent. She was not going to let her only interlude of happiness slip away because *it was wrong.*

'I should feel easier if you will allow me to chaperone you.'

'Must you? Please do not insist!'

'But you are putting yourself in danger. Will you not allow me to meet and speak with him?'

Olivia knew she would not leave the matter. Miss Trent was nothing if not persistent. 'Only if you promise not to tell anyone at all. Even the curate's wife. Promise me.'

'Of course I promise.'

'Very well. But not today,' Olivia said. 'I'll ask him first.'

Harriet nodded. She reasoned that this would be the most sensible thing to do in the circumstances. Olivia was a wife without choice in the matter and deserved a little happiness. But she also realized that Olivia had her own opinions, her own will, and no longer looked to her for guidance.

She supposed it was bound to happen. She hoped it would not cause too many dangers for Olivia as she truly believed that old Hesley would lock her away if he found out. At least until his grandson came back from abroad. The master had the capital he craved. Now all he wanted from Olivia was heirs. Harriet consoled herself that at midsummer she would have enough money to make a choice for herself.

Chapter 16

'Miss Trent has found out that I meet someone here.'

'Does she know who?'

'She guessed.'

'Will she stop you?' Jared had dismounted and tethered his horse at the back of their ruined cottage – he thought of it now as theirs. There was a broken gate in a dry-stone wall that had kept sheep away from the garden. In sunny weather they sat at the far side of it, leaning against the warm stones, out of sight of the trees and the track and the rest of the Riding.

Olivia shook her head. 'She will do my bidding.'

'She will tell your uncle.' His voice was harsh.

'I have made her promise not to.'

Jared wondered what a promise meant to a woman like Miss Trent. He heaved a sigh. He no longer thought of foolishness or danger in these meetings. He thought only of Olivia's need to know that he would do anything for her. She asked so little of him, just to meet and walk and talk. And now to include the governess in their secret.

'Will she keep her promise?'

Olivia nodded. 'Miss Trent cares for me as my own mother would.' There was an uneasy silence until Olivia added, 'She is content that it is you. I know it. She wishes to speak to you.'

What about? he thought, but simply said, 'Very well. Next week. Now, tell me, are you in good health? Is Hesley treating you well?'

Olivia's face darkened. 'If only he would not drink so much.'

'He does not beat you, does he?'

'No. He – he—' She looked down. 'Miss Trent says he will be more . . . well, that it will be better when he is older,' she muttered.

He saw the hurt in her eyes and his mouth curled down. 'I'm so sorry,' he said.

'Oh, don't be. He will leave within the month.' Her face brightened.

'Will you miss him?'

Not at all, she thought. I am looking forward to his going. 'I am used to being on my own. I have Miss Trent and – and you, if you will visit me? Will you?'

'You know I cannot come to the house.'

'Then we shall continue to meet here. As we do now. Every Sunday.'

'Perhaps you will be able to come into town on

market day?' Jared suggested. 'To the draper's or dress-maker's. In your carriage.'

'Uncle Hesley will not let me. Everything is sent out for us so there is no need, he says. Besides, it is safer here. If we are careful, no one will see us, and it is so pleasant when the weather is fine. Carters never come this way now and only a few horsemen cross the ridge.' She turned her head to peer through the broken stones. 'If it rains, we have the cottage. Our cottage. You can tell me about the mine where you work and what your sisters are doing at their lessons.'

Jared's spirits were raised by her cheerfulness and he pushed aside his worries about the governess. Olivia's happiness was all he cared about.

Harriet curtsied politely to Jared and watched him turn to Olivia, taking her hands in his and kissing them lovingly. She saw her blush in the mild spring air. He is too familiar, Harriet thought, with pursed lips. And Olivia appeared to welcome his embrace. Her eyes were sparkling and Harriet had not seen her so happy for a long time. It was, as she had suspected, more than a friendship.

There was an awkward silence until Harriet said, 'Mrs Mexton takes great benefit from her Sunday walking. I, too. Though I am surprised that you chose to venture so far out of town.'

'I ride these hills every Sunday to see Olivia.' He was looking at her in a questioning, challenging way.

Olivia interceded. 'Miss Trent has not told anyone. I said she wouldn't.'

Harriet scanned the hedgerow. 'I believe I saw some elderflower in bloom back there, madam. Why don't you gather some for cordial?'

'Will you tell old Hesley?' he asked, as soon as Olivia had gone.

'Why do you think I would?'

'Because you are his spy where Olivia is concerned, are you not?'

'No!' she retaliated sharply.

'You share his bed.'

'It is not my choice! Just as it was not Olivia's choice to marry his grandson.'

That seemed to shock him. He recovered quickly and went on, 'But you do talk of her when you are together?'

'I have learned to tell him only what I think he needs to know,' she answered stiffly.

'So will you tell him?' he persisted.

'Olivia has need of a friend.'

'Even one that her uncle has seen off with a gun?'

'I know you care more for her than her husband ever can.' She looked him squarely in the eyes. 'I want you to promise me that you will always put her interests before your own.'

'Of course—'

'Let me finish. You and I are the only ones who care about her well-being. And I – I shall not be her companion for ever.'

'You are thinking of leaving Hill Top House?'

'No,' she lied. 'The master will – that is, when Olivia is older there will be no need for me—'

He gave a half-laugh. 'I see. Old Helsey is tiring of you. It's hardly surprising since you are not to his usual taste.'

She ignored the taunt and snapped, 'That is no concern of yours.'

'It is, when you have such influence over Olivia.'

'But that will not be for ever. That is why you must promise . . . You must promise . . .' Miss Trent quietened. 'You will promise to stay close to her when I am gone from here.'

'I promise.'

He meant it, she thought. She had been right about him. He did care. 'You must promise me, also, that you will not jeopardize her marriage. There is no telling what Hesley will do if he finds out about you.'

'When does he leave?'

'Next week.'

Jared was encouraged by this. Life would be easier for Olivia with Hesley across the ocean. And the governess, despite her loose morals, seemed dutiful towards her charge. Perhaps there was good in the woman after all.

He gazed at the view. From here he could see down to the navigation where it crossed the meadows on its way to Tinsley. The sun glinted on the water in the distance. Complicity with this whore was a long way from the respectability of his own home or, indeed, those of his fellow workers at Kimber Deep. But he felt relieved for Olivia's sake that Miss Trent was loyal to her. He wondered why she cared so much.

'I shall ride this way every Sunday.'

'Take heed that no one sees you, sir.'

'Except you.'

'Yes. I shall chaperone you. Then, if you are seen, I can vouch that it was a chance meeting.'

'Thank you.' He bowed his head and walked away to find Olivia.

'You look very handsome, sir, in your summer riding jacket,' Olivia commented lightly. 'Do you like my new parasol?' She held it high and twirled it.

He smiled. 'Very pretty. It matches your cape. You are quite a lady now.'

'I am not so sure I wish to be a lady. This is my Sunday best. Can you see me dressed in silks and satins all week? With a maid to attend to my *toilette*?'

'It will suit you very well. You have intelligence and beauty.'

'You are only saying that to make me happy.'

'False modesty does not become you.'

Olivia laughed. 'Well, even Miss Trent looks beautiful in a silken dinner gown with her hair dressed.'

'*Even* Miss Trent? She is a fine-looking woman. As you are, with your silken fair hair and blue eyes.'

'Hers are grey.' She pushed him playfully. 'I shall tell her what you said.'

'Then tell her also that being beautiful is more than a pretty countenance. You need to be of good character as well.'

Olivia clicked her tongue impatiently. 'So righteous! Just like her.'

'What?' he exclaimed.

'Oh, never mind. Anyway, I need not be a society lady until Hesley comes home. I am enjoying being mistress of Hill Top House. I teach the servants new household tasks and I am talking to Matt about enlarging the garden for more produce.'

'Does your uncle approve?'

'Oh, yes. We are to have a carpet for the drawing room and new furnishings in the bedchambers.'

'Then you are more content now?'

'Content? Perhaps.'

'But not happy?'

'I am happy only when I am with you.'

Jared did not know how to reply. He wished for her happiness more than anything but he did not see how that was possible now that she was the wife of Hesley Mexton.

Olivia continued, 'Well, I shall not say that again if it makes you frown.'

'Was I frowning? It's the sun. The corn seed will grow well this year.'

She put her arm through his and hugged it. 'Let's go to our cottage. It's shady there.'

'That is the bell for evensong,' he cautioned. 'The trees are nearer.'

'Very well.' She sighed. 'Miss Trent has disappeared. How kind of her.'

She held his arm so tightly as they strolled that her closeness made him hot, even in the lightweight coat. He wondered if she could hear his heart beating. It seemed deafeningly loud to him. When they stopped, she allowed her parasol to fall from her grasp and clung to him, pressing her face into his jacket.

He looked down at her bonnet and placed a hand on the back of her neck. 'Let me go, Olivia.'

'No.'

'You must. I hear Miss Trent approaching.'

She looked up at him. Her cheeks were pink and her eyes bright with tears. 'I care only about you.'

Again, he did not know what to say. His heart was racing and he wanted to hold her. Closely. Lovingly. He shook his head slightly. 'Do not speak such things.'

They stared at each other, only for a few seconds but long enough for Miss Trent to see them.

'It is time for church, madam,' she said. 'Would you walk ahead of me? Hurry now.'

Jared watched Olivia retrieve her parasol and go. 'What else do you wish to say to me, Miss Trent?'

'She talks of you constantly when we are alone.'

'We are friends.'

He heard her sigh. 'I saw you together,' she said. 'You have the advantage of years, sir. It is not wise to become too – too friendly with her.'

'What is it you want of me, then?' he demanded. 'To be her friend or not?'

'To be cautious. She will be lonely while her husband is away.'

'She will not miss him! And she has you for companionship.'

'You will not forget that she is a married woman.'

How could I? he thought, and said, 'You may be assured of that.'

'But I am not. I see she attracts you, which is dangerous.'

'What are you suggesting?'

'She is easily led by you.'

'She is not! Olivia knows her own mind.'

'And so must you! I am not sure I can trust you with her.'

'You insult me by your insinuations. I care only for her happiness.'

'Quite so. It will not be a good idea for you to meet if I am not here as chaperone.'

He laughed harshly. 'You think I will lie with her as soon as your back is turned?'

'I think she would encourage you and that the consequences would be devastating for her if her uncle discovered it.'

'I know what he is capable of. Please do not judge me as you would him. I am a Tyler, not a Mexton.'

'You are a man, sir.'

'Not all men are like Hesley and his grandfather.' But he reflected that the governess had a point. He thought of Olivia all the time when they were apart and she was indeed much more than a friend to him.

Olivia had stopped along the track through the trees. 'What are you talking about?' she called.

Miss Trent raised her voice. 'News of your uncle Hesley, madam, for his sister.'

Olivia resumed walking towards the church.

'How she trusts you, Miss Trent,' Jared mocked. 'And you must trust me. I can understand how that must worry you.'

'Do not make fun of me, sir. Her husband will be gone for several years.'

'And old Hesley will pay you off before he returns.'

He saw that she looked uncomfortable about this and added, more kindly, 'I shall always respect her married status. Take whatever your master offers and make a fresh start in another county. I shall look after Olivia.'

She did not appear satisfied with this, but she seemed to accept it and left. Yet she had seen what he was refusing to acknowledge. Olivia would soon be in her fifteenth year. She was mistress of Hill Top House and was rising to that challenge in a way he admired. She was already beautiful. More than that, she was growing into a woman to be reckoned with, to be acknowledged as such and – at last, he admitted it – to be desired.

Harriet knew she could not endure her life at Hill Top House for much longer. It would tear her heart in two to leave, but Olivia had recovered her strength and had shown a blossoming independence and determination that Harriet admired. Harriet felt she could look forward to her own freedom, a little money of her own and a choice. She began to make plans for her departure.

Chapter 17

Harriet hurried down the track until she was out of sight of Hill Top House, and by six o'clock she could see the smoke from the chimneys in the town rising to meet her. She drank from a horse trough where her path joined the Sheffield way and widened. She was hungry and chewed on a heel of bread as she rested. A cart rumbled slowly down from the other track and the driver paused to water his horse.

'Hot again,' she observed.

'Aye. You on yer way to town?'

'Will you take me? I can pay you.'

By her own standards she had felt a rich woman when she had received a quarter of her increased annual stipend at midsummer. The coins chinked satisfyingly in the leather pouch tied to her waist. There had been a celebration of sorts for all the servants, with eating and drinking in the gardens, though none ventured further afield. Not even Matt or the farmhands.

The carter agreed a price, she placed her bundle on the cart and sat up front as they bumped their way down the valley. Hill Top House had slumbered in the breaking dawn as she had left at half past four and she was glad of the ride. Her heart ached for Olivia, who, she hoped, would understand why she had gone without a word. She had feared to leave a message lest her mistress might be implicated in her disappearance. It was best she knew nothing of her plans as the master would be vindictive in his revenge. Harriet had suffered deep anguish at leaving Olivia, and drew solace from her certain knowledge that Jared Tyler would look after her.

'Where you from?' the carter asked.

She gave the name of the village over the moor near Blackstone School.

'Long way from home.'

'I am looking for work.' A new future, she thought. No one owns me now. I am free to go where I wish with the money I have earned. She tried not to dwell on the means she had used to earn it.

The master's demands were too much for her to bear. He was ageing and losing his vigour. The apothecary thought his kidneys might have been injured in the pithead riot. At first the news had pleased her, but then she had realized that, while he did not have the energy for frequent activities in the bedchamber, his need for her special favours remained. She was obliged to perform tasks for him that she had never dreamed of, tasks that sickened her and for which he sometimes left an extra coin beside her bed.

As she recalled this, her lips turned down in distaste and the saliva gathered under her tongue. The first time she had left his payment there for a whole day and prayed. Then she had remembered Jared Tyler's words and a new life in the next county beckoned. So she had put the coin in her pouch and thought of her fresh start.

She inhaled the morning air. Hesley Mexton was her past now. 'I hear there is work a-plenty in the Riding towns,' she said. This was her new beginning.

'For the menfolk, aye.'

Her heart sank a little. As the sun rose higher, and she contemplated an unknown future, the sky darkened. 'Looks like a storm,' she said ruefully.

'It would clear the air.' The carter urged on his horse. 'I'll stop at the inn before I go up to the beast market. The innkeeper's wife'll know where you can find summat to do. You can trust her.'

'Thank you.' She wanted to travel on, to be further away.

It began to rain, large spots falling heavily on her best bonnet. There was a flash of lightning and a distant clap of thunder. The carter hunched his back

At the inn, Harriet hurried indoors and found the landlord's wife harassed by an influx of farmers and butchers arriving for the market.

'Work, you say? I've allus got need of another pair of hands in t'kitchen. But you don't look like a kitchen-maid to me. What can you do?'

'I've taught in school. I can look after girls.'

'Not much call for that in these times. Even the well-off folk have suffered lately. You'd best try the mission. There'll be a ladies' meeting today. They'll all be 'ere for the market.'

'Where is the mission?'

'Up Sheep Hill. Follow the track and ask for the Dissenters' House.'

It was just an ordinary house from the outside, built of local stone with a slate roof. Inside, there was a hall, and through that a large, open space where the walls had been knocked down, leaving massive wooden posts to hold up the ceiling. At the far end, a group of women were sitting at a table, talking earnestly to each other. They were soberly clothed in dark gowns. Harriet fingered the lace trim on her bonnet, which matched her light grey skirt, and grew nervous.

One noticed her and called, 'The meeting starts at ten o'clock.'

'May I wait here? It's raining.'

The woman nodded and returned to the discussion. Harriet leaned against a wooden post, feeling thirsty and weak. They looked like respectable ladies, reminding her of the principal's wife at Blackstone. They might help her find work and somewhere to stay. She caught snatches of their conversation, villages she had heard of, names of people she had not, and sums of money.

One or two other ladies wandered into the building, their bare heads protected from the rain by shawls and glanced in her direction. Her bonnet set her apart from them, more akin to the grouping around the table. She gave them a faltering smile.

When the meeting started they gathered to stand in the centre. Someone came round with a small wooden box and asked for a penny if she had one. Then they said prayers and had Bible readings, and the lady who seemed to be in charge talked to them. Harriet would have called it a sermon if it had been the Sabbath and she had been a minister.

At the end she came across to speak with her. 'Welcome, friend.' She smiled, holding out her hands. 'I'm Miss Holmes, but please call me Anna.'

No stranger had called her 'friend' before with such obvious sincerity. 'Harriet Trent,' she replied, grasping the hands firmly.

'Are you new to the town?'

'Yes. I am looking for work.'

'I see. It's mainly lodgings and coal mines for the women here.'

'I was hoping for something better.'

'Such as, my dear?'

'I am a teacher, ma'am. I can read, write and do numbers.'

Anna's tired lined face brightened. 'Do you have a testimonial?'

'From a school, yes.' Harriet hesitated. 'Lately I had work as a governess.'

Clearly Anna expected her to say more.

'My pupil was married and had no further need of me.' She felt uncomfortable as she said this and Anna noticed.

'But her parents gave you a letter of recommendation?'

Harriet bit her lip. She was beginning to feel faint with thirst and sagged against a wooden post.

'Have you come far?' Anna asked gently.

'No, not really, but I – I left at daybreak.'

'That was hours ago! I'll fetch you some water.'

Anna handed her a wooden ladleful from a small half-barrel in the corner. 'I don't suppose you have had much to eat, either. There'll be hot pies from a butcher's wife in the market square soon. Do you have money?'

Harriet nodded.

'I have need of a teacher.'

'Here?' She had hoped to be further away from Hill Top House.

'I'm afraid not. My mission is on the other side of the Riding. I'm returning there this afternoon.'

Harriet fished in the pocket of her skirt and drew out the letter from Blackstone, 'to whom it may concern', recommending her as a governess. She had removed it from Hesley Mexton's papers weeks ago. 'Please. Let me come with you. I can pay my own fare and ask only for board and lodging until I have proved myself to you.'

She held her breath as Anna read. 'This is dated more than a year ago. You have nothing to vouch for you since then?'

Harriet shook her head nervously.

'Why did you leave your position as governess?'

She blushed. 'I told you. My – my pupil was married.'

'Well, I shall not judge you until I know more, but you must answer one question truthfully.'

Harriet held her breath and waited.

'Are you with child?'

'No! Truly I am not!' But her cheeks reddened more as she said it.

Anna gave her a level stare. 'You are not alone in your sin. I follow the teachings of John Wesley. He believed that we all have sinned but can be saved.' She paused. 'I shall be on the carrier that leaves at four this afternoon from the inn. You may join me, if you wish.'

'Thank you, ma'am. I will be there.'

Anna nodded as though she approved. 'Now you must excuse me. I have mission business to attend to. The rain is easing. Go to the fair. It is Lammas Day and there are travelling players in the town square.'

Anonymous in the crowd, Harriet enjoyed her first day of freedom in the market. She bought a good length of cotton calico from the back of a cart. It was a strong weave and she took more than she needed. The traveller added a piece of sprigged muslin and some ribbon to her parcel and she felt pleased with her purchase. But the extra bundle was heavy to carry and she went to the inn to sit on a wall and wait for Anna. She had eaten well and drunk from the spring that filled the horse trough. Her heart lifted when she saw Anna approach with a gentleman companion, carrying a travelling bag.

'You are early. I said you would be. Harriet, this is my brother, Tobias Holmes.'

'Ma'am.' He set down the bag, took off his low-crowned hat and bowed.

'Sir.' She curtsied. 'Are you travelling with us?'

'I'm afraid not. I come only to see you safely on your way. The carrier is not due for an hour. Shall we take tea inside?'

He took one of her bundles as well as the bag, and they settled by a window so they could see the cart when it arrived. Harriet guessed that he wished to know more about his sister's travelling companion and prepared herself for more questions.

'My sister tells me you were a teacher at Blackstone?'

'Do you know of it?'

He nodded. 'By reputation only. You understand that we are Dissenters?'

'Oh, yes.' She found herself looking at his countenance with interest. He was a handsome man. In fact, a very attractive man. Harriet could not take her eyes off him.

'But Anna has not told you about her mission?'

'It is all God's work, is it not?'

'Anna has chosen a particularly difficult task.'

'I shall do my best for her.'

'But the people who—' He stopped as his sister put her hand on his arm.

'Toby, I shall explain to Harriet as we travel.'

'Very well. I shall ride over to visit you after next quarter day.'

Anna smiled brightly. 'Am I not lucky to have such a thoughtful brother, Harriet? Oh, good, here is our tea. And lardy cake, too. How lovely.'

They talked about the new chapel in town as they ate and drank, and of other missions that were setting up to serve families who laboured in the Riding. It seemed to Harriet that coal mines and iron works would soon be taking over the whole town. The cart was early. Tobias loaded their belongings, then embraced his sister warmly. 'I am so proud of you,' he said.

Anna smiled back and replied, 'And I of you. We shall see you in two months' time.'

He bowed to Harriet and stood back as they climbed into the cart and settled themselves with their luggage. The horses jolted them away. As Harriet looked back, she had mixed feelings. She was glad, oh, so glad, to be leaving Hill Top House and the unhappiness it had caused her. But when she thought of Olivia, she felt deeply saddened and guilty that she had left her. They had become like – she hardly dared to think it – like sisters in their support of each other. It had been all she had hoped for when she had first taken the position. She prayed that Jared Tyler would keep his word, respect her and care for her. For now, she could only pray.

She looked forward to working with Anna, even though Tobias had warned her of hardship. She deserved her sackcloth and ashes, and she would endeavour to redeem herself from her wickedness at Hill Top House. Perhaps God had not totally forsaken her. He had given her this chance to repent through Tobias and Anna's work. Suddenly she felt elated. It did not matter how difficult Anna's mission was. It would be her salvation. She was so lucky to have met them.

It was a long ride, and when they were set down at a tavern they had to wait for a messenger to fetch a trap for the final stretch of the journey.

As they lingered, Anna explained, 'You will live with me in my tiny cottage. It is just outside the gates.'

'Gates?'

Anna placed her hand on Harriet's. 'My mission is with girls and women who have been cast out by their families.'

Harriet thought she understood. Like some of the girls who had been at Blackstone. Those in danger of moral decay, and worse.

'You must understand that some cannot think for themselves. They have never been able to. But others, well, they are different. They were influenced by – by people, by events that led to their state of mind and . . . Well, you will see for yourself.'

'Where are we going?' Harriet asked.

Anna stood up. 'Here is one of the warders with his trap.'

'Is it a prison?'

'No, but the inmates cannot leave, though many wish to.'

Suddenly Harriet knew where she was going. 'It's an asylum, isn't it?'

'Yes. An asylum for the insane.'

Panic rose to Harriet's throat. 'But I do not see how I can be a teacher of the insane.'

'Please don't be alarmed. In my view not all of the inmates are insane. As I have said, some cannot think for themselves – indeed, cannot think at all. But there are others who are there because of things they have done in moments of madness.'

'Do you mean criminals? Murderers?'

'No. Their behaviour has been wild enough to cause their physicians to diagnose insanity and that is why they are here.'

Like Olivia, Harriet thought, whom everyone had said was wild but was simply lonely and unloved.

'Some have recovered,' Anna went on, 'but cannot leave unless the father or husband who sent them here agrees and will look after them. Those are the ones we can help.'

It was falling dark by the time the high stone wall loomed in front of them. The warder dropped them outside a small artisan's cottage and continued on to the high iron gates of the asylum.

Chapter 18

The following day the heavy iron gates creaked as they swung open.

'Don't be frightened, Harriet. You are quite safe. Besides, we are not allowed into the main building.'

Harriet was frightened. The insane were unpredictable. One of her pupils at Blackstone had been declared insane and taken from the school. She had attacked the principal with dressmaking scissors and cut him so badly they had had to call the surgeon. She wondered if the girl had been brought here.

The grey granite building was high and forbidding. There were three storeys with tiny windows, each with vertical bars, and she shivered as she tried to imagine the life of the inmates. She and Anna followed a laden supplies cart that trundled off to the right and around to the back of the building. 'We go to the left.' Anna led the way to a small grey house. Its cold austerity reminded Harriet of Blackstone, except that her school had been built of Pennine stone. At the time she had not appreciated the warmth in its hue, but she did now.

The warden's wife let them in, nodded briefly in Harriet's direction and said, 'My husband has told me about you. How do you do?' She was plainly dressed in dark grey, with hair that seemed the same colour. Her manner was brisk. Harriet returned the greeting and the woman disappeared into a room containing a large desk and cupboards round the walls. Harriet followed Anna up a narrow wooden staircase and into a small chamber set out like a schoolroom. She relaxed a little. This was familiar territory, except that the windows had iron bars fixed across them.

'Our pupils will come after they have finished their work in the kitchens. They are not allowed here unless they have shown themselves trustworthy.'

'Trustworthy? But they cannot escape.'

'Work in the kitchens is a privilege reserved for those who are not violent in their behaviour. There are knives in the kitchen.'

Harriet's nervousness returned. Anna unlocked a cupboard. 'I do not have many teaching materials, but there is a blackboard, some slates and an abacus.'

'Are there books?'

'The Bible. Here it is.'

'Just the one?'

'I shall have more. With your help in the classroom I can spend more time visiting local landowners for dona-tions. It is hard work because most of the charitable ones already give towards the upkeep of the asylum. Persuading them to pay for schooling is not easy Like you, they believe the insane cannot learn.'

'I'm sorry, I did not know.'

'Oh, you are right. Many cannot learn. But for those who can it is their lifeline to the outside world. I have women in my class who were educated before they were admitted and seek only to return to their former lives.'

'Will they do so?'

'Perhaps, if I can buy paper and ink for them to write letters to their fathers or guardians.'

'I see.' Harriet surveyed the paucity of equipment in the cupboard.

Anna saw the dismay on her face. 'Do not despair. Everyone here will be grateful for anything you can do.'

Harriet gazed at her companion. 'Your brother is right. You have chosen a most difficult task for your mission.'

Anna gave her small smile. 'I did not choose it, it chose me, and it would not be a mission if it were easy.'

'How many pupils should I expect?'

'It is never the same number. Attendance here is a reward and can be taken away. Sometimes we have no one to teach and sometimes as many as a dozen.'

'Only twelve? My classes were much bigger at Blackstone.'

'You will find each inmate difficult in her way.'

'What have you done with them so far?'

'Mainly they read the Bible to me. I tried giving

writing and counting exercises but I do not have teaching experience. This is where you can help.'

Harriet nodded and began to organize the slates. 'I shall find out what they can do first. There isn't much chalk.'

'Chalk isn't dear. We can buy more. Listen, they are coming up the stairs.' Anna went to the door. 'Only six today.'

They were dressed in the most awful brown gowns Harriet had ever seen. The material was as coarse as that used at Blackstone, and poorly sewn. The garments looked to be all the same size and with little shape to them so that they hung loose on some and were stretched tight on others. Harriet was shocked to see that every woman's hair was cut short under a dingy calico cap. But they were not children. They were grown women, all of whom watched her closely as she stood in front of them.

The warden's wife and a nurse came in with them and stood at either side of the group. They were both large women with big hands, and the nurse wore a heavy grey gown covered by an apron of the same colour. Nobody smiled as Anna told them about Harriet.

The warden's wife left immediately. Harriet had only four slates so the nurse selected three women for writing exercises with her, and Anna took the others to the far end of the room for reading. Shortly afterwards, the nurse went downstairs and Harriet heard voices from the office below.

The women sat at one end of the table and she

asked them to put their names on the slates. They obeyed silently. They wrote their surnames so she suggested they added their Christian names. They seemed hesitant. Harriet showed them hers on her own slate. Then one woman, she seemed to be the oldest, spoke. 'We are called by our surnames here,' she said.

Harriet smiled pleasantly. 'But you have another name. Can you write it for me?'

They did so, and Harriet walked around them to watch as they formed their letters. Isabel. Madeline. Bridget. 'What pretty names,' she said. 'Now write down where you live.'

'We live here,' the oldest one said.

'Where you came from,' Harriet added quickly.

As the lesson progressed, Harriet noticed one of her class was snuffling quietly. She had her head down as though concentrating on her slate and was breathing shakily. The older woman kept glancing at her and Harriet realized that the younger one was distressed. She was weeping in a silent, controlled way that indicated to Harriet she was trying not to show it.

'Be quiet, Wingard,' the older woman hissed.

Isabel Wingard wiped her nose on her sleeve.

'What is it, Isabel?' Harriet asked gently. But she realized, of course, that here it could be so many things. Isabel began to cry again. Harriet gave her a handkerchief, which only made her worse.

The older inmate moved to Isabel's side and spoke firmly: 'Hush now. They'll hear you downstairs.'

Isabel breathed in deeply with a shudder. 'I've stopped,' she said. 'I'm sorry, Miss Trent. Please don't send me back to the kitchen. It's – it's just that no one's called me Isabel since my brother came to see me.'

Later, when the lesson was over, Anna and Harriet were given bowls of soup with bread and cheese in a small room next to the kitchen. It was nearer to the cells where the inmates lived and they could hear shrieking and wailing, shouting and the clanging of doors.

'You'll get used to it,' Anna said, and kept her eyes on her food. 'The nurses eat here,' she explained. 'They will be in the refectory now. Everyone eats together, our pupils with poor creatures who can barely feed themselves. They rock backwards and forwards and cry out.'

Harriet frowned with sympathy. But she was full of admiration for Anna. 'Did they take you in there to see them? How brave of you to go.'

Anna hesitated before she replied. 'Not exactly, but I know how they suffer, and how they fight when they do not understand why they are here.'

Harriet thought of occasions at Blackstone when she had been called upon to calm a pupil who had rebelled against the discipline of school, and had kicked and bitten her teachers. 'Thank goodness for the nurses,' she responded. 'They all look very capable.'

Anna looked uncomfortable. 'Yes. They are employed for their strength.'

Harriet tried to imagine how it must feel to lose one's mind. She could not. 'But our pupils have some education. They speak well. Why were they admitted?'

'The oldest one ran away from home. Isabel – poor Isabel – is very highly strung and wept all the time at first. I believe she refused to marry the gentleman her father had chosen for her. The other girl in your group bore a child out of wedlock.'

Harriet thought of Olivia, who could so easily have ended up an inmate if she herself had not been able to tame her wild ways. She hoped that she would not disobey her husband in a similar manner. Harriet worried that she had deserted her too soon, that Jared would not keep his word, that Olivia might run away. She missed her dreadfully and wanted to go back and see her. She sighed.

'Our pupils have a little hope,' Anna reassured her. 'With your help, their lives may be better.'

They met with the warden and his wife after dinner to talk of their plans, then returned to their home outside the gates. The cottage was tiny and damp and Anna did not have a maid. After the relative luxury of Hill Top House it felt to Harriet as though she had returned to the poverty of Blackstone. In fact, in some ways it was worse for at Blackstone, and even in the poorhouse, they had had a cook and an endless supply of children to do washing and cleaning. Here, they had to do everything for themselves, as well as the mission work in the asylum. And they had very little money, save what Harriet had brought with her and what Anna could raise from benefactors. Their existence was frugal.

But, as promised, shortly after quarter-day, their lives were brightened by a visit from Tobias. He arrived on horseback, bringing small luxuries and supplies: tea, soap, a length of linen, a collar of bacon, which they boiled with dried kidney beans and feasted on for days.

He brought money as well. The cottage had only one room downstairs with a lean-to scullery at the back, so Harriet was there to see it change hands.

Tobias smiled at Harriet. 'It is our allowance,' he explained, 'from the investments left by our late parents. To use in our missions.'

'We divide it equally between us,' Anna added. 'It is not much, but it helps.'

Harriet gave a small smile. Tobias had had no cause to tell her about his affairs but she realized he did not see why he should not. They had accepted her as an equal, and she felt honoured and valued for that. He was, indeed, a very fine gentleman and Harriet warmed to him as she had not with any gentleman she had met before.

It was a strange feeling. Gentlemen had always controlled her life in one way or another: a distant cousin, who had removed her from the poorhouse but had not enquired for her since, the principal at Blackstone, a strict churchman and disciplinarian. Latterly, she reflected, it had been the master of Hill Top House, who had taken her virtue and turned her into a whore without a by-your-leave.

Tobias Holmes was like none of them. He did not seek to dominate his sister, or indeed Harriet, as the asylum-keepers did their inmates. Or, she reflected bitterly, as Hesley Mexton had done at Hill Top House. Tobias was a sincere, kind gentleman, who put the needs of others before his own. He treated her with respect, and after his first visit, she anticipated the next with eagerness and excitement.

When she saw his horse outside the cottage on her return from the asylum one month later, her heart swelled.

He sat with them at the kitchen table and asked how she was faring.

'I have settled well, thank you. The teaching is much the same as at Blackstone.'

'You are not afraid of the inmates?'

'I should be, I think, if I were asked to be a wardress or nurse. I do not know how they do their work. Sometimes I hear the inmates screaming and shouting, and the banging of doors. The nurses have the worst of it, I am sure.'

'One of Harriet's pupils has begun writing to her family,' Anna said.

'Really?' Tobias and she exchanged a glance.

Harriet hoped they were pleased with her progress. Since Isabel had started her correspondence she had hardly wept at all.

'Yes,' Harriet replied. 'Isabel Wingard. Her father is a landowner in the South Riding. He will have nothing to do with her, but her brother is more sympathetic, and now that he is of age and gainfully employed he is willing to care for her.'

'Her brother?' Tobias repeated, and his gaze became fixed on his sister across the table.

Anna gave a sad smile and Harriet thought her eyes held an unshed tear.

'Are you all right, my dear?' Tobias asked his sister. She nodded.

Harriet became concerned. 'Have I done something wrong?' she asked.

'No, of course not,' Toby answered. 'We are pleased for you. What does the asylum doctor say?'

Anna's sadness passed. A painful memory, perhaps, Harriet thought, and went on, 'She is well enough to leave. The board of governors will consider her case at their next meeting.'

'Why, Harriet,' Tobias smiled, 'this is your first success. We must celebrate. Boil the kettle, Anna, and make chocolate to drink.'

Harriet had drunk chocolate at Hill Top and adored it. It was warming and made her feel good in a way that nothing else could. Except, perhaps, strong drink. Neither Anna nor Tobias ever took spirits unless they were ill, claiming that it overheated the blood and led to sin. Harriet brewed beer in the scullery on the advice of the asylum doctor, who told her it was safer to drink than water. He believed that water could cause the fever unless it was boiled.

After they had drunk their chocolate it was time for bed, and Harriet damped down the kitchen fire while Anna pulled out a wooden pallet for Tobias to sleep on. The cottage had only two small chambers upstairs and Harriet was now in the smaller one. It had a tiny window that looked over the rear yard. Harriet blew out her candle and watched as Tobias went outside to his horse. There was an outhouse next to the privy where they kept their wood and coal and it was just big enough for a temporary stable.

She heard him pumping water. The moon was bright – a sign of a frosty night – and she lingered in the shadows by her window, waiting for him to emerge from the outhouse. She admired him so much for his devotion to his sister and her work. She wondered what he did at his own mission in the town. Wrapped in her calico nightgown and fortified by the chocolate, she climbed into bed and drifted into a pleasant slumber, thinking of the kind gentleman who was sleeping downstairs.

The following day the distant clang of the early-morning rising bell in the asylum roused her, and her first thought was of Tobias. She strained her ears, heard him raking the ashes and imagined him in his shirtsleeves, with stockinged feet. After a few moments of this indulgence, she flung back the bedcovers and moved about quickly to wash in cold water and dress in the chilly air.

Later, when they waved him off on his horse to return to his own mission, Harriet wondered how she would survive until his next visit. She did, of course, for there was much work to be done and it filled her head during waking hours. But alone in her bed at night, she dreamed of him and counted the days to the end of the quarter.

Chapter 19

Jared reined in his mare as he rounded the hillside. He had a good view of their cottage and the track from the trees behind the little church. He cantered down the slope, across the sheep pasture, dismounted and tethered his horse inside the tumbledown building. He stayed on the shadowy side. The summer days were long and many a hill walker crossed the ridge to visit kin over the moor.

He expected the governess to be with her, but Olivia was alone, dragging her feet and looking forlorn with her head down. When she saw him she broke into a run, stumbling towards him over the grassy hummocks and through the broken-down wall. Her bonnet ribbons were undone and her eyes red.

'What is it? What has happened?' He took her hands in his, drawing her back into the shadows.

'She – she's gone. She went without saying goodbye

to me.' The tears welled and threatened to spill over her flushed cheeks.

'Miss Trent has left Hill Top House?'

Olivia beat her fists against his chest. 'How could she, Jared? How could she leave me like this? I loved her as a sister, and she has deserted me.'

Jared's heart turned over as he saw how desolate she was. He stilled her fists with his own. 'You're not alone. You have me.'

'But she did not tell me she was going,' Olivia whispered. 'Not a word! Why?'

'I expect you would have persuaded her not to leave.'

'Yes, I would!' The tears spilled out and she leaned against him. 'What shall I do without her?'

He wrapped his arms around her and held her close to him as she wept. 'You are mistress of Hill Top House, Olivia. You are wise and strong, and you will manage quite well without her.'

'I know,' she cried. 'It's my fault. I tried to show her how capable I was, and how it would be better when my husband went away. But I only did it to stop her worrying! She was always concerned for what Uncle Hesley might do with me.'

'We all worry about that, Olivia. He is a vindictive man, as I'm sure Miss Trent found out.'

'Oh, yes, he was cruel to her. That was why I wanted her to know that she did not have to stay just for me.' Suddenly she collapsed against him. 'But I didn't mean her to go.'

Jared pressed her to his chest. He thought Miss Trent's departure might be for the best and wished he could do more to comfort her. 'I am sure she did not leave without good reason. But as your uncle's servant—' He stopped, unsure how to continue.

'I know she was my uncle's mistress,' she said, into his jacket. 'Do not spare my sensibilities. You forget that I am a married woman.'

'I do not forget that. Ever,' he responded evenly.

'Sometimes I wish you would,' she said quietly.

'Do not speak of such things.'

'Why shouldn't I?' She sniffed. 'I need you more than ever, Jared. It is so isolated out here and you are so kind.'

Jared did not reply. He was drawing on all his self-control to steady his breathing, to stop himself kissing her and loving her.

After a few moments, she took a deep breath and looked up at him. 'But you are not my husband. Hesley is, and everyone says how wonderful that will be for me when he comes home.'

'Well, he is a gentleman and now he is rich,' he pointed out.

'Oh, I know. He will have government compensation for freeing the slaves and then he will sell my plantation. Mexton Pit will have a new mine shaft and a steam engine, and all will be well. Everyone will be happy. Except me.'

'Perhaps Hesley will reform his ways.'

'Do you really think so?'

He shook his head.

She took his hand and held it to her cheek. 'I am happy only when I am with you,' she said softly.

'We can only ever be friends, Olivia. You belong to Hesley and nothing can change that.'

'He has no feelings except for himself. I am glad he went away. I wish he would stay abroad for ever. I'd rather be with you.'

'Do not say that. It is wrong.'

'Wrong? What is wrong? That I should prefer you to Hesley?'

'We cannot be friends if you think of me in that way.'

'Why not?' She expected an answer from him.

'You know why not,' he said shortly. 'You have a *husband.*'

'But he is not a husband! He is not here, and when he was he did not love me. Not tenderly as a husband should. Not like you would.'

'Olivia, this has gone too far. I shall not ride over here again if you behave in this way.'

'So you would desert me, too?'

'No.' He did not want to leave her, but he had to be firm. He wondered where he would find the strength.

'I wish you were my husband instead of Hesley.'

'You must not say that. You must not think of me in that way.'

'But I do! Hold me, Jared. Please.'

He could not refuse her. He held her as tightly as he dared, wondering if she was aware of just how much he craved her closeness. Her body moulded to his and her eyes insinuated her meaning to him. The temptation was too intense and he took her chin gently in his hand and kissed her. Desire flared out of control and his heart began to thump, strongly, steadily. It felt for a few precious moments as though she were his. His alone, not someone else's wife.

Olivia had never felt like this with Hesley as she responded hungrily to Jared's kiss. Hesley had not kissed her in this way. He had only made a pretence of kissing her in front of others. A brush of his lips on her cheek to please his grandfather.

He had been the same in the bedchamber. He did not truly want her as his wife. Any woman would have done for him. He had used her as he used his tavern whores and, she guessed, other women wherever he was now. She was not stupid about her charade of a marriage. His grandfather wanted her inheritance and an heir.

Jared's tongue searched for hers and she pressed against him. Her bonnet fell to the ground and she did not mind. She wanted to devour him, for his body to join with hers, to give her the kind of joy that Hesley never had – indeed never could. Hesley. Hesley. Why must she think of him all the time? Hesley was halfway across the world and Jared was here, his arms around her, holding her as though he would never let her go.

He stopped and drew back his head to speak. But before he could she whispered, 'Let's go inside.'

'No, Olivia, no.' He groaned. 'Do not tempt me.' He held her head to his shoulder, his fingers parting and loosening the coils of her hair.

'But I need you, Jared. I need you to love me,' she choked.

Her face was close to his and he could see the tiny hairs that were straying from her bonnet and catching on her eyelashes. He wondered why those damp lashes were so dark when she was fair. He marvelled at the blueness of her eyes, shiny and bright, and wanted to kiss away her tears. His desire to love her was so strong he could barely form his words.

'I must not,' he whispered. 'Do not urge me so.'

She watched his lips move and his stormy eyes darken. If she moved a little closer she would be able to feel the rasp of his chin where he had not shaved since morning. She had not noticed it before. Now she imagined how rough it would feel by evening, by night and, yes, by the following morning before he shaved again.

The urge to be near to him and to know him intimately overwhelmed her and she whispered, 'I need to be close to you.' Her hands crept around his neck and she clung to him.

His resolve ran away, like water on a hillside. His pulses quickened and when she opened her mouth to his, he bent his head and kissed her with a passion that he did not recognize as his own. His long-suppressed desire had taken away his reason, and he surrendered to his yearning to possess her.

She returned his hunger, her body urging him with its own language. His lips lowered to her throat and to the swell of her breasts. She tilted back her head with a strangled moan. Oh, if only they could be together . . . if only . . . His mouth returned to hers and she thought he might devour her, so eager were his kisses. Her knees buckled beneath her and they would have fallen as one to the ground, to the dry, springy grass, if only . . . if only he would let her.

He took her weight in his arms and drew his lips from hers. 'This has to stop. It has to.'

She saw the pain in his eyes and pleaded, 'You don't understand. I – I love you, Jared. I love you.'

His fingers covered her lips gently. 'You must not say that.'

She opened her mouth to lick and nibble at his hand. 'It is the truth. I want you to love me, too. I do.'

'You know it cannot be.'

'But I cannot live if I cannot love you.'

'Olivia, you must be strong about this. We may not be together. You belong to Hesley.'

'I do not love Hesley!'

'You are his wife.' The words restored his reason. If Olivia could not stand firm, he must find strength for them both. 'I should not have kissed you. We must not meet like this.'

But he could not move away from her. His passion was so keenly aroused that he thought it would never subside. He allowed himself a few more seconds of tortured bliss, then gently pushed her away. 'We must stop now. Before we regret our actions.'

'I should not regret anything,' she said quietly.

'Olivia, this will not do.'

'But you want me. I am a married woman so I know the signs.'

He held his head in his hands. 'No, Olivia. I have said no.'

'And I must do what the men say. I tell you, Jared Tyler, I am growing tired of doing as I am told.'

'Please, Olivia, take care. I fear for your freedom when you speak so. We shall not meet again like this. It is too dangerous for you. I shall go away.'

'No!' Olivia felt as though a knife had sliced through her heart. 'Don't leave me. How can I go on without you?'

'You have your house, the garden and the harvest to fill your days.'

'And my nights? How shall I fill those?'

'It will not be for ever. Hesley will return.'

'It is not Hesley I want!' she cried.

'Do not be angry with me, Olivia.'

'Oh, but I am.' She turned her back on him with a flounce and walked away.

He caught her arm and stopped her. 'Olivia! We should not part like this.'

She shook off his hand. 'Leave me be and go away. If you will not love me, do not taunt me with your presence.'

She marched off, her head held high. He called her name once but she did not reply or look back. She could not bear to see him, knowing he had refused her. Her heart ached for him, and as the distance between them widened, her tears flowed more readily.

He watched her until she disappeared, leaving a void in the air around him that seeped into his core. He prayed she would see the sense in what he had said. If they continued to meet she would not heed the risk. She would persist until she broke his resolve. And break it she would, for Olivia was headstrong and he was not made of iron. He would have to stay away from her. For her own protection. And he knew how.

Sir William had talked to him of lectures in Manchester, at the Institute. He wanted Jared to attend, to lodge there, work with engineers and learn about steam engines. It was a rare opportunity, and it would take him away from the South Riding for several years. And it would be a solution of sorts for him. But one he chose to follow with a heavy heart.

Olivia could not console herself with household tasks. Her isolation was matched only by the bleakness of the open moor. She did not revert to the wild ways of her childhood. In those lonely hours when she walked alone, she thought often of Miss Trent and remembered her counsel on devotion and virtue, reflecting that there was wisdom in her words.

But Miss Trent had not warned her that love could be destructive. Her hopes for Olivia had been for a brighter future with a mature, considerate husband. They were Olivia's only hopes now, as she excelled as mistress of her own household and as nurse to her ailing uncle. She endeavoured to forget her love for Jared and prepare herself to be a good wife for Hesley when he returned. Her happiness with Jared had been an interlude only, a short-lived escape from the desolation of Hill Top House.

PART TWO: 1837

Chapter 20

'Go to bed, Olivia. I have business to discuss with Grandfather.'

'Is it not my business, too? I should like to hear how my plantation has fared.'

Hesley's scorn astonished her. She had thought her husband would have been pleased with her interest. Instead he sneered, 'Pretty yourself in the bedchamber. That's what ladies do with their time, isn't it?'

She glanced at Uncle Hesley, who waved her away. Now that his grandson had returned he had no use for her to fill his time, reading news-sheets or mixing his medicines. In the years that her husband had been away her uncle had aged considerably. He had never recovered fully after he has been injured in the pit riot before her marriage. Her husband, also, had not weathered well. He was too thin. The sun had taken its toll on his skin and he looked much older than his eight-and-twenty years.

'Of course, dearest,' she replied, and rose to leave. He was tired after his journey and his grandfather was pleased to see him, if she was not. She had long since accepted that Hesley would never bring her happiness. But for a while now she had thought that a child might. She envied the mothers she met at church, and for a time had considered that when Hesley returned she might try to be a wife to him. Hill Top House echoed with emptiness and she wanted children, even if they had to be Hesley's.

She had offered to show him her house improvements and the garden she had made. But he was not interested in domesticity. He was not even concerned for the coal mine, which was now his main source of income. His tastes lay in drinking and gambling, traits he shared with his ageing grandfather and a group of like-minded South Riding friends.

Olivia had survived well enough without him, she thought, but not so well without Miss Trent and Jared. They had been her only true friends. She understood why Miss Trent had been forced away, but that she had gone without saying goodbye still hurt. She prayed she was well and often wondered where she was. Perhaps married with her own child by now. Olivia hoped she was happy.

And then Jared had left the Riding. When she had found out her heart had bled. Some misplaced sense of duty to her had driven him away. Hesley was no husband. He was a drunkard, a gambler, and selfish like his grandfather. But there was one thing she shared with them: the desire for a child. She did not look forward to union with her husband, but how else was she to bear him an heir?

In the bedchamber, Mary was laying out a silken nightgown. 'Shall I fetch your hot water now, madam?' she asked.

'Yes. And I need you to brush my hair tonight.' Olivia began to unpin her lace cap and loosen the curls.

The silk felt luxurious against her clean, scented skin as she lay awake, waiting. She was a mature woman now, not the young girl he had married.

She must have dozed for it was quite dark when she was roused by Hesley joining her in the bed. The smell of cigars and whisky reminded her of her uncle and she recoiled but he did not notice. He lay flat on his back and said, 'Grandfather wants an heir as soon as possible.'

'Don't you?'

'Does it matter what I want?'

Olivia did not know what to say. He did not seem to desire her in that way.

'Get on with it then,' he said. 'See what you can do.'

She was unsure what he meant and hesitated.

'Go on,' he repeated. 'Do you not remember what I like?'

Olivia was glad that it was dark. Her hand crept slowly round to explore him. He was soft and flaccid. She fondled him gently but there was no response. She did not know what else to do. Perhaps kiss him. She turned her head to find his lips.

'If you want to kiss me, kiss this!' His own hands had joined hers to bring on an arousal.

Shocked, she allowed him to push her fingers out of the way but still nothing happened. What was wrong with him? She remembered her wedding night when he had asked her to take off her nightgown and had been immediately aroused. 'Take off your nightshirt,' she whispered. She threw back the covers and lit the candle before slipping her silk nightgown over her head. Her body had matured and she stood for a second in the light.

She was further shocked by the sight of his scrawny white body and legs. He used to be so muscled and sturdy. What had happened to him?

'Use your mouth,' he breathed hoarsely.

She had no idea what he meant. 'Where?' she asked nervously.

'Oh, God.' He groaned. 'Must I show you *everything*?'

He gave up and rolled away from her. She was left staring at his narrow, curved back and bony shoulders. She didn't mind that he didn't want her. But if he was impotent, how was she to have a child? Perhaps the journey had sapped his energy. She replaced her night-gown and blew out the candle. Perhaps tomorrow would be better.

It was not. Nor the night after or the night after that. When she asked what she might do for him, he scorned her. She realized then that the drink had weakened him. He took so much of it. Much more than he had before he had gone away. She searched her books and journals for remedies and tried to discuss

272

them with him when they were alone in their bed, but he shouted at her to stop.

'Nothing works!' he yelled. 'Do you think I have not tried?'

'But – but how shall I become with child if you cannot—'

'If you dare to breathe a word of this to anyone, I'll kill you!' He said this with such venom that she really thought he might. 'The fault lies with you. Is that clear?' he added.

It was a statement that set the pattern for her new life as Hesley's wife.

Harriet thought Anna was nothing short of a saint. Her efforts for those less fortunate than herself were tireless, and the secret that Harriet harboured about her past became an increasing burden for her to bear. Anna did not press her for details, but it lay heavy on Harriet's shoulders, especially when they walked the three miles to the nearest chapel for Sunday service. Dissenters had different views about God's work from those of the church she had known at Blackstone and Hill Top House. But it was the same God and she listened with interest to their teachings.

All have sinned. All can be saved. All can know that they are saved.

All can know that they are saved. Harriet thought that Anna and Tobias had saved her, but if she had their forgiveness for her past, she would *know* that she was saved. Tobias and Anna were such kind and generous people that she could not keep her secret from them

273

for ever. They would be fair and not condemn her, only ask if she had repented and she had.

When Tobias visited them he embraced Harriet as warmly as he did his sister. He enquired about her work and they talked. They talked so much that Anna sent them for walks together while she prepared dinner and Harriet felt welcome at his side as he encouraged her conversation.

He praised her efforts in the classroom. 'The board of governors said, in their last report, that they continue to have the services of an excellent teacher supported by the Wesleyan mission. That is you, Harriet,' he told her. 'They sent a formal acknowledgement of their gratitude to the chapel elders. We have you to thank for that.'

Harriet was thrilled to be honoured in this way, and more so as the knowledge came from Tobias. 'I do what I can. I cannot help all the poor souls inside the asylum and there are many of them, I know.'

'The doctor and his nurses do their best.'

'Yes. I have suggested that a pupil teacher should help me. That is how I learned at Blackstone and an able gentlewoman is willing.'

'Really?'

'She is educated, although she was of a stubborn disposition until she started at my class. She is much improved now, but her father will have nothing to do with her. They have means and pay well to keep her here, so there is no hope of her leaving.'

'What does the doctor say?'

'He thinks it will be more fulfilling for her to be of help to others and has recommended it.'

Tobias stopped and turned to face her. He placed his hands gently on her shoulders and said, 'You have done a first-rate job here.'

Harriet's eyes sparkled at such a compliment from an educated gentleman she respected. Her feelings for Tobias were developing into more than those of friendship, and she dared to hope that one day he might return them. But she worried that she was deceiving him in not owning up to her past.

'I cannot do it without the benefactors Anna finds,' she replied seriously.

'Anna is the first to admit that she is not half the teacher you are. We are both very proud of you.'

Harriet gazed at the sincerity in his eyes. There were dark circles and lines around them, and his hair was greying at the temples, but in her eyes he was the most handsome gentleman she had ever seen, and he was strong. He was strong in mind as well as body, and she loved him. She must tell him of her sins. But when? she thought nervously. And how?

They had butcher's meat for dinner, boiled with barley, onion and carrot. Anna mixed dumplings on their return and when it was all ready the three sat down to a feast. After saying grace, they ate silently and hungrily.

'I have something to tell you,' Harriet said, when they had finished. 'Something about my past. Something sinful.'

Anna stacked the plates. 'I'll make tea,' she volunteered, without looking at her brother.

Tobias sat back in his chair. 'You are a good woman,

Harriet. We are celebrating your success. You need not distress yourself in this way tonight.'

'Oh, but I must. I know that I have sinned and that the chapel will forgive me if I repent. But I feel I am betraying your trust by accepting your goodwill without owning my past.' She looked down at her hands, twisting in her lap, and added quietly, 'I cannot deceive you any longer.'

Anna brought the teapot and stoneware mugs to the table. She poured in silence, waiting for Harriet to speak.

'If it will unburden your conscience, then we shall listen,' Tobias replied.

She took a deep breath. 'You did not press me about the time I spent as a governess after Blackstone and I am grateful for that. I was so – so proud of the work I did with my pupil and I – I tried so hard to keep it from her but – but—' In her anxiety, Harriet pulled restlessly at her fingers.

'We are your friends.'

It was Tobias who had spoken. She looked up at his serious face and wavered. He meant so much to her and she wondered if he would be able to forgive her.

'It – it was an evil house. The child was not evil. She was running wild and responded well to my direction. But – but . . .' Harriet's courage was failing her. The master was an evil man, she thought. And she had complied with his wishes. In the end she had been complicit in his sinfulness. She looked from brother to sister with wide shiny eyes. 'I sinned,' she said simply. 'Shamefully.'

Tobias said quietly, 'We have all sinned.'

'Oh, no, not like this!' Harriet said anxiously. 'The master was wicked, I knew he was, but I was wicked too! I gave in to his sin. I should have left, but I could not desert the child. She needed me and I – well, I went there for her sake. I had to stay – for her.'

'You did not say no to him.' This time Anna spoke. Anna had known at their first meeting what she was fleeing from: she had asked if Harriet was with child. Tobias, too, needed no further explanation.

'I did! He would not listen!' Harriet's voice dropped. 'He – he forced me. I told you. He was a wicked man.'

'You were there for more than a year. That is a long time.'

'My salary was paid to Blackstone until I became of age. I had no money of my own.'

'But you gave me money for the mission when you came here,' Anna pointed out. 'Did you steal it?' The shock in her voice was evident.

'No!' By now, Harriet was almost beside herself with anguish. 'He made me do it and I earned every penny!' They could not hate her any more than she did herself for what she had done. But she was so desperate for their understanding and forgiveness. That mattered to her more than anything.

'I thought – that if I could earn money quickly, I could leave sooner. He was willing to pay – to pay me well.' Her voice lowered to a whisper. 'If I did what he asked of me as a willing partner.' She dared not look up and the silence lengthened, until she added very quietly, 'I was never willing. You must believe me.'

'And that is how you came by the money.'

'Half of it was my governess stipend,' she said, in a small voice. 'I prayed for forgiveness every night.' She wiped away damp tears with the back of her hand. She had not realized she was crying. The tea was welcome and she picked up her mug.

'This is worse than I imagined,' Anna said.

'Anna!' Tobias chided his sister gently. It was worse than he had imagined too. But Harriet had been brave to tell them this, and he appreciated her courage and honesty. 'Did the child know?' he asked.

'She was married very young and grew up too quickly. She knew I was unhappy and – and gave me leave to flee. Otherwise I could not have left her. The master was a mine-owner, you see, and his pit was going bankrupt—'

'Mine-owner, you say?' Anna interrupted. Her breathing was laboured suddenly, and Harriet noticed Tobias staring at his sister.

'He owned Mexton Pit,' Harriet volunteered, but neither seemed to be listening to her now.

Tobias picked up Anna's mug and handed it to her. 'Please, try to calm yourself, dear sister.'

But Anna was not to be calmed and Harriet's eyes widened in alarm as her dear friend appeared so distressed. She seemed unable to catch her breath.

Tobias moved to his sister's side. He looked once in Harriet's direction and she saw fear and loathing in his eyes. Oh, no! Would he hate her for this? She attempted to explain. 'I did not know about Hesley Mexton's reputation when I agreed to take the position.'

Anna was making rasping noises in her throat and her face was darkening as her chest heaved.

'Run and see if the doctor is still with the warden,' Tobias pleaded. 'Fetch him at once. Quickly, Harriet!'

Harriet leaped to her feet and did as he bade. Anna was in some sort of seizure, brought on by her confession. Dear heaven, she had misread her situation. Neither brother nor sister had been prepared for her to admit to such shame. Perhaps they would forgive a woman who through her own foolishness had lost her virtue but not one who had compounded the sin by an unholy bargain with the master.

The asylum doctor was leaving. The iron gates had closed behind him and he was driving his trap away. Harriet ran after him, calling his name. He heard her and slowed the pony.

'Please come back,' she panted. 'It's Miss Holmes. She's very ill.'

The doctor leaned down and offered a hand to hoist Harriet beside him, turned the pony and whipped him into a trot. It was not far but he hurried into the cottage, leaving the reins trailing and calling for Harriet to secure the trap.

Inside, Anna was lying motionless on the pallet, her face ashen and her eyes closed.

'She isn't breathing!' Tobias exclaimed, as the doctor entered.

'Give me room,' he answered curtly. 'A seizure as before?'

'Yes. Exactly so. What is it, sir? Will she recover?'

The doctor did not answer him. He was opening

279

his leather bag and taking out an ear trumpet that he placed on her chest. He listened.

'Is she alive?'

'Quiet, sir!'

Harriet came through the back door of the scullery silently. She was shocked by what she saw and hovered in the kitchen doorway as the physician tended her dearest friend, watched anxiously by the gentleman she loved. She could not bear for anything to happen to either of them.

'She is in a deep faint, Tobias, but she lives.' The doctor reached into his bag, retrieved a small glass phial with a metal top that he unscrewed. He passed the open bottle backwards and forwards under Anna's nose.

She inhaled raggedly, then more substantially, and her eyes opened.

'Praise the Lord!' Tobias exclaimed, and took Anna's hand.

The doctor passed his hand over her brow. 'An hysteria.' He nodded. 'Suffered only by ladies. I have not seen your sister like this since – since, well, you know how much she has improved since Miss Trent arrived.'

'I fear Miss Trent is the cause of this.'

'How so?'

'She told us something of her past that – that shocked us both, Anna more than I. Anna has suffered worst.'

'You must take care of her, Tobias. You have seen that she is prone to these attacks. The asylum is not the best place for her mission. I have told you so before.'

'I cannot persuade her to give up her work here.

And she has been so much better in recent times until—' He looked down and shook his head.

'My advice is that she should go away for a time. Take her back with you. Miss Trent is more than capable of keeping her mission going.' The doctor was raising his patient to a sitting position, supporting her shoulders. 'As soon as you can, my dear,' he said to her, 'go to your bed and stay there until the morning. I'll leave you a sleeping draught and I'll call to see you on my way to the asylum tomorrow.'

Harriet stepped into the kitchen. 'I'll help her upstairs.'

But Tobias barred her way. He took her elbow and steered her back into the scullery. His face was pained and anxious. He looked older. 'You must keep away from her,' he whispered fiercely.

Startled by his tone, her heart sank. Was he blaming her for Anna's seizure? Was he not as forgiving as she had been led to believe? She had thought he and Anna, above all people, would have understood her need of their forgiveness. But it seemed they would rather not have known about her shameful past.

'I am so sorry, Tobias. I had to tell you. I thought you might find a little charity in your heart.'

He stared at her, agitated. 'Oh, Harriet, I do not blame you for this, but you cannot know what you have done and I cannot explain.' His voice was low but his anxiety was clear.

He could have warned her that Anna's sensibilities needed such protection. Yet Anna worked in a mission for the less fortunate. It did not make sense to Harriet.

Anna was a gentlewoman by birth, who had chosen, like her brother, to follow a hard road in life. Harriet had thought she had a steely core: Anna did not flinch from difficult tasks. She had been mistaken. Her confession had been too much of a shock for the other woman.

The more Harriet thought about this, the more she thought she was to blame. Perhaps Tobias was simply trying to make her feel better. If so, she groaned inwardly, she loved him more for it. But she feared Anna's seizure had been her fault and her misery deepened.

'You must keep her quiet,' she heard the doctor say as he left. 'Do not distress her with talk of others in less fortunate situations. She will recover. If you take her away from here, Tobias, it will hasten her restoration.'

'Very well. I shall. Tomorrow, if she is well enough to ride with me.'

'I'll mix her draught,' Harriet volunteered, and swung the kettle hook over the hottest part of the fire. When she had prepared it and sweetened the bitter drink with honey, she laid a small tray prettily with a clean napkin and an oat biscuit baked especially for Tobias's visit. She went out into the lane and picked a wild rose, which she placed in an empty glass phial on the tray.

Tobias came in from seeing the doctor off in his trap as Harriet was about to climb the wooden stairs leading from the kitchen to the bedchamber.

'I shall have to take that,' he said briefly. 'The doctor does not want her upset any more.'

How Harriet stopped the tears flowing she did not know.

'It is not your fault,' he said, quite kindly, 'but you have resurrected memories. I cannot say more than that, except that if anyone is responsible it is me. She was alone when our parents died and I should have been here for her then, not in America. We all have our guilty secrets, Harriet.'

Harriet sank into a fireside chair and stared at the glowing coals. She heard voices from upstairs, then silence. Tobias came down with a serious face.

'Do you wish me to leave?' she asked quietly.

He shook his head. 'Anna will return with me to my mission. We shall go tomorrow, while you are working in the asylum. That way she need not see you and become agitated again.'

'I – I am so sorry. I had no idea that my confession would cause so much upset.' She looked at her hands, twisting in her lap, and heard him sigh.

'I should like to tell you more. You are doing good work for the asylum and it is Anna's wish that you continue. The doctor has said he will manage the mission accounts for me. He will call on you from time to time.'

'I am to stay here alone?'

'I do not see what else I can do.'

'When will you return?'

'I do not know.'

'I am so very sorry, Tobias,' she repeated in a whisper.

'Yes, I am too, but it is done now and my sister's health is my first concern.' He lit a candle stub and gave it to her. 'I should like to retire now. Goodnight, Harriet.'

'Goodnight.' She said it so softly that she did not think he heard her. He was not listening anyway. He was already packing his bag for his journey tomorrow.

Harriet climbed the narrow stairway and ducked into her tiny room. She undressed slowly in spite of the chilly air and placed a nightcap over her hair. The sheets were cold and she was glad of her thick nightgown. She lay awake, watching the flickering shadows from the dying candle on the sloping timbers under the slates. At least the roof was dry, even though a draught blew in through the loose bricks in the end wall. She pulled down her cap and tucked her feet up inside her nightgown as the candle flame died and the shadows disappeared.

She was not saved. No one could save her. She had behaved too wickedly to be saved.

Chapter 21

Olivia heard horses outside on the cobbles. A carriage as well. The sound of loud voices drifted through the open schoolroom window. She often sat in there, reflecting on those distant days with Miss Trent. She had asked after her at the gownmaker's and draper's, even her uncle's lawyer's, but no one knew where she was. Or cared. Since Hesley's homecoming, Hill Top House had degenerated from the gracious family home she had made into a gambling-den for his friends. She had loved this house once, but now she hated it.

They came here from that place called Grace's down in the valley, gentlemen on horseback and in carriages, from the railway company and the government bureaux that now served the Riding so well. The town was growing out of all recognition, with foundries and glassworks adding to the iron works and forges, fuelled by the coal brought in from surrounding pits on the navigation.

Olivia knew the household servants would be awake all night, providing meat and drink while the gentlemen played their card games for coins and banknotes. And when they ran out of those they wagered their time-pieces and guns.

Her husband was already drunk. She hurried across the landing to give her uncle his medicine. She did not want him roused for he would wish to join them, which caused him such pain and anger now that he was too weak to do so. If only he would accept his advancing years and failing health. His apothecary recommended laudanum and he took it willingly, asking her every day if she was with child.

She did not linger long, for her husband ordered her to be with him when his gentlemen friends visited. And she obeyed because when she didn't his tantrums sorely vexed her maids. She was hardened now to his ways, but he whipped the servants for the least thing when he was irritated by Olivia's behaviour. So, she dressed in the fine silks he liked, curled her hair and painted her face.

He took her arm possessively and walked with her around their drawing room, pausing to pass his hands over the swell of her breasts above her gown and tilting her chin upwards so that she was obliged to look directly at some flushed lawyer or company agent he wished to impress.

To this end he had bought her beautiful gowns and jewellery, but she knew they were not for her benefit.

They were to show off his new-found wealth. That was what she was to him: one of his possessions to be exhibited along with his treasures from the West Indies. When the gentlemen began gaming she stood by the wall next to the ostentatious displays of valuable articles he had collected.

One of the gentlemen was making up the fire in the drawing room while others were helping themselves to strong drink and opening packs of playing cards. Money had been plentiful at Hill Top House since Hesley had received the government compensation for freeing the slaves. It had paid off some of the Mexton debts. Then he had sold her plantation and used the capital to pay for a new shaft at the mine with a steam engine to wind the cage.

He said he would invest more in machinery and railtrack for the mine: it still did not make enough profit. Olivia wondered why he didn't proceed with his plan instead of wasting money in this disgusting fashion on these disgusting people.

If only Miss Trent were here, or Jared, so that she could escape to their ruined cottage with him. But she had long since discarded any hope for either of them. They had abandoned her when she needed them most and, in doing so, had stiffened her resolve not to trust anyone ever again. She was alone in this God-forsaken life, but she was intelligent and strong and she did not need either of them now.

Mary brought in refreshments and Olivia sent her away, aware that some of Hesley's guests could not be trusted to behave properly towards the servants. She began taking round the salvers herself, keeping her eyes down to avoid the more voracious looks some of the gentlemen were casting her. She was still young and she had learned already that her youthful attentiveness was prized among Hesley's friends, many of whom were older than he.

Hesley was in high spirits for he seemed to be winning. The hour moved past midnight, and Olivia watched quietly from a shadowy corner as the others noted ruefully his mounting pile of coins and notes. At least he would be in a good humour when they left, she thought.

'We're not leaving yet, Mexton. You must give us a chance to win it back.'

'If you want to risk the shirt on your back.' He laughed.

The party divided into a small group wanting to win back their losses and others attracted by the spectacle. The players filled their glasses, lit cigars and sat down.

'*Vingt-et-un?*' one suggested.

'Higher stakes this time?'

Olivia knew that Hesley would agree to any stakes in his present mood. She came forward. 'Dearest,' she said politely, 'this will go on all night. I shall retire—'

'You will stay where you are,' he answered sharply, then noticed a few raised eyebrows and added, 'My dear.'

'As you wish.' She melted into the shadows again. She was angry. He did not care whether she was present or not. He was concerned only with showing his friends how obedient his young wife was. She did not mind if he hit her for disobeying him, but she could not bear it when he beat her young maids with his horse-whip. He did not need a reason to do so, except to punish her. She remembered how he had taken pleasure from it when she was a girl and hated him for it.

After an hour there were only two players left, Hesley and a man called Jessup, who raised the stakes even higher. Hesley's luck wavered. Twice he wagered heavily and lost, then won most of it back only to lose it again. He seemed more than unusually angry at this turn of events and stood up to leave the table.

'You can't go now, Mexton,' someone goaded him. 'You have to take it back from him.'

'He's out of funds, aren't you?' Jessup said. He was a young lawyer, who was making a name for himself in the town. He was the grandson of a farm labourer whose son had bettered himself and opened a butcher's shop in town. Jessup had proved an able scholar and had been sent to the grammar school by his ambitious father, then attended university at the same time as Hesley.

'And if I am?' Hesley responded belligerently. 'My credit is good at the bank.'

'If you say so. But you know our rules, Hesley. No promissory notes.'

'Very well!' Hesley sounded irritable. 'I have more valuable things to wager than coin. Look about you.'

Olivia thought privately it would be better for Hesley to lose some of his silver collection than more of her money. She knew their income from the pit was not inexhaustible, and all this entertainment was paid for by spending what was left of her capital from the plantation. She cared nothing for his possessions, but the mine needed more investment.

He slapped his hand on the table. 'Who will pledge their coin against one of my treasures? Lady Luck has not deserted me yet.'

Olivia wondered what had made him think that. Even when he had a good night, he never quit early and always lost. Tonight would be no different.

'I will,' Jessup suggested calmly. 'Twenty guineas on the turn of a card.' He piled his coins on the table.

Hesley eyed the gold and, in the candlelight, Olivia saw a pulse throb in his temple.

'If you win that, Mexton, you can play on all night,' someone suggested. 'So what's to be your stake?'

Olivia knew he would be unable to resist.

'My stake? I have silver to pledge worth a hundred times that. Choose your piece.' He waved his arm airily around the room.

Olivia guessed that Jessup could afford to lose his wager. His father had leased his butchery and now owned terraces for the workers in the iron and glass manufactories in town. He had bought his educated son a partnership in a law practice and, once set up, Jessup had made it his business to know everything about government and municipal regulation. He had cultivated the Member of Parliament for the Riding and other local dignitaries so he knew their thinking and was retained as their agent to institute new parish laws and deal with the resulting disputes. He was not of the gentry but he was powerful in the Riding.

She wondered idly whether he had good taste and which piece of silver he would choose. He walked over to the glass-fronted display cabinet beside her and peered inside. Suddenly she realized he was not looking at the silver: he was staring at her reflection in the darkened glass. She blinked and moved away.

'I choose this piece,' he said quickly, and took her wrist.

'Let go.' She tried to wrench her arm from his grasp.

But he dragged her to where Hesley was sitting at the card table.

'My wife?' he exclaimed. 'For twenty guineas?'

'An hour with her.'

The others, who had become bored by Hesley's lack of funds, brightened and regrouped at the table. Horrified, Olivia saw that Hesley was contemplating the wager. 'Hesley, stop this at once.'

'Fifty,' he said.

'Hesley!'

'Alone.' Jessup raised his eyes to the ceiling. 'Upstairs.'

'Agreed.'

This was a game, she thought, a jest. They did not mean it. They were simply using her as a means to goad him for their pleasure. The lawyer handed her wrist to another gentleman. 'Hold the stake. Let Hesley have first cut.'

'Hesley,' Olivia pleaded, 'you are taking this too far. You must not do this.'

'Be quiet,' he said. 'I feel lucky tonight. Who will shuffle the pack?'

She was enclosed in a circle of his so-called friends,

who were surrounding the card table with its single candle already burning low. The two gamblers sat opposite each other while a third stood with his fingers resting lightly on the deck of cards. The third man said, 'Aces high, high wins,' and removed his hand.

Olivia held her breath. Hesley cut the knave of clubs. High. He had a good chance of winning. There were only twelve cards in the pack higher than a knave. The lawyer cut the knave of spades. Olivia could hardly believe it. There was a huge roar from the other men.

'A draw, sir,' Olivia said to the gentleman holding her wrist. 'Let me go now. You have had your fun.'

'We'll cut again,' Jessup said evenly. 'Same stakes.' He looked to the staring faces for approval.

Hesley nodded, and the onlookers went deathly quiet as Jessup took the first cut. The seven of hearts! Olivia let out an audible sigh. Hesley was bound to cut higher than that.

A deuce. Cards didn't come any lower! The deuce of spades. This time there was no roar as the implication of Hesley's loss sank in.

'Mine, I think,' Jessup said, taking her wrist again. He picked up the silver candle-holder from the card table and dragged her after him out of the room.

'But surely you did not mean it, sir!' Olivia did not know whether she was laughing or crying. 'Hesley!' she croaked. But Hesley was rubbing the back of his head and frowning at the cards. The third gentleman had pushed a large glass of brandy into his other hand. From the hall she heard a lone voice urging, 'Call him back, Mexton, before it's too late. I'll pay him off for you.' She wondered who it was.

Jessup pulled at her arm. 'Come, my dear. We know of your husband's failings in the bedchamber. Let me show you what a man can do.'

'What do you mean?' How could they know about his failure in their marriage bed? She supposed because she was not with child. She blushed at the thought.

He laughed at her and hauled her up the stairs. 'Which room?'

She pulled away from him. 'Stop this at once, sir. You are no gentleman.'

He lowered his voice menacingly. 'But you are a lady and a prize worth having. Come.' He jerked at her arm. 'Let us see if you are a lady in the bedchamber. I do not want to waste a minute of my hour with you.'

He opened the nearest door. It was an unused guest chamber with the window curtains pulled back and no fire in the grate. He pushed her inside, locked the door behind him, put the key in his pocket and placed the candle by the bed, an ornate four-poster with brocade hangings.

He began to remove his boots. 'Take off your gown.'

'No.'

'Would you disobey your husband and shame him in front of his friends? He is proud that he always pays his gambling dues and he is not to be trifled with when he is displeased.'

Olivia knew that and was prepared to risk it. 'If you are any sort of gentleman you will not take your winnings. I am not one of his girls from the tavern. I am his wife.'

'Quite so. Your worth is much higher than that of a tavern girl. And he has a debt to pay.'

'I shall stay with you in this room for the hour, sir, and then you may tell him his debt is paid. I shall not disagree and he will believe you.'

He stared at her in disbelief. 'You think I would settle for that? My dear, you have no idea of the prize you are. If old Mexton had not been clever enough to wed you to his grandson before he left for the West Indies, there would have been any number of suitors queuing at your door. Including me.'

'Attracted, no doubt, by my money,' she snapped.

He moved close to her and stroked her cheek with a knuckle. 'Dowries like yours do not usually come with such beauty, my lady. We are all insanely jealous that an ineffectual runt like Hesley should have plucked you. I shall have my winnings, whether you co-operate or not.'

In the candlelight she saw him smiling crookedly. Then he became impatient with her, pushing her onto the bed and throwing her skirts over her head to claw at her drawers. 'You're wasting my time,' he breathed angrily.

She heard the fabric rip and struggled to breathe. He cared not for how she felt about the arrangement. He meant to have his due. She wondered if he would hit her if she fought him and guessed he might. She rolled away from him and half fell off the bed, intending to leave the chamber.

He was a lithe, agile man and caught her wrist again. He tugged down one of the cords that held back the bed curtains and began to tie her hand to the bedpost. He was agitated and talking breathlessly as he bound her. 'You may do this willingly or not. As you wish.'

When he took her other hand to tie that as well, she became frightened. Would he beat her into submission? She was helpless and exposed in front of this stranger.

She feared also for Hesley's respect of her. Her husband had set such little value on her virtue, yet it was not the quantity of coin that enraged her. It was that he had used her as a gambling stake without a second thought. He had gone too far this time.

Jessup stood by the bed and picked up a fly swat from the mantelshelf. It whistled through the air as he struck it against the bedpost. 'That is a warning. Next time it'll be your flesh.'

He would beat her! She had no wish to be injured. 'I'll do it!' she cried. 'I'll undress and do as you ask.'

He smiled at her, a sneering grin that caused her stomach to lurch as he unbuttoned his breeches.

'Untie me,' she asked quietly. 'Please.'

He freed her quickly and, frightened for her safety, she kept her word.

Shakily, she took off her silken skirts and lace drawers and dropped them to the floor. The buttons on her bodice were fiddly and her fingers trembled. He became impatient, and tore them away.

'And the corset,' he barked, and pushed her onto the bed again.

Quaking with fear, she unhooked the front, which fell aside, leaving her in a fine muslin chemise that skimmed her shoulders and reached her thighs. She sat on the edge of the bed, shuddering with despair.

Was this what her marriage had come to? She was being forced to give herself to a stranger to pay her husband's gambling debt.

She heard the lawyer take a ragged breath and in the candlelight saw his arousal. She could not do this. She had to get out of the room. Somehow. How far was it to the door? How many seconds did she need to unlock it?

'And this,' he ordered, hooking the fly swat under the edge of her chemise. 'Off.'

'No.'

He whipped the swat across her back. She winced and drew her chemise over her head. Then, suddenly, he was on top of her, his open mouth over her face as if he were trying to devour her. She turned her head away and he bit sharply at her earlobe.

He spread himself over her, his weight pressing her into the feather mattress. Her flailing arms made no impression on him as he grasped her thighs and pushed them apart. She struggled in an attempt to fight him off and her body recoiled when he mauled her private parts. She protested, shrivelling beneath him, tensing the muscles of her lower regions. But he laughed, with a harsh snarl that disgusted as well as frightened her. She did not touch him with her hands and when his face came near her as he shoved and rutted she kept her head turned away. Her eyes focused on the grotesque moving shadow cast on the wall by the candle flame and she wondered how much longer she could endure her life at Hill Top House.

As this stranger indulged himself with her body she remembered the pain of her wedding night. In her childhood innocence she had thought then that this was a kind of punishment to be endured as a wife. Miss Trent had assured her it was not, but she had been wrong.

Pleasure for gentlemen meant grief for their ladies. When she was used like this, it was the worst kind of pain for any woman to endure. It did not hurt her in any physical way. The ache went deeper, stamping on her core, killing any vestige of affection or sympathy she might feel for any life that had ever touched hers.

Jessup's use of her body was over quickly. But, unlike Hesley, he did not need her assistance to repeat his actions. Her eyes watched the flickering shadows on the wall as she pondered the irony of being grateful for that.

Her assailant was unaware of how much she hated him. She could not move beneath his weight as he fondled and invaded her until he was exhausted. Then he climbed off her and rolled onto his back, sweating silently in the cold, dark room. Presently, he reached for his jacket and searched for a cigar, which he lit from the candle flame. The smell reminded her of Uncle Hesley. She hated Jessup as much as she hated her uncle. She curled away from him. She hated her husband for humiliating her in this way. She hated everything in this house. Miss Trent had known what to do when she had suffered here. Miss Trent had fled. So would she.

At first light she dressed in a comfortable day gown from last year's wardrobe as though she would be spending the day pickling vegetables or making cordials. She asked Eliza to serve her an early breakfast before Mrs Cookson stirred. Then she went across to the stable and ordered the lad to harness the pony and trap. She thought no further than getting away from Hill Top House.

She wondered if she dare go to her aunt Caroline's. But she thought not. The Tylers were respectable, and however much they hated the Mextons, they would urge her to return to her husband. Perhaps even send for him to take her back. Why wouldn't they desert her, as Jared had when she needed him? She closed her eyes at the memory. Why couldn't he have loved her as she did him? They could have run away together and she wouldn't be alone like this. Cold, lonely and unloved.

Well, she didn't want anybody's love now. Not if they would let her down. From now on she would live her life on her own. She did not know how. Fearfully she wondered what she would do as she rattled down the valley through the early-morning mists. But she had decided on one thing. She would never go back to Hill Top House. Not while her husband or his grandfather lived there.

As she approached the town she realized how notice-able she was in the trap. Few knew her well for she visited rarely and only then for the draper and the dressmaker. The miller delivered flour to Hill Top House but he was out of the town on the Grassborough road. The butcher called, too, and stayed for refreshment with Mrs Cookson. He would recognize her. She stopped at a watering trough and tethered the pony. A farm cart rumbled by.

When the road was clear she pulled down her small travelling bag from the trap and, hitching up her skirts, climbed over the dry-stone wall to cross the fields, running for the sanctuary of a copse. She looked back when she was under cover of the trees. All was quiet. At the other side of the wood she shaded her eyes against the sun. The navigation glinted in the valley. Sheffield one way, or Doncaster the other? She had until nightfall to decide.

Chapter 22

The early sun had given way to clouds and by the afternoon she was hungry. She had not brought food with her. In her anxiety to get away from Hesley she had not thought beyond the little money she had and her jewels. They had belonged to her mother and she hated to part with them. But she had no idea how she would survive outside Hill Top House unless she sold them.

Cold stream water refreshed her and the hunger pangs receded as she took her rough descent through woods and fields towards the waterway in the valley. She was used to physical exercise from labouring in her garden, but fear of the unknown life before her made her tense and her body ached. She found a sheltered grassy slope to rest until nightfall.

The next thing she knew she was being woken by

rain on her face and it was dark. Very dark. She had never been away from the house at night. She had no lantern and clouds shielded the moon. For the first time since she had left that morning she was frightened. This was more than just the fear of hunger and fatigue. Vagabonds were out at night, with cudgels and knives, and she was alone.

But she was free. She was free of the humiliation that Hesley had heaped on her – and the freedom to starve was better than suffering at his bidding. But perhaps not the freedom to die. She pulled her hood over her bonnet and stealthily followed the stream downhill until a cluster of cottages loomed in front of her. She crept around them until she located a track. This, surely, would lead her into the town? But what would she do then? Already she was feeling faint with hunger again.

The stone buildings of the town square, dominated by the majestic spire of the church, were familiar although all was in darkness. Perhaps she could sleep in the church and be away before dawn. She remembered Mrs Cookson talking of a pie-seller who visited the beast market and began to climb the hill past the church, wondering if he had lingered, drinking his profits at the tavern.

'Boy! Come here,' Olivia called, to the ragged group hanging around the door, and held up a coin. 'Fetch me some food. Do not tell anyone who it is for.'

He took her coin and ran back to the tavern. But he did not go in, and the other children followed him as he ran past the entrance and disappeared into the darkness. How stupid of her! Servants obeyed her, but why should anyone else? She wondered if she dared go in herself. What if the butcher were in there celebrating a good day at the market? She approached a dingy window and lingered in the shadows.

'Are you looking for business? 'Cos if you are I'll thank you to move on. This is my patch.' A woman of her own age loomed out of the shadows. In spite of the chilly air her gown was cut low at the neck and half of her skirt was hitched into her garter to expose a worn shoe and a white leg without a stocking. The woman looked her up and down. 'You won't get no trade dressed like that, love. Pretty face, though.'

The woman smelled of drink but Olivia was too exhausted to be concerned. She placed her bag by the wall and leaned against the damp stone. 'I – I'm hungry.'

'Aren't we all? Wait there.' The woman went inside and, through the dimly lit glass, Olivia glimpsed the drinkers, men in moleskins and tweeds who should have been in their homes at this late hour. She heard their raucous laughter. She undid the fastenings on her cloak to locate her leather purse, lodged safely in the inside pocket. She would need another coin for the food.

'This one?' She was startled by the male voice. He had come outside with the woman and he flung back both sides of her cloak to look at her. Then he tipped her chin up towards the yellow glow from the window. 'Aye, you're right. She is a pretty one. Well, my dear, why don't you come with me?' He tossed the woman a coin and she disappeared into the tavern.

He was respectably dressed and reminded her of the pit manager at Mexton. But he also smelled of drink and tobacco, which reminded her of Uncle Hesley. She backed away, alarmed.

'Hey! Where are yer going?' He grabbed at her cloak and hauled her towards him. 'I've just paid good money for you.'

He had no food for her – he had bought her, as Jessup had last night. She kicked his shins and wriggled out of her cloak, leaving it trailing in his hands. She ran across the dirt track, soft underfoot with mud and droppings from the earlier beast market, and into the darkness of the buildings beyond.

'Come back 'ere!' the man shouted. She heard him yelp, and when she glanced back he had stumbled over her cloak and was cursing the mire on his own clothes.

She hid in the shadows and caught her breath. Her money was tied inside her cloak! And her jewels were in her bag, which was still by the tavern wall where she had placed it. She would have to go back. She waited for the man to leave and picked her way back through the mud. But her cloak and bag had gone. Taken, she guessed, by the woman.

She had lost her money and her jewels, and her boots smelled of the privy in high summer. She was cold and hungry. Her back, legs and arms were tired and sore. Dear heaven, she would not survive if she could not look after herself better than this. None of her reading had prepared her for life on the streets. She realized that she did not have the wit to survive in this dangerous place alone after dark. Not yet, she thought with determination. She would learn. Others had and so could she. But she dared not linger. Hunger must wait. She had to find somewhere safe to spend the night.

Olivia hurried to the back of the building where she might find an outhouse or stable. But this was a tavern, not an inn. There were no horses, no kitchen to prepare food for hungry travellers, only a locked brew-house and a stinking yard that was dark and empty. Too frightened to approach a door for help, she did not know what to do next. She sat on a mounting stone and thought briefly of her foolishness in leaving her home without a thought for where she would go and how she would survive.

No, she was not foolish. She could not, *would not*, go back to the humiliation and misery of Hill Top House. But cold fear crept around her heart. She had to get away from the town, where she might be recognized by tradesmen and word sent to Hesley. It would be better to go now, at night, when decent folk were asleep in their beds. She shivered. She no longer had a cloak to protect her from the weather. But she straightened her spine. Without her bag to weigh her down she could move more swiftly, more quietly, and out of sight.

She stumbled down the hill to the navigation, keeping close to the walls and avoiding any building with a glimmer of light at its window. After a while she forgot her hunger as her legs grew tired. She chose the Doncaster direction, she knew not why, only that she had heard Sheffield, though nearer, was the worst for smoke and squalor. And there was more farmland towards Doncaster in which she felt she might be safer.

She followed the towpath past the iron works and the wharves, past empty and laden barges moored for the night. She went around locks and under bridges until she was dropping with weakness and fatigue. She must not faint! If she rested she might fall asleep and freeze to death by the canal. She did not want to die. She shivered and wrapped her arms round herself for warmth. Then, with a flash of inspiration, she hoisted her skirts and stepped out of her thick petticoat. The cold air swirled around her legs until the heavy skirt fell back into place. Quickly, she slipped the warm flannel over her head so that it formed a cloak and tied the tapes about her neck.

It began to rain, a steady, soaking drizzle, so she found shelter under a bridge. It was dry at least, but the chill penetrated her bones. Why was it always colder by water? It weakened her so much that she could barely stand. She leaned against the brickwork for support. Her head spun and her vision, such as it was at dead of night, blurred. She was going to faint. Her eyes were closing. She must pray. Yes. Her prayers, learned by heart from Miss Trent, would keep her safe. The words came and went in her mind as consciousness ebbed. She was in God's hands now.

It was still dark when Olivia woke, stiff and thirsty, dishevelled and grubby. Her feet and hands were freezing. Her corset was digging painfully into her flesh where she had slept on it. She wanted to take it off, but she needed its warmth. As she emerged from under the bridge she saw that the sky had cleared and the first signs of dawn were easing away the blackness of the night.

She heard a distant voice – 'Gerrup, girl, goo on, goo on' – and glimpsed a cowman bringing in his herd for milking. A farm! Food and drink! She retreated under the bridge until he had passed overhead with his six cows. There was enough light for her to make out a cowshed in the distance and a barn. There would be a pump for water and warm straw, perhaps, to comfort her stiffness.

The cowman led one of his beasts into the barn; she was lowing constantly and her belly bulged on both sides. There goes my resting-place, she thought. He was unlikely to leave his beast for any length of time until she had calved. But a young girl joined him to herd the others into the milking shed. Perhaps she would let Olivia have a ladle of milk.

Olivia approached cautiously and leaned against one of the wooden stalls. 'Good morning, miss. I wonder if I may have some milk?'

The maid jumped. 'Ooh! Where you come from?'

'The canal.'

'Traveller, are you?

'Yes.'

'You got summat to put it in?'

She shook her head.

'You must be new on the barges not to know to bring a can,' the girl scoffed.

'Yes.'

'Well, it's not far. Go back and get one and I'll fill it for you.'

'May I – could I have some to drink first?'

'If you milk her yoursen, aye. Mam's poorly today and I'm on me own. There's a stool and bucket over there.'

Olivia looked around. 'I – I don't know how.'

'You don't know how to milk a cow? Blooming 'eck, I've been milking since I were walking!'

Olivia guessed this was not quite true. At Hill Top House she had learned how to scald cream and churn butter, but the farmhands, assisted by Mary and Eliza, milked the cows. Why hadn't she waited to plan her escape? Had she left in too much haste? Never! She could not have tolerated Hesley and his ways a minute longer. She had made the right decision and she would not go back. Ever.

But she must have food and shelter. And work of some sort for she had no money. Unless . . . She fingered her gold wedding band. 'I'm very hungry,' she muttered.

'Wait till this is full, then.' The young girl squeezed the cow's udder rhythmically for several minutes. Then she stood up, lifting the heavy wooden bucket with both hands.

'Perhaps a little of that?' Olivia ventured.

'Don't you go putting no dirty hands in there! It's for cheese.' She went through a gap in the stone wall and returned with an empty bucket.

'You have cheese?'

'You want some o' that an' all?'

'And some bread. How much will that be?'

'I'll have to go indoors for bread.'

'Please?' she begged.

307

The girl stared at her. 'You don't look like you've come off the barges.'

Olivia thought again of how hopeless she was at finding food and drink. She must do better than this or she would die. She felt faint and staggered. 'Some water, please.'

'Well, you walked past a stream on your way from the canal.' But she fetched her some fresh water in another bucket with a wooden ladle. While she was gone, Olivia tugged at her wedding band and when the dairymaid returned she held it out in her palm. 'Is this enough payment?' She added quickly, 'It was my mother's. She's dead now.'

'I'll ask me mam.' The girl took the ring and went off in the direction of a low stone building. Olivia wondered if she would steal from her as the street boy had. It seemed a long time before she returned.

Olivia sat with her back against the wooden stall as the cows, waiting to be milked, shifted and grumbled restlessly. The water refreshed her. She drank copiously and was on her feet when the dairymaid returned with two bread cakes, a hunk of cheese wrapped in a cloth and two apples.

'Me mam says you can keep the calico 'cos your ring was real gold.'

'Thank you.' Olivia began to tear at the bread with her teeth straight away.

'Ta-ra, then,' the girl said and moved her stool to the next stall.

'Good day to you. And thank you.'

The sun came up over the water meadows and she

sat in its rays to eat her breakfast. She had enough food for the day and lingered, trying to work out a plan. Although she felt bedraggled and must look a sight, her gown was neat and made of good cloth, which had impressed the dairymaid. She was clearly not some street woman like the one who had stolen her bag. And she had to earn a living somehow.

Fortified by food, she felt well again, and she knew she could work hard. But her demeanour and skills were those of a well-born housekeeper and no one would be foolish enough to give her a trusted position without knowledge of her background. She was obviously too educated to be a kitchen-maid or farmgirl.

There were not many options for her. But she was pretty – a beauty, Jessup had said – and that was something she could sell. After all, her body had been used for gain twice already in her life: the first time when she had become Hesley's wife so that he could have her fortune, and last night when he had not thought twice about forcing her to pay his gambling debt. She could not accept being used in that way, but an unscrupulous man like Jessup expected it of her. It was what men did with women they did not respect. And, she thought painfully, it was what women did for payment when they had no alternative. At the moment, she had none.

If she was considered a prize by her husband's gambling friends, others would pay for the privilege of using her body. Is that not what her uncle had done with Miss Trent? And with others before her? There must be more gentlemen like him, without a wife or, indeed, seeking comfort outside the marriage bed. She had an idea of what she was worth. Jessup's wager had given her an indication. She would be able to pay rent on a cottage and employ a servant. All she needed was to get away from the town where she might be recognized.

She reflected on these ideas as she walked along the towpath, dodging into hedges when heavy horses drawing barges plodded by. No doubt there was money to be made from bargemen, but that was not what she had in mind. A horseman, smartly dressed for business in town, had passed her and given her more than a passing glance. She wondered if he would ride back the same way at the end of his day.

The weather was cold but dry and she made good progress. When she spied a farm building set back from the canal, she trudged across the fields. She found that it was not locked and contained straw. She slept for a long time on the warm bedding and ate more bread and cheese when she woke up. She had no idea of the time as the clouds now hid the sun and the sky was grey. She found a stream, drank and washed, drying herself on the calico square. She had continued to reflect on her idea. Ahead, there was a lock and an inn. If she had money, she might buy a bed for the night.

She saw the rider returning on the towpath, which brought her to her senses. What was she thinking of? He might be as evil as Hesley. To be well attired meant nothing. Jessup had looked like a gentleman but had not behaved as such. She searched for a gap in the scrubby hedgerow in which to hide as the rider went by. In her haste her toes caught at a root, throwing her off balance. A searing pain shot through her ankle. She yelped and sat down heavily, choking back her annoyance. If she had wanted to attract his attention she could not have done better.

He reined in his horse. 'Good afternoon, ma'am. Are you in some difficulty?'

'No, sir. Good day to you.' She hoped he would continue his journey.

'You are in pain, I think.'

'No, I – I am resting.'

'In the hedgerow? I saw you fall. Does it hurt very much?' He dismounted and tethered his animal to the hedge. 'I noticed you on the towpath this morning. Have you been walking all day?'

Oh, no, she thought. She could not run from him. 'I am nearly home, sir.'

'Where is that?'

She looked away silently. Already the lacing on her boot felt uncomfortably tight. She couldn't even get to her feet without help.

'Will you permit me to examine your injury?'

'Very well.'

He knelt beside her, gently removed her boot and manipulated her ankle.

She gave a squeak of pain.

'There is swelling but it is not broken. You are new here, are you not?'

She nodded. 'I was making for the inn.'

'Alone?' He held out his hand. 'Let me help you to your feet.'

He took a step back and stared at her. 'The inn, you say?'

'I have no money. My purse was stolen.'

'Then you may stay with me until you can walk again.'

'No, thank you.' He was not a young man for he had greying hair, but she guessed he had expected her to trust him because he looked hurt by her refusal. 'What will your wife say, sir?' she asked.

'I have no wife, ma'am.'

She realized he was not like Hesley or his friends. He was a kindly gentleman. His horse was from good stock and well cared-for. Silently she picked up her boot.

'I have a sister,' he added, 'who will welcome you.'

'Then thank you,' she replied. He was educated and polite. But his dress was not that of a gentleman. He was more of a countryman, she thought. Perhaps a farmer.

He lifted her on to his saddle and mounted behind her, holding her between his arms as he took up the reins. She panicked when they reached the lock and he turned the horse's head from the canal towards the distant winding gear of the pit. 'Where are we, sir?'

'Mexton Lock. Do you know it?'

'Where do you take me?'

'To my home, as I have told you.'

'But you are riding towards a pithead.'

'Indeed I am. I shall turn off the track shortly. I live in a disused farmhouse a short distance from the pit village.'

He was taking her to within a stone's throw of Mexton Pit! No matter, she thought. Hesley never visited the mine and the manager she had known as a child had died. A younger man had taken his place and did not visit Hill Top House. All Hesley's mining dealings were done through Jessup's legal office in town. She smiled at the irony in this turn of events.

Chapter 23

'Have you news from Hill Top House, Father?' Jared had come home from Manchester to install new steam hammers at his father's forge. Sir William had released him from his position at Kimber Deep to study and he had used his learning to help his father expand their thriving concern.

During his absence from the South Riding he had tried to forget Olivia but could not. Finally he had asked after her in his letters home and had received news of Hesley's return. 'But what of Olivia?' he had asked again. 'She is mistress of Hill Top House,' was all his father would say. Neither would his mother be drawn. He guessed they knew of his affection for Olivia and feared for the safety of both. He recalled his father being very persuasive about Manchester and at the time it had seemed the right thing to do.

Now Jared was an assured and confident gentleman, respected among local ironmasters, but – oh, how he regretted leaving Olivia. Yet what else could he have done? He had no doubt that old Hesley would have locked her away if he had even suspected a liaison. Perhaps now that her husband was at home they might meet openly on social occasions. He wondered how Hesley would react to that.

Jared was living with his family again. They were drinking coffee in the drawing room after dinner. It was new to the household: Jared had acquired a taste for it in Manchester. His mother and sisters didn't like it, and had gone to help the maid put away the china.

'No,' his father replied, 'but it's interesting that you should want to know. Old Samuel Mexton's lawyer has asked to see me.'

'Mr Withers?'

'Yes. It's about your mother's half-brother, I believe.'

'I had heard he was very ill, Father.'

'Who from?'

'I met the pit manager from Kimber Deep. He knows Hesley's man at Mexton. I asked about Olivia but he had no other knowledge of the family. Do you know anything, Father? I'm worried about Olivia.'

His father gave him a long, hard look. 'So is your mother. She heard from the vicar's wife that Olivia had stopped going to that little church. Leastways, no one's seen her for a month.'

'Didn't they call on her to find out why?'

'No one goes to Hill Top House unless they're invited, these days.'

'Well, I shall. She may be ill too.'

'Wait, son. Come with me to the lawyer tomorrow. He will have news.'

'She left on her own? Why? What happened to make her go? I must find her! She will be in danger. Why has Hesley made no effort to look for her? Why haven't you?' Jared had leaped to his feet in the lawyer's office. What kind of husband did not search for his wife? Hesley didn't deserve her. Nobody did! She was too good for all of them.

Withers was frowning. 'Hesley Mexton doesn't instruct me now. He uses Jessup.'

'Then how do you know about old Hesley?' his father asked.

'He is dying and his apothecary asked me to visit. I'm still a trustee for the pit. That was in old Samuel's will. Young Hesley will take charge of his grandfather's mine.'

'He has a manager,' Jared said.

'The new one is not much older than you and he does as he's told.'

'Well, Hesley's university education will come in useful after all,' Jared went on wryly. But he didn't want to waste any more time worrying about Hesley or his grandfather. He was anxious to be away making his own enquiries for Olivia. Somebody must have seen her when she left. She couldn't just have disappeared. 'Have you finished with us, sir?' he added.

'Rum lot, the Mextons,' his father commented, as they left the office.

'Mother's one of them.'

316

'Aye, she is. Blood's thicker than water, and Mr Withers was right to tell us. She'll be wanting to see old Hesley before he passes on.'

'I'm going there now. I want to know what's happened.'

'Wait until after dinner, son. We'll all go.'

'No. It's been too long already. I'll ride ahead and meet you there at tea-time.'

'Good day to you.' Jared slid down from his horse and walked her towards the old walled garden. 'Are you from Hill Top House?'

The servant girl glanced towards him. 'I might be. What do you want?'

'Is your master at home?'

She tossed her head in the direction of the house. 'You'll find him there.' She sat on a rock to unlace her boots and ease her aching feet.

He led his horse into the yard, expecting Matt to appear from the stable. He tethered the animal himself, uneasy with the silence. No one answered the jangling bell at the front door so he walked unannounced into the kitchen where another girl was stacking crockery on the dresser.

'Who are you?' she demanded, startled.

'I'd like to see the master.'

'You'll have to ask Mrs Cookson.'

'Where is your mistress?'

The girl's eyes took on a guarded expression. 'She's gone.'

'Gone where?'

317

'Left. She took the trap into town one day and never came back.'

'That's enough, Mary.' Mrs Cookson had walked into the kitchen, carrying a foul-smelling pail covered with a pile of soiled linen. 'Take this bucket to the privy and find Eliza to wash these.' She turned to Jared. 'I wondered when you'd show your face again. Is she with you?'

'Olivia?' Jared felt anxious. 'No, she isn't. When did she leave?'

'A few weeks ago. I'd thought she'd gone to her aunty Caroline.'

'We haven't seen her. Why did she leave?'

'Not for me to say. I don't interfere between man and wife. But things weren't right, that's for sure.'

Jared remembered some of the things Olivia had said about Hesley. 'Did he beat her?'

'You stay away from him. He's got enough with his grandfather.' Jared caught the firmness in Mrs Cookson's tone and remembered how loyal she was to this household. His eyes followed the girl as she went outside with the linen. 'How is old Hesley?'

'He's dying. He won't admit it, and won't have it said outside the house, but it's true enough. Never been right since he took the rock in his back at the pithead.'

'I didn't know. Neither did Mother, I'm sure. Where's his grandson? I want to talk to him.'

'I don't advise it, sir. He's quiet at the moment, but you never can tell with him. The least thing sets him off.'

'Is that why Olivia left?'

'Couldn't say, sir.'

'Tell me, woman! What happened?'

'Honest, sir, I don't rightly know. I were over in t' stables wi' Matt. But it were after one of his late-night gambling parties.'

'And nobody has seen her since?'

Mrs Cookson shrugged. 'That governess was supposed to look after her and all she did was lead her astray. I knew about you two meeting of a Sunday, even if her husband didn't.'

Jared detected a sneer in her voice, which he ignored. 'You should have sent word to my mother. She's old Hesley's sister, for God's sake!'

'I had my orders, sir.'

'What does Adam Harvey say about old Hesley?'

'He says nothing to me or Matt, except when to give him his medicines.'

'You should have told us,' he said again, angrily, but his thoughts were with Olivia. Where had she gone and who was she with? The governess, maybe? He had no idea where Miss Trent was either. But maybe he could find out. A woman travelling alone would have been noticed.

Had they planned their escape together from Hill Top House? He thought not. Olivia had been devastated when Miss Trent had left. Perhaps they had corresponded since and Olivia had made up their quarrel. He wished he knew. Why had he listened to his conscience and stayed away? He could have helped her – he'd wanted to. But his misplaced respect for her sham of a marriage had kept him away. He had to find her, and prayed she would be in good health. He hoped he was not too late.

He tried the curate's wife at the little church. She had not seen Miss Trent or Olivia so he rode across the moor to Blackstone. Neither woman had been there either. It was past five in the afternoon when Hill Top House was in his sights again. As he approached the farmyard he saw his parents' trap making slow progress up the track from the town.

'I'll be in as soon as I've seen to the horse.' Jared held the mare's head as his father helped his mother down from the trap. They were anxious about this visit and pleased to see him. As he led the horse to the barn, he wondered again why Matt had not appeared from the stables. Another horse was already stabled there. Jared recognized it. Mr Harvey, the apothecary, was visiting too.

He went into the hall through the empty kitchen. The dining-room door stood open and he saw Mary sweeping up broken china. The chairs were all over the place. He was reminded of a time in his youth when he had been the cause of such destruction. She looked up in alarm as he stood in the doorway and surveyed the congealing food on the table and the floor.

'They're all upstairs, sir,' she said nervously.

As he went up he remembered his fight with Hesley and his anxiety for Olivia increased. He prayed she had come to no harm. He followed the hushed voices to old Hesley's bedchamber. He had not seen his uncle since he had run Jared off his land with a shotgun and was shocked by his gaunt features and sallow colour, yellow against the bed linen. His eyes were closed and his breathing rattled in his throat.

Matt was here, and Mrs Cookson. Mr Harvey was talking quietly to Jared's father, while his mother stared at her half-brother.

'Where's Hesley?' Jared asked.

His father steered him out of the chamber.

'What's been going on, Father? There's been a fight downstairs.'

'Not a fight, son. It's young Hesley, he takes too much drink.'

'He smashed the china?'

'Mrs Cookson says it's happened before.'

'Where is he now?'

'Sleeping it off.'

'Dear God, he's a drunkard. No wonder Olivia left him.'

His father was shaking his head. 'It's not only that. It's— Well, the apothecary says it's due to the heat in the West Indies. His brain was overheated . . . He has fits of anger, loses control and . . .'

'He's going mad?'

Benjamin covered his eyes with a hand. 'It comes and goes, apparently. But don't tell your mother. Her brother is dying and she worries for Olivia.'

'I should think Olivia is best away from this,' Jared said bitterly.

'Perhaps that was why she left. Matt confirmed what Withers said about the trap.'

'Where is she, Father?'

'I don't know, son. I am as troubled as you. You may be right about her going to the governess. That woman had a good head on her shoulders.'

'She was old Hesley's mistress.'

'Calm yourself, Jared. Olivia has covered her tracks. I think she knew what she was doing.'

'Her life here must have been unbearable for her take to such action. I must find her. I must!'

'Hesley might know something. He's in his chamber. Matt put laudanum in his wine to calm him.'

'I'll talk to him now.'

The stench hit Jared as he opened the door. Young Hesley was slewed across the bed, his shirt front covered with spilled food and vomit. One of the stable lads was with him. He had removed his boots and trousers, which were wet and soiled. He had placed them in a laundry pail and was attempting to wash the emaciated body and legs. Jared picked up the bowl of water from the washstand and held it closer to the bed.

'Thank you, sir.'

'How long has he been like this?'

'He's had these turns ever since he came back from the West Indies. Not as bad as this until just recent, though, sir.' The lad rinsed his cloth in the bowl.

Jared hated Hesley, but would not have wished this on him – not even on his worst enemy. He wondered again what Olivia had had to endure in this house and his anxiety deepened. Had Hesley harmed her? But Hesley was in no fit state to answer any of Jared's questions and he had to be content with what the servants could tell him. They were of no help. He had to find her soon! He hoped he would not be too late when he did.

'I told you, sister, I found her on the towpath.'

'She is educated, Toby, and from a good home. Someone must be searching for her. Has she said anything to you?'

'Only that her name is Livvy Smith and she has no family. Give her more time.'

'She has been with us for almost a month, dearest,' Anna pointed out.

'And you are sure you are happy for her to stay?'

'If she wants to. She will be useful in the house. I am not as young as I used to be.'

'Your mission manages quite well without you. It is right for you to spend more time with me.' Tobias smiled fondly at his sister.

'God has provided, as He always does. But I have been away for a month already this year. I shall return soon.'

Olivia listened through the open scullery door as she washed the pots after tea. They were chapelgoers, they said, and had a following in the village. That was the only danger, she thought. The colliers and their families gathered in the barn on Sundays.

She told them she was church and asked if they minded. They were good people, she judged. They gave her a Bible to read in her chamber on the Sabbath. She retreated there, staying away from the barn. There were other books in the house, too. She might be content here, she thought. When they offered her a position, she accepted without misgiving. She felt safe with them and had found employment.

Livvy Smith became housekeeper to Tobias and Anna Holmes. She covered her gown with a large jute apron and made a plain calico bonnet with a forward brim that shielded her face and hid her abundant fair hair. Anna gave her a shawl, which she knotted around her shoulders on cold days. When she caught sight of herself in a darkened window she thought she looked like a slighter version of Mrs Cookson.

At first their kindness made her weep. She relived her recent traumas every night but the rough, heavy work helped her to sleep and overcome them. It would take time and she was determined to go forward with her life. She became a hardworking housekeeper for her benefactors. She filled her days with cleaning, cooking, washing and ironing. In fine weather she dug the garden. Tobias brought seed potatoes from town and she discovered overgrown gooseberry bushes and lavender in the neglected garden.

In the evenings, they read by the fire. When the Holmeses had mission meetings in their house, Livvy took her book to her chamber and read until the candle guttered. She was not happy. She did not know how to be happy, she thought. But she was content. She was employed as their servant yet they treated her as an equal. Before long she was calling them Toby and Anna and she was Livvy. She became a different woman, a new woman with a new life. The past was gone. Only the future mattered now.

'Won't you come with us to town today, Livvy?' Anna asked one morning. 'Toby is taking the trap.'

'There is plenty of work for me to do here.'

'But you would enjoy the company of the other ladies at our meeting.'

'Perhaps next time.'

'Very well.' Anna turned to address her brother. 'While we are in town will you purchase more writing supplies for the Sunday school?'

Livvy stacked the breakfast bowls on a wooden tray as brother and sister talked of their needs for the Mexton villagers. She felt secure in their home and was willing to be their housekeeper, if it allowed them more time for their mission work.

They did not press her for details of her past, or insist that she accompany them to their meetings. They were tolerant of her need for privacy, and she thanked the Lord every day for her good fortune in meeting Toby on the towpath. She shuddered when she thought of what she might otherwise have become.

She enjoyed her solitude when Anna and Toby went into town. There was much support for the chapel among the tradesmen and artisans who relied on coal for their livelihoods and who saw the toll it took on families who mined it. They had regular meetings of mission leaders from the surrounding villages while their ladies planned ways to raise funds and organized their clothing exchange. At Livvy's request, Anna had brought her hard-wearing, coarse-textured servants' garb for every day and she repaired and pressed her old day gown to keep it for Sunday best.

When they returned, Anna came in first and went upstairs to remove her cloak and bonnet, leaving her brother to take off his coat and shake it out in the scullery. Livvy was sitting by the window with her book. 'Leave it in there,' she called. 'I'll brush it for you later.'

He walked into the kitchen. A stew of butcher's meat, vegetables and barley was simmering over the fire, and the scrubbed wooden table was laid for the three of them. Newly baked bread still warm from the oven was cooling by the hearth.

He surveyed the scene and thought how comfortable Livvy looked, how well she fitted in with their life and how skilled she was as a housekeeper. 'Our minister was there and very excited that the new act will soon become law. He has our application for chapel registration with York already. Any day now he expects to hear from them that he will be able to solemnize marriages in our chapel.'

Livvy closed her book and stood up, smiling. 'You have had a good meeting?'

'Yes, all our leaders were there. Tell Livvy about your ladies' gathering, Anna.'

Anna did, and added at the end, 'They talked of a gentleman making enquiries about a lady. He had visited them before, they said, looking for – for a relative, I suppose. Her pony and trap were found abandoned at the crossroads out of town and he is worried for her safety.'

'Oh! Did he say who he was?'

'He did not give his name. But he seemed anxious to locate her.'

'His daughter, perhaps?'

Anna shook his head. 'He said the lady was of age. He was only a little older than that himself. Her brother or husband, they thought. He was well-to-do and they felt sorry for him.'

'I should be concerned if Anna had disappeared like that,' Toby commented.

'Are there people who might care for your safety, my dear?' Anna asked Livvy casually.

'I'm afraid not. I wish it were so,' she replied honestly. But she feared Hesley was trying to track her. He would haul her back to Hill Top House to avoid a scandal. She did not want him to find her and fretted for several days about this news.

It hardened her resolve to stay out of the town. No one took any notice of her out here, in her dowdy work dress and the plain bonnet that hid her long, light hair. They would never dream she was the lady for whom he was looking.

She was no longer a lady and she was content. She was an ordinary working woman who enjoyed the toil and satisfaction of helping those less fortunate than herself. She had found a real home with a brother and sister who felt the same.

Anna waited until Livvy had retired to her chamber before broaching the subject again. 'But, Toby, my dearest, what are you thinking of? You know nothing about her.'

'I know that she is educated and well-bred. Her character and manner tell me that. She is fleeing from something or more likely some*one*. A tyrannical father or unwanted suitor, perhaps.'

'Then you must try to return her.'

'For her to flee again and risk falling into the worst kind of company? I tell you, sister, she had no idea of the danger she was in, out on the towpath all alone. She is educated, yes, but innocent in the ways of the wider world. I am sure she had not considered what might happen to her. Besides, she says she is of age. She is free to do as she wishes.'

'Unless she has a husband.'

'There is no wedding band.'

'No. I noticed that too. But I fancy there is a faint mark where she might have worn one.'

'I looked also, but could not detect a trace.'

'Even so, we know nothing about her.'

'Anna, you shock me! When have we questioned God's work? Do we not teach that all have sinned and all can be saved?'

'Dearest brother, you have brought her into your home, into your life.' Anna gazed at her younger brother. She had not seen him so enamoured of a task as this one. His mission to save this woman was as intense as any he had ever tackled. 'She is more to you than just a wayward soul to be saved, isn't she?'

'She stirs a passion in me that has been dormant for too long. It has been there from the moment I set eyes on her when I rode by that morning. I thought about her all day, and when she was still there on the towpath on my return, I knew it was God's will that she had waited for me and that I should bring her here.'

'And so you have.'

'Anna, dearest, I have determined to give my life to

the service of our chapel, as you have. As our parents wished us to. I had made a decision not to seek a wife, but I believe that God has sent Livvy to me for this purpose.'

'Had you not thought of Harriet in the same way?'

'Why, no! She is as a sister to me. I believe I could love Livvy as a wife.'

'Do take care, Toby. There is unhappiness in Livvy's eyes. It is in her heart and, I suspect, her soul.'

'She will unburden herself to me in time. I shall not press her, so please do not ask me to. She is an adult, and if she has a past she will not be the only one—' He stopped. 'I'm sorry, Anna. I did not mean to hurt you with those words.'

'Toby, my past is gone for good. If Livvy has endured anything like I have, she will be happy to turn away from it. But it may come back to haunt her. You should be prepared for that, my dear.'

'Of course.' He hugged his sister. 'You have come through, have you not?'

'Indeed I have. My faith has been my support. And I should return to my own mission. I have left Harriet for too long to cope on her own.' Anna paused.

'But she is more than capable.'

'The work increases every year. More mines and factories in the Riding mean more poor souls are forced from the countryside into the smoke-ridden towns. Many cannot make the adjustment. There is much to be done.'

'You will stay with me until I have settled Livvy's future?'

'As long as you make haste.'

Chapter 24

'Livvy.' Toby held out his hand. 'Come and sit with me by the fire.'

She looked up from the book she was reading by the window.

'Come, my dear. I wish to talk to you,' he added gently.

She put down her book and moved to sit on a chair opposite him. She thought he was quite a handsome man, although his face was lined and his hair was quite grey at the temples. She wondered what he had in mind for her.

'Are you settled with us here?'

'Why, yes. I am surprised you ask.'

'Have you thought about your future?'

She caught her breath. Was he going to ask her to move on? She did not want to leave. She dared not.

It would mean working in another mission, perhaps nearer the town where she would be recognized. 'I am content here with you and Anna,' she answered truthfully.

She saw a light come into his eyes. 'Are you? Are you truly happy here?'

Livvy hesitated. The household was not a comfortable one. Indeed, her life was frugal compared with Hill Top House and her daily routine was tiring. But she was valued here, and her wishes were considered to be as important as theirs. She worked diligently because she wanted to, not because she felt she had to do their bidding. This was a wealthy house, yet the wealth was not measured in money but in something much more valuable, and she marvelled that she had settled so quickly.

True happiness, though, was something she had known briefly with Jared. It pained her to recall those stolen moments with him because they would never be repeated. No, happiness was something she could not have. Nor did she seek it. Not any longer. It was not for her. But she had no wish to upset her friends and answered, 'Yes, I am.'

'Have you thought about your future, my dear?' Toby pressed.

'Are you going to send me away?' she asked tentatively.

'Do you want to leave?'

'No, but if it is your wish, I shall go.' She suspected that Anna would like her to work in her mission on the other side of the Riding. She did not say much about it and Livvy respected her silence, as they respected hers.

'And if it is my wish that you stay?'

'I shall stay and continue to work here.'

'Anna must return to her own mission soon.'

'Then you will have more need of me here.'

He smiled at her. 'Yes, indeed. However, we should consider your reputation if you stay here when Anna leaves.'

Livvy would have laughed if she had not thought it would cause him offence. What reputation had she? Toby did not know who she was or where she came from.

'I am your housekeeper, yours and Anna's. Can that not continue when she leaves?'

'Your young age and my unmarried status would set tongues wagging.'

She blushed. Such matters had never been discussed in this kitchen.

'Oh, but anyone who knows you would not imagine that you would ever—' She stopped, and there was an embarrassed silence. Of course, everyone knew what a fine man of integrity Tobias Holmes was. But they did not know about her. She guessed that they thought of her as a rescued street woman who was grateful for a home. They would think that she might slip back into her old ways, given half a chance.

While his sister was living in the household, Toby's followers were comfortable with her. But when Anna left? Oh, yes, they would fear for their leader's reputation, not hers. Did they think she would seduce him under cover of night? Become with child so that he would be obliged to make her his wife? The idea was laughable, but Livvy had the sense to see that it was a real dilemma for Toby.

She said, 'Of course, you have a position to uphold. I shall leave as you suggest.' But she wanted so desperately to stay that it must have shown in her tone. She was sure he did not believe her. He was a clever man, he had travelled widely and talked of his journeys, the people he had met. She guessed that he knew she wanted to stay.

'I am not suggesting you leave, my dear. You are happy here and so am I. Very happy.' He smiled at her again.

'But I cannot stay if, as you say—'

He was holding his hands palm down in the gesture that she knew meant 'Please be quiet and listen.'

'You can stay as my wife.'

She stared at him, wide-eyed, as he turned over his hands and reached out towards her. 'Would you consent to be my wife, Livvy?'

Wife? *Wife?* Of course she could not. She was someone else's wife, but she dared not say so. Toby was an honourable man, and if he knew her true position in the Riding, he would have no choice but to return her to her husband. She floundered, seeking the right words. At last she said, 'I am honoured and flattered that you hold me in such high esteem. But you must not take me as your wife because you feel sorry for me. You deserve better than that, Toby. You deserve better than me.'

'And when I hear you say such things I know I am right to ask you. Your concern for the sensibilities of others is commendable. I do not ask you to marry me because I pity you. I ask you to be my wife because I believe that I can love you.'

'You do not love me now?'

'I shall! I feel a desire for you that I have not known since I was – a younger man.' He remembered when he had indulged that passion with a young lady who resembled Livvy. And how she had loved him too. He added, 'I must be truthful with you. In the past I have loved a woman and, to my shame, I did not marry her. This time I shall not make that mistake.'

Eventually she said, 'I do not love you as a wife should love her husband.'

He looked disappointed but rallied: 'Is your heart elsewhere? In your past?'

'No,' she answered. But it was. It was with Jared. 'I love you as Anna loves you, only as a sister loves her brother.'

His voice was low and he did not look at her. 'If you will allow me through our marriage vows, my dear, I shall teach you how to love me as your husband.'

She did not mistake his meaning. That was not love. That was what husbands expected of their wives when they were married. To seal their vows and beget heirs.

She said, 'You cannot marry me. You do not know what I have done.' She hesitated and her voice dropped to a whisper: 'I am not a maid.'

'Do you think I had not guessed that? You were running from some*thing* or some*one* in your past when I found you. You had been ill-used by those who should have known better.'

Alarmed at this statement, she exclaimed, 'Why do you say that? What do you know of my past?'

'Nothing, my love, save what you choose to tell me. I hope that, one day, you will trust me enough to unburden yourself further and allow me to help you overcome your pain.'

'Please do not press me on that, Toby.'

His voice remained low. 'I shall not. You need not fear.'

This only increased her agitation at her deception. 'I cannot marry you.'

'Of course you can,' he argued softly. 'My forgiveness for what you were was given when I hoisted you onto my horse that day by the canal. I do not wish to live without you and I must when Anna leaves.'

'You will send me away?'

He sighed. 'You do understand what I mean when I say you should not stay in this house with me unless we marry? I desire you and I am not made of stone. You cannot stay unless you become my wife.'

Livvy understood only too well. She was already thinking she would have to run away, leave under cover of darkness, and she did not want that. Were she in the next county she might have said yes to marriage with him. She cared not for the laws of the land – they had served her ill in her short life. But a ceremony here meant the church in the town, a vicar who might recognize her and know she already had a husband, alive and well and seeking her return.

She swallowed and replied, 'I – I . . . If you wish it,

I do not seek your hand in marriage to give you the comfort you desire.'

The horror on his face startled her. 'Livvy! How can you even think of it? Would you give credence to the gossip? I am a mission leader! How can I betray my fellows in such a way? No, marriage is the only solution.' He softened. 'It is what I want for us. Please say yes.'

'I cannot.' She shook her head emphatically. 'I cannot stand in the church and make the vows . . .'

'Of course, I see. You are afraid of meeting with your past life in the town.' He knelt by her side and held her hand tenderly. 'Dearest Livvy, if you can bring yourself to agree to become my wife, to do this one thing for me, we shall be the first to have our union blessed in our chapel.'

'Not the parish church?'

'Why, no. As I said, we shall have notice soon from York that our chapel is registered for marriages. Our own Wesleyan minister will conduct the service. It will make me so happy.'

A marriage with Toby? Was it possible? She had found a safe and caring home with him and Anna. She gazed at him. If only he were Jared she would not hesitate. She would have lived with Jared outside marriage, even had his child outside wedlock. If that was wicked of her, then so be it. It was the only way she could ever be truly happy. But that was impossible for her. Toby was a fine man and would make any woman a good husband. He was strong in spirit and kind in heart, and she wondered why he had not

336

married. As his wife, she would have a proper name, a proper life.

No one who went to the chapel knew her as Hesley Mexton's wife. Chapel was for the artisan and labouring classes. She was Livvy Smith now, and Livvy Smith had not been married before. Toby knew she was not a maid and did not seem to mind. She would be protected from prying eyes and secure in a new life as Toby's wife.

She thought briefly that she would go to gaol if anyone found out. But, she considered rashly, it would be worth it to stay in this loving home. She put her doubts to the back of her mind and said, 'Very well. I will marry you.'

When he told Anna that Livvy had agreed to become his wife, she replied, 'I am pleased for you and wish you both every happiness.'

'You do not sound joyful.'

'There is a side of her that we do not know. Do not expect too much.'

'She has an inner strength, sister. When we are as one, she will open up to me, I am sure.'

Anna sighed. 'I hope so. Truly, I do.'

Livvy wore her old day gown, and trimmed a straw bonnet with flowers. The minister, misreading her nervousness and uncertainty, assured them that the chapel was now registered with York and their marriage would be a proper one. They had a simple ceremony, which Anna attended with them. She left directly afterwards to go back to her own mission and Toby drove the trap, carrying his new bride, to the empty farmhouse.

As soon as they were inside the door he embraced her tightly. 'Thank you, dearest, for agreeing to marry me. We shall learn to love each other as husband and wife. Let us begin now.' He led her upstairs to his chamber and the bed that they would share.

Livvy took off her best dress and laid it carefully over the wooden ottoman. She knew what her duty was, and while he was disrobing she removed her undergarments and slid between the sheets.

When he climbed in beside her he was wearing his night attire. 'My dear,' he exclaimed, 'where is your nightgown?'

'Is this not what you wish?'

'Well, I – that is, I had not expected to see you.'

She put her arms above her head and opened her legs.

He owned to being shocked, but he had a burgeoning hunger for her and he quickly shed his own garment. He wished he had taken longer, for his pleasure was over far too soon. He lay there afterwards, thinking how little she had responded to him. His memories of lovemaking as a young man were of eagerness and girlish thrills from the ladies. They had sought union as much as he. He was older now. But Livvy was not. Yet she had been willing. Perhaps he had rushed her, he reasoned. He must be patient. Tonight he would be better prepared, less anxious, and they would learn to enjoy each other in ways that only married people could.

But that night she was no different. The same passive offering and lack of passion. When it was over she sat up, drew her nightgown over her head, turned her back on him and went to sleep. He lay awake, fretting. There seemed to be no desire on her part. Livvy was compliant with his wishes, but she should expect more from him for herself, and he did not know how to encourage her.

If she did not warm to this part of their marriage how could he ever hope that she would love him? Would she tire of him and seek a more youthful husband? He did not believe that. Livvy, his adorable young wife, was a dispassionate and cold woman in the marriage bed. It shook him to the core.

Livvy was pleased he had got it over with quickly. Her previous experiences had been with rough, greedy men who called themselves gentlemen but did not behave as such in the bedchamber. Toby was different. He was vigorous, yet kind and gentle in his manner and his murmurings. He had said he did not mind if she preferred to wear her chemise or nightgown while he lay with her, so she did. This part of her new marriage would be tolerable if nothing else.

For nothing else was all she had.

'The coal stocks are low, Father.' Jared stood in the office doorway at his father's forge. He filled the space, blocking out the light and casting his shadow over the large oak desk.

'I don't know what's going on at Mexton Pit, these

days,' his father complained. 'The barges used to arrive regular as clockwork, but now I never know when to expect one.'

'The new seam is good, isn't it?'

'Oh, aye. As good as Swinborough's.'

'And the miners are back on full pay?'

'What's left of them. A lot of 'em moved on after the old manager died.'

'Well, it should be here, then! We can't run the steam engines without a regular supply of coal. If Mexton can't ship it, we'll go elsewhere.'

'Calm down. I expect it's young Hesley, having one of his turns.'

'He never goes to the mine. He leaves everything to the manager.'

'That's the trouble. They said at the lodge he dismissed the man.'

'What? He was young but he knew about mining.'

'There was a difference of opinion over the way he ran the pit. From what I hear Hesley wanted him to run the mine as he tried to run the sugar plantation.'

Jared gave a hollow laugh. 'When all his workers were slaves? The man's mad.'

His father remained silent.

'Can't something be done about him, Father? He shouldn't be in control of anything if he's drunk and filled with laudanum.'

'It's his mine, son.'

'It's as much Olivia's. It was her money that saved it.'

'Don't start on about his wife again. You couldn't find her, and Hesley doesn't want her. Wherever she is, she's probably better off than she would be with him.'

'If she's still alive,' Jared muttered bitterly.

'Don't say that. She'll be with the governess. You'll see.'

'That's what worries me!' He stopped and took a deep breath. He had searched tirelessly for Olivia but it wasn't his father's fault that she had disappeared. 'What are we going to do about this coal, Father? Shall I put in an order at Kimber Deep?'

'No, son. Why don't you ride over to Mexton Pit and find out what's going on there? See if Hesley's found a new manager yet.'

Jared decided his father was right. Nobody was holding the reins at Mexton. What was Hesley thinking? He could sell all the coal he could mine, and for a good price now.

Jared had not ridden to Mexton Pit for years. As he walked his horse slowly along the towpath he remembered Tobias Holmes and his sister with affection, but Olivia had kept him away from their mission. The new pithead was a couple of miles from the old one and the coal had to be carted further to the canal for transport to the forge. Kimber Deep had its own rail lines for drawing coal carts to the barges, but the Mexton cart track, laid with stone excavated from the new shaft, was already lined with ruts and littered with pot-holes. There was some activity at the engine house.

'Halloo!' he called. A working man came out to him. 'Are you in charge?'

The man pushed back his cap. 'You might say that. What's your business?'

'Is Mexton about?'

'Who's asking for him?'

'Tyler. He supplies coal for our forge.'

'Then you'll know he's badly.'

'Not the master, his grandson. Is he about?'

'He's never set foot in this place and never likely to.'

'Who do you answer to, then?'

'I keep the records and Jessup in town has the other papers. He sends one of his clerks to pay the men.'

'Well, your shipment is overdue.'

'That's as may be.'

Jared dismounted. 'I see you've a steam engine now.'

'When it's working. I do me best, but t' old manager that left knew more about it than I do. Horses are more reliable any day.'

'Shall I have a look at it for you? I worked with the engine at Kimber Deep.'

'They 'ave a proper engineer to keep it going. And that isn't you, sir. You leave my engine alone.'

Jared let the matter drop. 'When d'you think you can get a barge of coal down to us?'

'End of the week, I reckon.'

Jared led his horse to the water trough. The Mextons were feckless. They needed a better steam engine and twice the number of miners. He remounted and rode back to the town, arriving at the Red Lion as the carrier came through. He recognized one of the passengers straight away.

'Sarah?'

She looked up from checking her bag as it fell from the cart. She had hardly changed, he thought. Pretty and personable. Plainly dressed in a simple bonnet and cloak. 'Jared Tyler! My, how handsome you've grown!'

'You too. Teaching must suit you.'

'It does.'

'Where is your position?'

'County Durham. And you, are you still at Kimber Deep?'

'With my father at the forge.' A thought occurred to him. 'I don't suppose you've come across a teacher by the name of Trent, have you?'

Sarah shook her head. 'Can't say I have.' She frowned. 'Although now you come to mention it, I believe I have heard . . . What's her Christian name?'

'I don't know.'

'Trent . . . I'm sure I've heard it somewhere.'

'Where? Try to remember,' he said anxiously.

She looked at him steadily. 'It may come to me later. I must go home now. My mother is ill.'

'I'm sorry to hear that. I hope she recovers.'

'Thank you. Why don't you join our Sunday meeting in the barn this week?'

Jared agreed. If Sarah remembered and he found the governess, he might find Olivia too.

Chapter 25

'Who's there?' Harriet was used to being alone in Anna's cottage outside the asylum now. But night had fallen and she was not expecting a visitor.

'Open the door, Harriet. It is I. I am come home.'

'Anna!' Harriet leaped to her feet, drew back the bolts and turned the key. She grasped her arms and pulled her into the kitchen. 'Praise be! Where is your box?'

'It will be here tomorrow, with supplies for the mission. The post was delayed, and I did not wish to stay a night at the inn so I walked.'

'You must be tired. Come, sit by the fire. I'll fetch a log.'

The wood was damp and the flames hissed and spat. Harriet lifted the heavy blackened kettle and shook it. 'There is a little warm water left. And I have honey.

You won't believe the gifts I have received from the asylum governor's wife! But more of that later. Are you quite well?'

'I said so in my letter, did I not?'

'But that was weeks ago and — and you have stayed away for so long.' Her voice dropped. 'I always fear the worst.'

'Dearest Harriet, it is not my health that has kept me away. There is much to tell you.' Anna flopped into the fireside chair and undid the bow on her bonnet. 'I should really like a drink of warm water and honey.'

Harriet stirred in a little elderflower cordial, too, and handed it to her. 'You have not had any attacks while you have been away?'

Anna reached out to take the mug. 'I have not. You need not worry. I had the weakness when I was young. The physician who attended me then said I would grow out of it and I did.'

Harriet would have preferred it if she had not been the one to cause Anna's relapse. But she had recovered and not had another. 'Drink,' she urged.

Anne moulded her hands around the warm stoneware mug. 'Delicious.'

'Is — is Tobias well?' Harriet asked tentatively.

'Very. Never better.'

'He will miss your help now you are here.'

'Indeed he will not! That is what I have to tell you. He is married!'

Harriet felt as though her heart had stopped as she absorbed this news. The room was silent. She could not hear the crackling of the fire or the soft whistling of the wind through the shutters. The darkness of the room deepened so that she could no longer see her friend sitting opposite her. She was conscious only of a tiny glow, an ember at the edge of the fire. Her vision centred on it as she tried to focus her thoughts.

Tobias had married. He had found someone else to love. Someone other than her. If she had harboured thoughts of them ever becoming more than friends, those hopes were now extinguished. He had never said anything to her to encourage her affections. He had not needed to. He just had to be there. As he was. A gracious man, who cared more for others than he did himself, and she loved him. The silence continued. It was probably not for very long but it seemed like an age to Harriet. She could think of nothing to say.

'Yes, I was rendered speechless at first, too,' Anna added. 'I had believed he would not marry, that his calling took all of his attention. But, you see, my dear, we must never make up our minds too quickly about our fellows.'

Why not? Harriet screamed silently. She had known from her first meeting with Tobias that she loved him. From the way he had hoisted his sister's box onto the carrier's cart and taken his leave of her – nay, of them both – with such tender affection. She'd thought his affection for her had grown. *She knew it had.* But not in the way she wished.

She was his second sister, that was all. Where Anna was the elder, she was the younger, and she had basked in that, never having experienced such regard before in her life. But she loved him as a woman loves a man who is her husband, not her brother, and she had continued to hope that that kind of love might be returned.

'Harriet, my dear, you are upset.'

'I – I . . . Well, no. That is, of course I am pleased for Tobias. It is such a surprise. There has been no betrothal, no celebration.'

'No, my dear. Miss Smith is a private, shy person, and she was content to wed in the chapel, which has given us all a great deal of pleasure.'

The daughter of another mission leader, perhaps, whom he had encountered at a chapel meeting. 'Has he known her for long?' she asked.

Anna shook her head. 'He is more than forty, my dear, and has met many suitable ladies in his time. He made his decision almost as soon as he met her. She – she is very beautiful.'

As though that explains everything, Harriet thought. Unconsciously she stroked her hair, tucking in a few loose strands, and looked down at her plain skirt. She was not beautiful, she was presentable. Cleanliness and tidiness had always been important to her. What was beauty, anyway? Tobias was beauty to her, but clearly she did not inspire the same feeling in him. A deep sadness seeped into her heart.

'Miss Smith is agreeable, too?' she asked.

'She is Mrs Holmes now, my dear. I find her a little withdrawn but she is very hardworking. Prodigiously so. She spends her days washing linen and scrubbing floors, even digging the garden in fine weather. Do you know? She reminds me of you in her ways. Clean and tidy, and so very thorough in everything she tackles.'

347

Perhaps she was a pupil at Blackstone, Harriet thought miserably.

'She will make him a very suitable wife. And, well, he is like a youth again in his demeanour,' Anna finished, with a smile.

This served only to deepen Harriet's sadness. She wondered if she had been right to confess her past to him. Had it made a difference to his affection for her? She would never know. She heaved a great sigh. From now on she could be no more than a younger sister to him and would have to be content with that. But she was tired of being content with her allotted role in life. She pasted on a smile. 'Then I am happy for him. You must be exhausted, Anna. I have kept you from your bed. I shall tell you news of the asylum in the morning after you have rested.'

'It is from Toby.' Anna came back from the front door with the letter. 'What can be so urgent that he must write?'

Harriet hoped he was not ill. There were so many with the fever. 'Good news, I trust.'

Anna adjusted the spectacles on her nose, slid a knife point under the seal and unfolded the thick paper. Her eyes roamed quickly through the writing.

Harriet held her breath until she could stand the suspense no longer. 'Is he well?' Her voice came out as a squeak.

Anna looked up sharply. 'Why, yes, of course. Bad news for some, I'm afraid, although you may not find it so. Nor I.'

'How so?'

'Hesley Mexton is dead.'

Dead. Old Hesley had died. Nervous relief washed over Harriet. He was gone for ever and she was free of him at last. Perhaps she could return to Hill Top House and see Olivia. She would like so much to do that. She was overcome with emotion and could not reply.

'You look pleased,' Anna remarked.

'I suppose I am. The man was evil. Do you not think so?'

Anna did, and this surprised Harriet. 'I would not expect you to be so uncharitable, Anna. He was a wicked man, but does not God ask us to forgive the sinners among us?'

'Sometimes He asks too much.'

Harriet could only agree where Hesley Mexton was concerned. 'I can never forgive him.'

'Nor I, for what he did to me.'

'To you?' Harriet was astonished. 'Did you know him?'

Anna did not answer her. 'There is to be a funeral in the town,' she said, 'at the parish church. Gentlemen from all over the Riding will attend.' Suddenly she thrust the letter at Harriet. 'I – I can't read any more.'

'Anna, you are quite pale. What is it?' Harriet feared she would have another attack and got up to fetch her smelling-salts. 'It's him, isn't it? You did know him. It was the mention of his name before that caused your relapse. I am surprised that your brother wrote to you of him.'

'I am well. Truly. Toby knows this news will please me. As it does you.'

'You wished him dead, too?'

'He wanted the same of me once. You see, he blamed me for his only son's death. He said I stopped his son riding and shooting so he was not a good enough horseman for the hunt. But his son was a quiet, studious gentleman. He did not want to hunt. His father made him do it.'

'Old Hesley's son was thrown from his horse,' Harriet said slowly. 'How well did you know him?'

'He came to our readings in the old Dissenters' House. We shared so much,' Anna said. 'I became his wife. Our son was a babe in arms, not long born, when he was killed and I was so *angry* with old Hesley. He was grieving too, I realize now, but we argued and shouted and fought, and I – I attacked him with a dinner fork. The tines were sharp. I drew blood and, at the time, I was not sorry.' She shuddered and swayed a little in her chair. 'But I should have been.'

Harriet was astounded. She would have liked a strong drink to calm her agitation, but that was not possible in this house. She moved a chair to sit beside Anna and put an arm about her shoulders. 'This is too distressing for you. Do not go on.'

'I must. It has been a secret from you for too long. Of all people you will understand. After I had attacked him, he took my baby from me and had me put away in the asylum.'

'In here?' This was too much to bear. 'Oh, Anna, how dreadful.'

'Toby was in America, our parents had died and old Hesley would have nothing more to do with me. I wanted to write to Toby, but I had no paper or ink. Or anyone to help me. He came home eventually for reasons of his own, and I thank the Lord every day for that. When he found me, he took me out. But I could not go back to my son. Or even acknowledge that he is mine. Old Hesley had insisted on that.'

Then her son must be young Hesley, Harriet thought, and wondered how much Anna knew about him. 'What happened to your baby?' she asked.

'I do not know. Toby wrote to the lawyers to ask if I might see him, but they refused. I suppose old Hesley brought him up. Another Hesley in his image. He was keen on his blood line.'

'Oh, Anna, this must have been so awful for you. I had no idea. How on earth do you get through your days knowing you have a son you cannot see?'

'I help others. It gives me hope of a kind, and I have my faith. But I should dearly like to see my son.'

Harriet blew out her cheeks, wondering if it were possible now old Hesley was dead. His cruelty had held no bounds, she thought angrily. 'I should like to dance on old Hesley's grave,' she whispered.

'I too.'

'Then I shall,' Harriet responded firmly. 'I shall go to his funeral, watch as he is lowered into the ground and bury that part of my life with him. I shall lay his ghost to rest for both of us.' Harriet glanced at the letter. 'But women don't go to funerals as a rule.'

'They are not expected to, I grant you, but it will

be a grand affair and no one can prevent you watching from beneath the trees.'

'Can I be spared from here?'

'Indeed you can, now that I am here. We have a capable teacher in the inmate you have trained. The governor wrote of it to Toby. The asylum doctor is to approach the trustees about including our lessons as part of the treatment for some, and providing more funding. Thanks to you, my work here is a success.'

'I shall not be gone for long,' Harriet said.

'Well, Toby will not be at the funeral. His mission is with the Mexton labourers, not the gentry. You need not see him if you do not wish it.'

'Why should I not wish to see him?'

'As I told you, he has a wife now.'

'So?'

Anna gazed at her frankly. 'I did not realize you cared for him in that way until I spoke of his marriage.'

'I don't know what you mean.'

'You do.'

Harriet sank on to her chair. 'It is true I had harboured hopes for more than friendship with him, but he has made his choice and I must live with that. I will stay with one of the leaders in the town, at least until he and his wife are more settled in their home.'

'We shall visit them together, later in the year, when the weather improves,' Anna suggested.

Chapter 26

Harriet watched from the trees as the polished oak coffin adorned with brass was lowered into the ground. She thought that black ebony would have been better for him. A cold black coffin for a man with a cold black heart, like the cold black coal he mined.

It took her several minutes to identify young Hesley. He seemed so much older and thinner, and he staggered as he took up his position as chief mourner. She remembered how his grandfather had dominated his life and wondered if he had ever asked about his mother, or been told the truth. She considered the possibility that Anna might be able to see her son now that old Hesley was dead and gone.

Mr Harvey, the apothecary, was standing beside him, supporting his elbow as he swayed. Then they were lost from view as the grave was surrounded by dark-coated gentlemen in tall black hats, clustering around the vicar.

With a start she recognized the principal from Blackstone. She shrank back into the trees. Dear heaven, she did not want to meet him. He must have been aware of the reputation of Hill Top House, and also that she had been keen to go there. He had probably known all along what would happen to her. She did not notice the tall gentleman behind Hesley at the back of the gathering until the service was over and he detached himself from the group to walk in her direction.

Jared was standing next to his father when he spotted her, half hidden beneath the trees, to see her former lover buried. He supposed she had heeded her conscience in the end and left before she was sent away, after Olivia had married. Still, he expected that old Hesley had paid her handsomely for her services. He might have been mean with his miners but he was not so with his women. The vicar had finished and the mourners were moving away.

'We are invited for sherry and biscuits at the Red Lion,' his father murmured in his ear.

'You go ahead. There's someone I want to talk to.'

'Hesley first.'

'Of course.'

Jared approached Olivia's husband, offered his hand and a few words of condolence. Hesley's grip was weak and his eyes vacant. Jared had not seen him for several weeks and was shocked by the deterioration in his appearance. He looked enquiringly at Adam Harvey, who shook his head to urge him to move on. Clearly it was more than grief that was bringing Hesley down. Jared turned his attention to the woman in the trees.

Even though he had disapproved of the governess as old Hesley's lover, he owned to thanking God that she was there. In fact, his heart was racing as he approached her. She might know where Olivia was. Perhaps she had come on Olivia's account, even, to report on how her husband was faring. Why else would she wish to pay her respects to a man she claimed had corrupted her? Could Olivia be living with her? He frowned. If they were together he was anxious about the life they might be leading.

As soon as Harriet saw Jared her heart soared. He would have news of Olivia! She waited patiently for him to reach her.

'Miss Trent.' He nodded curtly. He did not sound friendly.

'Sir.' She curtsied. 'I trust you are well.' He nodded, but his face was stony and she rushed on, 'Mrs Mexton is also in good health?'

His expression changed so suddenly and so alarmingly that she blinked.

'Is she not with you?' he demanded.

'With me? Why should she be with me?'

'Because she idolized you. You must have known it.'

Harriet felt a thrill of pleasure course through her, which was quickly followed by regret that she had had to leave her – and then anxiety.

'Hesley would not have expected her at the funeral, would he?' she asked.

She watched the colour drain from Jared's face and his expression turn to grief. His eyes looked haunted.

'You have not seen her?' His voice was hoarse. 'You were my last hope. I was certain you would know where she was.'

'Surely Hesley made arrangements for her in the town?'

'Hesley has no care for her, and has not since she left him.'

'*Left* him?'

'She walked out one day and has not been seen since.'

'Olivia is no longer living at Hill Top House?'

'She disappeared some months ago. She took the pony and trap out early and it was found abandoned on the Sheffield road.'

'No!' Tears sprang to Harriet's eyes. 'But where did she go?'

'I thought you might be able to tell us. I thought she would be with you.'

'Did not Hesley search for her?'

'I believe he tried. I have been looking for her ever since I heard she had gone. When someone said you had been to the new chapel in town I hoped she had gone after you. The alternative does not bear thinking about.'

Surely she cannot be dead. 'Was there no trace of her at all?'

Jared shook his head.

'*Then where is she?*

'I wish I knew. I have even travelled to Bristol. Olivia's grandmother came from there. I guessed she might have fled to her. She is dead, but no one had seen Olivia.'

'Were they not concerned for her well-being?'

Jared guffawed. 'Olivia's Bristol kin didn't approve of her grandmother's marriage to Samuel Mexton in the first place. They thought that coal was dirty and beneath them. Olivia's father might have been a lawyer but in their eyes he was of the same standing as a servant. They believed he had married Olivia's mother for her fortune.'

Harriet knew about how Olivia's grandmother had prevented Olivia's father squandering her fortune by forming the trust for her. Perhaps with good reason, she thought wistfully.

'Besides,' Jared continued, 'they have plenty of sons and she was a girl, someone else's responsibility. They were slave traders, you know. I was relieved, in a way, that she hadn't run to them. Did you send for her?'

'No! I was unhappy about her marriage, but I thought Hesley might come back from the West Indies as a more mature gentleman.' Her eyes were glassy.

'But you knew his grandfather. Did you expect him to turn out differently?'

'I hoped he might, for Olivia's sake. Has no one seen her?' She looked him square in the eye as the first tears spilled onto her cheeks.

Jared thought her grief was genuine but he was not sure whether it was for Olivia or the old rake who had just been lowered into the ground. He glanced over her, taking in her appearance for the first time. She was neatly dressed in a quiet, understated way. Plain gown, well cared-for, polished boots peeping out as she lifted her skirts from the wet grass, a cloak that was not opulent but made of decent cloth and serviceable. This was the dress of a housekeeper, he thought, and wondered where she was employed.

'Not a soul,' he said. 'I was sure she would try to find you. She was devastated when you left.'

'I – I had to,' Harriet said. 'The master was a wicked man. I only stayed as long as I did because of Olivia.'

Jared remembered how Olivia had blamed herself when Miss Trent left. 'Where did you go?' he asked.

'There's an asylum on the far side of the Riding. I found a position there.'

This was not what he had expected and his eyes widened.

'I work with a mission, and some of the inmates,' she continued.

A mission? That was how Sarah had heard Miss Trent's name. Suddenly he knew how important it was to make friends with the governess. She held the key to finding Olivia. She knew Olivia better than anyone and could ask questions of other ladies where he could not.

'Are you staying in town, Miss Trent? We should talk more.'

Harriet answered truthfully, giving the leader's name, and adding, 'You may reach me through the meeting room near the beast market.'

Jared offered his arm. 'May I walk you into town?'

'Thank you, but I shall stay here a little longer. I want to watch the sexton fill in the grave.'

'Just to be sure?' he queried lightly.

She nodded, and gave him the vestige of a smile. 'I will help to tamp down the soil.'

Jared moved through the mourners at the Red Lion until he was standing beside his father. 'Have you asked about Olivia?'

'No one's heard anything and no one seems to care apart from us. Whom did you meet in the churchyard?'

'The governess. She hadn't seen Olivia either and she was my last hope.'

'You talked to her?'

'She was at the burial.'

'I didn't see her.'

'She was watching from the trees.'

'So she cared for the old goat after all.'

'Hardly. She wanted to dance on his grave.'

'I see. And she knows nothing of Olivia?'

'No. But she is as concerned as we are. She was very close to her. For a governess, at any rate.'

'What is she doing now?'

'She teaches at the asylum, of all places.'

'Are folk in there capable of learning?'

'Some of them must be. I'm going to speak more with her. She knew Olivia and I will not give up hope. I mean to find her and, together, we shall search until we do.'

Chapter 27

'Are you awake, my dear?'

Livvy feigned sleep, knowing that Toby was too well-mannered to wake her. But as she listened to him drawing on his nightshirt she knew that if she did not do her duty tonight he would expect it of her in the morning. If anything, he would be more vigorous then.

She loved living at the old farm and she was able to tolerate being his wife in all respects but this. It was because she did not love him as a husband that this aspect of her marriage was distasteful to her. She felt used by him and it was her own fault. She had thought that her lack of love for him would not matter. But it did. Without desire, without passion, she felt as though she was selling herself to him for the price of a home. It was no different from Hesley's wager, when Jessup had so cruelly invaded her body. At first she had been able to endure Toby's attentions, but she despised him for his appetites.

The following morning she woke early and slipped out of bed to wash and dress, disturbing him.

'Why so early, Livvy? Come back to bed.'

'I must get the fire lit.'

'Not for another half-hour, surely.'

'It's chilly. There is a north wind blowing.'

'Half an hour, my dear.'

His tone was firm and she knew what he meant. 'I already have my corset on.'

'Then take it off. You are my wife.' It was the first time he had spoken to her in their chamber in such an authoritative fashion.

But she could not obey him. Silently she stepped into her gown and buttoned the bodice. He slid up the bed and watched her with a grim face. She picked up her stockings, garters and boots and went downstairs.

The fire was drawing well when he joined her in the kitchen and she turned to him with her best bright smile. 'Oh, you are dressed. The water will soon be hot and I was going to bring it upstairs for your shave.'

'Sit down, my dear.' He stood in front of the window, blocking out the grey dawn.

She looked at her hands, grubby from laying the fire. 'I must wash—'

'Please sit down.'

He did not say it loudly, but his tone told her she should obey and she sank into the fireside chair.

'Are you quite well?'

'Of course.'

'You were like this with me once before.'

She looked down and swallowed. It was nothing to do with that. A few months after their marriage ceremony her monthly courses, never regular, had been so much more than usual and very painful. A repetition of a similar incident after she was married to Hesley. No one had explained to her what was wrong then, not even Miss Trent. She had told her what Mr Harvey had said. It was because she was so young to be a bride and all would be well when she was older. The matter had not been discussed again.

She could not find the words to explain to Toby and had hoped he would understand. He had not questioned her and she had recovered, without an apothecary, to resume her wifely duties. However, she was unable to respond to those duties in the way that he wished, and it was then that she had begun to resent his demands on her body.

She did not have such an excuse today, only that she did not want him. She wished she did. He was a good man and she felt that she should be able to love him as a wife. He had been so kind and gentle with her, but she could not forget the trauma of that last night at Hill Top House. Toby wanted her so desperately to love him and she couldn't. She feared he was losing patience with her.

'I – I – sometimes I—' She stopped. She wanted to tell him that she simply did not want him to touch her, but knew she could not. He would be hurt and angry, and rightly so. She tried to think of something to say.

When he spoke again, his voice was a little louder. 'Do you think you might be with child, my dear?'

She was startled. 'No.'

She was not even sure, now, that she still wished for a child. She had realized months ago that she had not fully considered the consequences when she had agreed to marry him. Certainly not the possibility of becoming with child. Surely it could not happen so soon. But her knowledge in these matters was sketchy. She dropped her gaze to her grubby fingers, entwined and hovering above her lap, and realized that it was always a possibility.

But she had long known that men did not regard the act as necessary only for begetting children. The urge was much stronger in men than in women. They did it for pleasure. Miss Trent had told she would eventually enjoy her unions with her husband, but she did not.

She was glad that her hands were not clean, for otherwise she would have placed them on her skirt over her belly as she contemplated the possible consequences of Toby's regular demands. Her body's responses were not a reliable indicator in this matter, but she believed she had answered him honestly.

Toby's voice softened. 'You have never spoken of your traumas before you came here, and I have never pressed you. But when you turn away from me I wonder that you have been ill-treated in the past. My attentions distress you. Do they remind you of those times?'

She would have to say something. She knew him

well now and he would persist until she answered him. She kept her eyes on her hands. 'No. Quite the opposite. You are thoughtful and – and loving. It's – it's – I am not used to such frequent attentions. You tire me.'

'Tire you?'

'You have such energy. All the time.'

'I am pleased you think so. I hope I am not yet an old man.' There was lightness in his voice as, she guessed, he tried to cheer her. He was not condemning her as another man might have. She fretted again that she did not love him.

'No,' she agreed. She was being unfair to him. She was his wife and his demands were not excessive. But it was becoming more and more difficult for her to be a willing partner.

'Perhaps you are working too hard in the house. This is a large old building for you to keep clean without a girl for the rough work. Shall I find one from the village to help you?'

Livvy shook her head emphatically. Work was her salvation. It saw her through the day and gave her a purpose. She wanted more to do, not less. 'No. Thank you, dearest, you are very kind but I can manage. I like to do it myself. Besides, the miners' children work with their families down the pit as soon as they are able, and I would rather you did not spend your money here when you can use it to better effect in the mission. In fact, now there are only two of us, I have more time to help you in this work.'

'Really? You do not think it will fatigue you even more?' His tone was ironic now, challenging, even.

364

Oh, Lord! She had said too much, protested too strongly. He would know that she was not being truthful about her tiredness. She deserved the sarcasm for lying to him and dared not look at his face. 'I am sorry,' she replied.

After a short silence, he murmured, 'Maybe I do ask too much of you.' His voice had softened again and she knew she was forgiven.

'I really should like to do more for the mission,' she ventured. 'Anna used to visit the injured and sick in the village.'

'You would be willing to go into their cottages?'

'If they will have me.'

'Of course they will. You are my wife.'

She thought that she would rather they invited her because of how much she helped them than because of her position. She said, 'I believe some may be missing Anna's care now she has left us.'

'I shall speak with Mr Wilton.'

'He is in mourning for his wife.'

'Yes, but he is our strongest supporter and knows the people well.' He paused, then added, 'I was thinking, though, that I might stay longer with Anna when I next visit her.'

Livvy smiled. He was going away for a while. 'That will be pleasant for you both.'

'And take you with me. A change of air, of routine, might help you.'

She didn't want to go. 'There is nothing wrong with me! Besides, you said she has an asylum teacher living with her, and their cottage is tiny. Surely the two of us would crowd them. And it is too far to take the trap. Think of the expense of the carrier! I'd rather stay here as I am and work in the mission.'

'Perhaps you would welcome some time apart from me?'

He was such a perceptive man. 'I should like to stay and work in the mission,' she repeated. She heard him sigh.

Toby watched her with a frank expression on his face. His desire for her had not diminished, but he had been wrong to believe he could make her love him. She would rather do anything else than lie with him. He could not, *would not*, force her, though there were times when he was sorely tempted. He was, however, prepared to do anything to make their marriage a happy one for both of them. It was *he* who had to be away from her. He could not share a bed with her and not want her as his wife. He hoped she would miss him and behave differently towards him when he returned.

'Mission work is arduous. You will become old before your time,' he said.

'I am well grown and strong.'

He could certainly agree with that. 'I shall speak to Mr Wilton tonight. His daughter is with him and they will look after you while I am gone.'

She dared not look at him and show her joy. 'Anna will be so pleased to see you,' she said.

'There is one more thing.'

Livvy waited patiently for him to continue.

'My investments have fallen in value and I can no

longer afford the lease on this house. I shall be travelling to Lincolnshire to see what can be done but until I have more funds you will not be able to live here.'

'Perhaps Mr Wilton will welcome a lodger?'

'Could you live in a miner's cottage after this house?'

Livvy thought she could live anywhere as long as it was apart from Toby. 'If Mr Wilton and his daughter would have me.'

'I shall ask him.'

'I don't know what I'm going to do wi'out me missus. Our Sarah has to get back to her school.'

'I'll look after you, Mr Wilton. I should be pleased to, now I'm lodging with you.'

Livvy had settled easily into her new home and set about the scrubbing and polishing that had been neglected during Mrs Wilton's illness. The cottage was only a quarter the size of the farmhouse and a tenth that of Hill Top. She had energy to spare and laboured in the long back garden as well. Physical exercise had always been her salvation, from walking on the moor to beating carpets and scrubbing floors. It cleared her head and gave her strength, rather than sapping it. She prided herself on doing everything well, even the most menial tasks.

'Ee, Mrs Holmes,' Mr Wilton replied, 'I don't mean the jobs around the 'ouse. I mean down the pit. Mrs Wilton used to do all me hurrying afore she were tekken poorly.'

'I'm staying a few more days, Father,' Sarah said, as she poured the tea.

'I'll not have you back down the pit now you're a teacher.'

Livvy had mixed scones, then scrubbed the kitchen table while they baked. They were sitting around the still damp wooden surface waiting for them to cool.

'What's "hurrying", Mr Wilton?'

'Carting the coal when it's dug out,' Sarah answered. 'I used to help me mam until I went away to learn about teaching.'

'Don't you have any other children?'

'Aye. Two full-grown lads. Gone away from here, though.'

'Mam and Dad wanted better for all of us than the pit or service,' Sarah explained. 'The mission helped. They got me the place as a pupil teacher in a proper school up in Northumberland.'

'Her mam, God rest her soul, were proud of our Sarah. So am I, lass. Me and yer mam managed quite well on what we could earn from the pit between us, wi'out having to rely on the children, an' all.'

'Where are you sons now?'

'My lads? Oh, I do miss my lads. I'm afraid your good Mr Holmes was part to blame for them leaving the village. They worked down t' pit wi' us until we had a travelling preacher from America. He fired their ideas, he did. And Mr Holmes told them of his times out there, too.'

'They are in America?'

'Aye. Me and Mrs Wilton told them not to worry about us. They must go if they wanted to, and they did. We have letters telling us how well they're getting on and our Sarah writes back to them. We're right proud of all of them, Mrs Holmes, that we are.'

Mr Wilton reached for a warm scone and Sarah poured the tea. 'I on'y need a few days a week down the pit to pay me rent,' he went on, 'but I need somebody to hurry fer me now.'

'I'll send you money for rent, Dad,' Sarah said.

'Nay, lass. You don't get that much yersen and I'd rather you saved it fer coming 'ome once in a while.'

Sarah gave Livvy a despairing look. Livvy sympathized, but Mr Wilton was right. She thought about it for a moment and realized there was nothing to stop her going down the pit. If Mrs Wilton could do the work, she was sure she could. And she wanted to. She wanted to prove to herself that she was as able as the villagers, that she truly belonged to this community, labouring alongside them as an equal.

'I'll do it for you, Mr Wilton,' Livvy said.

'You? Hurry for me dad?' Sarah asked, surprised.

'Why not?'

'You? Go down t'pit?' Mr Wilton echoed. 'Don't be daft, lass. You 'as to be born into pit work.'

'You mean they won't let me?'

'Well, folk round here like to keep it in t' family, like.'

'Were Mrs Wilton's people all miners, then?'

'Now, there you got me. Farm labourers, they were. But she married into a pit family, you see.'

'Well, I've settled in the village. I belong here now, and I promised Mr Holmes I would do whatever was needed while he was away. I do so want him to be proud of me.'

'It's hard work, lass.'

'I shovel coal, dig the garden and scrub floors every day. If you need a hurrier, then at least let me try.'

'Well, if you put it like that . . . I don't know what the overseer'll say, though.'

'Will he question your choice in this, Mr Wilton?'

He shook his head. 'If I say you'll do, you'll do.'

'Then that's settled, isn't it?'

Father and daughter looked at each other. 'I don't see why not, Dad,' Sarah said. 'I'll lend her Mam's thick trousers with the hide stitched on the knees.' She turned to Livvy. 'Leave off your corsets. You'll only want a thin old chemise under me mam's thick tunic 'cos it gets hot down there in the stalls. Some of the men work in nothing except what they were born with. Don't look so surprised, Mrs Holmes. It's dark down there. Anyway, Mr Wilton'll keep his underdrawers on, won't you, Dad?'

Mr Wilton managed a chuckle, which turned into a cough. 'You'll be safe enough wi' me, lass. My, I'll be right pleased to get down there again. I like mining coal. It's in me blood.'

'I'm catching the evening carrier tomorrow to get the overnight stage from Doncaster,' Sarah said. 'I'll leave a pot of stew on the fire. It'll keep you both going for a few days.'

Livvy felt a strange excitement as she prepared for the following day and looked forward to her toil.

'Who's she?' The overseer was a gruff bear of a man who kept a tally of the tubs of coal and supervised the steam engine that lowered them down the shaft. He carried a lantern that flickered as he held it aloft.

'She's hurrying fer me. Joseph's lad'll do the trap-doors fer us.'

'Tha'd best all go down together, then.'

They had walked two miles to the new mine shaft and it was not yet light enough for Mr Wilton to see the fear on Livvy's face. She had thought only of toiling in the dark and the dirt, not the journey down the shaft on a shuddering wooden platform.

'Hold firm to the rail, lass, and get one leg over t' gap. Don't want yer slipping down the side, do we? Gi' us th' snap tin and I'll put it wi' me pick and shovel.'

In spite of her thick clothing, Livvy was cold without her shawl. Nervously, she climbed onto the unsteady platform and clung with more than a little desperation to the wooden rail.

Mr Wilton handed her his snap tin and a can of cold tea, which she clutched with her free arm. 'Lean inwards and tha'll not tip thissen out. And keep th' arms and legs away from t' shaft wall as we go down.' Nimbly he climbed in next to her and was followed by a dozen other men, women and children until the trembling platform was crammed.

Their descent was alarmingly fast, only slowing as they reached the bottom of the shaft. They landed with a jolt and clambered out into the cold blackness. Livvy shivered and drew in her breath.

'Tha'll soon warm up, lass. Foller the lantern. I'll light me candle when we get to me stall. Keep th' 'ead down.'

The coal seam ran along the low tunnel through the rock. Low stalls were dug sideways into the wall of coal, each closed off by a small wooden door. When they reached their stall, Mr Wilton lit his candle and got down on his hands and knees.

'Crawl in after me, lass. As soon as me tub's full, put t' harness on and drag it down t' tunnel to t' shaft. Bring back an empty 'un fo' me. Joe's lad'll open t' stall doors for thee.'

He set about the wall of black rock with his pick until there was enough loose coal to shovel into the tub. Livvy's eyes were better used to the dim light by now and she hoisted on the leather harness connected by chains to the tub.

'I made this for me missus.' He lit a candle stub in a holder fixed to a leather strap. 'Tie this round yer 'ead so yer can see where yer goin'.'

At first she could not budge the tub, but once Mr Wilton had pushed it out of his stall and into the tunnel the going was easier. A woman came out of the next stall and dragged in a stooped, half-standing position. But Livvy found she needed to be on her hands and knees to keep the tub rolling.

'This yer first day down 'ere?' the woman in front asked, when they reached the shaft.

'Yes.'

'Here. Have a lend o' me gloves and, if yer can, rub yer hands and knees with raw spirit of a night time to build 'em up.'

'Thank you.'

'Aye, well, can yer come out inter t'tunnel when yer

372

stops fer yer snap? Talk to me little lad fer a minute or two. He's new down t'pit and he'll fret on 'is own till he gets used ter being in t'dark.'

Livvy agreed. She made a point of saying something to him every time she passed. If her job was arduous, his, poor mite, was lonely and boring, sitting in the blackness without a candle and waiting for the rap on the door to tell him when to open it.

At snap time, Livvy ate her bread and cheese with blackened fingers and crunched on the coal dust that came with it. 'It's good fer yer, lass,' Mr Wilton said seriously. 'It helps the digestive, they say. Swill it down with some cold tea from yer can. How yer doing wi' the hurrying?'

She ached in places she hadn't known existed in her body, but managed to return Mr Wilton's smile in the candlelight. 'Well. What about you?'

'I'm used to it. And this coal's easy to dig out. Good stuff an' all. Best thing that happened to our village was sinking this new shaft. It's worth the extra walk ter get 'ere.'

Livvy sat back against the rough rocky wall. Uncle Hesley had married her to his grandson to pay for this. Perhaps he wasn't such a bad man, after all. His grandson was, though. He had wasted the rest of her inheritance on drinking, gambling and his dubious friends. At least there was no chance of him ever visiting the pit. And she would earn a few shillings for her work that she could put to good use in the mission.

She smiled at the irony of her situation: she would rather be down here in the dirt and the dark than living in that house at Hill Top with those degenerate so-called gentlemen who had sought to control her life.

She wondered if they were still looking for her. She didn't think so. She would wager that neither was interested in having her back or even in avoiding scandal. The Mextons were expected to behave scandalously. Well, she hadn't let them down in that respect, she thought triumphantly. Except that she was a woman, and women were not expected to cause scandals. It was a pity they didn't know what she had done. She would have liked to see the fury on Hesley's face.

She tired significantly by the end of the day and her trails to the shaft became slower so that the time to fill the tub between journeys was shorter. But she kept going and heeded her neighbour's advice on hauling. Her legs and back were screaming when she heard a thump and a yell from Mr Wilton.

'What's wrong?'

'Lump o' coal.'

She scrambled over towards the candle.

'Just fell out. Shift it, can yer?'

It had trapped his right arm and he was trying desperately to push it off with his free hand. Between them they rolled it away. He was wincing with pain. 'Might be broken,' he wheezed. 'Mek way and let me crawl out.'

Joseph, in the next stall, came to look. 'Better get you up to the bone-setter,' he said.

'Go with him, Joe,' his wife added. 'There's enough

coal dug fer me ter fill another tub and then I'll foller you wi' the lad.' She held her candle high. 'Tek the lass an' all.'

'Fetch me snap tin up, will yer?' Mr Wilton called.

Livvy crawled back into the stall and gathered the cans. She could hear the shovelling in the next stall and marvelled at the strength of the pit women. Perhaps if she mined coal every day she would become as strong as them. She wondered how long it would take her. She was certainly exhausted today – drained. She leaned back against the stone wall and closed her eyes.

She heard a man call her name. Joe, she guessed, but she was too tired to crawl out and reply. He wouldn't wait. He'd get Mr Wilton to the surface as quickly as he could. She'd just rest a few more minutes, then go up with Joe's wife and the little boy. She must have dozed for she thought she heard a voice, but wasn't certain. 'You still in there?' A pause. 'Come on, then, lad.' No, it was a dream. All was quiet. She hunched her shoulders and slipped back into her doze . . .

She opened her eyes to total blackness and couldn't think where she was. Her hands and feet were cold. After a few seconds she remembered. The candle stub on her headband had burned away. She scrambled towards the stall door and opened it into more blackness. Not a flicker of light from a hurrier or an open door or anyone. Cold fear clutched at her heart.

'Halloo!' she called. 'Is anybody there?'

Silence. She strained her ears for the grating of tub wheels or the distant creak of the shaft pulley. Nothing except a darkness so black she could not see her fingers when she held them up to her face. She waited for her eyes to adjust but they didn't. She could not see or hear anything. It was then that she felt a sharp pain jab at her stomach.

Chapter 28

'Really, Father, we can't go on like this! The coal barge is late again. We'll have to get some from Kimber Deep.'

'But Mexton Pit depends on our trade.'

'What can we do, then?'

'All it needs is a decent manager. The colliers there are good workers.'

'Is Hesley doing something about it?'

'Why don't you ride over and have another look?'

'It's Hesley who should be doing that.'

'He's not well, son. He has that Jessup fellow to do everything now – and he's too busy talking to the railway company.'

'But the mine will fail again if somebody doesn't do something.'

'As I say, son, why don't you see what you can do?'

Jared thought about this. It was not only Hesley's

loss if the mine closed. There were other furnaces and forges that wanted coal and were too small to pay Kimber Deep prices. More than that, the village would die. The mission would not be able to save it and the people might starve. He couldn't let that happen. Surely Hesley wasn't short of capital? All Mexton Pit needed was a bigger steam engine and a railtrack to the canal. 'I'll ride over this evening,' he said.

'Nights are drawing in,' his father reminded him. 'Go in the morning.'

'No. Something's wrong and I want to find out why. I'll talk to the men first. There's an alehouse in the village now, where they slake their thirst.'

It was a small place, a former cottage at the end of the terrace nearest the track to the new pit. After a day's work and a two-mile walk home, the colliers were ready for a tankard of ale. Some went in straight away and stood in the back room behind the barrels with their blackened faces and clothes. Others went home first to the missus for a wash at the pump in the scullery and a plate of stew from an iron pot hanging over the kitchen fire. Then they put on cleaner trousers and flannel shirts, were given a copper or two by their wives, and joined their fellows in the front-room saloon.

Jared stepped inside. There was a fire going in the grate and a bucket of coal in the hearth. Several serious pairs of eyes, still rimmed with coal dust in washed faces, looked up. They were hostile, he thought, and became edgy. This was working men's territory. He nodded briefly from side to side as he walked to the counter, looking for the engine-house keeper he had met before. He was not there.

'How do, landlord?' he said. 'A pint of your best.'

The alehouse keeper liked his title. 'Haven't seen you in here before, sir.'

'I'm from Tyler's Forge. Our coal's late again. Is summat up?'

'There's allus summat up here. Gin-house man's not 'ere, though. Maybe trouble with t' steam again.'

'Aye.' Jared picked up his tankard and turned around, leaning against the counter. The door opened again and a brawny young man came in.

''Ey oop, Sam,' a drinker called. 'Your missus let you off the leash?'

A ripple of amusement crossed the room, then someone added, 'Old Wilton all right, is he?'

'Aye,' Sam replied. 'Bone-setter says so. Nowt broke. Got a problem, though. We've left somebody down there.'

'What – down t'pit?'

'He'd tekken this lass to hurry fer 'im, wi' 'im 'aving no missus now, like, and when somebody asked where 'is missus was, they said 'adn't they 'eard she'd passed on? So nobody knew we'd left the lass there until my missus asked me if she were all right, like, on her first day.' He stopped to draw breath and added, 'If yer get me meaning.'

'I think so, lad. Did yer say it were her first day? Aye, well, now she knows what it's like, she'll not let herself get left behind again.'

'We can't leave her down there all night,' Sam said.

379

'Why not? She won't be the first. Who is she, anyway?'

'Not their Sarah, is it? I've seen her about these parts recent, like.'

'Nay, their Sarah's a teacher now.'

'She used to go down pit, though, when she were a nipper, like, afore the mission were set up.'

'Aye, well, a night down there'll be no hardship fer her then, will it?'

Sam looked worried. 'It's not their Sarah, though, is it? Are you gunna just leave her there?'

'Have some ale, lad, and stop yer fretting. It's only fer one night. Besides, the gin-house man in't here so nob'dy can go down fer her.'

The men went back to their ale and tobacco.

Jared frowned. He didn't think it would be Sarah but, even so, he didn't like the idea of any woman being left on her own all night down a coal mine, even if she was used to it. He turned to Sam and asked, 'Do you know the lass?'

'She's new. I think it were her first day.'

Jared addressed the whole room. 'We ought to fetch her out.' He couldn't ask any of these men to go down again. They were all tired out. He would have to go. 'Take me to the engine-house keeper's home, Sam,' he said, and swallowed the remains of his ale.

The pit engineer had just finished his dinner and was lighting a pipe by the kitchen fire. His wife was in the scullery and her four children were helping with the pots and scrubbing the table.

Jared introduced himself.

'Tyler's Forge? I remember you. I can't get the coal to you any quicker. I've only just finished fer the day, what with old Wilton hurting his arm an' that.'

'Yes, I heard. Trouble is, you've left his hurrier down there.'

The man scratched his head. 'I can't help that. If she can't look after herself she shouldn't be down there. She'll not do it again, will she?'

'She might be injured, too.'

He considered this, then grumbled, 'I've just settled in fer the night, y' know. I have to do everything round here now. It's not like Kimber Deep, with proper supervisors and the like. The wages clerk's always late, keeping the men hanging around when they want to get off 'ome, and we can't get enough wagons to get the coal to the barges fast enough.'

'How long has it been like this?'

'Since the old master passed on and that Jessup took over.'

'Is Jessup responsible for everything now?'

'Just about. Why?'

'You have your pipe. I can work a steam engine, if you'll let me have your keys.'

'Only if you don't let on to Jessup I did this. He'll have me out on me ear as soon as look at me.'

Jared thought that it was probably all Jessup's doing that the mine was in such a poor state. He'd have a few things to say to him when he got the chance. Mexton colliers were some of the best in the Riding and he was frittering away their livelihood. 'Don't you

381

worry about Jessup,' he said. 'Come on, Sam. You'll help me, won't you?'

Sam looked alarmed. 'I'm not going down there at night on me own.'

Jared took a deep breath. Sam had been working hard all day and he was lucky to have his help. 'I'll get the engine going, then you can work it for me. He can do that, can't he, sir?'

'You'll have to show him first.'

'I'll do that, then go down.' Jared had been down Kimber Deep several times. 'Are your lanterns over there?'

Livvy thought she was dying. The pain in her belly was much sharper than anything she'd had before and it cut her in half when it struck. And she was bleeding. She could feel it and smell it as it soaked through her thick miner's trousers. She yelled, which helped her to endure it. But no one came to help her. No one.

When she thought the pain would never fade, it eased and she fell back against the rough rocky wall, frightened and exhausted. This was worse than her childhood nightmares. She had grown out of them eventually, thanks to Miss Trent. Miss Trent . . . It was always when she was in despair, when things went wrong, that she thought of Miss Trent. Why must she always associate the hardships in her life with Miss Trent? She missed her dreadfully.

But as Livvy drifted in and out of consciousness, with the ebb and flow of the pain, she thought of the good times as well. Walking through the trees and in the pasture before evensong when Jared came riding over the hill and Miss Trent had left them to talk. Those had been the best of times.

If she was going to die she wanted to die remembering Jared, and how her desire for him had increased when he had refused her advances. Even though she had hated him for it when they had parted, she would have welcomed him back. Always she would welcome him.

The pain returned, making her screech. Tears of agony flooded down her cheeks. No one would hear her. No one would come for her until morning. She might bleed to death before then. She was so cold . . . and she could no longer think clearly.

She was under the sea. Yes, she had drowned and sunk to the bottom of the ocean where there was a black rocky cave full of blackened faces. She was a child again. Black faces frightened her. They had taken her mama and papa and they spoke in a strange language. But when she recovered consciousness it was not soft, hot sand under her back. It was cold black rock, hard and unyielding. The stony floor and walls of this dark cave dug into her flesh.

Perhaps this was Hell? She had been wicked, she knew. She had spurned her duty. She had married another man while her husband lived. God would punish her for that. Now she understood. She was on her way to Hell. The pain was her punishment. It returned with a vengeance and she fainted.

Jared thought he would never reach the bottom of the shaft. The engine cranked and hissed and the platform creaked and groaned as it swung about, slowing as he neared the bottom. He had been down Kimber Deep often, but never alone, and he understood why Sam would not do it. The lantern cast weird shadows and revived childhood stories of ghouls and ghosts that lurked in corners, ready to pounce.

'Pull yourself together, man,' he chided himself.

He climbed out. Sam had described the layout of the pillars and stalls to him, and he began his trek along the tunnel, feeling his way along the rough black walls.

'Halloo!' he called. 'Where are you?'

Soon he had to bend his neck and then his back as he progressed. Twice he cracked his head on the roof and cursed, rubbing the bruise with his blackened hands. He was sweating. His body, folded almost double, was taut with tension. He wiped the sweat off his face, cursing again when coal grit scratched his eyes.

'Halloo!' he called again, and stopped to listen. Not a sound. Was Sam mistaken? Was no one here? Was this a futile journey? How foolish not to find out her name before he had come down. Well, he would search the tunnel to the end to make sure.

He had resorted to his hands and knees, crawling as best he could with the lantern in one hand, when he thought he saw a heap of ragged clothes piled against the wall. As he drew closer he saw it was a person, dressed in the thick trousers and tunic of a hurrier. Her head, covered with a close-fitting miner's cap, had dropped on to her breast and she lay still.

When he reached her, he put down the lantern and shook her gently. She flopped to one side and he had to move quickly to stop her head hitting the rocky floor. Then he smelled blood. Fresh blood. My God, she was injured! He hoped he wasn't too late. His mind raced. What should he do? Get her to the surface as quickly as he could. But how could he carry her, bent over in the tunnel?

He sat with his back to the wall and laid her head on his lap. 'Wake up! Please try.' He shook her again. She was like a rag doll in his arms. He had to stop the bleeding. He stretched out for the lantern so that he could see her more clearly, but it was just beyond his reach.

Then she began to groan, yell and scream, so loudly he thought she must be dying. Her body jerked as she brought up her knees and rolled away from him. He grasped her and pulled her back. In the dim glow from the lantern he saw her eyes open briefly, wide and frightened, pale in the coal-blackened face, and her screams became louder.

For Livvy the pain was like a wild horse that she could not deflect. It came at her at breakneck speed. It aroused her from her faint and she wished it hadn't. Soon it would overwhelm her and she would welcome the oblivion it brought. She jolted as it hit her and opened her eyes. It was dark, but not pitch black now. There was a soft glow in her cave. And a black face was staring at her. She screamed again. But it was not a face from her childhood nightmares. She knew it. She had dreamed of it recently. This was a dream. It was . . . She fell back onto the hard rock floor.

★   ★   ★

Jared stared at her. In the second when her eyes had flashed open it was as though a bolt of lightning had struck him. He had seen those eyes before and had not forgotten them. He would never forget their shape, the colour, the way they were set well apart in her face. It was just a glimpse. Surely he was mistaken. Feverishly, he laid her gently on the floor and scrambled for the lantern.

He held it close, searching his jacket for a handkerchief. Carefully he tried to wipe away some of the coal dust but it did not make much difference. As he moved the lantern closer he saw that there was no doubt. It was Olivia. At the bottom of the mine and half dead from her injury, but it was her. Her now-blackened face was the one he still dreamed of and thought about constantly in his waking hours. It was the face he longed to shower with kisses and to love. He had found his Olivia! Dear Lord, he had found her at last.

A turmoil of emotion washed over him, making his body tingle with relief and joy, then with the fear that he might be too late to save her. She was the most precious person in his life, and until this moment he had thought he had lost her for ever. But his beautiful, darling Olivia was here. Not ten miles from home. He had yearned so long for her that he could not lose her now. He would not let her die. She was his life, his love.

He had to get her to the surface. But how? How could he carry her and the lantern back to the shaft? Kimber Deep had canvas slung between poles kept down there for just such a purpose. Mexton Pit had no such help. Dragging her would take the skin off her back before he reached the shaft. If he hoisted her into a coal truck how would he drag her out again without doing further damage? The bone-setters' advice was always to leave an injured man be, if you could.

He hardly knew what to do. The roof was low so he hoisted her flaccid body on to his back, securing her arms about his neck, and took the lantern in his teeth. The heat from the candle rose and burned his face as he crawled on his hands and knees until the black tunnel joined with another and widened. As soon as he could stand he did so, dispensing with the lamp and walking into the dark with her in his arms.

He had found her. She must not die now. A dozen questions raced through his mind, but he pushed them away, concerned only with reaching the surface while she still breathed. Feeling his way with his body and legs, he lowered her onto the platform and climbed in beside her, yanking at the pulleys to signal to the surface. He could not see the ropes tighten but he felt the sway as the platform began its slow ascent.

Her clothes were soaked with blood and he felt the stickiness on his hands. God help her, what had happened down there when she was left alone in the dark? This was Jessup's fault. Sir William would not have let this happen in one of his pits. They had a proper supervisor and checks against this happening. They wanted their colliers to work another day.

She groaned again and he sank beside her, holding her head. 'You're safe now,' he whispered. 'Safe.'

He wished he believed it, because she was in a bad way. As soon as she was at home he would ride for Adam Harvey himself. He wondered where her home was. He took her left hand and felt for her wedding ring. Well, that was still there so she had not dispensed entirely with her former life. He wondered what she had said to the people of Mexton and was astonished that word of her whereabouts had not got out.

His neck ached from looking upwards. His eyes stung from the falling grit, but eventually he detected a pale hint of moonlight penetrating the blackness. He stood up. 'Bring another lantern. Quickly! Help me here. Secure the platform first.' He picked her up in his arms. She was groaning again, weakly now. 'Take her from me. Careful, man, she's hurt.'

Jared hoisted her limp body across the gap and Sam took her from him. He clambered out. 'Here, give her back to me. Do you know her?'

Sam held the lantern close. 'Oh, aye, that's the new lass. Went down with old Wilton this morning. You don't suppose she were hurt an' all and never said owt?'

'It's likely. Where does Mr Wilton live?'

'Farmhouse Lane. End cottage afore you get to the cobbler's house.'

'I'll take her there. You turn off the steam pressure as I showed you and lock up. Make sure the keys go back.'

'Right, sir.'

Jared didn't hear him. He was already on his way.

He fell against the cottage wall, his arms and back aching. 'Mr Wilton!'

The door opened, casting a shaft of candlelight over the threshold.

'Sarah?'

'Jared!'

'I thought you were leaving.'

'I was on my way to the carrier but one of my dad's neighbours caught up with me and I came back. Dear Heaven! That's Livvy!'

'She was left behind and I fear she is badly injured. There's a lot of blood—'

'Wait a minute. I'll clear the kitchen table. Here, put her there for now. Can you light me another candle? There, on the mantelshelf.'

When he had done that and placed Olivia as gently as he could on the table, he said, 'I'll fetch the apothecary.'

'No, there's a lot of blood. I might need you. My father's asleep and there's no one else. I'll send Sam from next door.' Sarah picked up a heavy metal ladle and knocked on the kitchen wall.

'He can take my horse.'

They heard the wail of a child through the wall. 'You'll wake your father, too,' he said.

'I've given him a sleeping draught. I – I've decided to take him with me to Northumberland. He can't stay here with a bad arm.'

Sam came in through the open door and Jared despatched him for help. 'Give Mr Harvey this guinea and impress on him the urgency.'

'What shall I tell him?'

'Say nothing. Tell him it's for Mr Tyler.'

When he had gone, Sarah asked Jared what had happened to Livvy.

'I don't know,' he replied. 'She was left behind when they brought your father out. She may have been hurt at the same time.'

Sarah was searching Olivia's near-lifeless body for wounds. She lifted her tunic and unbuttoned the thick trousers, peeling them away from the bloodied skin. She had seen this before when helping her mother in the village and frowned. Jared could hardly believe there was so much blood. 'What is it?' he asked anxiously.

'She's not been injured by falling rock. She's lost a baby.'

Chapter 29

'Lost a baby?' Jared breathed.

'I'm certain. And is still bleeding. She'll die if we don't stop it. I'll fetch more linen.'

His eyes searched hers as though for a sign that this was not true. 'What can you do?'

'My mother kept a mixture in the cupboard. I'll make it up.'

Jared now wished he had gone himself for Adam Harvey. He paced the kitchen, listening to the clock on the mantelshelf tick away the minutes. He supported Olivia's head and shoulders while Sarah spooned the potion between the pallid lips. It seemed to revive her and she groaned again.

She opened her eyes first, and her mouth to scream, but no sound came. Her eyes rolled and she fell back in another faint.

'Will she live?' he asked anxiously.

'I don't know. Ask your Mr Harvey when he gets here.'

'Should we get her upstairs?'

'Can you carry her?'

Livvy roused again as Jared lowered her onto the narrow bed. She drank some water and groaned as anxious eyes stared at her in the candlelight. She was too exhausted to scream. Her mind was jumbled with memories of stormy seas and dark mines. There were black faces everywhere, black faces with white teeth, and white eyes looking at her. Then they had walked away and left her to die. Her body ached. She was hurting all over, alone and frightened, and she heard a distant sound in her head, a wailing, long and whining . . .

'Hush, Olivia. Be still. You're safe now.'

Olivia? Who was Olivia? A name from the past. A voice from the past. She opened her eyes again. A face from the past. But this face was no longer black, except for the rings of coal dust that clung round his eyes. Then the familiar features were gone, replaced by a woman's, a stranger who pushed pillows behind her back and spooned a bitter tincture between her lips.

'At least she's still alive,' the woman muttered.

Jared had never felt so weary. His lips were pale in the candlelight. As he sat with her in the dimness, watching her every move, he wondered how long she had been in Mexton, toiling in the pit that bore her husband's name. All the searching he had done! Had she been working down the mine all this time? He had never thought to look for her here. Neither had Hesley. She had disappeared right under their noses. He guessed that the colliers did not know who she was. He wondered if they knew the father of her lost child.

He should not have left her. He had thought at the time it was the right thing to do, but if this was the result he had been wrong. God keep her alive, he prayed. Where was Harvey? He should have been here by now.

The apothecary arrived on horseback, ahead of Sam, and came straight into the kitchen.

'Oh,' he said, as soon as he saw Jared, who hurried down to meet him. 'I expected your father. What is it?'

'A miscarriage, I believe, sir.' Jared picked up a candle and led him up the narrow stairs to the small chamber. Sarah stepped away from the bed.

'But this is—' Adam Harvey exclaimed, as soon as he saw his patient. Then he snapped his mouth shut and set about his task of examination and administration, giving orders to Sarah as he did so. When she went downstairs to make up the couch for herself in the front room, Harvey turned to Jared. 'How long has she been here? She's been missing for more than a year.'

'I found her by chance. I can scarcely believe it myself.'

'Was it your child?'

'No, sir, it was not. I had not seen her for years until now.'

'But you found someone to help her get rid of it.'

'What sort of man do you think I am?'

'The woman did it, then?'

'Sarah? Certainly not. She's a chapel teacher, home to see her father. Olivia – er – Mrs Mexton was hurrying for him.'

Now it was the apothecary's turn to be surprised. 'Mrs Mexton was down the pit?'

'That was where I found her.'

'How long ago?'

'Two hours, maybe three.'

'Well, you were already too late for her child, but you saved her life.' He handed Jared his brandy flask. 'I attended her before, a good few years ago, not long after she was married, for something similar.'

'You mean she has already been through this?'

'As I remember it wasn't so bad. She was very young. I thought she would grow out of it. You're sure nobody helped this along?'

'I told you, I found her a few hours ago down the mine. Surely such work would bring it on.'

'Colliers' wives keep going until their waters break.'

'But they are born to it. Mrs Mexton is not.'

'Aye. There's something in that.' Adam Harvey handed him a glass phial. 'I've stemmed the bleeding for now. Keep her still and give her five drops of this in boiled water every two hours. Sarah has a good head on her shoulders. She'll tend her well enough and I'll call back in the morning.'

'Thank you. Just one more thing.'

'Yes?'

'It is best if her husband does not know of this. Or where she is. Not yet, anyway. Can I count on you for that, sir?'

Adam Harvey gave a tired half-laugh. 'You haven't seen Mexton for a while, then?'

'Not since his grandfather's funeral. You were there with him.'

'He's worse now. It is more than just the drink. He is hardly sensible most of the time.'

Perhaps that is why Jessup has so much power, Jared thought. 'I did not know he had deteriorated so quickly. Why was my mother not informed? She is his great-aunt.'

'Believe me, sir, it is better that she does not see him. His new lawyer handles the banking – that jumped-up butcher's son.'

'Jessup?'

'That's the one. A gambling friend of young Hesley. He took over the family affairs after old Hesley died.'

'Withers is no longer needed?'

Adam Harvey shook his head slowly and deliberately.

'Jessup is no pit manager! He is the reason the mine is going to rack and ruin. He must be stopped. I'll speak to him.'

'Take care, Jared. Jessup has influence in the town with the parish and the railway company. He can make life uncomfortable for those who cross him.'

'Then perhaps it is time someone made life uncomfortable for him. But he can wait. Olivia is my concern now. Will she recover?'

'She's strong in mind and body. Or she was when

I last attended her at Hill Top House. These things can affect ladies in different ways.'

'She needs to be with people who care for her. I'll take her home with me.'

The apothecary shook his head. 'You must not move her until she has healed enough to travel. Do you know who the baby's father was?'

'She hasn't said. She may tell me. Or Sarah.'

'Sarah has her father to deal with.'

'And she told me she has to return to her school. She was already on her way.'

'Mrs Mexton needs someone with her at a time like this,' Adam Harvey advised.

'I do know someone.'

'Well?'

'I'm not sure that she is the right person, though.'

'Why not?'

'They did not part on good terms and − she had dubious morals.'

'Who is she?'

'The woman who was her governess.'

'I remember her. Miss Trent. Capable, I always thought. My impression was that she was very moral. Schooled at Blackstone, I believe.'

'She was old Hesley's whore!'

Adam Harvey gave a short, dry laugh. 'You do not see the world as I do, young man. The child Mrs Mexton lost was not her husband's. Is she a whore, too?'

Jared was silent. He could not believe that of Olivia. But where was the baby's father? Eventually he said, 'I'll stay with her tonight and ride into town tomorrow to ask Miss Trent if she will take over from Sarah.'

'Why did you not tell my father how bad things were at the mine?'

Jared had breakfasted early and left Olivia in Sarah's care. He rode hard, intent on a visit to Jessup. If Adam Harvey was right that Hesley was barely sensible, it would be hopeless trying to reason with him, but Jessup was a lawyer and would surely listen to advice. The man had no experience of running a mine and Jared had. From what he had seen, improvements at Mexton Pit were urgent if it was to stay in profit and pay its colliers. Jared insisted on an immediate audience with Jessup, and his standing in the town ensured that he got it.

'I answer to Mexton and Mexton alone,' Jessup protested.

'When did you last see him? And what were his orders?'

The lawyer went quiet. The skin around his mouth turned white as his lips tightened. 'How dare you march in here and make demands of me, sir?'

Jared ignored the question. 'Why have you not employed another manager?'

'That is none of your affair.'

'My mother is his kin, you charlatan!'

'I warn you, sir, I do not have to receive you in my office.'

'Nor the colliers, it seems. They need an engineer for the winding house.'

'And who would pay him? The miners themselves?'

'You are not talking to one of Mexton's lackeys now. That coal is good and I know what you charge my father for it. Where are the profits going?'

'It is not your business, sir. If that is all?' He raised his voice. 'Clerk!'

A youth in a poorly cut jacket, ill-fitting breeches and worn shoes came in immediately. Clearly, he had been waiting by the door and listening.

'Show Mr Tyler out,' the lawyer ordered. 'Good day, sir.'

'This matter isn't concluded, Jessup.'

The youth looked at his feet as he led Jared through to the front of the office. But when he held open the outer door, Jared heard a soft whisper: 'Gambling, sir.'

'What did you say?'

The youth kept his eyes firmly on the ground. 'Nothing, sir. It's a chill wind out there today, sir.'

Jared nodded. Of course. Jessup was one of Hesley's drinking friends. He wondered how much Hesley owed in gambling debts. Perhaps nothing. Perhaps he was using the mine profits to pay off his creditors. That was a more likely explanation. He walked slowly to his horse, immersed in thought.

The only way forward was to see Hesley and try to reason with him. What had Adam Harvey said? Hardly sensible? Well, he would find out for himself. But first he had to make sure Olivia was looked after discreetly. He must find Miss Trent.

It was surprisingly easy. A visit to the mission hall next to the beast market brought him face to face with her again. 'I thought you'd gone back to the asylum,' he said.

'I am staying with one of the leaders and his wife. I have been speaking with other leaders here and I am to have my own mission – a school, when funds can be found.'

'Congratulations, Miss Trent. You must be pleased. May we talk privately?' He took her elbow and steered her into a dark corner.

'You have news, sir?'

'Can you leave here? Can you move out to Mexton? Someone needs your help.'

'Mr Holmes has a mission there,' she said.

'Holmes? Do you know him?'

'Of course. His sister was my benefactor when I left Hill Top House.'

'They are both gone. The farmhouse is shut up.'

'He has been visiting his sister while I am here. With his wife, I expect. He married, you know.'

'Did he? I had not heard.' Jared lowered his voice. 'It is not Holmes I speak of. I have found Olivia.'

Harriet's eyes rounded. 'You have? Where is she? May I meet her? Will she see me, do you think?'

'She is not well and needs someone to care for her.'

'She is the one you spoke of? In Mexton? So close and I did not know! What ails her? Take me to her immediately.'

'Wait. Finish your business here and come outside. There is something you must know first.'

Minutes later they were standing beside his horse, deep in conversation.

'She has lost a child. The apothecary believes it was several months in the womb. She had a great deal of bleeding and is weak.'

'Olivia has lost a child?'

'She almost died. This might not have happened if you had not deserted her so soon, if she had not run away . . .'

'But you know why I had to do it! Th-that cruel, selfish man – I had to get away from him. You advised it yourself at the time.' Her voice ended in a whisper.

'I wish I hadn't. It was Olivia who suffered.'

'I thought she would be all right. Truly I did. I should not have left her otherwise.'

'Well, you were wrong.'

'You cannot blame me for everything! You were her friend. You told me you would look after her. I trusted you with her.'

'She – she asked too much of me. She wanted me as her – instead of her husband.'

'She . . .' Jared saw realization dawn on Miss Trent's face. 'It was your child, wasn't it? Yours!'

'No! Why does everyone think that? I cared for her but I would never have disgraced her in such a way. I did not lie with her!'

'So it was Hesley's child.'

'No. She has not lived with him for more than a year. I do not know who the father is. She may confide in you.'

'If she will see me. We did not part as I would have wished.'

'Well, she needs you now,' Jared stated flatly.

400

'She has asked for me?'

'No.'

'So it is you who is asking for my help?'

'I know you can be discreet and you were very close to her once.'

'Will you take me to her, please?'

Jared untied the reins tethering his horse. 'We shall be quicker on horseback.'

'I – I do not ride, sir.'

'But you will do it for Olivia, I am sure. There's a mounting stone by the water trough.' He took the halter and swung into the saddle with ease.

Miss Trent eyed his horse and swallowed. He leaned over towards her, offering his hand. 'Put one foot on my boot and swing the other leg over the horse's back behind me. I shall not let you fall.'

She grasped his arm and he smiled at her, making her blink. He had never smiled at her before. She landed behind him with her skirts awry, showing her boots and stockings and – her eyes widened – the edge of her drawers. Carefully she shuffled about until she had covered as much of her legs as she could.

If Jared had not been so concerned about Olivia he might have been amused by her show of modesty. He said, 'Now put your arms about me and lean forward. Hold on tightly.'

They set off at a walk and eventually she relaxed her grip.

'That's better,' he said. 'I thought you would squeeze the breath out of me.'

'I prefer to ride in a cart.'

'Well, you had better hold tight again because now we are going to speed up.'

He grimaced. He could hardly believe he was doing this. He was taking old Hesley's former mistress to look after the woman who was so precious to him. Why? Because he knew she would put Olivia's welfare before her own. No, more than that: because a bond had developed between them since she had first gone to Hill Top House as a governess.

He supposed they had both been ill-used by Mexton men, had both fled the comfort of money to be away from them. Miss Trent had found solace in religion and good works. And Olivia? What had she been doing for more than a year? Who was the father of her lost child? Who had deserted his responsibilities when she needed him most?

With a guilty start he realized that Olivia had accused him of the same thing when he had ceased their meetings at the ruined cottage. But surely he had not been misguided in his desire for her to maintain the sanctity of her marriage. To walk away from her then had been the most difficult action of his life. He had done it for her, for her future happiness, and now she hated him for it. No, it would not be Miss Trent that Olivia refused to see. It would be him. Her late uncle's mistress would be more worthy in her eyes than himself. He deserved Olivia's rejection.

Chapter 30

Harriet slid thankfully off the horse and stumbled before she picked up her skirts and hurried into the Wiltons' kitchen, where she introduced herself briskly to Sarah.

Sarah was pressing linen with a flat-iron on the kitchen table. She directed Harriet upstairs to the back bedchamber, where Olivia was awake but pallid.

Harriet was so relieved to see her again that she could hardly speak. She approached the bed softly. 'Madam! What has happened to you?'

'Miss Trent?' Livvy could not believe her eyes. Miss Trent was here? Dear Heaven, she had come back. *Come back to her.* Now she could explain how she had never wanted her to leave. 'What are you doing here?'

'I'm going to look after you.' Harriet marvelled at how wonderful it was to say it. To have a chance to make up for the guilt she had felt when she had left her. To make good their friendship.

'Look after me here?'

'Oh, Mrs Mexton, you have no idea—'

'Do not call me that.' She lifted her head to see around her visitor. 'Is anyone with you? No one here knows who I am and you must not tell them.'

'But why not?' Harriet began to feel anxious. Had she been in hiding all this time?

'I'm known as Livvy. You must call me Livvy.'

'Very well.'

But Livvy began to worry about what Miss Trent would do when she found out the truth. 'How did you get here?' she asked. 'Who else knows about me?'

'Stay calm, my dear. Jared brought me.'

'Jared? He is here too?' She remembered seeing his blackened face through the pain It had not been a dream, after all. They were both here! What did they want? To take her back to Hesley, where she belonged? She couldn't go back. Not now.

Harriet saw the anxiety and distress on Olivia's face and it worried her. Olivia had trusted her. She had betrayed that trust and deserved the censure. But she had thought she would be pleased about Jared.

'We shall both care for you until you are well again.'

'No! Go away! I have managed quite well without you, these past years.'

'I'm sorry I left, but you know why I had to go, and I have missed you so much. I often wondered how you were faring as mistress of Hill Top—'

'Quiet! No one here knows of my past life.'

'Past life? But why did you have to leave?'

'Hesley came home.' Olivia tried to sit up and Harriet moved to aid her. 'I do not need help.'

'You do. This happened only yesterday and you have lost a great deal of blood.'

'You know what happened?'

'Jared told me.'

'He mustn't tell anyone else.'

'He won't.'

'I should like to speak with him.'

Harriet smiled. Olivia had not lost her spirit and for that she was grateful. 'Wait until you are stronger,' she said.

'Do you still think you know what is best for me?'

'I think you will become too agitated with him. You should rest.' Harriet began to straighten the bedding.

'I am already agitated. Please stop doing that and go away.'

Harriet sighed but did as she was bade. She understood Olivia's anger. 'Very well. If that is what you want.'

'It is.'

Reluctantly, Harriet went down the stairs. Jared had seen to his horse and was now in the small cottage kitchen, emptying his saddle-bags of brandy, sugar and scented soap from the town, and questioning Sarah about Olivia.

'May we speak frankly, sir?' Harriet said.

'Of course.'

Sarah put her iron to cool in the hearth on its heel

and picked up a pile of undergarments. 'I'll go to my father. These are for travelling.'

As soon as she had gone, Harriet turned on Jared. 'Did you tell me the truth? Was it your child?'

'I have already answered that question.'

'But you did lie with her?'

'I gave you my word,' he said evenly, 'and I have not seen her since she left Hill Top House.'

Harriet put a finger to her lips and raised her eyes towards the ceiling. 'You promised you would take care of her.'

'I did what I thought was best for her. And I have searched everywhere. Believe me, I have been out of my mind with worry.'

Harriet gave a wry half-laugh. She might have said the same before she had seen what it was like to lose one's mind. A thought struck her. 'You do not suppose Hesley was going to lock her up and that was why she left?'

'That is a possibility. Jessup would have arranged it for him, especially if she was having another man's child.'

She picked up an empty blackened kettle from the hearth. 'I'll fetch water. Make up the fire, would you? I want to know what has been going on since I left.'

He poked at the dying embers and added fresh coal from the bucket. He needed answers too. It had not occurred to him that Olivia would run away from Hesley. Or end up working in her husband's pit.

Harriet slung the heavy kettle on a hook over the fire and asked, 'Did Hesley look for her?'

'He said he did. But who can believe anything he says?'

'What do you mean?'

'You have not heard about him?'

'Only what you have told me.'

'He is manic, and I am told he is getting worse.'

'Who says he is manic?' Harriet demanded. Not someone who had seen what 'manic' meant, she thought.

'Adam Harvey. An overheated brain, he said.'

'I see.' She respected the apothecary's opinion. 'She is worried about something, a secret. She has asked to speak with you.'

For the first time that day he brightened. 'Really? I'll go up to her now.'

'Wait. She is already annoyed with – with me, and that is not good for her recovery. Wait until she is less anxious. I'll make tea for us all. That will help.'

Jared paced about the kitchen. 'Sarah has agreed that Olivia can lodge here – she says her father is well enough to travel and she wishes to leave today. Will you stay with her tonight?'

'Of course. Perhaps you would fetch my things from the town.'

He nodded briefly. 'I'll go now.'

'Have some tea first.' After a short silence, Harriet added, 'I may not be the person to help her get well.'

'You know her better than anyone else.'

'She is not pleased to see me.'

'Can you blame her?'

Harriet was spooning tea into a brown earthenware

teapot. She stopped, remembering her anguish at the time. 'I believed you would look after her. And also that Hesley would grow, like you, into a mature and responsible gentleman. I suppose it was foolish to expect such a change in him. In any event, I could not stay.' Her voice dropped to a whisper. '*I could not.*'

'I see that now.'

'Do you?'

'Of course. You were trapped by him, once you were there.' He frowned at her. 'What I do not understand is why you went there in the first place. Old Hesley's reputation in the Riding was widespread.'

Harriet wished she could tell him, tell anyone, even tell Livvy. But she had kept it to herself for too long to unburden herself of her secret now. It would only add more pain to this unfortunate situation. Over the years she had grown used to its weight on her shoulders. 'I had my reasons,' she answered shortly, and added, 'Will you tell your mother about Olivia?'

'Of course. She is as worried as I am.'

'Please wait a little. Until we know more about her. About the child.'

'And her lover?' Harriet saw a look of pain pass across his brow. 'Surely a lover would not have deserted her. Perhaps he did not know about the child.'

'Even so, where is he? More importantly, who is he?'

'She may never tell us.'

'Have patience, Jared. I hope she will. Eventually.'

He took a few coins from his waistcoat pocket and placed them on the table. 'For anything Olivia might need. I'll ride into town for your belongings. I cannot sit about drinking tea. Adam Harvey will visit later this morning.' He stopped at the back door and said, 'Look after her, Harriet.'

'I shall.'

'She is much better. The bleeding has stopped. Mrs Mexton is a sturdy young woman, but keep her in bed for two weeks. Give her butcher's meat and plenty of porter from the alehouse.'

'It is a cold morning, sir. You will take a drink yourself before you leave?' She offered Mr Harvey hot tea laced liberally with Jared's brandy.

'Thank you, Miss Trent. I am pleased Jared found you. I always thought you such a sensible young woman. Mrs Mexton did not seem as content after you left.'

'Do you think her unhappiness was my doing, sir?'

'Her husband was difficult.'

'I saw you with him at the funeral.'

'You were there? I feared for the pit after old Hesley died. His grandson is a weak man and he – he . . .'

'Yes?'

'We all believed that sending him to the West Indies would have an improving effect on his character, but he came back a dissolute and sickly man.'

'Sickly?'

'A tropical fever ruined his health and he will not see sense about his habits. I have said too much, but this pit village is dying when it should be thriving and it is his responsibility.'

'Does Hesley not care about the profits? They were always foremost in his grandfather's mind.'

'It is my belief that Hesley no longer has a mind of his own. Others order his life for him now.'

'Then who runs the mine?'

'Jessup, his gambling friend and now his lawyer. Hesley signs anything he puts in front of him. And Jessup makes sure that one of the servants is there to witness it. He's even asked me on the occasions I have been present.'

'Do you know Jessup?'

'He dresses and behaves like a gentleman. And he is clever with all these new laws. Rich, too, they say. But over-fond of the horses and the card table, which is how he came to meet Hesley.' Mr Harvey drank again and seemed to relax in Harriet's company. 'He's cunning. He hangs about Hill Top House, eating and drinking until Hesley has a more lucid moment. Then he talks about horses and bloodstock, and persuades him to bet huge amounts on the races.'

'Does he ever win?'

'Jessup tells him he does, even if it's not true, so that he will wager more. I believe Jessup pockets the money. Or feeds his own gambling habit with it.'

'Can nothing be done about him?'

'Have you any suggestions, madam?'

Harriet chose her words carefully. 'Is it Hesley's sickness that affects his mind?'

'Do you know of these things?'

'I have worked in an asylum for the insane and often talked with the doctor there.'

'You have courage, madam. That is difficult nursing.'

'I helped with the ladies who were showing signs of getting better.'

'Really? We must talk again. I should like to know more of your experiences there.' He stood up and swayed.

'Are you well, sir? Shall I fetch your horse?'

'No, thank you. I am quite all right. It is simply that I am not as young as I was. Tend your patient. She is in need of cheering.'

Harriet thought that she was the last person who could raise Olivia's spirits. 'You will not tell Hesley that she is here?'

'No, madam, I shall not. Mrs Mexton has begged me not to.'

'Nor Mr Jessup?'

'Hesley's money may be his business, but his wife is not.'

'Thank you, sir.'

She watched him straighten his back and mount his horse, then settle in the saddle with a sigh. He ought to be using a trap at his age, she thought, but he must be too proud to give up his horse.

'I do not need a nurse,' Olivia muttered.

'Mr Harvey has said you do.'

'What would he know? But, then, I suppose that because he is a *gentleman* he thinks he knows best what is good for the ladies.'

Harriet was surprised at this. 'He's an apothecary. You are distressed. You will feel differently when you have rested.'

'I have rested all night and most of the day.'

'If I may say so, Livvy, you are a difficult patient.'

'I was a difficult pupil, wasn't I?'

'Sometimes.'

'And you were always very kind to me.' She sighed. 'Firm, but kind. You put up with such cruelty for my sake. I wonder you stayed as long as you did. I do not forget what you did for me, Miss Trent. You were so devoted to me.'

'I am still devoted to you.'

'Are you? I have not been very nice to you.'

'I understand you, perhaps better than you do yourself. Can you forgive me?'

'Of course I do! Jared, too. But I fear you both wish to persuade me to return to my dutiful place as Hesley's wife. Well, I shall not go. I shall throw myself into the cut first.'

Harriet stopped tidying the bed. So that was it. They had both encouraged her to make the best of her marriage and Olivia thought that was their motive now. She said calmly, 'I have heated some porter for you. The doctor says you must drink it.' She held out the tankard, but Olivia did not take it. 'Mr Harvey is a good apothecary, in spite of being a gentleman. It is his bidding, not mine.'

Olivia shuffled up the bed, took the warm drink with both hands and sipped. Harriet supported her back and plumped up the pillows. After a few more sips, Olivia said, 'That's nice.'

'Honey and cinnamon. I found it in Mrs Wilton's cupboard. It is well stocked, for a collier's household.'

'She treated many of the villagers. They all miss her.'

Harriet watched her finish the porter and yawn. She took the empty tankard from her and said, 'Try to sleep. I have to walk into town for food. You must eat well, too.'

'I'm not going back.'

'Where?'

'Hill Top House. Not while Hesley is there. You can't make me.'

'No,' Harriet agreed quietly. But she couldn't stay here for ever, either. 'We'll talk about that later.'

Olivia yawned again and slid down the bed. 'There is nothing to talk about.'

Harriet raised her eyebrows but did not respond. She remembered how determined Olivia had been as a child. And how, when she had left her to mull over her choices, she often came to a reasonable solution. But she could not think of a sensible way forward for her, except to return to her husband and her home. It would be difficult to keep her presence here secret now. And Hesley, no doubt, was like his grandfather, a vindictive man, even in the throes of ill-health, and a gentleman with powerful friends.

She had seen what could happen to wayward girls and women at Blackstone and in the asylum. Running away and working in the pit were enough for Hesley to commit her, if he so wished. His grandfather had done it to Hesley's mother. It was the Mexton way. To have carried a child that was not her husband's would seal her fate. Harriet racked her brain for answers as she found a basket in the scullery of the Wiltons' tiny cottage and set off for the market.

*　　*　　*

'Who's there?' Livvy raised her head from the pillow and called as loudly as she could.

A gentleman's voice came up to her: 'Do not fear. It's Jared, with your supplies.'

She heard him moving about downstairs, then the tread of his boots on the stairs.

'May I come in?' he said softly.

She wondered if Miss Trent had sent him to change her mind about returning to Hill Top House.

He pushed open the door and filled the space with his tall frame. 'How are you?' he asked gently.

She felt fragile and hardly dared to move, but her heart leaped in her breast at the sight of him. Yet she was wary of his concern for her: she remembered why he had left her. 'Have you seen Miss Trent?' she asked.

'I passed her on the towpath. She has been to market and was struggling with her purchases.' He tried to lighten his tone. 'She wouldn't ride with me. She preferred to walk, so she'll be here later.'

'She'll tell Hesley where I am. Or you will. Or Mr Harvey.'

'No, we shan't.'

He sounded indignant and she peered more closely at his face. He looked old and haggard, worn beyond his years, and she wondered if he, too, had been working down the pit when he had found her. 'Would you fetch me a drink, please?'

He jumped smartly to attention. 'Yes. Something warm?'

'I'm to have porter.'

He had gone before she could say more. She heard

him raking the fire and shovelling coal. Then she heard the pump creaking and squeaking in the yard. She wondered if any of the neighbours had seen him and covered her face with her hands. He didn't have to tell anyone about her for them to find out. Folk around here were not stupid. She was the talk of the village. They would put two and two together and work out who she was. She had thought she would be well away from prying eyes down the pit but she had only drawn attention to herself. She should have gone away with Toby.

Toby. Dearest Toby, who had been so kind to her and whose love she had shunned. How could she tell him the truth? He was devoted to her and it was his child she had lost. Her child, too. Tears pricked her eyes as she remembered. She had not wanted Toby's child, but she now that she had lost it she knew that she *had* wanted her child, her own flesh and blood, to look after and cherish. And she had lost that child through her own foolishness.

She should have paid more attention to her body. She should have known she was with child. But other women toiled in the mines and the manufactories with huge bellies, so why couldn't she? She was strong and worked as hard as they did. Indeed, she had prided herself on that since she had come to this village. And through that silly pride she had lost a child, her child, a child she would have welcomed and adored as her own mother had loved her.

She had lost a part of herself with her child. She tried to stem the tears and could not. They spilled out of her eyes, down her cheeks and over her lips until she was choking with sobs. Her shoulders heaved under the blanket and her whole body shook with grief. She could not stop. The room became a blur and in the mist she saw Jared, but she could not still the shuddering in her breast.

'Please don't weep, Olivia. I cannot bear to see you so unhappy.' He was kneeling by the bed, his face contorted with grief.

'I – I l-lost my b-baby,' she wailed.

His arms hovered over her. Then he leaned forward and lifted her head on to his chest. The buttons on his waistcoat pressed into her cheek. It felt solid underneath and smelled of warm wool, horses and leather. She grasped at his jacket, bunching the thick tweed in her fists, and wept.

How long she held onto him she did not know. Or when Miss Trent arrived. But after a while the sobbing subsided and she released him. She heard him plead, 'What can I do?' and Miss Trent reply, 'I do not know,' then fell back onto the pillows. Her gulps and shudders continued. It seemed that everything she could ever hope to love was destined to be taken from her.

Miss Trent walked over to the fireplace and touched the metal tankard resting on the mantelshelf. 'Why don't you drink this while it's warm?' she suggested. 'I'll light a fire up here. Jared, would you bring up some coal?'

She packed the pillows behind Olivia's back and handed her the tankard. 'I have a piece of brisket from the market for dinner. And apples for a pudding.'

She glanced up. Miss Trent sounded brisk, but she

416

was frowning. She's wondering what to do with me, she thought. She heaved a sigh. So was she.

Mr Harvey had been right about porter: it cheered Olivia and gave her strength. Miss Trent sent Jared on his horse to track down other delicacies for her. She ate some porridge and, later, beef brisket stewed in the pot over the fire with barley and vegetables. The smell of baking bread drifting up from the kitchen was appetizing and Miss Trent came to make up the fire.

'What will happen to me?' Olivia asked.

'I do not know,' Miss Trent replied, as she drew the curtains against the gathering dusk. 'I fear you will be in Hesley's hands.'

'He is quite mad, you know.'

'What do you mean?'

She did not answer at first. It hurt too much to remember. 'I wish he was dead,' she said. 'I hate him.'

'Strong words.'

'You don't know what it was like with him!' she retaliated.

'Then tell me.'

So she did. She told Miss Trent of Hesley's more erratic behaviour and his irresponsible gambling. But not about Jessup. Or Toby. She could not face Miss Trent's total condemnation yet and, if she were honest, she was too ashamed of herself.

She talked until the light faded and Jared returned with chocolate, honey and rare oranges. Olivia dozed and Harriet went downstairs.

'What can we do?' she asked.

Jared shook his head. 'I don't know. Hesley owns the pit and this village. She has humiliated him in the worst possible way.'

'If he finds out she is here, he will have her put away.'

He looked up sharply. 'We must not let that happen.'

'But how can we stop him?'

'She could go to Ireland or France.'

'Is that the only way?'

'It is all I can think of.'

Harriet sighed. A life abroad was preferable to the asylum. But there had to be another way. She busied herself with chores and finally said, 'Jared, will you come and sit with Olivia tomorrow afternoon? I wish to call on the apothecary.' She told Jared about her idea.

Harriet had planned what she would say to Adam Harvey. 'You know I am acquainted with the doctor at the asylum. It is only natural that you would wish to seek a second opinion about Hesley's illness. Will you do this?'

'I should certainly like to discuss the case with him. I shall write immediately and ask him to visit.'

'Er, you will not mention this to anyone? At least, not before the doctor is here?'

'Jessup will be angry if we do not tell him.'

'He will stop us if we do.'

'Perhaps Hesley's aunt Caroline should be told.'

'Say nothing to her! Not yet. Please! The fewer who

know the better. If Jessup finds out and is difficult, Jared will support you, I am sure.'

'Miss Trent, you are indeed a true friend to Mrs Mexton.'

Harriet looked at her hands. More than that, she thought.

Jared went to see Mr Withers about the state of Mexton Pit. He had handled old Hesley's affairs and Jared wanted to know exactly how much power Jessup had.

'All is not well, sir,' Jared told him. 'The mine is losing production while Hesley's so-called friend gambles away his money.'

'Sit down, Jared. My powers are limited. However, I was an executor of old Samuel's will and I still manage the family trust he set up. But I cannot influence how the assets are disposed of once they are released. Hesley is quite at liberty to invite whomsoever he wishes to assist him in spending his income. Jessup has influence over that, but no legal power of attorney on his behalf,' the lawyer told him.

'Can you be sure of that?'

'The pit was entailed in old Samuel's will and I am a trustee. I would have to be involved.'

'What about Mrs Mexton?'

'Ladies did not exist as far as old Samuel's will was concerned, so she has no right to any of Hesley's wealth except what he chooses to give her as his wife.'

'Not even the money from her own plantation?'

'You know about that?'

419

'At home we all did. Are you saying it won't make any difference if she comes back?'

Mr Withers seemed unsettled. 'If she were sitting here in front of me I should advise her not to return.'

'Never?'

'The Mextons are proud gentlemen, and Hesley cannot be seen to condone her behaviour. He – he would have her in the asylum.'

'Others say so too.'

'It's been done before by the Mextons and Jessup would arrange it for him. He would not want her interfering with his authority.'

'You must help us, Mr Withers. Is Jessup within his rights?'

'More than that, he is within the law. He is simply acting as Hesley's agent.'

'Can he sell the mine?'

Withers shook his head. 'He can only spend the profits, and only according to Hesley's wishes, such as they are.'

Jared nodded. 'Could Jessup apply for power of attorney?'

'Under what circumstances?'

'Well, if Hesley was . . . incapacitated in some way.'

'Mad, you mean? He could. So could I, and I should.'

'What about my father?'

'You are a better choice. You have Mexton blood through your mother and you know more about mining.'

Jared stood up and held out his hand. 'Thank you, Mr Withers.'

'Keep me informed,' the lawyer said. 'It's time something was done about Mexton Pit.'

Two days later, a solemn group of gentlemen gathered in the gloomy drawing room at Hill Top House.

'Mr Tyler is aware of his responsibilities,' Mr Withers began.

'My son is more than capable, sir,' Benjamin Tyler said. 'He worked at Kimber Deep for five years and attended lectures in Manchester. He is the son of a gentlewoman.'

Jared maintained his silence. His mother's connections did not make him a gentleman, and he knew it. Four pairs of eyes turned on him. None of these men was a true gentleman, he thought, not even the asylum doctor. The one born to that status was a wreck, languishing in his bedchamber, stupefied by medicine. But quiet. For now.

Mrs Cookson brought in a tray of glasses and some brandy. When the door opened they could hear the tick of a casement clock standing in the hall. Only the smaller, more portable of Hesley's treasures had been removed and sold. Presumably by Jessup, Jared thought.

Adam Harvey spoke next: 'He continues to deteriorate. Since the housekeeper called me in I have consistently applied all my knowledge and skill.'

The asylum doctor held up a hand to silence him. 'There is no question of your devotion to the patient, sir. I have examined him in detail and spoken at length to his housekeeper and his servants. He is insane. He should be in my asylum for the safety of himself and of others. He has a wife?'

'She left him a while ago,' Mr Withers said quickly. 'Are we in agreement?'

They nodded and drank their brandy. Mr Withers stood up and walked to a table where the papers were laid out. 'That is settled then, gentlemen. Jared, you will assume responsibility for Hesley's affairs immediately. All of them, not just the pit. You will find that they are in dire need of your attention. If both doctors will sign the medical declaration, Jared can sign the power-of-attorney document. Benjamin, will you witness the signatures with me? Thank you. I had not expected this to happen so soon, but the situation here and at the pit can continue no longer.'

As soon as the signing was complete, Jared bowed to the others. 'If you will excuse me, gentlemen, I have urgent business in Mexton.' He went outside to his waiting horse. He was in charge of the pit and he was eager to take up his responsibility. But he had more important things on his mind. He was impatient to see Olivia, to tell her the news, to hold her in his arms, kiss her and love her. He had waited too long already, and spurred his horse into a gallop.

Chapter 31

'You are not strong enough to come downstairs yet.'

Olivia steadied herself on the handle as she closed the kitchen door that led to the bottom of the staircase. 'I am here now, Miss Trent, so do not send me back to bed. I am not a child.'

'No. But you have lost a great deal of blood, which weakens the body.'

'Do not scold me, Miss Trent!'

In the ensuing silence, Olivia realized that Miss Trent was right. She was feeling very shaky.

The older woman noticed. 'Meat and drink will put you to rights. Sit at the table. There is good broth in the pot.'

Olivia did not obey. She was shivering in spite of the thick shawl over her nightgown. Her feet were bare so she crossed to stand on the rag rug by the fire.

Miss Trent pulled a low chair nearer to the coals and rummaged in the alcove cupboard. 'Here, put these on.' She handed her a pair of old felt slippers, then ladled some broth into a bowl.

Olivia waved it aside. 'I cannot eat. Not just now.'

'Try some brandy. It will revive you.'

'Have we any?'

'Jared brought some. I'll fetch it now. You should not be out of bed. You are trembling.'

'Where is Jared? He said he would call today.'

'He – he had urgent business this morning.'

'And it is tea-time already.'

'He has a forge to run.'

'You are always making excuses, Miss Trent. You forgive everybody their sins, don't you?'

'It is not a sin to go to work. He said he would call and he will.'

Olivia did not reply. She stared into the flames licking the base of the blackened broth pot. She stretched out her hand with the empty brandy glass. 'A little more this time, please.'

'Have some broth, Livvy. Please.' But she poured the brandy.

'Thank you.' Her eyes lit up. 'That's a horse outside. Is it Jared?'

Miss Trent moved to the kitchen window. 'He's brought his mare to the back.'

A minute later he was in the kitchen. His face was even greyer and more haggard than when she had first seen him. But he was here, which was all that mattered to Olivia.

Her arms snaked around him and her wrap fell away as she pressed herself to his solid frame. She had always thought of him as her rock, her staff, her anchor, and that was why she had been so distraught and angry when he had left her. But he was back now. Here. With her.

Jared took her slight frame in his arms and held her so close that she could hardly breathe. He held her as though she was the last living thing on earth, and she welcomed his embrace. 'Hesley cannot touch you now,' he whispered into her neck. 'You're safe from him for ever. You're safe. You're safe.'

She wondered what he had done that he could say that, but she didn't care. Her questions could wait. She was so happy to be in his arms that she could not speak. In a moment he would kiss her, she was sure. She raised her head to meet his lips.

Jared savoured the moment when he held her in his arms. He loved her so much, had yearned for her so desperately during their years apart, that he hardly dared kiss her for fear of releasing the caged animal of his passion. Hesley could not separate them now. She was safe from the asylum, from his neglect and cruelty. One day Jared would make her his. One day Hesley would die and she would be free. He was vaguely aware of a rap on the door, of Miss Trent leaving the room, of other voices in the house. The next thing he knew, a strong, masculine voice was demanding, 'What are you doing with my wife, sir?'

The voice was familiar.

'Jared Tyler? I do not believe my eyes! This lady is my wife!'

Olivia felt cold air swirl over her as Jared relaxed his grip. She heard him say, 'Holmes?' and then, incredulously, 'Your wife?' before she slithered down through his arms to the floor. The next thing she was aware of was the heaviness of blankets settling over her in her bed. And then welcome oblivion.

It was dark when she awoke but a candle was burning near her head and a familiar figure dozing in the chair next to it. Wide awake, she struggled to sit up. 'Anna? What are you doing here?'

'I came with Toby. He was worried about you.'

She sank against the pillows as recent events flooded back. 'What happened? Did I faint?'

'You should not have been out of bed.'

'Now you are telling me what to do.'

'Someone must,' Anna responded gently.

'What have they said to you?'

'Who? Jared Tyler and Harriet Trent?'

Harriet? she thought. Was that her name? How odd to think she had never known. Olivia thought it suited her.

'Well, they have told me quite a story,' Anna continued.

'So Toby knows who I am.'

'Livvy . . . Livvy, why didn't you trust us?'

'You would have sent me back.'

Anna stroked Olivia forehead with her soft fingers and murmured, 'What shall we do with you now?'

Olivia had no idea. But the magistrate would send her to gaol when he found out about her marriage to Toby. She didn't want that. She wanted to stay here with – with . . . Not with Toby, to be sure. She wanted to be with Jared. But how could she say so to Anna? Anna was the most saintly woman she had ever met and she had deceived her and her beloved brother most cruelly.

She answered, in a small voice, 'I'm sorry. You were both so kind to me. I – I just wanted to stay.'

'Of course. You must look to getting strong again and not worry.'

But Olivia did worry. She worried greatly. 'Does Toby know about the baby?'

'He is very distressed and has gone back to the farmhouse.'

Olivia's guilt for deceiving him ran deep. An apology was not enough. She could think of nothing to say and the silence lengthened. Eventually she said, 'I thought the farmhouse was closed up.'

'We have raised money to renew the lease. That is why I am here.'

Olivia brightened. 'Oh, some good news at last. We need you. You know about Mrs Wilton? And Mr Wilton's accident?'

The door opened and a sleepy Harriet Trent came in with a candle. 'I heard you talking.'

Anna looked over her shoulder. 'All is well, Harriet. Go back to bed.'

Olivia yawned. 'Do you know each other?' She saw them exchange a smile.

427

Anna said, 'We'll talk more tomorrow. Go back to sleep now.'

The next morning she felt stronger. The magistrate was not yet aware of her bigamy, but she guessed that someone would inform him. Then the constable would be looking for her. Toby came to see her in the afternoon. He tried to smile but his face showed his disappointment in her.

'I'm sorry,' she said again. It seemed she had to say that to them all, but to Toby more than anyone else. He and Anna had welcomed her into their home without question, and they had trusted her. She had betrayed their confidence for her own selfish reasons. 'I do not expect your forgiveness,' she added.

'Why did you do it?' he pleaded. 'Why did you agree to marry me?'

'I did not want to, but you were so insistent.'

'I loved you.'

'Loved?'

His chin dropped and he shook his head. 'It is difficult to keep loving someone who deceives you. You never truly returned my love, did you?'

'I tried.' Her eyes filled with tears as she remembered his kindness and patience.

'You pushed me away. Constantly.'

'I'm sorry.' She did not know what else to say. Or do.

'I don't think you ever wanted me as a husband, did you?'

She remembered Hesley making similar comments in the early days of their marriage. She must be honest with Toby now. She had always been compliant but had not known what else he had expected of her. Sadly, she shook her head.

He seemed to calm himself and continued, 'I am truly sorry you lost our child. I thought you would grow to love me eventually. But it was not to be. I see that now.'

'Do you know what will happen to me?'

'You will have to go abroad.'

Olivia felt panic rise in her breast. She did not want to leave the Riding and her friends, no matter what they thought of her actions.

'Jared has offered to take you,' he went on.

'He has?' she responded hopefully.

'But he cannot. He has the coal mine to run now. Harriet will explain it to you. Your – your husband is very ill.'

'I want to stay here.'

'Do not be stubborn about this, Livvy. The word is out in the village as to who you are. If you don't leave soon it is only a matter of time before the magistrate hears and sends the constable to arrest you. Jared is asking Mr Withers's advice about this on the pretence of it being for one of the hurriers at the pit.'

'But it wasn't a proper wedding,' she protested, 'in the parish church. The minister who performed our chapel ceremony has gone to Africa, hasn't he? Only you and I are left.' When she saw how much these words hurt him, she covered her eyes with her hands and fell back into her pillows. How thoughtless she was! She had not meant to be so unkind.

His frown deepened. 'We cannot deny that a

ceremony took place. Chapel marriages are legal now and recorded in a special book kept for the purpose.'

'A book?' She did not remember there having been a book at their wedding.

'It's in the law that allows our chapels to celebrate marriages. They have to be recorded.'

'Who keeps the book?'

'That new lawyer, Jessup. He deals with all the legislation for the parish.'

Jessup. The name triggered memories and she went quiet. If he had behaved like a gentleman that night and not insisted on his winnings, she might never have left, might never have met Toby and never have been in this situation.

Jessup owed her, she thought, and she wanted revenge. Before she went to gaol. She wanted to expose him for what he was. She did not know how, but she would think of something. She wondered where he kept his precious book.

'Did you hear what I said, Livvy?'

'I was drifting a little.'

'We must part for ever now.'

Although she did not love him, she felt a slight constriction in her heart. Toby had treated her with tenderness and respect. She met his eyes and said, 'I am very sorry I betrayed your trust and hurt you so much. I was – I was quite desperate at the time.'

He nodded. 'I do understand. I shall not visit you again. If you decide not to go abroad I shall speak up for you at your trial.'

'Thank you, Toby.'

'Stay here with Harriet until you are strong enough to travel. She will care for you and keep me informed. Jared will be at the pit every day if you need anything.' As he left the room he half turned and spoke over his shoulder. 'Do think again about leaving England.'

But Olivia's thoughts were elsewhere, with Jared. She knew with certainty now that she did not want to be apart from him. Just seeing him again had told her so. When he had held her in his arms, for those short, sweet moments, he had confirmed what she had known all those years ago. She loved him and she wanted to be with him for ever.

She wondered if he felt the same. She had thought he did until Toby had interrupted their embrace, and now she fretted about her past behaviour. What would Jared think of her? Would he still want her now that she had lived with Toby as his wife? She could not bear it if he spurned her.

She had made it so easy for him to reject her. She was a bigamist who would soon be tried and gaoled for her crime. Why should he even speak to her? She almost began to sob, then tried to pull herself together. She could not run away from her life any more, and did not wish to. Her conversation with Toby had given her an idea. She didn't know if she was brave enough to see it through, but she did not want to be parted from Jared. Or from Mexton Pit. It had been expanded and run on an inheritance that was rightfully hers. But her plan meant confronting Jessup and she wasn't sure she could do that. Yet she had to. If it meant winning her freedom, she had to.

Jared, also, tried to persuade her to run away. She was still in bed and regaining her stength quickly when he came to talk about her future. He bowed formally as he entered her chamber. She yearned for him to touch her, to hold and kiss her, but he sat in a chair several feet from the bed.

'I know your marriage to Toby took place in the chapel,' he argued patiently, 'but it was lawful. The chapel is registered with York and the recorder was there to witness the ceremony.'

'Recorder? What recorder?'

'The lawyer who keeps the register. Jessup.'

'He wasn't there.'

'Are you sure?'

'Of course.'

'But did you not sign your names in his book after the ceremony?'

'There was no book.'

'He should have been there with his register. That is the law now.'

'Well, he was not.'

'How can you be sure?' Jared persisted. 'Do you know Jessup?'

She wished she didn't, but replied, 'Oh, yes. I know him. No one else was there.'

'I do not think it will make any difference. He probably wrote the record afterwards, and who will argue with him?'

'I will. And Toby said he would. He did not sign any book either.'

He smiled at her sympathetically. 'The book is

evidence that the ceremony took place. It will be at your trial. You cannot do anything about it, Olivia.'

There was an uneasy silence.

'I don't want to go to gaol,' she said eventually.

'You could live in France. English people have settled there, soldiers and camp-followers who stayed on after Napoleon's defeat.'

'I won't go without you, and you cannot leave the pit. It needs you. Mexton folk need you. I shall not run away.'

'But what will you do?' Jared pleaded.

Olivia gazed out of the window and wondered.

Chapter 32

It was the end of the day, cold, dark and damp. The glow of lamplight in windows was as welcoming as the smell of soup or stew wafting across the street. Jessup's offices were in a new stone building close to the town centre. The upstairs chamber was used as a courtroom.

Olivia had been on edge all day. She was frightened of Jessup, but she had to do this. And she could not ask for help. She could not involve her friends in such a risky venture. She had waited until after dinner, until Harriet had gone to have tea with Anna in the farmhouse, before she left.

Now, her heart thumping, she approached Jessup's office cautiously, her face hidden by her cloak hood. She stayed in the shadows and watched his clerks leave one by one. Through the window she saw him move from his desk to close the shutters. She slipped inside, giving a saucy wink to the youth who was letting himself out to go home, and turned the key in the lock behind her.

'Who's there?' The door to his office opened and a shaft of light fell across the passage.

'Mr Jessup?' She kept her voice light. 'I must speak with you, sir.'

'Who are you? What do you want?'

'May we speak, sir?'

'Where is my clerk?'

'He has just left, sir.'

He held the door wide open. 'Come into the light where I can see you.'

When she saw him she wavered. The memory returned of his brutality and her humiliation, raw and real. She breathed in deeply to quell her fear, and as she did so, her eyes narrowed and her mouth set firm. When faced with difficulties she had always done what she'd had to to get through and now was no different. Somehow, she found the strength to step forward.

When her hood fell back he was astounded. 'You? So the rumour is true. You did not leave the Riding.' His tone was disrespectful and mocking. 'You know that the constable will be after you before long.'

'That is why I am here.'

'I cannot help you. I represent the law, madam, not the law-breaker.'

'I am told you keep the register of marriages that take place in the chapel.'

'So?'

'May I see it?'

'Certainly not.'

'But I wish to inspect the entry you made for my marriage,' she continued firmly, 'and the date when you attended the chapel.'

'That won't help you. You went through the ceremony, which makes you guilty.'

'But you were not present, were you? And you should have been. Where were you? There was a race meeting at Doncaster that day. Were you there with Hesley?'

'And if I was?'

'You will not want the magistrate to know that, will you? If you show me the book I shall know that you were present in the chapel. Otherwise I did not see you there, sir.'

She smiled sweetly and let her cloak slip from her shoulders. She had chosen her gown carefully. It was the day gown she had worn when she had escaped from Hill Top House and kept for Sunday best. It was made of good cloth. It covered her well with extra lace at the neckline – but it fitted her closely, too, and he noticed.

'Show me the record, and I need not say that to the magistrate,' she repeated, undoing the ribbons of her bonnet.

'Why would you not tell him?'

'I have little to gain, whatever the outcome. I prefer to have you as my friend rather than as my enemy.' She leaned forward and lengthened her neck to show the swell of her breasts. Jessup had been greedy for her body once and she hoped he would remember. 'You have influence, sir, with the magistrate.'

He gave a short laugh. 'You are offering me your body? You were a cold fish last time.'

'It was a shock, sir. I did not know you and was not willing. Not at first . . .' She raised her eyebrows. 'But now I am sure I shall be different.' She pulled at the lace covering the swell of her breasts. It came away in her hand.

He walked around the desk. 'Here?' he asked. 'Now?'

She straightened. 'Show me the book first.'

He laughed again and went to a cupboard, selected a heavy ledger and laid it open on his desk. 'There. Recorded, signed and –' he sneered again '– legal.'

Her signature certainly looked like her own. And Toby's. She supposed Jessup must have copied them. It would have been easy enough for him to get hold of originals. There were few other entries. Most couples, even chapelgoers, still celebrated their marriage in the parish church where the vicar kept his own register.

As she examined the damning evidence of her crime, he took hold of her neck and bent to search under her skirts.

She stepped away from him. 'A kiss, sir, is all that I meant. I need a little more in return for – for what you want.'

'You are in no position to bargain.'

'There is the matter of your wager with Hesley. It was not the behaviour of a gentleman with responsibility for keeping parish documents.'

'Who will believe an adulteress and bigamist?'

'Does it matter if they don't? The town matrons will ask questions and I have no reputation to lose.'

After a short silence he asked, 'What more do you want?'

'I need your help before the magistrate, sir.'

'You are guilty, madam. You will go to gaol.'

'But you would not wish me to be there for a long time?'

'Why not?'

She inhaled steadily to slow her hammering heart as she unhooked the fastenings that held her skirt in place and it slipped down over her full petticoats. 'Tonight will be only the beginning.' Her hands moved to the buttons on her bodice. 'So many of these, sir. Will you help me?'

His fingers fiddled feverishly and she could feel his breath fanning her face. 'You are offering to become my mistress when you are free again?'

'If you will speak to the magistrate on my behalf. Quietly, beforehand.'

'That will not keep you out of gaol.'

'But my stay need not be so long. And when my sentence is over I shall be available for you.'

Surely he could hear how loudly her heart was beating as he loosened her bodice. She faced him in the lamplight, noticing the darkened gleam in his eyes as he contemplated her body. She wriggled her hips and her overskirt slipped to the floor. 'Is there . . . somewhere more comfortable?' she murmured.

'The supper rooms upstairs, where the courts are held.'

'How perfect! During my trial we shall be reminded of the pleasures to come.' She paused. 'When I am free.'

She took a backward glance at the book on his desk, at her cloak, skirt and bodice lying abandoned on the floor. Her mind was in turmoil but she noted that he locked the door after him. She saw also that he needed a key for the upstairs room, which he left in the lock. He had hung his office key on a hook by the door. He carried a lamp up the stairs, went into the chamber and placed it on the large, polished oblong table. There were chairs around the table and couches against the walls.

'Close the shutters,' she asked, and as he did so, she took her chance.

Swiftly she retreated, locking the door behind her and retrieving the office key from its hook. She sped downstairs with both keys in her hand. She heard him shout and thump on the door and knew it would not be long before someone else heard him and investigated. In her haste she fumbled with the office lock, losing precious seconds.

The room was darker than the stairs had been. She focused her eyes as best she could, found her cloak, wrapped it round herself and rammed her bonnet over her hair. Swiftly, she crossed to the desk, closed the book, wrapped it in her bodice, then her overskirt, and fled out of the building, locking the front door behind her and clasping three heavy keys in her hand.

Jessup had already opened the shutters and was wrenching at the windows. She ran for the shadows of an alley and melted into a doorway to pull on her skirt and bodice, leaving many buttons unfastened. Quickly she made her way to the canal and, with all her strength, flung in the keys and the book. The keys plopped and disappeared quickly. The book gave a satisfying slap as it hit the water, causing ripples to spread around it.

She panicked as it seemed to float, but, slowly, it sank beneath the oily black surface. She felt a pang of guilt for those couples whose entries she had destroyed. But she was desperate and hoped they would forgive her. Without the book how could anyone prove there had been a marriage? There had been no other witnesses. No one, she hoped, who would speak against her in favour of Jessup.

There was no evidence for a trial.

Chapter 33

'What were you thinking? Taking Toby's trap into town on your own!'

Livvy was sitting by the fire, reading a news-sheet that Anna had brought. She called regularly, returning Harriet's visits to the farmhouse. Livvy did not join them there. She respected Toby's wish not to see her again and welcomed this time to herself, to read and to think. And, on this occasion, to go into town.

She had fretted all the way back to Mexton about the repercussions of her visit to Jessup's office. Perhaps she had made the situation worse for herself. But word was out in the town about Hesley's state of mind and of how Jessup had neglected his affairs while he was supposedly looking after them. She guessed he had a reputation to salvage.

Jared came to see her on his way home from the

pit. He called when he was able to get away early enough, bringing her small luxuries. A book, a piece of lace or a length of ribbon and, once, a tiny porcelain pot of the lightest salve she had ever used. He said it came from London and Adam Harvey had recommended it for ladies' complexions in the colder months. He was waiting anxiously when she got back from town and came outside with a lantern to take the horse.

'Toby said I might use his pony and trap when I was well again,' she replied. 'He brought it over himself.'

'You have spoken with him?'

'No. He did not come into the house.'

'I was worried about you, Livvy. It is well past dark.'

'It is not late. Night falls early at this time of year.'

'All the more reason for you to make haste.'

'I am home and safe now, am I not?'

'Where is Harriet? She should have gone with you.'

'She's at the old farmhouse with Anna and Toby. She visits them often and helps them in the mission.' She paused. 'As I used to.'

Jared handed her the lantern and she watched him secure the horse beside his own. She didn't want him to be angry with her. She wanted him to take her in his arms. But since Toby had returned and uncovered her disgrace, Jared had seemed distant. She hoped he would not start giving her orders, as Hesley had done. When she handed back the lantern and he had helped her down, he said, 'I'll return the pony and trap for you.'

'There is no need. Toby will walk back with Harriet and collect it.'

'He is a good man, Livvy.'

'I know.'

'You used him badly.'

'I know.'

'Will you not think again about leaving the country? I could arrange to go with you. Until you are settled.'

She would have liked that more than anything in the world. But she shook her head and said, 'You're needed at Mexton Pit.'

'Perhaps Harriet will travel with you.'

'I would not ask her to leave Anna and Toby. Anna has passed on her asylum mission to others and they are talking of a new venture at the old farmhouse.'

'I cannot bear to think of you in gaol.' She detected anguish in his voice and realized he knew the conditions she would have to endure.

She had caused him too much distress. 'It will not be for long.' But as she spoke she thought of how she had stolen and destroyed the record book, and that if Jessup got her before the magistrate he would now be her enemy. He would be vengeful, she was sure. 'They will not hang me, will they?'

'Not for bigamy.'

'Or transport me to the colonies?'

'You will be locked up, I am afraid. The magistrate is harder on women than men in these matters. More so, if a husband is obliged to cast aside his wife, as Hesley is.'

Livvy stood by the gate that led to the cottage's back yard and kicked restlessly against its wooden post.

She wanted to take his hand and hold it, draw strength from it. But she feared he would push her away. In the yellow glow from the lantern she noticed Jared's riding boots, scuffed and dusty from his long day's work at the pit. His head was bare and his hair was long, curling over his collar. He must be exhausted, waiting for her to return before he rode home. But she was pleased that he had, and responded brightly, 'The constable has not come for me yet.'

He raised the light and peered closely at her face. 'Do not treat this matter lightly, Olivia. Mr Withers says that if criminals are repentant for their actions they find favour with the magistrate.'

'Of course I am repentant! It was wrong of me to marry Toby. I did not wish it and I told him so I offered to live with him as his wife without a ceremony.'

The horror on Jared's features silenced her. What would he think of her after such an admission? But it was the truth and she could not hide it from him.

'You must not say that in front of the magistrate,' he replied. 'It will make matters worse for you. And it will ruin your character for ever.'

'Oh, I see. It was all right for Uncle Hesley to keep a mistress in town, but not for me live as one?'

'It is the way things are. You must see that too.'

'Oh, yes. I see that very well.'

'Please try to be calm. I have a solution that may help you.'

'What is it?'

'You must demonstrate your repentance.'

'You sound like Harriet.'

'Be sensible, for Heaven's sake! Hesley is your lawful husband. You must return to him and live in his house.'

'Never.'

'Where is your reason? If you show the town that you have mended your ways, you have a chance of a more lenient sentence.'

'I cannot live with Hesley. Or, indeed, in that house. It will destroy me. My memories of it are all bad.'

'All?'

There was such kindness in his tired eyes, and such gentleness in his voice, that a sharp response died on her lips.

'I believe you were happy there once,' he murmured.

'Before my marriage. When Harriet was my governess. And – and you were my friend.'

'I am still your friend.'

She did not doubt it, and loved him even more for not deserting her now. But was that all he was to her? She wished so desperately that he was more than a friend, that they were lovers and could run away together to France, to live as husband and wife, and never return to her terrible memories at Hill Top House.

She wondered if she could persuade him to take her abroad. She believed he would if she insisted. But as the notion flitted through her mind she knew it could never be. She could not ask him to abandon his responsibilities at the pit. The livelihood of too many folk depended on him. The Mexton colliers respected him and, in time, he would take over his father's forge as well. The South Riding needed him as much as she did. She must stay and take her punishment. 'I'm frightened, Jared. I've done a wicked thing.'

She was thinking also of Jessup's book at the bottom of the canal. Her impulsive gesture had compounded her already uncertain situation.

'Try not to worry,' Jared said quietly. 'Mr Withers says he will speak for you at the court.'

'You have told him I am here?'

'He guessed. He had heard the rumour and I – I have been seeking his advice.'

She pulled her cloak closer around herself. 'He is a law-abiding gentleman. He will have to tell the magistrate.'

She was right. Jared knew he had to persuade her to return to Hesley, no matter the cost to himself. His hand moved of its own accord to hers and she clasped it tightly, causing his pulses to race. He breathed deeply to quell his pounding heart. 'Let us go inside to the warmth. There is something else we must talk about.'

They went into the kitchen of the Wiltons' terraced cottage. The fire burned brightly and she lit a candle. In the increased light she saw that not only were Jared's boots dusty, but his jacket and trousers rumpled and greasy. She took off her cloak and bonnet and hung them behind the door, realizing that her own appearance was dishevelled and grubby. Hastily she took down a large apron, tied it over her bodice and skirt, then pulled on a cotton cap.

Jared drew two chairs closer to the fire 'Hesley is still your husband and there are decisions to be made about his – er – future.'

'Not by me, surely? You and Adam Harvey can do that.'

'You are his wife.'

'But he has disowned me! No one will listen to me so why do you ask?'

'Hill Top House needs you too. It is your home, where you belong. If you return to Hesley and show you have reformed, it will help Mr Withers to plead your case at the trial. You might find a little happiness there. Somewhere.'

If you were there I should, Livvy thought. She had been truly happy there for such a short time, from the Christmas when she had met Jared and sat in her grandfather's coach with him, then on the slopes beyond the little church until he had ordered her not to think of him as more than a friend. She would willingly have given him all her love, all of herself. She would do it now if she had thought he would accept it.

She thought he might have loved her before Toby had found them together. But he had a position to uphold in the Riding and he would suffer if he was associated with her in that way. He would seek companionship and love from a genteel, respectable lady, like his mother or sisters, not from a bigamist adulteress who was now also a thief. Lord, what had she become? She was lucky to have a friend like Jared, who would not snub her in the roadway. She wondered how much longer she could suffer the frustration of having only his friendship.

'And you were, at least, content with Harriet at Hill Top House?' he continued.

'Perhaps,' she said. 'I enjoyed learning.'

'You have a right to return. You are Hesley's legal wife.'

'Surely he will not have me over the threshold?'

'He is mad, Livvy. Insane. I am his legal attorney.'

'You? I thought that was Jessup.'

For the first time that evening she detected a smile on his lips. 'I have the power to make Hesley's decisions for him. That is why I am running the mine.'

'Do you own Mexton Pit? And Hill Top House?'

He gave a soft laugh. 'I do not *own* any of it. I am simply responsible for it.' He stopped smiling and added, 'And you.'

'So that is why you visit me here? Because I am your responsibility?'

'Is that what you think? You are a suspicious woman.'

'You would be suspicious if you'd been through what I've been through.'

He glared at her. 'How do you know what I've been through since you disappeared?'

She covered her eyes with a hand and pushed the cotton cap back from her brow. She could feel the agitation rising in her breast. Fear of the future was always uppermost in her mind, he should know that. She heard him get up and rummage is the cupboard by the fire.

'Have you finished the brandy?' he muttered. 'That is the only thing I have against the Methodists. They do not keep spirits in their houses.'

'If you'd seen Hesley and his grandfather together, you'd know why.'

'Have a little sympathy, Olivia. I was at the pit at five this morning, getting that steam engine up to pressure.'

Livvy stood up and took a metal tankard from the dresser. 'Harriet brews beer. It's in the scullery.'

Jared found a stone bottle of porter in the cupboard. He poured it into another tankard, then filled a wine muller with hot coals and warmed it for her. She took it from him, gave him the beer and they resumed their seats by the fire.

'Do not quarrel with me, Olivia. This is difficult enough as it is. You must understand that returning to Hesley is your best chance of a light sentence,' Jared persisted.

She sipped the porter. There was no honey in it but its warmth and robust bite were welcome. He was at the pit every day now, Harriet had told her, but she had not known he was there so early. Output was rising already, Harriet had said. The colliers welcomed Jared Tyler's efforts.

'I want to stay here, in Mexton,' she said. Near to you, she thought.

'No, Olivia. You have caused a scandal. You will be shunned.'

'I'll help in the mission,' she suggested.

'With Toby? You cannot do that to him. This is as painful for me as it is for you, but you must go back to Hesley.'

'I can't.'

He frowned. He could not persuade her and she would suffer more as a result. 'Can you tell me what you want for Hesley?' he asked. 'I have to make a decision about his future.'

'He is sick. Let the doctors decide.' She heard a noise and voices in the scullery. 'That's Harriet. It sounds as though Anna is with her. They were carrying over curtains from the farmhouse for one of the villagers.'

'What do you want me to do about Hesley?' he persisted.

'I cannot help him,' she said. 'No one can. Hesley will have to go to the asylum.'

'No!'

Olivia and Jared turned. Anna was standing in the doorway to the scullery. 'Not the asylum,' she said.

Harriet was standing behind her. 'How bad is he, Jared?' she asked.

'I have no experience of these things,' he replied, 'but you have, both of you. You will know what to do and I should welcome your counsel.'

'I should like to see him.' Anna said softly, and Harriet reached for her hand.

'Olivia?' Jared queried. 'Will you come with us?'

She looked at the three waiting for her answer. It would mean going back to Hill Top House and she had vowed never to do that while Hesley was there.

'I do not like that house . . . My memories . . .'

'Then we must replace them with better ones,' Jared said. 'It is only a building made of stone and slate, wood and lime. Old Hesley made that house a bad place to live, but he has gone.'

She would be with Jared and she trusted him. He would not deceive her and use her as others had.

450

He had always wanted to do what was best. For her, for Hesley even, and for the pit. Perhaps it would not be such an ordeal for her to return there if Jared was with her.

She nodded.

'We'll go tomorrow,' Jared decided. 'After I've been to the pit. I'll bring the trap from home. We must make haste before the constable catches up with you.'

'Madam! Ee, you made me jump.'

'How are you, Mrs Cookson?'

The housekeeper was rummaging in the pantry and had not noticed them arrive. 'I never expected to see you up here again. Are you back for good?'

Olivia didn't answer.

'You'll have heard about the young master?'

'That's why I'm here.'

'I've heard a tale or two about you, an' all, but I'm right glad to see you.'

Olivia looked around the untidy shelves. 'Are Mary and Eliza still with you?'

'They are. But they have to do most of my work now I see to the master.' Mrs Cookson appeared much older and her face was lined and tired. 'Are you coming back, madam? We're in a right pickle without you, these days.'

'We'll see,' Olivia replied. 'Miss Trent is with me. Will you take us up to him?'

They went into the hall, where Jared, Harriet and Anna were waiting, and climbed the dark wooden staircase to Hesley's bedchamber. He was quite peaceful as he slept.

451

'He's quieter nowadays,' Mrs Cookson told them. 'He has medicines that do it and he doesn't take the drink. But he needs seeing to all the time. It's like having a newborn, with the feeding and the changing and the washing.'

'Does he know who you are?' Harriet queried.

'Sometimes. Sometimes not.'

'Will he die?' Livvy asked.

'We all die eventually,' Mrs Cookson responded. 'Are you going to take him away?'

'He doesn't have to be in the asylum,' Harriet said. 'He can be looked after here.'

'Will you do it, then, Miss Trent?' Mrs Cookson demanded.

They stood in silence around the bed. It was only then that Livvy noticed Anna, staring silently and – *weeping*. She was not mistaken. Tears were rolling down her cheeks.

'I'll do it,' Anna said in a low voice. 'I'll look after him. If I may.'

'Why would you want to do that?' Livvy asked quietly.

Anna lifted her head. Her eyes were bright and her gentle lined face filled with sadness and pain. 'He is my son,' she said.

'Anna, why don't you sit down?' Harriet had been the first to speak.

Livvy said, 'Hesley's mother died when he was a baby. Shortly after his father was killed.'

'No, she didn't – *I* didn't.'

Jared moved to stand before her and took her hand. 'Are you saying that you are Aunt Sukie?'

452

Anna nodded. 'Susannah. I was baptized Susannah. After John Wesley's mother. She was known as Sukie, too.'

'Uncle Hesley said you were dead.'

'I was to him.'

Jared put an arm round her shoulders and led her to a chair. 'Why didn't you tell us? This is too much for you to bear.'

'You have been at the mission all the time?' Livvy said.

Harriet intervened: 'Anna was a patient at the asylum. Old Hesley put her there.'

Livvy choked with horror. 'My God! If he were not dead I should kill him myself. Poor Anna.'

'Poor Hesley.' Anna stood up, walked to the bed and stroked her son's sunken, pallid cheek. 'Let me do this for him now.'

Harriet moved to the bed to be beside her and said quietly, 'Jared, would you take Livvy downstairs? I'll stay here with Anna.'

Standing in the gloomy hall, Livvy's heart was thumping in her breast. 'I should like some fresh air,' she said.

He ached to hold and comfort her, yet he dared not. Her renewed devotion to her marriage vows must be unmistakable to everyone. 'We'll walk together,' he said. But apart, he thought.

She set off with him, past the walled garden with her fruit bushes and vegetable rows, now neglected and overgrown, and up the hill towards the little church on the moor. The wind was keen and they wrapped their cloaks closely about them as they climbed.

'I can hardly take this in,' she muttered.

'Nor I. A lifetime of separation. A whole lifetime.'

'And Anna's mission at the asylum, too. To go back to the scene of so much of her suffering and help others in their misery. She is too good for this earth.'

'She is a Methodist. They do not flinch from their duty. I admire them for that.'

'You would make a good Methodist, Jared.'

'Don't say that to my mother.' He laughed gently. Then he became serious. 'Poor Anna. You will agree to her request to look after Hesley, won't you?'

'Of course. She has endured such hardship. I shall help her where I can.'

'Does that mean you will move into Hill Top House?'

'Why, yes. If Anna is determined, I shall return.' Livvy stared at the rutted track beneath her feet. 'But it will not be long before I am taken away.'

Her words sliced through him like a knife. 'I hardly dare think of it. It pains me so,' he muttered.

It pained Livvy, too, to think that her actions were the cause of Jared's unhappiness. But her heartache amounted to nothing compared with Anna's. She inhaled sharply, straightened her back and quickened her pace. 'Do not grieve for me, Jared. I am young and strong. Whatever I have to endure, I am sure it cannot be as dreadful as the asylum.'

But he knew he would suffer every day that she was away. He said, 'I shall make it known in town that you have returned to be with your ailing husband.'

454

'Hesley will take Anna from her new venture in Mexton.'

'Harriet is helping Toby to set up his mission school at the farmhouse. As soon as the pit is in profit again I shall be able to support them with money.'

'You are a good man, Jared. The miners' children will have an education.'

'I hope so. The pasture is dry today. Shall we go across to our cottage?'

Jared was silent as they walked. She wondered if he was remembering the last time they had been there together. They had quarrelled because he would not kiss her and love her as she had wished him to.

'I thought about you all time I was away,' he said quietly.

'I thought I saw you sometimes. In the distance. I always hoped it was you, but you never came back. And that made me more angry with you.'

'We both know what would have happened if we'd met without Harriet to chaperone us.'

Yes. Yes, yes, yes! She had wanted it so much that she had ached for his touch. She glanced sideways. Her passion for him had not dimmed with their years of separation and her body still yearned to be possessed by his. She wondered if he could tell by looking at her. 'They were good times, weren't they?' she said at last.

'The best.'

She stopped and turned to face him. 'Do you think so? Really?'

'Truly.'

They stared at each other. Jared did not know where he found the strength to keep his hands at his sides until Olivia moved on and they continued to the dry-stone wall that surrounded their cottage garden. 'Shall we sit a while?' she suggested. 'The air is wonderfully fresh out here today.'

They looked at the view in silence. Then Jared said, 'Hill Top House is where you belong, Olivia.'

'I know,' she agreed, and thought, You too. You belong there with me. She said, 'Will you live there while I am in gaol?'

'Me?'

'It is your responsibility now, is it not?'

'It is too far from the pit.'

'Cross-country on horseback? Surely not.' She took a deep breath. 'If you do stay there, I shall come back and live with you when I am freed.'

'Another scandal – won't it worry you?'

'You have power of attorney for my husband. It is right that you should be there.'

He passed a hand over his brow. 'I cannot think beyond your being in gaol. I hate to think of you locked away. What shall I do? I love you. I have loved you so much and for so long that it hurts.'

Had her ears deceived her? 'You love me? Oh, Jared, I have loved you since that first Christmas we met. Say it again!'

'I love you, Olivia. I always have, but you are married. It is impossible for us to be together.'

'Not any longer, surely?' Suddenly she reached over to grasp his hands and pull him close. 'The constable will arrive for me any day now. Let us not waste this time alone together. Hold me, Jared. Hold me close. Kiss me. Love me.'

He had kept two paces distant from her as they walked. When they sat on the wall, he had placed himself with enough space for Harriet to sit between them, had she been there. And now he did not know whether he wished she were or was glad that she was not.

He wondered how much more his heart could take. It felt as though it were being wrung out, twisted and squeezed until he was sure it would expire from exhaustion. He was elated that they should be together so naturally and so comfortably, walking, talking, sometimes sharing an easy silence. But he was dashed to the ground and broken by the thought of her locked away.

Yet when she had talked of past good times his heart had soared. He had thought it would burst out of his chest when she agreed to return to Hill Top House. And then to ask him to live there with her was too much for him to bear.

Yet bear it he must, for soon she would be taken away from him. And though she would have the worst of it, and he grieved for that, he did not know how his tortured heart would survive without her. Not now that he had found her. He knew he wanted never to let her out of his sight. So when she pulled him towards her, his well-meaning resolve to respect her married status bolted away on the breeze.

He had control enough for both of them, he knew that, and had relied on it over the years, sometimes in wretched anger that it must be so, but mostly because he loved her. He knew also that if he had the control of two men he had also the passion of ten, and she was right. He should not, would not, *could not* waste this precious time together.

He kissed her hands first, each palm in turn, then her lips, exploring their sweet softness with an ecstasy born of longing. She slid to the ground, pulling him after her and he rolled onto his back. Once joined, their lips did not part as she undid his heavy cloak, then her own and pushed them aside on the crushed grass.

She fumbled with the buttons on his jacket and trousers, and he helped her. And when he was free of such encumbrance he searched beneath her skirts for the tapes of her drawers. Her skirts – there was so much of them! His heart, his poor wrung-out heart, was pounding so loudly in his ears that he thought they would both be deafened by it.

She kicked aside her drawers and fell away from him, onto her back, and for a few seconds the cold air intruded between them. But she was smiling at him. Her eyes shone with tears of happiness as, already, his hands explored the warm flesh of her thighs above her garters. And beyond.

They were not kissing when they became as one, and his eyes seemed to close of their own accord as he began to love her, nervously, gently, tentatively at first, then with growing urgency and a confidence that enabled him to look at her again. The expression of wonder in her eyes was matched only by his own feelings. Then her breathing deepened and her body arched. She wrapped her legs around his back and his instincts took over.

Olivia had loved him and yearned for him to love her for so long that she hardly believed this was happening. It did not matter that they were in the open air, cold breeze seeping through the gaps in the stone wall, their bodies entangled with their clothing. What mattered to her was that this was one realization of love on her part and – oh, joy – on his too. He kept whispering it between kisses. He loved her.

And as he showed her that love, she experienced it with a sensation that astounded and eventually overcame her. She had so much wanted to give herself to him that her body opened like a flower. Her whole being tingled, first in anticipation and then in a desire so strong it frightened her. She moved with him, finding a posture with her back and legs that she had not even known was possible. He was taking her on a journey she had not travelled before and she let herself ride in freedom with him. Her reward shuddered through her to burst in her head like a whole heaven of stars.

Afterwards he wrapped her in his cloak and sat with his back against the dry-stone wall. He was breathing shallowly, but steadily. She felt drained of all her energy. But loved. She loved and was loved. It was all she needed. She could not speak. She had no words.

'This is not how it should be,' he said quietly.

She supposed he meant out here in the open, beside a tumbledown cottage, in the lee of a crumbling wall.

For her, it did not matter where they were, only that he loved her, she loved him, and he had fulfilled that love as none before him could.

'Yes, it is,' she replied firmly. If she were less ashamed of her recent behaviour she might have added, 'This is exactly how it should be. Take it from one who knows.'

He put his head on one side. 'I've never loved anyone else as I do you, and I never shall. This is for ever. We are for ever.'

She smiled at him, a satisfied smile, and began to pull on her drawers. 'You will have to be my looking-glass,' she said lightly.

'It will be my pleasure.' He returned the smile and retrieved her bonnet from where she had tossed it.

Chapter 34

It was several days before he visited again and Livvy's overriding fear was that the constable would come for her before she saw him again. But she occupied herself gainfully as mistress of Hill Top House, feeling that gaol would not be quite so bad with Jared's love in her heart. She was helping Anna to change the linen on Hesley's bed when she glanced out of the window, as she often did, and saw Jared riding up the track from the town.

'Go downstairs and receive him,' Anna suggested. 'I'll finish here.'

'He will have news of Toby and Harriet. Join us as soon as you can.'

Livvy removed her apron, tidied her hair, and hurried to the kitchen. 'Mrs Cookson, we have a visitor. I'll let him in. Make up the fire in the drawing room and bring some warmed ale. And Anna will want tea when she comes down.'

She opened the heavy front door as he approached and almost fell into his arms. 'Let me take your cloak. There is a good fire waiting.'

He kissed her first, a warm, passionate embrace, then took her hand and led her into the house.

'I have good news. I saw Mr Withers this morning and he is optimistic that you will not be summoned to trial for bigamy.'

Her heart turned over. Could this be true? Might she be tried for another crime instead? She dared not raise her hopes until she knew more. She hoped she sounded calm, even though she did not feel it, when she said, 'Why is that?'

'It seems that there is only rumour about your marriage to Toby. Jessup was not as thorough in his duties as he should have been and could not produce any record of the ceremony.'

'Really?' She tried to moderate the squeak in her voice.

Jared nodded. 'Mr Withers went to his office and demanded to see the evidence. Jessup said that you had stolen it but no one believes him. He has fallen from favour with the town gentry as he is constantly distracted by the races and the card tables. Who would want to steal a record book, anyway?'

Livvy stared at him. He had to know the truth. 'Me,' she answered quietly. 'That day I borrowed Toby's trap. I threw it into the canal.'

'You did?' He swallowed. 'You take far too many risks for my liking.'

'But you do not despise me for it? You will not send me away?'

'How could I? I love you. I would forgive you anything.'

'I – I was desperate. There is more to tell you about Jessup.'

He placed a finger lightly over her lips. 'Perhaps I should not know. It will stir my anger and I should want to kill him. As I wanted to kill Hesley. Then I should be the one in gaol.'

She thought that she would tell him at some time in the future. But she would not spoil their joy today with more miseries from her past. 'So, I do not need to watch and listen for the constable any more.'

'You were not at the top of his list anyway. There are still plenty of folk in town who do not think chapel ceremonies are proper marriages. Their bigotry plays in your favour.'

'Hush! Do not let Anna hear you say that.'

'But it's true,' he whispered. 'It'll take years for the South Riding to change its ways.'

'Well, in that case, I shall never be accepted as respectable by the town's matrons, shall I? I am an adulteress, if not a bigamist. It is hardly a lesser crime in their eyes.'

'You will not go to gaol for adultery and I, for one, shall thank the Lord daily for that blessing.'

They sat in companionable silence, staring into the fire. Mrs Cookson brought in their ale. 'The tea will be a few more minutes, madam,' she said. When neither replied, she bobbed a curtsy and retreated.

Jared got up to pass Olivia some ale. 'Perhaps my

mother will relent when my sisters are married. She is very shocked by our relationship and fears you will corrupt them. My father is more understanding and – and when— Oh, never mind.'

'When what?'

'I was thinking about – well, about Hesley.'

'When he dies, you mean?'

'I'm sorry, it was insensitive of me.'

'But it will happen,' she said. 'What do you want to say about when he dies?'

He had returned to his chair and stretched out his feet towards the hearth. 'We shall marry, of course.'

She had hoped he would say that. 'Yes, we shall,' she agreed.

She smiled, sadly in a way, because they must wait. But they had waited so long that a little more time would not be such a hardship. Not now they were together. She noticed that working at the pit had taken its toll on his fine leather riding boots. He needed new ones.

After a few more minutes' staring into the fire, she asked, 'Shall we live in the town?'

'Do you want to?'

'No, but Hill Top House will belong to Hesley's heir, whoever he is.'

'Oh!' Jared sat bolt upright, almost spilling his ale. 'I forgot the other thing Mr Withers told me. I'm the heir. It's in old Samuel's will. I'm the nearest male relation. Actually, the *only* male relation. That is why Mr Withers suggested I run the pit. Mexton Pit and this house will be mine.'

Olivia sipped the ale, enjoying the warmth that

spread through her veins. It wasn't just the ale, she thought. Her life was beginning to glow. She could think of no one better than Jared to inherit. 'There is some justice in this world, after all,' she murmured, 'but I shall miss the mission.'

'Now that you live here you can have your own mission.'

'My own?'

'You can do something to help the poorer folk and their children in these parts.'

'Such as?'

'Well, I don't know, but I'm sure you, Harriet and Anna can think of something. If anyone can turn this building into a house of help, you can.'

The next time Jared visited he brought the trap and took Anna to visit Toby. When she returned to Hill Top House, Harriet came with her.

'Shall I ask Harriet to live here with us?' Olivia queried, as she and Anna tended to Hesley in his chamber.

'I don't think she will want to. She spends much time at the farmhouse, getting it ready for the new school. With Toby.'

'She has talked about him all the time since she arrived. Your brother is a fine gentleman. I am truly sorry I treated him so badly. I hope he does not think ill of Harriet because of me.'

'Quite the opposite. He speaks highly of her when she is not present, her ideas, her teaching and her sound sense. I have not seen him so genuinely enamoured of a lady before. Not even you.'

'We didn't truly love each other.'

'I know. Harriet loves him, though. She has loved him for a while, now, and I believe he has fallen for her, too.'

Livvy stopped folding the sheets and straightened. 'Oh, I am so pleased for them both. They will suit each other well.'

'Yes, they will.' Anna smiled and carried on washing her son.

Livvy relayed this conversation to Jared as he rubbed down his horse in the stable.

'Well, that is good news. Toby has often talked to me of Harriet's beauty,' he said.

'Her beauty?' Livvy remembered a conversation years ago about beauty, on one of their Sunday walks when he had reproached her for her false modesty and mentioned Harriet's appearance. 'He sees beyond her pretty face, then. Into her good character as well.' She added lightly, 'I hope you did not feel you had to put him right.'

Jared glanced at her and remembered. 'He knows of her past and I – well, I was hasty in my condemnation of her.'

'And of me.'

'I did not condemn you. Ever.'

'Not even for marrying Toby?'

'I know why you did it. I admire your courage.'

He stood back from the horse to look at his handiwork. As he did so, she reached up on tiptoe and stole a kiss from him, intending to step back straight away. But he did not let her. He gathered her in his arms and returned her kiss, deeply, passionately and lovingly.

He paused for breath and whispered, 'Let's climb up to the hayloft.'

She groaned. 'I cannot. Harriet has something important to say to me. We are to have tea together. Alone,' she said. 'In the library.' Before he could speak, she rushed on, 'When are you coming to live here?'

'As soon as I can arrange it.'

'Sooner,' she replied, and he nodded.

Harriet was standing in the gloom of the bookshelves, the place where she had lingered and watched on the day she had arrived at Hill Top House. The place where she had first met Olivia, a scruffy little urchin who would have seemed more at home scavenging by the canals and was now a beautiful young woman, who had survived such dreadful events and had, at last, found happiness. Harriet watched her with pride and love.

Olivia carried in the tray and set it down near the hearth. 'This is where we first saw each other. Do you remember? You didn't beat me and I knew from that moment you were different.'

'You were wary of me, though.'

'I didn't know you. But I realized quite soon that you were special to me.'

'Special?' Harriet's heart surged.

'You always tried to protect me, and I was a difficult child, wasn't I?'

'You were intelligent, strong-willed and sometimes too impulsive.'

'I'm sorry—'

'No, don't be.'

'I was going to say that I am sorry I was so cross with you when you found me in Mexton. You stirred the anger I had when you left me. I missed you very much and I am so pleased we are friends again. In fact, we have something more than friendship, don't we?'

Harriet felt tears well in her eyes and her words stuck in her throat.

When Harriet didn't reply, Olivia stood up, walked over to her and wrapped her arms around her. 'We are like family to each other. Now, come and pour the tea while I toast the bread. What is it you want to say to me?'

Olivia thought Harriet was going to tell her about Toby. She was happy that Harriet had made a match with him. So she was surprised when her friend said, 'Do you remember your father, Olivia?'

'Not really. My mother, yes. But he – he was a shadow in the background.' Olivia knelt on the rug and skewered a piece of bread on a brass toasting-fork.

'At least you knew him.'

'You knew yours, didn't you? Until the fever took him?'

'He wasn't my true father. I was farmed out to the Trents when I was born. They were my foster-parents.'

'You were a foundling?'

'I was born out of wedlock to a servant.'

'Who told you that?'

'No one did. Did you ever wonder why I came here?'

'To get away from Blackstone, I should imagine.'

'But why here?'

'Harriet, what is this?'

'When I was a teacher at Blackstone I had privileges. Teachers were trusted to clean the principal's office where the keys were kept.' Harriet came into the firelight and picked up the silver teapot. 'And papers about the pupils. Including me.'

Livvy turned the piece of bread carefully on the fork. 'Nothing in your past will make me think ill of you, Harriet.'

'Perhaps I should have told you before now,' Harriet said quietly. 'The principal had letters and notes from a gentleman to my foster-parents, which had, at the time, enclosed sums of money for my care. They were from a Mr Copley. Oliver Copley. A drayman who delivered coal to Blackstone once mentioned a Copley girl living at Hill Top House.'

Livvy's hand dropped and the half-toasted bread fell off the fork into the fire. 'That was me. My father was Oliver Copley.'

'Yes.'

'And he knew your father?'

'He was my father.'

Livvy watched the bread burn away in the flames. 'Are you sure?'

'In two of the letters he refers to the money for his – for his daughter's upkeep. The letters and money stopped in the year he and your mother were lost at sea.' Harriet replaced the teapot on the tray without pouring. 'I was sent to the poorhouse after my foster-parents died. I was an orphan so I think my real mother must have died when I was a baby.'

Livvy was staring into the fire, unable to comprehend what she had just heard.

Harriet went on: 'When I discovered I had a sister, I wanted to find her. And when I did I wanted to be with her and care for her.' Her voice dropped to a whisper. 'That is why I could not leave you, even though it was so hard for me to stay.'

'You did it for me. You put up with all that cruelty for me,' Olivia said quietly. Then she jumped to her feet. 'We are sisters,' she cried. 'Oh, Harriet, I *knew* there was something special about you! You are my sister, my own family! I have longed for a family of my own. I could not wish for more. Come here and let me hug you again.'

They stood in the firelight, tea and toast forgotten, arms wrapped round each other, holding each other tightly for a long time.

Read on for an extract from Catherine King's wonderful new saga, *A Mother's Sacrifice*, available from Sphere in December 2009.

Chapter 1

1835

They were prettied and ready by mid-morning. Their cottage kitchen was clean and tidy and a cut-up fowl was simmering slowly with barley over the fire. Quinta finished slicing carrot and onion at the kitchen table and stood up to tip them into the blackened pot. Her best gown was covered by a large apron. She was worried about the bottom edge of the skirt getting dirty if she had to help Farmer Bilton with Darby, but her mother had insisted she wore it.

'Come to the front window, Quinta,' Laura called. 'I can see him. He's got a new horse, a beauty he is too. Just look at that beast.' She coughed then added, 'Spring's on its way now. A bit late this year but the trees are greening up nicely.'

Quinta frowned and handed her mother a horn beaker of warm water with calming honey mixture. It was time she threw off that cough. But even when she was poorly, Laura Haig managed to look beautiful. Her skin was lined but still smooth and flawless. Unconsciously, Quinta passed her fingers over her own cheeks.

'Did you put your salve on this morning?' her mother asked.

'Not yet.'

'Go upstairs and do it now, dear.'

Quinta sat down in front of her mother's looking glass and took the cork out of a squat stone jar. Mother made the precious salve herself, using wool fat and rose petal water and applied it every day without fail. Quinta spread it quickly over her face and neck, rubbing it in vigorously until the greasiness had gone. She stared at her image in the spotted glass. Folk said she looked like her mother, although she couldn't see it. She had the same hazel eyes, but Quinta's hair under her cotton cap was darker; a rich burnished brown, thick and glossy, which she plaited and wound around her head. She wondered if, now she was fourteen, she might coil it differently and curl the front.

'Hurry, dear, he's here,' her mother called.

A large black hunter carrying its smartly dressed rider ambled into their grassy yard. Mother and daughter stood outside the cottage door as he dismounted, tethered the animal at their lean-to woodshed and removed his saddlebag. Quinta watched seriously as he slid his shotgun out of its long holster. He wore a thick buttoned coat, breeches and leather gaiters, and nodded formally as he approached them. 'Good morning Mrs Haig, Miss Quinta. Where is he?'

'Down by the stream,' Quinta replied. Darby had not moved all night and Quinta was relieved his pain would soon be over.

'Best get on with it then.'

'We are pleased to welcome you here, sir. Will you stay for your dinner?' Laura asked politely.

He sniffed the air, looked from one to the other, nodded slightly and answered, 'Don't mind if I do.'

Quinta noticed her mother brighten and smile. Even if she didn't like Farmer Bilton, she knew that, as their landlord, his good opinion of them could be their salvation. Mother had been right to make an effort for his visit.

'I'll take the lass with me, Mrs Haig,' he said, adding, 'I might need an extra pair of hands.'

'Very well. Take care with your gown, my dear.'

Quinta ran ahead towards the stream. Forgetting about her skirts she knelt beside Darby, quite still beneath his canvas blanket, and fondled his ears as she held back her tears. She had ridden on his back as a child, sometimes sitting precariously on top of bulging sacks going to market before father had made the cart. Farmer Bilton loaded his gun. At least Darby's end would be painless and quick. Quinta pressed her lips together as he approached.

'Move away from him, Miss Quinta. There's bound to be mess.'

She got up and stood on the muddy bank, unable to watch. Five Acre Wood across the water was still and quiet apart from . . . from . . . She narrowed her eyes, detecting a movement in the shadowy trees.

It was too big for a fox. A deer, perhaps, but she thought not.

'Oh!' The shotgun went off, causing her to jump. The trees came alive with flapping, squawking birds. It was over. She turned round in time to see the splintered bone and flesh, oozing with Darby's blood, and her face grimaced in grief. Farmer Bilton drew the canvas cover over his mutilated head. She told herself that Darby was only a donkey, but she had loved him nonetheless. She took a few deep breaths to calm her distress. 'Thank you, Mr Bilton. Will the Hall take him away?'

'Aye. The kennelman will send a cart over.' He rested the butt of his shotgun on the ground, surveyed the scrubby pasture and remains of a copse, and their small stone cottage roofed with red tiles. 'I'll take a look at the cowshed while I'm out here.'

It had been built by her father in a similar fashion to the cottage, and fitted with wooden stalls inside. Father had learned carpentry as a labourer on the Swinborough estate before he became a smallholder. Holding the Top Field tenancy had been a step up for him; he had been lucky to gain it and had worked hard to make it profitable. But he had passed on two years ago and it was a struggle for Quinta and her mother to work the land without him. Farmer Bilton said little as he inspected. His expression told Quinta all she needed. He did not approve of what he saw.

'Will you come inside now, sir?' Quinta suggested eventually.

'Aye. That dinner smells good.'

He looked around with interest as they stepped into

the cottage. Quinta drew out their largest chair, the one father had used, and said, 'Please sit down, sir.'

He did and Quinta brought over plates of stewed fowl and vegetables from the fire. Mother placed warm oatcakes on the table and said grace. The food tasted as good as it smelled and Quinta ate hungrily for a few minutes.

Farmer Bilton broke the silence. 'I can see daylight through that cowshed roof.'

Her mother looked anxious and explained, 'I lost some tiles in the winter storms. My late husband would have mended it by now if he were still with us.'

'Aye. It's hard for a woman living on her own.'

'She's not on her own. She's got me,' Quinta said firmly.

'And a bright little lass you are too,' he responded.

'If it were the cottage roof, you would send your man to fix it,' Laura added.

'I might. But Joseph Haig put up the cowshed himself so it was his job to mend it.'

Quinta and her mother did not argue. He drained his metal tankard of ale and Quinta poured more from the jug.

'Will you want payment for killing our donkey, sir?' Laura asked.

'This dinner is payment enough. I've sold him for the dogs at the Hall. He's not worth much, but I'll credit your rent for what they give me.'

'Thank you, sir. I'm sorry there is no bread. We have no flour left and it is too dear to buy until the harvest is in.'

He picked up a corner of oat biscuit and bit into it. 'This suits me well enough. I'm a plain living man—' He stopped and added, 'That is, I mean, gentleman.'

So he was rising to his new wealth, Quinta thought. He had been working his farm for as long as Quinta could remember and was now reaping the benefits of his efforts. Mother had told her that gentlemen farmers had always owned this part of the hillside. But Farmer Bilton was a distant cousin on the female side. It had taken the lawyers two years to find him when the old farmer died and he'd had to change his name to Bilton to inherit. It was said that he was only a farm labourer in the next county before then.

He sat back in his chair and looked around. 'You have a pretty little place here; a pretty kitchen for a pretty lady.'

'Thank you, sir,' Laura replied.

Quinta thought that the ale was having a good effect on him. He didn't usually say anything to them that might approach social conversation. She got up quietly to refill the jug from the barrel in the scullery.

'It is small compared with your farmhouse, sir,' her mother added.

'Aye. I'm thinking of building on to this cottage.'

Quinta heard this and her eyes widened. Was that the real reason he was here? He could have sent his farmhand to see to Darby for them. 'But you'd put up the rent,' she protested as she returned to top up his tankard.

'Aye.'

Laura said, 'Well, an extra room is a kind thought,

but I am a widow, sir, and hard pressed to pay the rent as it is, sir.'

'I know that.'

'We can find it, Mother!' Quinta responded. 'I can do more. Perhaps Mr Bilton could let us have a nanny or two in exchange for our donkey?'

'Shush, dear,' Laura said as Mr Bilton shifted his eyes from mother to daughter.

He shook his head slowly. 'You were a respectable little family, madam, when your husband was alive. But you neglect your duty on the farm, and on the Sabbath.'

'Mother has been ill!' Quinta protested. Her winter cough had persisted this year and the climb back from church was too much for her. Laura glared crossly at her interruption.

'You are wasting good land,' Farmer Bilton went on. 'You need a man here.'

Quinta began to feel uneasy. This was not at all what either of them had expected and she didn't like Farmer Bilton's disapproving tone or the way he called her mother 'madam'.

Laura looked down at her plate in silence.

'I want a man here, too,' he went on. 'And a fitting rent for my property.'

The silence lengthened until Laura lifted her head and said quietly, 'I can't afford any more, sir.'

'I know folk who can, though. They can work the land and turn it back into profit. The town is spreading with newcomers, with labouring men and their families who need feeding.' He speared a chunk of fowl from his plate and chewed on it slowly. 'I'll not have you wasting another year.'

'You want us out.' It was a statement from Laura, rather than a question.

'That's about it, madam.'

'But where would we go?' Quinta exclaimed.

Farmer Bilton looked sideways at her and, although he did not smile, she thought his features softened a little. He said, 'I'm not a harsh landlord. I've let you stay for two years, watching you struggle.' He shook his head and pursed his lips. 'No man to turn grass for hay, or clear the stream. It goes to rack and ruin, you see.'

'We have done our best,' Laura explained. 'We till a large garden and sell eggs and – and make cheese too when we can get the milk.'

'But only one donkey on all that pasture. And now he's gone, you think only of a goat.'

'Or two,' Quinta interrupted.

'Be quiet, dear. It is all we can manage, sir.'

'Aye.' He resumed his eating and appeared to be enjoying his dinner. After another gulp of ale he asked, 'Will you have my rent at midsummer?'

'I shall have half of it, sir.'

'But will you get the rest?'

Without a donkey to take their produce to market Quinta knew it would be difficult. She heeded her mother's wishes and stayed silent.

Laura had hardly touched her stewed fowl but she remained composed and replied, 'I can work for you, sir, to make up the difference. I am clean and frugal in my ways. Look around you, sir. You can see that I am a good housekeeper.' She hesitated, took a deep breath and continued. 'You have good standing as a farmer in the Riding, if I may say so, sir. I wonder, does the vicar ever pay you the compliment of calling on you, with his sister?'

Quinta saw him frown and begin to look uncomfortable and she knew he did not. He was a bachelor and his farmhouse was ill-furnished and unkempt. The vicar's sister had caused a stir in the village when she had come to live there, for although she was a spinster lady of maturing years, she trimmed her bonnets lavishly and it was said she was seeking a husband.

Laura went on, 'How welcome they would feel if you had a parlour maid to offer them a glass of sherry wine in your drawing room. I was a servant at the Hall before I wed, sir. I know how to do things properly for you.'

Quinta looked closely at him as his face set in a grimace. He was about the same age as her father had been when he died two years ago. His face was weather-beaten and lined to be sure, but his wrists looked sinewy and strong and his hands were straight. Not like the knobbly gnarled fingers of his bent old farmhand.

'And would you leave here?' he asked.

'I should not wish to unless my daughter comes with me. I have taught her all I learned from my time at the Hall. She would not be a burden.'

Quinta watched his face as he considered Mother's offer. He pulled his mouth to one side and nodded slightly. Then he said, 'Can she graft?'

'Yes sir,' Quinta answered swiftly. 'I can till a garden, milk a cow, churn butter and make cheese.'

He glanced at her. 'Aye. I believe you.'

'However, I should like to stay in my home, sir.' Laura went on, 'The old Squire promised my husband—'

'He made promises to me, too. Nigh on fifteen year ago, when I first came here. Did your husband tell you that?'

Mother did not talk of the past much and the old Squire was dead and gone. But Quinta knew her father had done him a great service and in return he had persuaded young Farmer Bilton to grant him a tenancy for Top Field. Bilton Farm had been neglected before its new owner arrived and three years advanced rent from the old Squire was a welcome sum to get the farm going again.

Her mother became flustered. 'You were glad of the Squire's help at the time. As indeed we were. Quinta, would you pour me a little ale, dear?' When she had taken a drink, she added, 'I am a respectable widow, sir, and I should serve you well as housekeeper.'

Farmer Bilton seemed to recover from his former uneasiness and looked from mother to daughter and back again. 'Aye, you might at that.'

'You – you will consider me, sir?'

Quinta gave him more ale. He drank again and leaned forward. 'Do you know how old I am, Mrs Haig?'

'No, sir.'

'Past five and forty, madam. The years have run away from me. Now I am reaping the fruits of my labour.

482

I visit my neighbours and the shopkeepers in the town, and I see how they all have ladies wearing pretty bonnets to walk out with them.'

'As I say, sir, I can keep as good a house as any from round here.'

'I want more than a housekeeper, Mrs Haig.'

'My daughter and I can tend your garden and orchard, as well as your dairy, sir,' she added.

'I am looking for more than a servant.'

Quinta stopped eating her dinner, a forkful of fowl halfway to her mouth. What more did he want? Surely . . . surely he could not mean a *wife*? This was not what mother had expected at all and her normally serene features had frozen into a surprised query. 'Please speak plainly, sir.'

'Come now, Mrs Haig. You womenfolk know of these things before we menfolk have even thought of them. I am looking for a wife, madam. A wife.'

'And you have come to me?'

'I have.'

Quinta watched the look of disbelief on her mother's face, closely followed by a nervous smile. Neither had expected this and wariness came into her mother's eyes, but she remained calm. 'You honour and flatter me, sir. But I had not thought of you in such terms. If you will allow me time to consider—'

'Time? Forgive me, madam. That is something I have little of. I have learned that ladies do not discuss their ages. But I must. You are, I fear, older in years than I?'

Her mother's face stilled. 'I have a grown daughter, sir.'

483

'But can you bear more children?'

Quinta was astounded by his forwardness and watched an angry flush creep up her mother's neck, around her chin and over her face, making it blotchy and unattractive.

'Please do not speak so when my daughter is present,' Laura said tightly. She looked away and then down at her hands. Finally she returned her attention to him, as he calmly soaked up the last of his gravy with an oat biscuit, and said quietly, 'You are disrespectful, sir. Quinta, would you fetch me some water from the barrel?'

Quinta rose to her feet.

'Sit down, Miss Quinta. This concerns you as well as your mother.'

Laura Haig turned her serious face towards their visitor. 'I do not deny my age. I am sure I would suit you well as a housekeeper. But that is all.'

'You mistake my meaning, madam. Yes, I shall take you as my housekeeper and be pleased to do so. But my greater need is for a wife.'

Quinta noticed that her mother seemed to relax at this remark. She did too. He must be thinking of marrying into gentry and his lady wife would expect a woman to run the household for her. They had both misunderstood his needs and Mother rallied in her response. 'I shall of course be happy to housekeep for whomsoever you choose for your wife, sir.'

Quinta watched him nod his head slowly. 'Do you think I have the makings of a good husband, Mrs Haig?'

'I do not know, sir,' her mother replied shortly.

'I am accumulating wealth and I have no kin to benefit from my fortune. Toiling in my fields has given me little time for courting and my years seem to advance more quickly nowadays.'

'Please do not prolong this interview, sir. Either you wish me to work for you or you do not. If you have finished your dinner, I believe our business is at an end.'

He ignored her plea, apparently intent on finishing his speech. 'I need more than a wife. I must have offspring, madam. Fruit of my own loins.'

'Sir!' Laura Haig was affronted by this airing of his thoughts. 'Do not continue this conversation when my child is present.'

'Child? She is no child. She is rising fifteen, is she not?'

'You will be kind enough to guard your tongue. She is a maid, sir.' Quinta recognised a firmness in her mother's tone that told her she was angry.

'Quite so. Your daughter will suit me as a wife down to the ground.' He turned to Quinta and raised his eyebrows. 'What do you say, Miss Quinta?'

Other bestselling titles available by mail: